Praise for Davis Bunn

"*My Soul to Keep* grips the reader with heartrending power and poignant insights . . . envelops readers, drawing them ever deeper into this memorable tale. Bunn's portrayal of Hollywood is astonishingly real and offers a dramatic portrayal of faith at work in the entertainment industry. Bravo!"
—Ted Baehr, Founder and President, *Movieguide* Magazine

"The prolific inspirational novelist Bunn (*The Lazarus Trap*) is an able wordsmith, whether penning a historical romance series (HEIRS OF ACADIA) or a sweet seasonal novella (*Tidings of Comfort & Joy*). But he's at his best in this absorbing faith-based suspense thriller. . . ."
—*Publishers Weekly* (about *The Imposter*)

". . . authentic, touching, and entertaining. *My Soul to Keep* opens up the world of filmmaking in a fascinating and believable way. . . . characters came to life for me . . ."
—Michele Winters, Reviewer

MY SOUL
TO KEEP

—◆—

DAVIS BUNN

BETHANY HOUSE PUBLISHERS
Minneapolis, Minnesota

Published by Bethany House Publishers
11400 Hampshire Avenue South
Bloomington, Minnesota 55438

Bethany House Publishers is a division of
Baker Publishing Group, Grand Rapids, Michigan.

Printed in the United States of America

Paperback: ISBN-13: 978-0-7642-0435-7   ISBN-10: 0-7642-0435-1
Hardcover: ISBN-13: 978-0-7642-0436-4   ISBN-10: 0-7642-0436-X

Library of Congress Cataloging-in-Publication Data

Bunn, T. Davis, 1952-
    My soul to keep / Davis Bunn.
        p. cm.
    ISBN 978-0-7642-0436-4 (alk. paper) — ISBN 978-0-7642-0435-7 (pbk.) 1.
Actors—Fiction. 2. Businesspeople—Fiction. 3. Screenwriters—Fiction. 4. Motion
pictures—Production and direction—Fiction. I. Title.
    PS3552.U4718M9 2007
    813'.54—dc22   2007023565

THIS BOOK IS DEDICATED TO THREE FRIENDS AND TEACHERS:

CHUCK COLSON, *Prison Fellowship*

RAYMOND HALL, *Prison Book Project*

AND

KEN HOWARD, *National Center for Fathering*

———◆———

By their example, they lead.

DAVIS BUNN enjoys unique involvement in the global film industry, thus providing an authentic voice to this fascinating novel. He is an award-winning and bestselling novelist, and his books have sold over five million copies in fifteen languages. His work spans reading genres from suspenseful action thrillers to heartwarming relationship stories in both contemporary and historical settings. Bunn is a sought-after lecturer in the art of writing and serves as writer-in-residence at Regent's Park College, Oxford University. He and his wife, Isabella, divide their time between Florida and Oxford, England, where they teach and write.

By Davis Bunn

The Book of Hours
The Great Divide
Winner Take All
The Lazarus Trap
Elixir
Imposter

SONG OF ACADIA*

The Meeting Place
The Birthright
The Sacred Shore
The Distant Beacon
The Beloved Land

HEIRS OF ACADIA†

The Solitary Envoy
The Innocent Libertine
The Noble Fugitive
The Night Angel
Falconer's Quest

*with Janette Oke

†with Isabella Bunn

rent Stark liked a lot of things about Austin. He liked the washed Texas sky at dawn, china blue and so big he could lie on a fresh-cut lawn and fly away forever. He liked waking up sober and free. Two huge words for a man who had once lost sight of both. He liked the life he had carved for himself since coming out of those big steel gates, walking under the razor wire that last time, taking that first breath of freedom. He liked having the last of his three penitentiaries a stone's throw away, close enough to remind him whenever that hunger started gnawing at his gut. Which happened less and less these days. But still.

"Amen."

Brent raised his head with the others. Giving thanks was a big part of these dawn AA meetings. All AA meetings followed a similar course, but each held a different makeup. This particular one was unreservedly Christian. Folks who wanted their higher power in more liberal doses were directed elsewhere. This particular meeting was led by the same man who had mentored Brent ever since he had arrived at the Texas federal pen. Stanley Allcott was a former convict himself, and a former pastor. He spoke a con's language, but with a Bible in his hand.

Brent Stark liked this place just fine.

After the closing prayer, Brent was moving down the central aisle when it happened. A woman Brent hadn't noticed before planted herself in his way and declared, "You're him."

Stanley glided over with remarkable swiftness for such a big man. "And you're new, aren't you, ma'am."

"But it's *him*. The movie star!" She had an alcoholic's ability to laser-focus on what she wanted. She ignored entirely the pastor blocking her path. "Oh, oh, what's your name, it's right here on the tip of my tongue."

Stanley had a Texan's inbred courtesy. And a pastor's ability to criticize gently. "We don't talk about lives we once had, ma'am. Not unless the other members—"

"Oh, I know all that." She scrabbled through her purse. "All I want is his autograph."

The group leader inserted himself more completely between Brent and the woman. "We are glad to have you join us. But if you ever want to come again, you'll have to abide by our rules."

"But—"

"There are no exceptions. Each of us comes in here with a past, and whatever that past may contain, it's confidential unless we choose to share." Stanley displayed his ability to command gently but firmly. "Your only choices are coffee and doughnuts, or the door. Take your pick."

Brent slipped around them and headed for his truck. These days, getting sideswiped by fans mostly happened after they aired one of his films on cable. But his guard was down in the meetings. Especially this morning.

The parking lot was typical for AA, with everything from heaps like his truck to a hundred-thousand-dollar status-on-wheels. Brent rolled down his window in a slow steady motion, his mind caught by recollections of the glory days. Back when he really was what that lady had called him.

A star.

The image flashed then. Of that last night, the last drive, and a woman whose hair shone like spun moonlight. That night Celia Breach had laughed from the seat beside him. She laughed a great deal back then, a beckoning sound that gunned his heart rate up to redline and beyond.

In these recollections, Brent always thought she told him to slow down. To pay attention to the road and not to her. Offering advice he had been too stoned to either remember clearly or obey.

Brent shut his eyes and shuddered through the rest of the memory—a flash of red from an oncoming car, a scream, the wheel spinning from his hands as they jumped the curb and smashed through a picket fence. Suddenly a stucco wall loomed before them, followed by an explosive impact. Then shattering glass, crushing metal, pain . . .

"You okay there?" The pastor waited for Brent to open his eyes to continue, "Today of all days."

"I'm fine."

Stanley leaned one elbow on Brent's open window. "We could pack up and leave for the hill country right now."

Two years previously, Brent had been out four months and three days, with six weeks left on his parole. Stanley had displayed a telepath's ability and known Brent stood on the abyss. So he'd packed Brent up and taken him into the most beautiful region of Texas and walked him until Brent had forgotten what day it was. Almost.

Stanley went on, "I've been begging God for a reason to get back up there where a man can breathe easy."

"That was a good day," Brent replied.

"The kind of day we're supposed to focus on." Stanley gave his friend a piercing inspection. "Instead of the regrets, the if-onlys, and the thoughts that stab us in the night."

Stanley Allcott had been out for seven years. He had recently been promoted to associate pastor of the church where this AA meeting took place. He was back in the pulpit again, leading the

Wednesday evening services almost against his will. The services were packed.

Brent said, "Thanks, but Liz Courtney invited me to a get-together tonight with some friends."

"What kind of friends?"

"From the amateur theater group. They know who I am, and they know what I've done, and they know I'm clean."

"You sure about that?"

"I'll be fine, Stanley."

His friend patted the truck's side, like he was gentling a restless steer. "You get that itch, I'm five minutes away."

Brent started his truck, waved his thanks, and eased his rig out of the lot. He saw his friend standing there still and knew Stanley was praying him away. Brent waved his arm in a Texan farewell, a lazy drift up and back, showing an ease he did not feel. The day ahead was anything but easy. There were too many memories eager to batter him into oblivion.

Five years ago tonight, Brent had stood at the back of a crowd of cons hooting at a television screen housed in a wire cage. He'd watched as his former producer and drinking buddy had walked forward and accepted Brent Stark's Oscar for best supporting actor. On behalf of the pal who was in San Quentin, doing three to ten.

———•———

Liz Courtney was, among other things, a mover and shaker in the Austin business scene. She was also Texan to the core, a sophisticated lady who had hunted first with her daddy and then with her husband, and still stalked birds and wild boar with her grown sons. When her husband died from a massive coronary five years back, Liz had inherited the family bank. Trained as an accountant, Liz had already worked for years in her husband's office. To the astonishment of many and the dismay of some, Liz had refused to sell out, but instead led the bank through successive years of steady growth. She was fanatic about her church, her family, her bank, her town, the local theater, and her friends.

Brent had met her soon after his arrival in Austin. Brent's parole officer had found him work with a tree trimmer who drank. One Saturday morning, Liz had watched Brent work around her house while his boss sat in the truck and nipped from a bottle. Liz had a talk with Brent and liked what she heard enough to set Brent up in business for himself. Liz had treated it like it was the most natural thing in the world to give an ex-con a fresh start. As though a felon's friendship was the only thanks she'd ever want.

Her home was modest by the standards of Texas rich, a low-slung ranch set on nineteen fenced acres. When Brent arrived, the house was already jammed with people, many of whom Brent recognized from the local theater. He stopped to say hello to his latest leading lady and shook hands with her bored-looking teen-aged son. Helping himself to a soft drink, Brent left the crowd and stepped out into the backyard. A giant television played on the patio by the barbecue pit. The screen flickered with pre-show commentators and fashion naysayers. Brent did his best to tune it all out. He picked up a Frisbee and tossed it to Liz's Irish setter. The teenager came out and joined them.

About a half hour later, Brent was witness to a very strange event. His AA mentor, Stanley Allcott, arrived with two strangers in tow. Liz saw them through the rear glass doors and came close to launching herself through them in her haste to get there. "Stanley!"

"Hello, Liz."

"You don't know what it meant to get your call." Liz took the oversized man in a fierce embrace. When they finally let go, both of them swiped at tears. Liz's voice was a half inch from breaking as she said, "Hearing your voice after all this time was as close to heaven as I've been in a long time."

"I'm glad I had a reason to call."

"You don't need a reason. Not now, not ever." Which was good for another hard embrace.

A few minutes later Liz pried Brent away from his Frisbee game. "Stanley says to tell you his being here is a last-minute thing."

"Why doesn't he come tell me himself?"

"There's some big mystery about the two men he came with." Liz walked him down to where the cottonwoods anchored the riverbank. Some of the trees were older than the state. Liz stared out at the meadows and the rushing water with a tragic expression.

"What's the matter?"

She hugged both arms tightly around her middle. "Stanley was pastor of our church. The year I was appointed church treasurer, I discovered he was stealing to support a secret gambling habit."

"Oh boy."

"I didn't know about the gambling, of course. Just the missing funds."

"You turned him in?"

"I didn't have to, which I still count as a tragic blessing. I had to testify at his trial, though. That was the only time in my entire life I ever took sleeping pills, making it through that week. I went to the prison afterward and asked his forgiveness." Liz swallowed hard. "He came by the office once, you know, doing that AA thing."

Brent nodded. "Making a list of the ones we've wronged and meeting them face-to-face."

"It was about three years ago. I hadn't laid eyes on him since." Liz shook her head. "My husband and I thought the world of Stanley. It was good seeing him walk through my door tonight. Real good."

Brent wished he could focus entirely on what she was

sharing. But he had an ex-con's fear of trouble. "Did he say anything about those men?"

"Only that the request came from somebody he couldn't say no to, and they've been asking questions around town about you."

"Are they cops?"

"Stanley didn't say. They claimed they're here to observe you, whatever that means."

"That doesn't make any sense. What do they think I've done now?"

Liz shook her head. You want my advice?"

Above him, the bare winter branches trembled. "Always."

"Don't let them get you alone."

———◆———

Soon after his release, Brent had made the rounds of Austin's regional theaters. The early roles had been unpaid walk-ons, with theaters that wanted him for the scandal value of showcasing a genuine Hollywood has-been. For some people, it might have been a bitter humiliation. For Brent, it was acting.

Later, Brent appeared in *Romeo and Juliet* at the Austin Playhouse. He did *Copenhagen* at the University of Texas. *Music Man* at the Austin Musical Theater. He did two commercials. He did one-liners. He held no hope of ever making it back to Hollywood. As his former agent told him the one time they spoke after his release, Hollywood studios were not in the business of second chances.

He took what he could get because he loved acting. Going to prison had not quenched his thirst for the lights.

Brent's favorite stage was the Zachary Scott Theater on Toomey Road. The place might have less history than some of the others, but it was a wide-open house with room for newcomers' explosive enthusiasm. They had treated him oddly at first—some with resentment, others awe. Brent took two small one-line roles and thanked them sincerely for the chance. He was respectful of a first-time director in well over her head. He made no suggestions unless asked. He stayed sober. He refused liaison offers from both women and men and ignored how some labeled him the village eunuch. Slowly but surely, he earned his place as one of the gang.

Liz and her late husband had shared a passion for the theater. Every other month they had flown to New York and gorged on Broadway. Since losing her husband, Liz fought her solitude by actively supporting all the local theater groups. She nurtured talent wherever it arose. Even in the heart of a former felon.

By the time the pre-shows ended and the commentators worked the red-carpet crowd, Liz's Oscar party was in full Texas swing. Caterers flitted about as though on Rollerblades. People with heaping plates clustered around the screen on the patio and another in the oversized den. The largest crowd occupied the living room, which had been transformed into a theater with room to sit or sprawl before a wall-size screen. The crowd hooted as the lights dimmed. Stanley and the two men he'd brought remained in the back corner. They neither approached nor spoke. But they also did not let Brent out of their sight.

He drank his share of ginger ale and laughed at the banter. When friends asked him about the ceremonies and the parties, he did his best to respond. But his fears would not let him alone. There might come a time when he could be easy around cops, when he did not constantly fear the wrong step that might land him back inside. But he wasn't there yet.

After a half-dozen awards, Brent finally gave up and left by the side door. The crowd's noise followed him as he crunched down the drive to where he'd left his truck. His isolation bit hard.

He knew twelve of those up for the top slots, had acted with two of the leading ladies, and had performed under three of the directors. There was an exquisite agony to seeing their faces painted and smiling on a night he yearned for and knew would never be his again.

But something even stronger than memories drove him away from the house, stronger even than his fear. He had been acting back there. Playing the role for the two sets of eyes at the back of the room. Honesty was one of those vital components of his new life. If he couldn't be honest, he had to leave. There was no going back on certain promises.

A lingering image chased him down the drive, of a woman with white blond hair, gemlike gaze, and the finest smile Brent had ever known. As he drove into the night, Brent could not say which was worse—not seeing Celia Breach among the glittering Oscar crowd or knowing she was absent because of him.

———•———

Celia Breach sat in the dark house and winced at the television's flickering images. Aiming her remote at the screen, she pushed the channel button as though shooting a fatal bullet. The awards show vanished, only to be replaced by the image of her own face, a closeup in a cable rebroadcast of one of her films. The image filled the screen with painful perfection. She snapped off the TV altogether.

Setting her wine glass on the coffee table, she rose and crossed the room on shaky legs. She halted before the gilded hall mirror. She should have asked Manuela to take this thing down long ago. A crack snaked down one corner, a souvenir of her rage after *his* last visit. She traced a finger along the scar that snaked down from her hairline, its pattern eerily similar to the crack in the mirror.

When she saw the tear reflected in the glass, she angrily swiped it away. "No." She spoke aloud, the single word echoing in the empty house. *I will not let you do this to me. Never again.* . . .

rent's AA meetings were held at dawn and dusk at Sacred Heart Methodist Church of Austin. Brent came mostly to the early session, since the theater claimed a lot of his evenings. The morning AA meeting was a protected sort of place. Being protected did not mean being isolated. Quite the opposite. Isolated AA meetings tended to bring in the sort of people who had hit rock bottom and started to dig. Such people knew their only alternative to sobriety was a one-way ticket to the meat lockers downtown. Such AA meetings held a desperate edge. Delirium tremors and heated exchanges were as much a part of those places as doughnuts.

Being protected meant a person could attend this AA meeting, feel safe, and not be found out. It was a haven for the businessman who woke up to discover his wife and children had been forced out by his affair with scotch and cocaine. Beside the businessman might sit a lonely housewife who had taken revenge on her husband's infidelity by diving into a martini glass the size of her swimming pool. Next to her could sit a former movie star, the genuine deal, who had ridden the high life all the way to the federal pen.

But in the hallway outside this meeting, the sign by the door was just another Magic-Marker placard reading *Morning Meeting 101*. Two doors down was the young mothers' Bible class, and across the hall was the nursery. The men's breakfast group met in the cafeteria one floor up. New AA attendees could pretend they were just another church member with normal daily problems, the kind that they didn't need to hide beneath blankets of shame, the kind that weren't whispered about whenever they left a room.

Protected.

Before his very public downfall, Stanley Allcott had led one of Austin's largest churches. Currently he shared an office with three other junior pastors. His salary paid for a studio apartment in a section of town where English was a visitor. If he minded the decline in status and pay, Stanley gave no sign. If someone asked, Stanley talked about the servant's role. To Brent's mind, Stanley knew more about service than just about anyone alive.

After the morning meeting, Stanley led Brent into his office and pointed him to the chair opposite his own. "I got a call from Kevin Phelps, director of Prison Fellowship for the southeast. We've been friends a long time. Kevin asked a personal favor. Wanted me to host a couple of men visiting Austin."

Brent said, "We're talking about the two guys you brought to the party last night."

"That's right." Stanley spoke with an ex-con's brutal frankness. Such direct words coming from a man the size of a Texas longhorn meant Stanley could talk very softly and be certain most listeners would hang on every word. "I asked who they were. In reply, Kevin asked if I trusted him."

"What kind of question is that?"

"The kind I don't need to answer. Which is exactly what I told Kevin. Kevin's response was if I trusted him, I needed to help these two guys out and not ask why."

Brent felt the creepy-crawlies emerge from his gut. "What did they want?"

"Access."

"To me?"

His nod was almost lost to his mug. "They asked about your time in prison and your life now. I had the impression they already knew a lot of the answers before they asked the questions."

"Feds?"

"I don't think so."

"Who else would do deep background on an ex-con who once had a shot at success?"

"Hey." Stanley set down his mug with enough emphasis to spatter the desktop. "Regret is just a sneaky road to ruin. The words on my wall are the real deal."

Brent did not need to read the plaque. *One day at a time.*

"You got to remember something important here. Kevin Phelps is our kind of man. He wouldn't send these guys out here unless he was certain they were on the up and up."

Brent rose, forcing his watery legs to function. "I better go start my day."

"You're not alone in this, brother. They want you, they're gonna have to crawl over my sorry carcass first."

That night was the last performance of *Fried Green Tomatoes at the Whistle Stop Café*. Brent played Ed Couch, the lead character's hapless husband. It was the sort of role he would have shunned back in his heyday. Brent's role was to be a foil for the star's lighter moments. He bumbled about, blind in a distinctly macho way to her feminine needs. He had to play himself down, make himself unattractive, form a human backdrop against which she could shine.

The deeply ingrained lessons in humility served him well.

His character was on stage for only twenty-two minutes, but these appearances were spread through both acts. In between, he normally retreated into a corner and read. But tonight the backstage area was a rustling happy scene, full of barely suppressed whispers and the electric jitters following a successful run. They had played to full houses for two weeks, including four matinees—a rare success for regional theater. Actors, stagehands, set designers, and hangers-on watched from the wings, barely suppressing whispers and laughter as the actors ran through the final scenes.

Only Brent did not share in the gaiety.

Liz Courtney, his host from the previous evening, sidled over. "You all right?"

"Why, did I miss a line?"

"Of course not." She lowered her voice. "What happened to you last night?"

"I went home."

"I know that, silly. Was it something I said?"

Brent turned from his inspection of the audience. "Not at all. I just wasn't feeling a hundred percent."

Liz was both strong and caring, a singularly Texas kind of woman. "Where does it hurt?"

"Third row, seats on the left-hand aisle. Two men in jackets and ties—Stanley's pair. I think they're from Washington."

"They came by the bank this afternoon. They wanted to know what I thought about you." Liz directed her words at the pair out in the audience. "I answered them because Stanley asked me to. I told them you take the people around you to a higher level by the way you handle yourself on and off the stage. You carry a genuineness with you everywhere that keeps the less talented among us from feeling overwhelmed."

Brent no longer watched the world beyond the curtains. "That's maybe the nicest thing anybody's ever said to me."

Twelve minutes and two scenes later, it was over. The actors gathered in the wings for a parry of quick hugs and handshakes, then trooped on stage for the final bows. When it was his turn to step forward, Brent felt the applause wash over him. That was the singular thrill of live stage, the one boost that could never be gained from film. It was the cleanest high he had ever known. Brent smiled and reached out as to embrace them back, basking in the only job he had ever loved.

The glow disappeared far too soon.

Hugs and farewells were passed among the troupe along with directions to the closing-night party. As the merry clamor faded, Stanley came up the side stairs with his two strangers in tow. The pair wore Mutt and Jeff expressions, frowning in unison at the sight of Liz Courtney standing alongside Brent.

The taller of the pair bore a pigskin briefcase and said, "We wish to speak with Mr. Stark alone."

"If wishes were fishes we'd move to Bimini," Liz replied. "You've gotten this far because an ally of Stanley's vouched for you. But this is Texas, and Brent's a friend, and you're not."

Stanley said, "Maybe we should invite them to have a seat."

"If they don't come straight with who they are, all they'll get is the legal version of a boot out the door." She held out her hand. "Show us your badges."

The shorter man said, "You think we're cops?"

"Sorry to disappoint." The taller man handed Liz a card. "I run the Nashville office of Woodman and Weld."

"Is that a fact." Liz said to Brent, "Woodman and Weld are a leading east coast law firm. They handle some of the nation's biggest companies."

Stanley waved them to folding chairs stacked by the curtain ropes. "Why don't we all grab a chair and you can tell us what's going on here."

When they were all seated, the taller man said, "My associate here is Jerry Orbain. We represent a group that is in the process of putting together a major new venture. And that is all I'm permitted to say."

Liz declared, "If Woodman and Weld says it's valid, you can stick it in your wallet."

"Orbain," Brent said. "I've heard that name."

"I'll take that as a compliment." Jerry Orbain was a small-boned man in his mid to late thirties. His face held the sullen tension of a man who wished to be elsewhere. "I directed a series for Hope-TV."

"Hope is a defunct Christian network," Brent explained to Liz and Stanley.

"Not defunct," the director corrected. "Absorbed. They've been bought out."

"I hadn't heard that."

"You weren't supposed to."

Liz said, "Let's circle back to earth here and explain what brings you to Austin."

Orbain said, "We were sent here to gather information on Mr. Stark."

"We already knew that. Who sent you?"

The lawyer responded, "The people I represent."

"Who you don't plan on naming."

"I'm specifically instructed to keep their names out of this for now."

Liz looked from one to the other. "I gotta tell you, I feel like an armadillo chasing her tail through high grass. Lost, confused, and growing hot under my shell."

The Nashville attorney said, "We came up here tonight to ask Mr. Stark if he'd travel to Nashville tomorrow."

"For what purpose?" Liz demanded.

The attorney shook his head. "My client wishes to have a look for himself before revealing what he has in mind."

rom the moment Jerry Orbain seated himself on the Nashville-bound plane to when the taxi deposited them at the downtown office building, the diminutive man did not utter a word. Brent assumed the man disliked playing step-and-fetch-it for a drunk, a felon, and a has-been.

Nashville in late February defined weather-bound misery. Sullen clouds slumped upon the hills and tallest buildings. The air stank of diesel and coming snow. A mist thick enough to choke off breath clung to every surface. The taxi took them to a building Brent scarcely saw. Inside, however, everything changed.

The building's lobby was adorned with framed gold and platinum albums and autographed concert posters. Flatscreens imbedded high in marble walls played a collage of music videos. The atmosphere held the electric quality of entertainment in the making. The people were young, extremely attractive, and used their conversations to claim center stage. Even so, every eye turned and watched them pass. Brent had been around the Hollywood scene long enough to know they were watching Jerry and wondering who Brent was to be with him.

Jerry led Brent to the last in the bank of elevators, the one that only opened when he fed a plastic card into the slot. Inside, he did the same thing. The elevator held no buttons. But from the way Brent's ears popped, he knew they were climbing quite a ways.

"Will this take us above the clouds?"

"Not in February. Come back next month, you won't recognize the place." Jerry tapped his fingers nervously on the brass railing. "A word to the wise. These people might look friendly and talk nice. But they are the real deal. If they say no, you can waltz back to Austin and spend the rest of your days on the dinner theater circuit. Far as they're concerned, you're just another road they didn't take."

"Thanks a lot," Brent said. "I was really worried before you told me that. Now I'm doing just great."

The executive suite's lobby was adorned with interior-decorator art and a sterling silver centerpiece. The colors were muted and sterile. The secretary wore a designer-name suit and a million-dollar smile. "If you and your guest would please wait in the boardroom, Mr. Orbain, the others will be with you shortly."

"No problem."

"There are soft drinks and coffee on the side table. Shall I come serve?"

"We're good, thanks."

The room was severely ornate and the two oils on the wall behind Brent's chair were both original Chagalls. Across from him, the wall of glass showed a dismal gray afternoon. Brent had scarcely settled into his chair when the boardroom door opened and a man bounded in.

"Jerry, my man. Good trip?"

"I'll let you decide." He waved at Brent. "Brent Stark, Bobby Dupree."

He had all the energy of a Hollywood agent and none of the edge. He was almost as tall as Brent, and Brent's height had often been a problem in a world where most leading men were, to put it mildly, tall only in the ego department.

"I'd like to pretend I'm not spooked, meeting a hero of the silver screen." Bobby's grip was solid. "But I don't want to start this meeting off with anything but the truth."

As far as Brent could tell, the guy was a hundred percent genuine. "If you're looking for a hero, Mr. Dupree, you got the wrong guy."

"Call me Bobby."

"I'm just a fellow trying to make it through the hours God gives me."

"You know what? I like that a lot."

"Can I get you a coffee?" Jerry asked.

"Nah. My wife has me on a strict diet. I get one cup to start my engine and then I'm cut off. She says if I have any more I'm harder to handle than our thirteen-year-old. I'd like to think she's exaggerating, since having a teenager in the house is just one long session of crisis control." He slid into the seat next to Brent's. "Did Jerry fill you in on why you're here?"

"I didn't tell him a thing," Jerry told him, "just like we agreed."

"That was the lawyers talking, not me." Bobby Dupree glanced at his watch, then started swiveling his chair back and forth, a kid in a suit. "I guess we better wait for the others. Tell me something about yourself, Brent. You mind if I call you that?"

"It's my name. What do you want to know?"

"What are you doing these days?"

"Running a lawn care company. Staying sober. Taking whatever roles the local theaters will give me."

"You don't like the idea of acting in front of a camera anymore?"

Brent took a breath. Bobby Dupree's question was casual enough. But Brent had no doubt about the truth behind Jerry's warning. The easy attitude masked a get-it-done guy. "I'd like nothing more. But these days, all drama is sourced through one system. And Hollywood has shut me out."

Bobby liked that answer as well. The guy had a gaze that reminded Brent of a clear-running stream, so guileless the color was unimportant. Bobby was starting to say something when the door opened and four others walked in. Two men, two women. One man and a woman were African American. Brent thought he recognized the woman from an album cover, but he couldn't be sure. They were followed by the Washington lawyer and Bobby's secretary. Bobby saluted them and joked with them and introduced them to Brent. The names came in a rush. Brent knew he wouldn't remember them and didn't try. If it proved important, he would have another chance. Right then he was too busy reading the room.

They were easy with their power. Brent knew the attitude well enough. He had schmoozed enough of them on his climb up the film ladder. Now, he cut their lawns. Rich folks came in all shapes and sizes. These were all drawn from the top drawer—genuine, honest, direct. Brent sensed all this in the time it took them to fill their cups and find places around the table.

Bobby kept doing his duck and weave in the suede swivel chair. "Okay, folks. The court's open and the ball's in play. Patrick, we did just like you said. The guy don't know a thing. But he's here and it's your move."

The lawyer seated across from him was the most ponderous of the lot and the only one wearing a vest. "Are you staying sober, Mr. Stark?"

The African-American woman said, "Nice opening, Pat."

Bobby said, "That's what I sent you down to Austin to figure out."

"It's a fair question," Brent said. "Seeing as how he's addressing a drunk and a felon. And the answer is I've been sober since the day I was arrested. Five years, six months, and three days."

"Good for you, honey." The woman had a model's magnetic

beauty and the ability to mute her makeup so that it looked like natural perfection. "We've all been around folks who've fallen and gotten up again. Isn't that right, Pat."

The man across from Brent flushed. "You heard Stark. It was a fair question."

"Give my lawyer room," Bobby said. "And Pat, the man goes by Brent."

Brent nodded, both because he liked how Bobby Dupree maintained order with an easy tone and because he recognized the woman then. She was a former R&B diva, referred to in the trades as the woman most likely to inherit Aretha Franklin's crown. Brent recalled several arrests for possession, followed by a stint in a rehab center, followed by a highly public conversion. She started doing Christian music after that and he'd found some of his own hard truths spun out in the woman's lyrics. Brent was surprised he hadn't recognized her at the outset. He said, "Your music got me through some real dark times, ma'am."

"Thank you, honey. That pretty much makes my day."

The lawyer cleared his throat. "What I want to know is can we trust this man to deliver?"

Bobby nodded. "Leave it to an attorney to get down to the brass tacks. Jerry, you want to tell us what you think?"

The man who had accompanied Brent back from Texas in silent hostility said, "Two days isn't enough time to answer that question."

"When we're after miracles, we know where to go," Bobby replied. "Give us your take. That's all we're looking for here."

Jerry Orbain occupied the seat at the table's corner by the window. He had pushed his chair back far enough to cross his arms, distancing himself from Brent as much as he could and still remain at the table. "I've got three observations. His acting, his business, and his friends. His acting was superb. He took a small role that could easily have been hammed into oblivion. He was by far the strongest actor and could have dominated the stage.

Instead, he became a throne for this woman to rest on. He was not just a consummate actor, he was the glue that held the play together. And he did so by disappearing. Nobody noticed him."

"Except you," Bobby said.

"That's why you sent me. To observe him. He was superb."

The atmosphere around the table eased a notch. The lawyer in the vest and the tight attitude said, "I have to confirm everything Jerry has said."

The singer said, "Don't gush all over the guy."

"We're talking about a huge investment," the lawyer countered. "Two days is not enough time to make a definitive decision."

"The decision ain't yours to make," Bobby countered. "Go on, Jerry."

The man in the corner shifted in his chair. "Observation two, his business. Brent runs a lawn care company. He has a silent partner named Liz Courtney. Local mover and shaker. Solid rep. A real theater buff. The partnership is over two years old. Financially, it's solid."

The lawyer broke in, "The company's no headline grabber, but consistently in the black."

Jerry went on, "Ms. Courtney is also Brent's friend. When we asked to meet with him, Liz basically put herself in the firing line."

"That says a lot about the guy," Bobby said. "I can't think of all that many partnerships I've funded where I'm still pals two years in."

"We're taking an awful chance," the lawyer said.

Brent felt tiny shards coalescing into a sudden realization. These folks had a project. A *film* project. And they were considering Brent for the role of director. Or star. Brent swallowed. Or both.

A second realization followed an instant later—Jerry Orbain's sour attitude had nothing to do with Brent's fractured past. Jerry wanted the director's slot. Plain and simple.

Despite that, Orbain had done both an honest and a thorough job checking him out. That fact shone a lot stronger than any reservations the board might be putting forward.

Bobby Dupree studied his colleagues through a trio of swings to his chair. Then, "Give us the third observation, Jerry."

"We talked with those who'd speak. There was some criticism from the theater crowd, which basically has to be discounted."

"I don't see why," said the man across from Brent.

The singer said, "People in the arts world stab fast and deep."

Bobby rolled his finger. "Let Jerry finish here."

"But nobody I spoke with could point to anything definite as a serious drawback. He doesn't party. He doesn't date. He doesn't drink. He lives to act, and he gives every role his absolute best. The worst criticism I heard was that the man is a shadow."

"What do they mean by that?" Bobby asked.

"My guess is, Brent's holding back because he doesn't want anybody to see him as usurping control."

Brent gave a fractional nod. The man's appraisal was dead on target.

Jerry went on, "I found how they acted a lot more important than what they told us."

"Which was?"

Jerry nodded to the lawyer at the table's opposite side. "You say it."

"They protected him," the attorney replied. "They were hostile to us because they thought we were cops."

"Cops?"

"They misunderstood our intro, is all," Jerry said.

"We saw the same thing at the Oscar party, and backstage at the theater. These people *care* for him. They're family."

Bobby let that sit for a while. "Anybody got more questions?"

The singer smiled. "A man with a felony rap finding family. That's a hard act to follow."

"Patrick?" Bobby said.

The lawyer tapped his pen on an empty pad. "Given everything we have managed to uncover, I cannot raise a single objection to our continuing."

Bobby straightened in his chair. "Okay. Before we get to round two, what say we all join hands and take this to the altar."

wo days after the Nashville conference, Brent attended another AA meeting. Only this one took place in an open-sided chapel overlooking a Pacific Ocean dawn.

Ever since the prayer time had ended in Bobby Dupree's boardroom, the world had spun at the speed of fractured light. As Brent watched the sun rise over the pristine blue waters of Hilo Bay, he felt the Nashville group's final prayers resonate in his chest.

A fragile morning breeze rustled the leaves on wild palms. The chapel was simple in the extreme. The altar was carved from a tree trunk, the benches were rough-hewn slabs, the floor concrete, the roof thatched. Brent sat next to a sumo-sized Hawaiian named Eddie Pikku, his host at the meeting and his guide for what was to come next. The trip to Hawaii and his contact had been arranged by the folks in Nashville. Brent had asked, they had phoned. Simple as that.

After the AA meeting ended, Eddie drove him back through Hilo, capital of the Big Island. Away from the glitzy seafront and the picturesque fishing port, Hilo was a time-warp of a town. Rusty clunkers shared potholed streets with barefoot children and mangy dogs. Eddie Pikku's arm rested on the open window, so that his hand could rise and fall in lazy greeting to people who called out as they passed. Pikku himself said almost nothing. He was a gargantuan presence on the other side of the vintage Dodge, so large his belly pressed against the wheel.

They pulled up in front of just another dilapidated shack. A wiry teen separated himself from a group and came over to stand by Brent's window. Eddie spoke to Brent for the first time since leaving the AA meeting. "Give the kid ten bucks."

Brent did not bother to ask why. The kid took Brent's money, leaned through the open window, and asked Eddie, "He's gonna bring this back, right?"

Eddie nodded. "The money is his, but the promise is mine."

The kid shrugged and walked around back and popped the trunk. Brent swiveled the mirror on his door. The kid stowed his dirt bike in the voluminous trunk, then banged it shut. "What's going on?"

"You'll see soon enough." Eddie gunned the motor and pulled away. "That kid has just done saved your life, man."

They left town by a road that swept through a valley of pineapple fields. The rise on the valley's other side was gentle at first, traversing ritzy housing developments and pristine golf courses. When the slope grew steeper, they passed several coffee plantations. Brent asked, "How do you know the folks in Nashville?"

"I don't know nothing 'bout Nashville but country music, and I hate country music." Eddie's car chugged determinedly through increasingly tight turns. "I got a call from people I trust. They said to trust you." He glanced over. "I can trust you, right?"

Most of the time, they traveled through a verdant tunnel. Occasionally the cliffs ate at the road's side, and Brent was exposed to a thousand-mile view. The earth dropped away in swooping green ribbons. Down below he saw miniature settlements with puny buildings, then blue. Far in the distance, the ocean was dotted with other cloud-rimmed islands. Then the green curtain swept closed again. Still they climbed.

They crested what Brent assumed was just another rise, only this time the road jinked once and swooped down into another world. The jungle was replaced by a vast field of broken black rock. A sign on the main road directed visitors to turn right into a national park. Eddie hooked a left onto an unkempt lane. Within a hundred meters, they left the last green behind. The rock was sculpted into a billion molten shapes and glinted like frozen glass in the sunlight. Up ahead, a sullen black cone stained the sky with smoke. Brent asked, "What's that?"

"Kilauea. Over there is Mauna Loa. What, you never seen a volcano before?"

"When was the last eruption?"

"Relax, man. These smoking ladies have stayed calm since eighty-four. Lot of history to this place. The old people, they've had an altar up here for centuries. They still come up on that day when the seasons change—I forget the name."

"Equinox."

He shrugged his unconcern. "I left that stuff behind with the ganja weed, man. It's God and me now. Got to know which rope to pull when you're looking for air, am I right?" Eddie simply stopped in the middle of the rutted lane. He cut the motor, then gave Brent a careful look. "How you know the Lava Lady?"

"Who?"

"Candace Chen. That's who you're up here to see, right?"

"She was a screenwriter in Hollywood."

"Sure. I heard that somewhere. You one of them actor fellows?"

"I used to be."

"Okay. Here's the word, man. You might have a pass from people I owe. But you hurt the Lava Lady, you don't leave here alive."

Brent only needed one look into that moon-shaped face to respond, "I believe you."

"Candace Chen lives up here on the land of her grandfather, who was a chief. You better be listening, because this is important, what I'm telling you. Her home was where they had their temple, back before the tribe got saved. The locals might joke about her and call her Lava Lady, but you hurt her, they'll do you, man. I mean it. They'll toss you into the fiery pit and walk away."

"I'm not going to make trouble."

"Get your gear out of the back and head straight down that path. Follow it right to the end." Eddie tapped his watch with a finger the size of a pick hammer. "You got three hours. Don't make me come looking for you neither."

———•••———

The so-called path was a level track that wound between three lava mounds, then disappeared around the bend. A rising wind moaned its way through the bizarre landscape. Brent's way was clear enough, a gravelly indentation in a sea of sculpted glass. Occasionally smaller paths extended off. These alternate routes were marked by cairns of rocks and hand-painted signs that dripped the words *Keep out*. Brent kept the kid's dirt bike in low gear.

Three miles later, he came to a rise steep enough for him to have to dismount and push the bike to the top. The problem was not the grade so much as the slippery lava rock. Cresting the rise, he found himself on the lip of a rain-fed lake. The path looped around to the north and ended by a round-shouldered trailer that had been extended until only the camper's front wall was visible. The additional rooms were a hodgepodge of junk and wood and rough-hewn stone. Between the camper and the lake was an outdoor kitchen-patio rimmed by a knee-high wall. The wall was decorated with plastic buckets filled with blooming plants. The blooms formed a raucous splash of color against the black rock wilderness.

The camper's front door squeaked loudly as the woman stepped outside and squinted into the sun. Brent called, "Ms. Chen?"

"Do I know you?"

"We've met."

She was much the same as the last time, and completely different. Which, Brent supposed, pretty much summed him up as well. He parked his bike by the side wall. "I'm Brent Stark."

"Been a long time."

"A lot of miles," he agreed.

Candace Chen wore cutoffs, sandals, and a T-shirt washed until the logo was illegible. She crossed her arms. "If you made the trip wanting to sell me on Hollywood, the lady's not home."

"I live in Texas now."

Her eyes glinted as dark as the surrounding lava. "I heard you did time."

"Three years and a month."

"I suppose that'll buy you five minutes."

"I'd appreciate it."

She turned to the butane stove. "You take honey with your tea?"

"Whatever you're having."

She served tea on the veranda. Brent drank from a scarred Bell jar. His rock bench was padded with a faded boat cushion. Candace turned a hand crank and unfurled a tattered canvas awning. Crystal chimes sounded so loud as to almost shatter the empty sky. The lake shimmered occasionally under the moaning wind. The water's surface reflected two smoldering peaks. Brent struggled to find something both nice and honest about the place, and could only come up with, "You must have an amazing sky at night."

"The moon is bright enough to read by," she agreed. "The whole world turns silver."

The speech seemed to be sucked from him. Every question that came to mind seemed wrong. But he could feel her eyes on him. He knew she was taking careful aim. Ready to shoot him down.

"I found a lot of unexpected enemies inside the pen," Brent said. The admission surprised him. He never talked about his time in prison. Not ever.

But the empty vista was made for harsh confessions. He cradled his tea and said, "One was how time doesn't move like it does on the outside. That was a big one. Then how the place acts as a nuclear power station for rage. And how danger is everywhere. I'd heard about it but never realized what it meant to live in fear all the time. No, not fear. A sense of . . ."

When he struggled for the words, Candace said, "Dread and caution."

Brent did not want to risk looking up. "That's right. You're the writer."

"Was," she corrected. "Was a writer."

He let that pass. "Small things became as hard to handle as the big. Like the noise. And how you're never alone. Being alone means you're prey. So you stay constantly surrounded by people and noise, night and day, a crashing echoing mass of noise, like some beast that's caged inside the steel and wire and concrete with you."

Brent stared out over the lake. "Never in my wildest dreams did I ever think I'd find a place this lonely, or this quiet."

"Your thoughts can get awful noisy."

"I don't doubt that," Brent replied. "Not for an instant."

He let himself really look at her then. Her naturally golden skin was tanned as dark as sourwood honey and her black hair was cut no-nonsense short. She was smaller than he remembered, tall yet as slender as a new moon, worn down to a tight lean nub.

The bouncy excitement he recalled was gone. Candace Chen had aged far more than the years since their last meeting. Another thing they had in common.

Seven years earlier, Candace Chen had arrived in Hollywood bearing a promising script and the most amazing pitch anyone had ever seen. A writer's ability to verbally sell a story was often as important as the written script, because many producers simply did not read. With a background in off-Broadway theatrics, Candace Chen did not so much pitch her idea as perform it. Her third day in Los Angeles, a powerful female producer dragged Candace into the office of a studio chief by the name of Sam Menzes. Menzes watched in silence as Candace performed her pitch about a prima ballerina who loses a leg and must re-create her life. By day's end, Candace Chen had landed a contract for her first script and been given a firm commitment on her second story. Her agent urged her to strike while the players were lined up. Candace agreed. The contract called for a hundred thousand dollar up-front payment against three quarters of a million dollars on final purchase—Hollywood-ese for first day of principal shooting.

Sam Menzes and Galaxy Studios also happened to be in charge of Brent's current project at the time. Brent's star was on the rise, and the studio wanted to wrap him up. Brent was willing so long as he could direct as well as star. By that point he'd directed two low-budget films, one of which had won at Sundance, and the studio was willing so long as they could keep the budget within bounds and locate a suitable story—or "vehicle." The studio chief brought him in and had Candace pitch her second concept.

Initially Brent had trouble getting beyond the young woman's incredible energy. She did not pitch her story so much as sing her enthusiasm. But the more he listened, the more Brent was certain this was the project he'd been after.

Her story was about Daniel Boone. Daniel Boone the

explorer, the frontiersman, the leader, the hero. She'd created a drama that swept aside decades of revisionism and political correctness. She'd returned the man to the pedestal, and in so doing restored the sense of adventure to America's history. It was a no-holds-barred return to the heyday of Hollywood epics, told about a man big enough to truly fill the silver screen.

Sam Menzes saw the story's potential instantly and wanted it for himself. Sam was notoriously two-faced. He could display all the charm of a snake-oil salesman, wrapped in the skin of a man who ran one of Hollywood's most powerful studios. But the other face of Menzes was that of pure danger. If a cobra wed a rabid lion, the result would be Sam Menzes in a rage.

And nothing got Sam so mad as not getting what he wanted.

Menzes and his team pressured them to wrap it up fast. Overnight Candace Chen went from owning all the rights to her screenplay to holding a check for more money than she'd ever had at one time.

Brent had been tempted to warn her of what would probably happen next. But Brent had wanted a piece of Candace's talent as well. So he had kept silent.

Candace's next stop was the home office of a major star. The actress was incredibly taken with Candace's concept about the dancer who loses a leg. She not only wanted to act but direct.

That was when things started to slide. And when things went bad in Hollywood, they did so in a spectacular fashion.

The star sent Candace thirty-one pages of alterations. Candace protested to the studio, or tried to, but Sam Menzes was no longer accepting her calls. That was bad enough. But the actress then secretly hired her favorite writer and sent him the same list of alterations. Candace's rewrite, a heart-wrenching four-month attempt to adapt her story to the star's requirements, was never even read.

Instead, the actress's favorite writer ditched the gentle moral and transformed Candace's story into a star vehicle.

Candace had made a few allies inside the studio. One of them secretly gave Candace a copy of the shooting script.

Candace hired a lawyer. She was savaged but not defeated. She could do nothing about the lost first story. But she wanted her second one back.

Sam Menzes did not willingly relinquish his hold on the Daniel Boone script. But Candace's lawyer was a shrewd Hollywood player. The lawyer pushed the only button that would work with Sam; she threatened Menzes with a page-one scandal.

Sam relented, but he made Candace pay. She was forced to return every cent she had received from the sale of her initial script. Her name was erased from the credits. Her agent dropped her. Candace left Hollywood seriously in debt. She was swiftly forgotten, just another jaded dreamer sent fractured and limping back to America's hinterland.

The Candace Chen who returned Brent's gaze had lines he had never seen before. But the calm was as steady as the surrounding rocks. She asked, "Are you here for Menzes?"

"Absolutely not."

"I didn't think so. But I needed to ask. I heard he did a number on you too."

Brent tasted his tea. "You heard right."

"I heard something else." Her gaze was strong enough to trace an artist's line about his form. "I heard you found God inside."

"That's also correct."

"You bring it back outside with you?"

"So far."

She liked that enough to nod. "I lost Him for a while. My faith and my talent were so tight in there, you know, using the gift for His glory—when I walked away from one I walked away from the other."

Brent set down his jar. "And now?"

"I've been spending some time reading about the early

church. They talk about God speaking in the silence, when you can be quiet enough to listen beyond the realm of words." Her whole body was nodding now, a soft motion, a gentle cadence. "I try to be ready in case He has something to say. It goes a long way to filling the empty hours."

"You're not writing anymore?"

She motioned inside the caravan with her chin. "I have a little table facing the window and the sunrise. I get up most mornings and sit there for a while. I finally moved my Bible over there to give me something to do, because I'm sure not writing. Five and a half years I've been up here. I still haven't filled my second note-book."

"I'm sorry to hear that."

She looked at him with eyes that revealed as much as they studied. "What if God doesn't want me to write anymore?"

"If I believed that, I'd get up from this bench and walk away and never bother you again. I can't ever come between a person and God's will for their life. Not ever again."

She drained her mug, pinged one fingernail on the rim, and said, "So why don't you tell me what it is you're doing up here."

"If it's okay with you, I'll lay it out like it happened."

When the sun vanished behind the rim of the lava lake, Brent biked back to Eddie's Dodge. He handed Eddie a note Candace had written and said, "She'll take me back down when we're done."

Eddie slapped the Dodge into gear. "Way to go, man."

"It's not what you think."

"All I'm saying, you got a lady who lives for privacy to sit and listen this long, you're good." He gunned the motor, lifted his arm in a lazy farewell, and bounced out of sight.

By the time Brent had returned to the trailer, the side of the patio opposite the outdoor kitchen had been transformed. Mosquito nets had been unfurled from the canvas overhang, separating off a sleeping area. A bedroll had been laid out beneath the cabin's barred front window. The message was clear enough. If a guest stayed for dinner, he stayed the night.

Candace used a battered wok to cook them a plate of brown rice and chopped vegetables over the butane stove. She slipped the steaming plate in front of him. "You're telling me they held hands around the boardroom table and prayed?"

"Not just prayed," Brent corrected. "Prayed for *me*."

"Get out."

"Like it was the most natural thing in the world. Like asking for miracles was what they did every day of the week. Which, to be honest, is what I think may be happening there." He tasted his meal. "This is great."

"Hard to find a fast food that'll deliver up here. It was either learn to cook or starve."

They ate by lantern light. When they finished, Candace relit the stove and put on a pot of water. She spooned in fresh tea leaves, then poured the boiling contents through a strainer. She handed Brent his tea, lowered the lantern flame to a muted glow, and reseated herself.

Dusk faded with a tropical tardiness. Night came in lazy stages. Yet already the stars were a portrait of wonder. Brent sipped from his Bell jar and studied the woman who stared up at the sky. "What happened to you?"

She could have brushed him off with all the questions he had yet to answer. Instead, Candace set her tea to one side and said, "I came out here because I was angry and wounded. I stayed because . . ."

Brent said softly, "I understand."

"Happiness became something that happened to people down below. The ones who stayed in the beachside hotels and managed to keep hold of their dreams. For me, loneliness and misery were the sweet elixir to life's wrongs. I know that is too close to crazy to be said out loud."

"No, Candace. It doesn't sound crazy."

"What happened to you, Brent?" she asked quietly.

"I live a small life. I found God. I stayed sober. I learned to be happy with the small triumph of a good day."

She turned back to the night sky. "That doesn't sound small to me. Not at all."

A sliver of moon emerged from a horizon of jagged silhouettes. "The day you pitched your story in Menzes' office, I was stoned as usual," Brent told her. "I'd gotten up and had a couple of lines with my OJ. Actually they weren't lines. I used this solid gold nasal spray, as though the rich man's toys made it all right to stay permanently high. My driver knew to stock the fridge with champagne—it was all I drank in the daytime. I only switched to vodka when the day's shooting was done.

"Anyway, it was just another day for me, headed to the studio to hear just another pitch. I was hearing so many back then, they all sort of ran together. Yours didn't, though. It *captured* me. And it wasn't just the story. It was you. When I got back to the limo, I remember sitting there staring down at my hands. The gold coke dispenser in one hand, crystal glass of champagne in the other. What I heard, though, was how you'd talked of God. How the word came out so naturally it was like He was this friend you'd left out in the waiting room. A buddy. I told myself you were just some squirrelly writer, and took another snort. But your voice kept echoing through my head. You and God. Friends."

She took her time answering. "I was furious with God when I left LA. He'd given me this gift, then let the world trample on it and on me. Why hadn't He *protected* me?"

Brent saw the words swim through his brain. The Bible passages. The things he might have responded with. Maybe he should have. But what he said was, "I'm so sorry, Candace."

"You didn't stomp on me. It was Sam Menzes."

The way she said that name caused his gut to quiver. "I was part of the food chain."

She let that slip into the night and disappear. "I got over the anger. I found my way back to God. But I never did recover." Her face glowed soft and fragile in the lantern light. "I stayed up here because I am still afraid of what life can do to you."

She took Brent's silence as enough of a response to say, "I guess that brings us back to your visit to Nashville."

"I guess it does."

She sighed her way around until she sat almost primly. Back straight, feet together, hands folded in her lap. Despite the dim light, Brent knew the strength of will it took for her to remain where she was. "So tell."

"They are a group of Christian businessmen and professionals from all over the South. They pray for one another. They hold each other accountable. They invest in mission work." Brent measured the words and kept his tone steady. "This time last year, they felt God calling them to become involved in the entertainment industry."

"The group that meets in Nashville?"

"No, Candace. The group nationwide."

"What, they got together somewhere?"

"No again. They felt God calling to them in these different groups that were meeting in cities all over the country."

"All at the same time?"

"Apparently so."

"How many groups are we talking about here?"

"Over a hundred." He waited until he was certain her questions were done for the moment. Then, "They have a copy of your script. Jerry Orbain brought it to them. He runs a music video production group, used to direct small-budget productions for Hope-TV."

"They went bust."

"Actually, the name and the studio were bought by this

organization. They want to do your story as their first project. When they prayed over me, they asked for a sign that all this was God's will. When they were done, I asked for one too."

"Did you get it?"

"I'm still waiting to find out." Brent took a long breath. "I said I'd get involved if you agreed to come on board. No questions, no objections, no fight. That you'd just walk down this hill and join me in turning your story into a movie."

hari Khan survived the Hollywood jungle because of what she called her hyper senses. She liked to think these catlike qualities were a gift of her Persian grandmother, her father's mother. Shari stood by the window in the secretary's office and fingered her favorite brooch, a gold panther with ruby eyes. She wore a Fendi suit of midnight blue, a perfect backdrop for her amulet.

Shari extended the tip of her tongue, tasting the air. She sensed the same pungent force that had carried her through the past twenty-four hours. The air's charge was like the instant before lightning struck, so dense she was amazed no one else in the crowded room could taste it. But Shari knew hers was a finely honed talent. She was one in a million. And her time had come.

"Ms. Khan? Mr. Menzes will see you now."

Shari walked through the double doors. The chairman's aide smirked at her from his position beside the big man's desk. Shari could guess what he was thinking. She was only a production assistant to Bud Levinson, one of several administrative vice-presidents. The chairman's aide smirked both because he was higher up the food chain and because he assumed Shari was about to be shot down. Shari had of course been in the president's office before. But she had never opened her mouth. A PA in Hollywood was expected to remain still, silent, and subservient. Hollywood PAs worked eighty-hour weeks for guppy wages. The fact was, a hundred thousand others would have *paid* to have Shari's job.

As Shari seated herself, the chairman's aide mouthed, *Been nice not knowing you.* The aide's name was Brad. Her first week on the job, Shari had refused his advances in no uncertain terms. Shari was not interested in a relationship with anyone's aide. A girl had to have standards. Especially in this town. Brad had not taken well to Shari's turning him down. Now Brad's expression said it all. He was going to enjoy this. A lot.

Shari focused on the man seated behind the desk. There would be ample time to scour the aide with her talons once she had passed him on the way up.

"Ms. Khan, is it? You wanted to see me?"

"Thank you for your time, Mr. Menzes." Until last year, Shari had been assistant sales manager to the largest books-on-tape producer in Los Angeles. Shari had taken a cut in salary and an even larger cut in title to work as Bud Levinson's PA. All for this. The chance to seat herself at the narrow conference table that grew like a thumb from the center of Sam Menzes' desk. "Something's come up that I think you'll agree can't wait."

"You heard from Bud?"

"He's still in traction, Mr. Menzes."

"How long?"

"Another three weeks." If her boss could survive that long. And if the nursing staff didn't murder him in his sleep. Bud was not being a good patient. Shari had that firsthand.

"Skiing, right?"

"Yes, sir. Aspen. Broke his right femur in three places and shattered his hip."

Sam Menzes glanced to where his aide sat against the side wall, notebook in hand. "We send flowers?"

"Twice."

"Good. Okay, Ms. Khan. What's up?"

Shari took a breath and tasted how the electric force had intensified. The thunderbolt was soon to come crashing down.

The aide smirked at his notebook. He no doubt expected her to use her boss's absence to claim she'd received a new job offer, yet she felt loyalty to this company and would so like to stay, if only, yada, yada. Sam Menzes did not pay for loyalty, because loyalty was a flower that did not grow in Hollywood soil. Sam Menzes paid for results. And Brad assumed results were one thing a guppy like Shari Khan could not produce. Only he was dead wrong. Emphasis on the word *dead*.

"*Iron Feather,*" she said. "Our Daniel Boone project."

"What about it?"

"We have competition."

Sam Menzes glanced at his aide, who was no longer smiling. The Boone project had been in turnaround for almost two years. Shari knew about the delay but could only make an educated guess about the reasons. It might be problems with the script. Or casting problems had ground things to a halt, if the actor wanted for the role was trapped in a contract with another studio. Delays often bred more delays. Filmdom had another word for long-term turnaround. They called it the boneyard.

The only thing that had kept this project from being relegated to the boneyard was Sam Menzes. He had a personal interest in this film.

That the film had finally emerged from turnaround was a carefully guarded secret.

Unlike most of the other major studios, Sam Menzes bank-rolled many of his own films. He often shared risks by drawing in other investors. But not always. *Forbes* estimated the Menzes fortune at three billion dollars. Sam personally bankrolled films he thought were going to be hits. That meant he could keep hold of lucrative distribution rights and DVD sales rights until the best and most profitable moment to sell. He took a personal hand in selecting stars and green-lighting their contracts. He was a hands-on CEO. If a director or producer didn't like it, Sam Menzes was happy to show him the door.

His level of control meant projects he chose to fund himself could remain highly confidential. Other studios could not rush a competing project into production and siphon off his advance publicity.

Menzes asked his aide, "Did you tell her about this?"

Brad stiffened in his chair. "Not a chance!"

"Actually, sir," Shari said, "it was through my own confidential source."

Menzes looked at her then. Actually *looked*. His regard seemed purely professional. She wondered if he even noticed she was an attractive young woman with honeyed skin and slanted eyes—the eyes of a cat.

"Universal finally get their project off the ground?" he asked.

"Their project is about Thomas Paine, Mr. Menzes, not Daniel Boone. Same intended audience. And no, they are still in turnaround. This competing project is from a new studio. An indie."

"You know anything about this?" Sam asked Brad.

"No, sir. Which makes me wonder how real this could be."

"It's real, all right." Shari kept her gaze on the chairman. Brad no longer existed. "And they've bought the Chen script."

The renowned Menzes calm finally cracked. "I own that story."

"Actually, sir, you gave up all rights in exchange for Candace Chen returning every cent she earned from the first script."

"You're sure about that?"

"Yes, sir. I withdrew the documents from Contracts yesterday. I have a copy with me, if you want to see it."

"Show it to Legal, see if they can find a way to battle it." Menzes drummed his fingers on the desk. "All right. Give me what you have."

"It's a Nashville-based group, so new they haven't even named the production company. They acquired Hope-TV, basically to get their hands on the cable network stations."

Brad sneered, "So we're blowing smoke over a made-for-TV puff?"

Shari did not bother to glance at the aide. "They are doing a major feature."

"Who's directing?"

"They have approached Brent Stark."

Brad huffed. "He's a drunk! A one-hit wonder of a scriptwriter has teamed up with a has-been who's made headlines with every tabloid on earth. PR will eat them alive."

Menzes ignored the young man seated by the wall. "You get this from Bud?"

"No, sir. I've developed these leads on my own."

"Have you informed him?"

"Last night." Which in and of itself had been Hollywood perfect. Shari had discovered in Bud Levinson's night nurse a woman who shared her own frustrated loathing for the man. The nurse could not do what she wanted, which was to smother the Hollywood exec with his pillow. But she could tell Shari when Bud would be completely zonko from his nightly cocktail. Shari recorded a conversation in which she relayed everything she had uncovered, and finished with the high note that she had scheduled a meeting with Menzes. Her boss, who was so paranoid about somebody stealing his slice of power that he had long ago ordered her never to set foot in the executive elevator without his express permission, had last night mumbled his agreement that this information simply could not wait and that she should hire herself some outside detectives to check things out on the ground. "He said to tell you hi."

"Did he." Menzes drummed a second longer. "So walk me through it."

She knew it was a test, that he half disbelieved it, a production assistant who had never opened her mouth in a director's meeting before had come up with a scoop like this all on her own. "A source revealed that you had finally green-lighted the Daniel Boone project and started production."

"A source."

"Yes, sir." She pressed her jaw out more firmly. If he asked, she would indignantly decline to answer that her source was another guppy working on the studio's back lot.

But Menzes didn't ask. "Go on."

"I heard through another source that Hope-TV's new owners acquired the old Angelini studio."

Menzes rocked back in his seat. "You're sure about that, are you?"

"I have written proof." Dino Angelini had prospered on the back of tough-guy films and handed a successful company over to his daughter, who had proceeded to make a series of true cinematic bombs. *Variety* had described her last three-hour epic as "a waste of perfectly good celluloid." Shari withdrew the photocopied pages from her slim portfolio. "The deed of sale."

"I never thought Dino would let that go."

"He had no choice, sir. The company was hemorrhaging money at the rate of a million dollars a week."

"Where are they located, Virginia?"

"Wilmington, North Carolina."

"So they have a studio and they have a cable outlet and they have a project."

"But no name," Brad sneered.

Menzes glanced at the young man, as though trying to remember why he was in the room. He turned back to Shari and said, "This is your baby. Rock it."

She could have hit an operatic high note. "You got it, sir."

"Updates, Ms. Khan. I want to know everything."

"Soon as it's mine, it's yours."

"Find us a weakness. Something we can exploit."

"I won't let you down, Mr. Menzes." She stood, zipped her portfolio shut, and waited for Sam Menzes to turn away before smirking her silent farewell. Bye-bye, Brad.

he next afternoon, Candace Chen drove Brent back to Hilo in her dust-caked Jeep. When they arrived at the airport, she halted far down the sidewalk from the departures entrance. Overhead, clouds grazed on the blue sky like airborne sheep. The airport's rhythm was island slow. Candace pulled the keys from the ignition and played with them like worry beads. "I'm going to stay with my folks here in town for a day or a week, until I have a genuine sense of what needs doing here."

"I couldn't ask for more."

"You meant what you said? If I don't come, you won't direct?"

"Precisely."

"That's a heavy burden to lay on a gal."

In the stark Hawaiian daylight, Candace's face was stronger than he remembered, and her eyes held a cautious note. Her bubbly enthusiasm was gone, but in its place was a calm certainty. Brent felt no hesitation in saying, "I'm not laying this at your feet, Candace."

"Sounds that way to me."

"I've set it at the altar. I've put this in God's hands. Maybe you should spend some time praying about this."

Her hands stilled. "Hearing that from a Hollywood star makes me quiver all over."

"I told you. This isn't Hollywood. And I'm not a star."

She started to respond to that but checked herself. Whatever was there in her shining dark gaze, her thoughts remained unspoken.

Brent asked, "You want to have a word of prayer together before I leave?"

This time the shivers were visible. "Go for it."

When they were done, Brent shook her hand, thanked her for the dinner and the bunk and the stars, and headed inside. Throughout the check-in procedure, as he passed through security and waited for his flight to be called, he debated whether he had been as fully honest as he should. He tried to convince himself that there had been no lie in omission.

But the whole truth was, Brent had laid two fleece upon the threshing floor. And the greatest impossibility he had set before God was not Candace Chen at all. Instead, it waited for him in Beverly Hills.

———————◆———————

The residential section of Beverly Hills was an exclusive island of Imperial palms and emerald lawns. The streets seemed paved in velvet rather than asphalt. Most houses had neither numbers nor names. Privacy was secured behind drapes drawn over bulletproof front windows and steel doors masked by oak veneer. Tiny security shields were planted in every front lawn. Brent turned his rental off Sunset, took the first right, the next left, and parked. He wanted to pray. But right then his heart hammered so loud all he could really do was stare at his hands. Finally he looked at the sun-splashed windshield and said, "You *are* in this with me, right?"

A bird warbled. A car passed. The clock in the dash flicked through another meaningless number.

"Yeah, that's what I figured." Brent rose from the car, hit the lock, and started up the path. Everywhere he looked, the scene was mined with the shrapnel of memories. He stopped at the front step and recalled another bright California morning. One when he had woken up to discover he had spent the night right where he now stood. On the front lawn beside the flower bed. He still had no idea how he'd gotten home.

Home.

The house was built in the old Spanish style, a one-story ranch surrounding an interior courtyard. The patio area contained an indoor-outdoor living area paved in rough-cut marble, an outside kitchen, a second dining area, a small pool, and a huge jacaranda tree ringed by a cedar bench. The second year Brent had owned the house, the tree had contracted some awful wasting disease. He had spent almost ten thousand dollars in tree surgeons and vitamin injections. He pressed the doorbell and wondered if the tree still lived.

His former maid answered the door. "Hello, Manuela."

"She no see you, Mr. Brent."

He nodded. "How have you been?"

"She say to tell you—"

A voice from the shadows said, "Oh, go ahead and let him in, Manuela."

It was hard to tell who was more surprised, the Guatemalan maid or Brent. Manuela stepped back from the doorway.

He entered his former home and immediately saw her, seated on a white leather sofa in the sunken living area, an open magazine in her hands. "Hello, Celia."

She looked back down at the magazine and casually flipped a page. "Manuela, keep the phone handy. If he does anything suspicious, call the cops."

"I'm not here to cause trouble," Brent said.

"You heard what I said, Manuela."

"Yes, Ms. Breach."

She turned toward him coolly. "Will you say your piece and never bother me again?"

"Yes. If that's what you want. Send me away this time, and I will never come back. Ever."

Either his words or the way he spoke them caused the woman to say, "You might as well come sit down."

"Thank you."

Celia Breach had a star's ability to find the best possible light. She sat with the doors to the courtyard behind her. The sunlight backlit her, hiding the scars that ran from her temple to her hairline.

The scars he had caused. In the accident he could barely remember. The one that had landed them both in the hospital and, eventually, him in jail.

And wrecked both their careers in the process.

It had been during the fourth week of shooting a feature for Sam Menzes. Brent had been both starring and directing. Galaxy Studios took a serious hit, claiming Brent's madness had cost them seven million dollars. The publicity had been stupendous. The film was recast and went on to make a killing at the box office. Brent had never brought himself to watch it.

He had already been on probation for two previous drunken driving offenses, the second of which had cost him his license. This third time, he had driven his car through the front wall of a family home, coming within four feet of an infant's crib. There had been drugs in the car. And a gun in the glove box. The judge had sentenced him, saying, "Mr. Stark, it appears to me you've been begging somebody to send you away. This time I am happy to comply."

Celia asked, "Why do you insist on bothering me?"

Brent nodded his thanks to Manuela for a coffee Celia had not offered. "I came before just to apologize. It's one of the steps.

To seek out those I've harmed and ask forgiveness."

"I'll never forgive you. Not in a billion years." She spoke with a detachment that made her declaration even more cruel. "If I could push a button and sentence you to death by a thousand cuts, I'd do it."

In a different era, Celia Breach would have been one of the *It Girls,* pinned to lockers and the controls of fighter planes by young men a long way from home. After her first film was released, one journalist described her as having a face born to demolish an entire generation of male hearts, and a body to match.

Celia was still beautiful. But Hollywood was full of beautiful women. The accident had kept her from the public eye for almost two years. Her remaining scars were only the final relics. By the time she was ready for the lights, the public had moved on.

"Eleven surgeries. Nine reconstructed bones. Sixteen weeks in the hospital. You think I could forgive that?"

Brent did not answer because he was not expected to. He sipped his coffee. Even here the memories were potent. Manuela made the finest cup of coffee he had ever tasted, spiced with chicory she roasted herself and sweetened with raw cane sugar.

"I was on the cover of every tabloid right around the world. You destroyed me. Not my career. Me. You deserved a lot worse than the judge gave you."

A woman's ire was never harsher than when it turned frigid with carefully tended rage. Even so, Brent counted the fact that he was seated here a genuine miracle. "You're right."

She wore a sleeveless lavender turtleneck of summer cashmere. Her white blond hair was pulled back and fastened tightly at the nape of her neck. This was no woman to adopt a hairstyle that partially masked her scars. "There's another reason why you showed up this time?"

"There is. Yes."

"I suppose you're going to tell me you've gotten together the money to buy me out."

"No, Celia. The house is yours. I'll never live here again."

"You've got that right. I'd poison that silly tree and rent the place to UCLA students for a dollar a year before . . ."

She stopped then. Her elbow rose to rest on the back of the sofa. Her hand patted the skin where the plastic surgeon had not completely erased the damage. Brent waited, expecting another cool stab.

Instead, Celia turned slightly, so that she angled away from him. It should have been her most unflattering angle, silhouetted such that her age and the scarring showed. Brent knew she was thirty-two, seven years younger than he, and perhaps the most beautiful woman he had ever known.

She said to the sunlight, "What's the use?"

Brent felt his heart squeezed until he could scarcely breathe. A woman born to perform, to shine. Trapped inside a house, on the fringe of a world she was banned from ever entering again. "I'm so very, very sorry, Celia. I'd give anything to turn back the clock, stay sober, drive you home, or at least if I had to destroy myself, drive alone."

She gave no sign she had even heard him. Dust motes danced in the still air. "What are you doing these days?"

"I run a lawn care company."

"You're kidding, right?"

"In Austin. I was paroled there."

"Are you doing anything on the stage?"

"Every chance I get. Mostly local stuff."

"They must love that. The disgraced Hollywood actor, doing walk-ons for a local theater troupe."

"My first year, I got a lot of that. But they can only hammer that nail so long. It's pretty much died down now."

She still spoke to the empty dining room and the rear doors. "How can you *stand* it?"

Brent understood her perfectly. "Being arrested, tried three times, convicted and imprisoned taught me how to handle shame."

"Three?"

"The trial, your civil case, and the court of Hollywood reporters." He sipped from his cup. The coffee had gone cold. "Once in a while a local reporter regurgitates the whole story before getting to how I performed onstage. It still hurts."

"You still read the trades?"

"Not the Hollywood ones. But the locals, sure. I'm an actor—I'll always care what the critics say."

Celia turned slowly, as though drawn by unseen hands. She called, "Manuela."

The woman appeared in the kitchen doorway. "Yes, Miss Celia."

"Get Brent another coffee."

"I'm fine, thanks."

Manuela was already moving. "Is no problem, Mr. Brent."

Celia made a process of tucking her legs under her. The maid reappeared bearing a fresh cup. As Manuela set it down, Celia said, "I dreamed about you last night."

Manuela's hand jerked, slopping coffee onto the saucer. "I'm so sorry, Mr. Brent. I'll go get another."

"Leave it, please." He dabbed at the saucer with his napkin. "Sorry, Celia, you were saying?"

"It lasted about ten seconds. We were somewhere. A restaurant or someplace, I don't know. You said you'd come to rescue me. When I woke up, I discovered I was crying."

Brent heard Manuela's quiet footsteps padding away. "Is that why you saw me today?"

She might have shrugged. "Is it true what I heard, you got religion?"

In the jail in LA County, while awaiting his sentence. The desperate act of a desperate man. "Yes."

"You're staying sober?"

"I haven't had a drink since that night."

"I wish I hadn't. Every time I do . . ."

Brent finished the thought for her. "Flashbacks?"

She reached for the embossed box at the center of the coffee table. She pulled out a cigarette and a slender gold lighter, and made a performance of lighting up. Brent remembered that lighter.

Celia exhaled smoke with her words, "So now you're going to give me the religion spiel, try to get me down on my knees?"

"Nothing would give me a greater honor. But no, that's not why I came. At least . . ."

She seemed to lift her gaze to his despite herself. "Go on."

"To be honest, Celia, I came to have you shoot me down."

The smoke turned her voice to a honeyed rasp. "Happy to oblige."

"I've been given a chance to get back into the business. I'm here because I'm looking for a reason to run away."

"You've been offered a role?"

"Act and direct both."

"Which studio?"

"It's an indie production."

"You want to turn it down? You just said you lived for the lights."

Brent found it necessary to set down his cup, as his hands had started trembling. "I've learned to live with the small gifts. A sober day. A few good friends. A couple of minutes on stage before a local audience. A night when I don't wake up sweating and scared because I don't know where I am or how I got there. A job I'm good at."

"Cutting grass."

"I'm outdoors. I keep places looking nice. There are worse things, Celia. A lot worse."

She leaned forward and stabbed the ashtray. Hard. "So just

exactly why am I the one holding your fate in my hands?"

"Because." Brent dragged his sweaty palms down his pant legs. "I told God I'd take this on only if you agreed to be my costar."

'm terribly sorry, Mr. Dupree." Though Liz Courtney's secretary had no idea who Bobby was, she
could also see this was a man who wasn't used to
being kept waiting. "Ms. Courtney has phoned
again and says she should be here in five minutes, ten at the
most."

"Ma'am, I tell you the truth. If I thought I could get this
much work done every day, I'd move my office into your waiting
room. You wouldn't mind that, would you?"

She almost managed a smile. "I'll have to get back to you on
that, Mr. Dupree."

Bobby Dupree laughed far too easily for a man who'd been
sitting in the Courtney lobby for almost three hours. "You do
that, ma'am."

Fiona Bridge, Bobby's number one assistant, had basically
taken over the waiting room area. The coffee table was piled with
files and spreadsheets. Her laptop computer was plugged in and
linked up. Every ten to fifteen seconds there came another click,
noting the arrival of yet more email. She had two cell phones
open and a Bluetooth remote fitted in either ear. Bobby Dupree
hated the immediacy of modern business. He liked using Fiona

as his buffer. When he needed time to think, it was Fiona's job to isolate and protect. Which meant his staff had come to loathe her. Around Bobby Dupree's sprawling empire, Fiona was known as Drawbridge.

Fiona said, "Jerry Orbain is checking in."

"I better take that." He accepted the phone. "How's tricks, Jerry?"

"I just got off the phone with Mr. Stark. He's back in LA and has met with Celia Breach."

"I don't have enough to chew on, Jerry. Give me the full load."

"He also met with Candace Chen in Hawaii. She's a maybe. Brent says she's coming in to hear more. I'm flying out to meet them in LA."

"Well, that's good news, wouldn't you say?"

"I suppose."

Bobby Dupree suppressed the sigh and the anger behind it. Jerry's tone of voice said it all. The man was still sore over not being given the top directorial slot. "Jerry, I want you to think about something. I gave Brent my card and even wrote my direct line on the bottom. I know you remember that because I saw the glare you gave him."

"I didn't—"

"But it wasn't me he called, now, was it? Brent Stark did what he set out to do, and then what happened? Who did he phone, Jerry?" Bobby gave that a double beat, then said, "Seems to me the man is bending over backwards, not just to make peace, but to make sure you're included. So I'm only gonna say this once. We're not stopping with this one project. If it goes, we're gonna be building for the future. Which means we need folks who can run their own rig, especially folks we raise up from inside the group. But you've got to make this first one work. I hope you're listening real good, because I don't aim on ever telling you that again."

He tossed back the phone. "I do declare, if I could find a vaccine against sulking, I'd be a kazillionaire."

A strong female voice said from over by the elevators, "I got me a passel of folks I'd like to shoot full of that stuff. Or maybe just shoot." For a lady wearing a skirt, she made swift progress across the reception area. "Liz Courtney. I can't tell you how sorry I am to keep you waiting."

"Bobby Dupree. Don't give it another thought, Ms. Courtney."

"I'm Liz to everybody I know. Especially those I keep waiting."

The banker's secretary said, "Ms. Courtney, I'm terribly sorry."

Liz tried to wave her away. "Whoever it is, they have to wait."

"Ma'am, it's our people in Tulsa again."

The banker deflated. Her shoulders slumped and all the air sighed away. "God sent these days to test us, isn't that what they say?"

"Sounds a lot better at poolside with a lemonade in your hand and the day done and put to bed," Bobby replied.

"The biggest deal in my bank's portfolio is unraveling." Liz Courtney walked to the secretary's desk and reached for the phone. "This is Liz." She listened for a minute, then, "No, Wayne. I can't just drop everything and go out there. You know how hard it is to get a flight—"

Bobby broke in, "I got a jet fueled and waiting on the runway."

Liz looked over. "Hold on a second, Wayne."

"What can I tell you," Bobby said. "I'm a man who likes his toys."

"You mean that?"

"Wouldn't offer if I didn't."

Liz said, "Wayne, I'll meet you at the Tulsa airport in two hours."

———•———

Bobby Dupree was born without a father or a middle name. His mother worked nights at a Union 76 truck stop outside Memphis. She loved truckers, gamblers, honky-tonks, and the sort of good times that left her forgetful of her boy. Bobby was saved from going seriously bad by a missionary pastor tending the truck stop chapel. The preacher was like many of his parishioners: a bearded, tattooed man with the jagged features and sawdust voice of a true hard timer. The only differences between this man and the ones who stole Bobby's mother away for a night or a week were the light in his eyes, how he used the Lord's name, and the way he taught Bobby that it truly was okay to hurt and to care. When Bobby's mom finally vanished for good, the pastor formally adopted the boy who already lived more with him than in the empty trailer home.

Bobby read voraciously, topped his school in all math competitions, and spent his summers on the road with his missionary-trucker dad. Bobby graduated from high school two years early. He got a job as a dispatcher at his dad's trucking company, the largest in Tennessee. Nights he enrolled at the local community college, taking all the business and accounting classes they had to offer. Six years later, after his latest promotion landed him an office with Vice President on the door, Bobby married a schoolteacher studying for her master's at the same college. Two years after that, the trucking company's four directors were sent to prison. Bobby Dupree put together a group of local businessmen to salvage the almost bankrupt company. He was twenty-four.

Bobby had an infectious optimism, a bear trap of a brain, and an energy level that drove his team to exhaustion. Why anybody would want to sleep more than four hours a night baffled him. He was soft-spoken, hated the limelight, made his donations through blind charities and his local church, and quietly gobbled up company after company. By the age of thirty-seven, Bobby Dupree's net worth topped a quarter of a billion dollars.

He was also, in his own words, bored out of his tiny mind.

"What am I gonna do for the rest of my life?" he'd asked his wife the previous winter. "Buy more companies and make more money? Been there, done that. I can't spend what I already got."

Darlene Dupree was the sort of country lady whose exterior calm hid a core of solid steel. She still ran the church preschool because she felt called to the duty. "You'll work it out."

When Bobby was at home and worried and pacing, his speech returned to the patterns of his early days. "I been talking to God like you told me. How come He don't say nothing?"

"He will. In His own good time."

"You're so all-fired sure about that?"

Darlene looked up from the papers she was sorting through. "Don't you go picking a fight with me, Mr. Dupree."

"I was just saying—"

"You know who's gonna win that one. Nobody."

He sank down in the chair across from her worktable. "There's got to be more to life than making money."

"Have you ever thought God is the one putting this screw to your brain?"

Bobby opened his mouth and shut it. Twice. Because no, to be honest, he hadn't. "You mean, like Paul's got that thorn?"

"Possibly, honey. But I doubt it." She set down her pen. "You're already too busy. You've got people begging for every scrap of time you can throw them. But here you are, hunting hard as you know how for something else."

"Something more," Bobby agreed.

"Did it ever occur to you how blessed we are to be sitting here having this discussion?"

Bobby rose from his chair. "There you go. Adding guilt to the cauldron."

It was not until five months later that the head of Nashville's teaching hospital introduced him to Christian Round Table. CRT was not so much secretive as cautious. The group had been founded forty-two years earlier in Baton Rouge, hardly a hotbed of moral living, a fact that was not influenced in the least by the town's ratio of one church for every fifty-six inhabitants. CRT did not seek new members, yet it grew steadily, until by the time Bobby was invited to a session it had groups in all fifty states and nineteen foreign countries. There was no political affiliation, though many members were deeply involved in politics of both parties. It had no religious affiliation, though most of its members were elders or deacons or lay leaders—right across the spectrum of contemporary Christian churches. Nor was race or gender an issue. A third of the group were women, a quarter came from various minorities.

"If this group ever adopts a motto," Bobby's sponsor told him after his first meeting, "we could do worse than 'It's lonely at the top.'"

The rules suited him right to his bones. No solicitations. No business or personal agendas of any kind. No judgment of any member based upon the stand they took, politically or socially or otherwise.

The creed was six words long. *Prayer. Discipleship. Study. Accountability. Service. Support.*

The night after his second meeting, Bobby told his wife, "I do believe God was listening after all."

———•———

Liz Courtney was having a hard time not being impressed. Which was why, when the co-pilot sealed the door and the pilot swung Bobby's jet onto the runway, Bobby said, "First time I sat in this thing, I worried if I'd forget to keep my feet planted on the rock. My wife told me not to fret, that was her job."

Soon as they hit level flying, Fiona set out a linen tablecloth, silverware, crystal, and a cold plate of salads and sliced filet mignon. Liz smiled genuine thanks. "If it were my decision, I'd give you that interest-free loan you're obviously after. But that's why God gave us a board of directors."

"I ain't after your money, Mrs. Courtney."

"Call me Liz."

"But I do need your help."

While they ate, Bobby Dupree told her the story. About the prayer time. And the mission. Liz Courtney patted her lips, nodded thanks when he refilled her cup, and said, "You all had the same impression?"

"Impression's too weak a word. But vision don't work. And nobody I know of actually heard God speak out loud. But we all knew it was Him just the same."

"He said for you to go start a film company."

"I tell you what it was like. One minute I was sitting in the meeting room, listening to that evening's leader. The next, I felt God's call. Felt it like a divine weight placed on my destiny."

"Is that what the others saw?"

"Saw, heard, felt, smelled. Call it what you like, none of the words fit all that well. And the answer is, more or less. I called around. Some of them said they'd been feeling that way for a while. Others said it first came to them in a dream. Others in prayer time. But they all felt another impact that same night as me. So yeah, I suppose you could say it hit us all pretty much at the same moment."

She stared at the passing clouds. "How many of you are there?"

"Couldn't say, and even if I knew, I'd be wrong to talk about it. We're not after numbers. We're after brothers and sisters in Jesus. People who walk the road with us. There to help, there to pray."

She felt her own internal walls crumble. "Do they take people like me?"

"As in people of the female variety? You bet."

"Is that why you're here? To ask me to join?"

Bobby grinned. "Could be. That ain't why I came, but hey, God's got His own agenda sometimes."

She turned back to the window. "My husband died five years ago. He'd been ill for some time. The bank was more than just a company. It was his life. As his energy slipped I helped him run things. Gradually I took over more of the day-to-day. When he passed, most of Austin sat back and waited for me to fail." Her jaw came forward. "Our turnover is up fifty percent. We're opening three new branches a year. And we turn down an offer from the nationals about twice a week."

Bobby understood what was not being said. "But being right don't make the lonelies disappear, do they. Or explain why God left you down here when half your life is already up in heaven."

Liz Courtney studied the clouds for a long moment, then, "What is it you wanted from me?"

"A handle on Brent Stark."

"He's as fine a man as I know."

"That'd work fine if all I wanted was a pal. But I'm about to trust that man with God's mission. And I need to know if I'm doing the right thing."

She nodded slowly. "I'll tell you what I know, and then what I think."

"Couldn't ask for more than that."

"Brent came out of prison a broken man, rebuilt by the strength of his faith. When I fronted him the money and called some friends to find him clients, I figured there was a fifty-fifty chance he'd last six months. He's proved himself to be so solid, I've begged him to let me move him into something bigger. But his life is on the stage. He knows if he accepted more responsibility from me, it would mean less time for acting. And that's what he lives for. He can't get back in front of the camera. So he takes whatever role he's offered and he throws himself into it. And he *shines*."

This was why Bobby had taken the time to come down here. So he could sit here with his fancy leather seat swiveled around and study below the surface. Liz Courtney did not speak because she thought this was what he wanted to hear, or out of some misplaced loyalty for a handsome young man she might have a hankering after. She spoke out of conviction. She spoke because she cared.

"The only problem I have with Brent is he won't give himself a chance. He's turned down two offers to direct pieces."

"He's afraid of letting people down?"

"Probably. Either that or he's just . . ."

"I'd appreciate it if you'd go ahead and say it, ma'am."

"I think he's ashamed. Of who he was. Of what he's done. And the result is he won't let himself have another chance."

The co-pilot opened the door and said, "We're beginning our descent into Tulsa, Mr. Dupree."

Bobby thanked the man and waited for the door to shut again. "Is that all you were going to say about what you think?"

"No." Liz Courtney closed the distance between them. "Brent has no idea how strong he is, or how good. He's ready for this chance. Been ready for over a year, in my opinion. He's been treading water. Running his little business, helping raise the quality of our local theater groups by a quantum level or two, praying hard, trying to pretend this is all he ever wants from life. All he ever *deserves*."

"You like the man."

"I couldn't be prouder of him if he was my own son."

Bobby hesitated over the next question. "What about women?"

"I've wondered about that. Because he doesn't go out. And a guy that handsome, he could be a serial murderer and still have chances. But he's a nice guy, he's intelligent, and he's open about his mistakes. Half the single women in church have tried to wrangle a date and the other half wish they had the nerve. The theater group has been a lot more direct, and a lot more diverse, if you get my meaning."

"He just says no."

"In a nice enough way to keep most of them from getting upset."

"Hard to do."

"I think it's because he's so sad when he says it. Like there's something there, the one bad thing that is so big and so raw he can't talk about."

"Maybe it's not bad."

"Yeah, that's what I keep hoping. But I've wondered about this. I'd be lying to tell you otherwise. The guy lives like a monk."

Bobby waited for the wheels to touch down and the motors to rev through the braking process, then asked, "Why do you figure he went off to Hawaii to start on this project of mine?"

She pondered that while the co-pilot opened the jet's door and extended the stairs. "Did you tell him you felt God call you to do this?"

"Yes, ma'am."

"He'd take that very seriously."

Back in the days when sniffing out a new company had been the high point of his year, Bobby had occasionally known a thrill so strong his blood actually created music in his head. He knew it was crazy. Probably nothing more than a sign of dangerous blood pressure. But he'd loved it then. And he loved it now. This very moment. Because Bobby felt his blood sing a little. Not a full-blown symphony. But a quiet little hum. A *real* good sign.

Bobby asked, "So this feeling of mine that God is behind the project might push Brent to put aside his fears?"

"Maybe, if he thought he was doing this for God instead of

for himself." But saying the words turned her sad. "Where did you say you'd sent him?"

"First Hawaii and now LA. But I didn't send him anywhere. He asked to go. Insisted on making the trips all on his lonesome."

The news only made Liz Courtney sadder still. "Maybe he traveled out there planning to fail."

hari Khan had never felt so completely out of place in her life. And considering some of the situations she'd landed in since coming to LA, that was saying a lot.

The AA meeting was exactly where her tame detective had described. The church was two blocks off Sunset, in a section of Hollywood that was downshifting from rough to creepy. As soon as she entered the room, Shari recognized Brent Stark. She didn't need to consult the photograph stowed in her purse. The former star was seated in the third row, doing his best to blend in. But even here, in a loser's dungeon of a church basement, the man held a visceral force. Shari saw other people glance at Brent and knew she was not imagining things.

But compared to Sam Menzes and the combined power of Galaxy Studios, this almost-ran and the Nashville company backing his movie were a minor nuisance at best.

Even so, a girl on the rise couldn't be complacent.

Which was what she had repeatedly told herself on the drive over. But truth be told, another big reason for coming here was morbid curiosity. After all, when would she have another chance to see a man trying to rise from a Hollywood grave?

The man at the podium was a veteran of battles Shari didn't even want to think about, with a voice and scars to match. She could smell dust and fresh paint and a vague body odor, as though the foulness of past mistakes emanated from the gathering. The speaker with his raspy grit-encrusted voice unsettled her. He spoke about God as if the two of them had survived the same war. He used words that never entered her normal life—words like *suffering, deliverance, enduring, patience, redemption.* Shari shifted in her uncomfortable metal chair and stifled an urge to yell at him to shut up, get a life, put a sock in it, whatever.

Then it was over. The suddenness caught her completely by surprise. Which was why Shari was unprepared when Brent Stark turned her way.

His gaze filled her with a perverse shiver. She knew so much about him. He, on the other hand, saw just another woman hiding in plain sight behind her Max Mara shades.

Even so, he held her with a knowing stare. The intensity seemed capable of reaching beneath her calm mask and wrenching out her motives. Shari broke the look by rising and heading for the door. She had the ridiculous sensation of his eyes boring into her back. Which she knew was absurd.

When she reached the door, she could not help but turn back.

Brent Stark was still watching.

———————

Jerry Orbain arrived in Los Angeles bearing a set of DVDs and an attitude. Brent drove them back to a hotel booked by Fiona, Bobby Dupree's secretary. It was a sixties-style two-story affair whose one major asset was its location—just off Sunset in Bel-Air, two blocks from the north-south interstate. Recent renovations had broken down walls, doubling the room size. Brent's room was on the upper level, overlooking a postage-stamp garden and pool. It was the sort of place filled with film wannabes and indies struggling to survive on the fringe. Back in his fat days, Brent would have avoided the place at all costs. Hollywood was all about image, location, and status. This place had none of them. Brent liked it just fine.

Brent borrowed a DVD player from the front desk and played three episodes from Jerry's work. Brent did not need to see three hours' worth of television drama. But he did it just the same.

Jerry had directed two shows—one through two seasons, the second through three. It was a good starting position for a new director. Which was the first thing Brent said when the final program ended. Jerry responded with silence, staring at the empty screen, avoiding looking at Brent.

"With anybody else," Brent went on, "I would have watched the first act of one, the second of another, and the climax from the third. I would have asked my colleague to summarize the plot and point out what I needed to see. But I was concerned you might not give me what I needed. Would you?"

Jerry rose from his chair. "Is there anything to drink?"

"Coke and ginger ale in the fridge."

Jerry walked over and opened the mini-fridge door. The harsh LA sunlight formed a jagged frame along the base of the window curtains. "Bobby should have given me your job. I earned it. I brought them Candace Chen's *Long Hunter* script. I helped them set up the company. A year and a half I've been putting this together. It's mine."

"I appreciate your being honest about this," Brent said, and meant it. "Do you think it would make any difference if I quit?"

Jerry popped the top. "Probably not."

"What makes you say that?"

"Couldn't tell you. Bobby hasn't even said why I didn't get the job in the first place."

"But you've worked with him for eighteen months. Make a guess."

"Because he doesn't know the business!" Steam vented as he spoke. "He doesn't know what it's like to work on drama when you're given a budget of a quarter of a mil per television hour!"

Brent made no effort to disguise his astonishment. "You shot that for two hundred fifty thousand an episode?"

"They cut the budget on me. To the bone."

"That's amazing work, Jerry."

He guzzled his ginger ale. "I know."

"No, I mean it. I would have guessed twice that, maybe more." Brent ran through the sequences in his mind. "Untrained no-name actors. No rewrite time. How'd you keep down the overhead?"

"We shot at Biola. Ever heard of the place?"

"Sure. The Bible college."

"They've got a great arts program. We used their sound stages, hired a lot of students as apprentices and worked them like they were full-timers. We rehearsed forever, so when the cameras and the lights were brought in, we were more than ready."

Brent heard the pride in Jerry's voice. And understood why. "You did good work."

"That's right." Jerry met his gaze for the first time. "I did."

"But you've said it yourself. Bobby won't give you the top director slot. Is there anybody you'd rather work with than me?"

Jerry stared at the drink in his hand. "I haven't thought about that."

"While I was still in Bobby's office, I asked God for two signs. It looks like He has given me both of them." Brent told him briefly about his contact with the two ladies.

Jerry could not mask his astonishment. "Celia Breach is costarring?"

"We'll know soon enough. She's now meeting with Candace Chen."

"For real?"

"Let's focus on the here and now, Jerry. I can't go back to

God and say, 'Wait, I need another sign after you've given me what I asked for.' But it's how I feel. I need . . ."

Brent stopped. His chair was pulled up so close to the television his outstretched feet almost touched the stand. It was standard placement for professionals inspecting work, getting so close to the screen the rest of the world was excluded. Close enough that the screen *was* the world.

He looked down at his hands. His callouses were permanently stained with a mixture of grass and fuel. Not a star's hands. Not by a long shot.

"I went out to Hawaii both expecting and hoping Candace would shoot me down. I came here as desperate for Celia to ax me as I was for her to say yes. I've got a lot more than a director's slot riding on this project."

He looked up to discover Jerry staring back at him. Hostile, yes. But listening hard. "My guess is Bobby took these DVDs to somebody in the business. You want to hear what I think they probably said?"

Jerry was probably not much more than thirty-five years old. At that moment, however, he aged twenty years. "Go ahead."

"The work is good. But it's not film." Brent wasn't sure he was doing the right thing, giving it to him straight. But no other option came to mind. "It's one thing to handle a television crew of, what, maybe fifteen? Twenty?"

"Try twelve."

"One camera crew. Three guys on lights and reflectors. You weren't working union, so no time clock. Long as you finished the episode for that week, you could handle the shooting schedule however you wanted. No-name actors, so no egos. Internal sets. How am I doing, Jerry?"

He drained his can. Crumpled it. Set it down on the counter.

Brent ticked the points on his work-stained fingers. "We'll have a film crew of sixty-five, maybe seventy. Three full camera teams. One interior stage, possibly two. And two location crews.

One will be setting up, the other handling the shoot itself. Do you see where I'm going?"

"You don't know what the budget is."

"I don't need to. I know the story. This is what we'll require. To stay on budget, we'll have to work out a production schedule. I'm thinking a shoot of fifteen weeks. Jerry, think what that means. Even if we run a nonunion shoot, which is what I'm guessing Bobby is after, we'll be looking at double your entire episode budget for *every day we shoot.*"

Jerry looked at him then. The hostile veil was gone, at least for the moment.

His own words crawled around Brent's brain. Every day *we* shoot.

This thing was happening.

Brent heard the tremor in his voice as he said, "I need an assistant director I can trust, Jerry. You will be off on your own for more than half the shoot, working with the second team."

"Bobby hasn't said anything about what role I'd take on the set."

"Bobby strikes me as open to suggestions. If this is what you want." Brent pointed at the screen. "I know what you're think-ing. That you have what it takes to *shine.* And I think you're right. So the question is, are you willing to give what it takes as my AD, then go on to direct your own production next go-round?"

* * *

Brent gave Jerry two solid hours with Candace and Celia. He did not join them. Instead, he sat in the shade of the jacaranda tree and worked on three notebooks. One was story. The second was schedule. The third he did not give a name. This third set of issues covered too great a range. If he had been forced to give it a title, he would have called it "Trouble."

When Brent finally gathered his work, the murmur of voices from inside brought to mind long-ago conversations, when Celia had revealed terse splinters of her past. Celia had cast out the bitter fragments like junk she wanted to leave at the roadside. Her father had been a construction worker injured on the job. Celia had never mentioned her mother at all. She had been born in Reno, a place for which Celia had not a single kind word. As Brent rose from the cedar bench, he recalled how she had once told him that everybody aiming for the big brass ring needed something they hated so bad they'd do whatever it took to never go back again. She might have even said it their last night together. Which was good for another piercing regret.

Brent knocked on the glass door and waited. Celia walked over and said, "It's been open the whole time."

"I wanted to give you folks ample warning," Brent replied, "in case you were talking about me."

"As a matter of fact." Celia did not smile. That would have been asking too much. But she did speak without the previous razor edge to her voice. "You want a coffee?"

"If it's no trouble."

"It'll make Manuela's day, you know that." Celia did not do the standard Hollywood act of calling out or ringing a buzzer, or if the house was large enough, using the intercom. Instead, she crossed the living room and disappeared into the kitchen. She came back to add, "I asked her to make sandwiches. Anybody vegan or whatever the latest trend is?"

Today Celia wore a plain white T-shirt and stone-washed jeans. No logos, no shoes, no makeup. A rubber band held her hair in strict ponytail order. Her lips were pale in the manner of a Scandinavian blond. Celia displayed an amazing ability to capture the light and *possess* it. The center stage was wherever she happened to be.

Interestingly, Candace Chen and Jerry Orbain both wore almost identical expressions. The two sat across from one another, staring into their own respective inner space. Both looked shaken to the core—it was hard not to be rocked by a star.

Brent took this as his signal and entered stage left. "Forget the sandwiches. Jerry and I need to be leaving for the airport, and there is something we need to take care of first."

"Careful there, Brent," Celia said. "You're almost sounding like a director."

"That is the question, isn't it. Whether I'm going to run this gig."

"You're asking us?"

"I sure am." He smiled his thanks to Manuela. Sipped his coffee. "Two of you I've let down in the worst possible way. Jerry wishes I had never surfaced on his radar screen. Each of you have excellent reasons not to speak with me, much less agree to four months of fourteen-hour days. But my God is a mover of mountains and a shaker of the earth's foundations."

"Sorry, sport," Celia said. She reached for the gold box and lighter. "That argument doesn't work for me."

"It's the only one I've got," Brent replied. "It's the only thing that's brought me this far. And it's the only reason I'm here."

Celia lit up, blew her smoke, observed him carefully. Her eyes were neither blue nor gray, but a mixture all her very own. Cloudy when storms arose, crystal when the moment called for guileless. Brent had played enough closeups with her to half believe the claim that she could change their color at will.

Celia held the moment a beat longer than was comfortable. "You're saying I have to convert to act?"

"No, Celia. I'm saying we're going to work together along faith-based lines. We will be honest with each other. Starting here and now. We will strive for harmony and a solid working relationship. We will have no agents on set. Or lawyers. If you have something to say to me, you do it directly. No star tantrums."

"Wait. I get it. Let me feed you the next line. You're using this religion thing as a way of cutting my pay?"

Brent saw the narrowing of her gaze, the way her chin jutted, and knew she was preparing for a fight. He nodded at Jerry. "Why don't you tell them what Bobby told me."

"All the senior staff will receive the same pay." Jerry gave them the figure, which was barely above scale. In the film business, the minimums for each top specialist—actor in starring role, screenwriter, director, producer, cinematographer—were set by the guilds. The expectation was that they would negotiate upward from this legal base rate.

Jerry went on, "All senior staff will also receive four percent of the gross after distribution costs."

Celia was caught in the middle of erupting. "You mean four points of *net*."

"He means what he says, Celia." Producers and financiers were loath to give up points. Net was the best most actors could ever hope for. A cut of net meant a percentage of the film's earnings after expenses. And in the film business, expenses were a flexible item. Profits from big hits were scaled back by factoring in studio losses from other films. The executive jet could be used one time to bring in the director and star and still have the plane's annual operating budget charged off a film. Net had another word in the film trade. To those on the receiving end, net was called smoke. As in, vanishing into thin air.

Jerry went on, "The next tier down will receive one percent. Again, this is gross revenue after distribution costs." The idea of sharing revenue after distribution had often been discussed as a means of halting the scams endemic in the current studio accounting system. But the studios, which made a killing out of promising a share of profits that never appeared, constantly balked at the idea.

Brent said to Jerry, "Now give them the rest."

"There's more?" Candace asked.

"Bobby wants all of us to sign a standard corporate contract," Brent said, watching Jerry. "Tell them."

"In any other business, an employee has to promise that he won't compete against the guy paying his salary. Bobby wants to put all of us on a four-year contract. Your pay will be in monthly checks, drawn from the film company. You agree not to compete. As in, no acting for other companies during this period."

Celia stabbed out her cigarette. "I seem to recall this was tried and killed by the courts."

"The old system was unfair in the extreme," Jerry said. "Actors were tied up for seven years, plus whatever time they had on suspension. They were loaned out to other studios and all profits pocketed by the contract holder. They could be fined for non-acceptance of a role."

"You've studied this, have you."

"Bobby has. His aim is not to cheat but to promote a product and an idea. Value-based entertainment, with actors and actresses known for only these sort of projects."

"You can go for other roles," Brent said, "but only when they don't conflict, either time-wise or value-wise."

"And who decides that?"

"For the moment," Jerry replied, "it's Bobby. But he's the king of delegating. He'll find somebody he can trust and hand it over."

"Sounds to me like I need to meet this Bobby," Celia challenged.

"Yes," Brent said. "You do."

Candace asked, "You're telling us this is an all or nothing deal? We sign on for the long run or we don't play?"

"You're gonna love this." Brent motioned to Jerry. "Tell them."

"Bobby can't guarantee there'll be a company beyond this one film. He's still feeling his way. Since he can't promise, he can't expect you to either. He just asks that you'll enter into the spirit of the agreement."

"The spirit," Celia said.

"Yes."

"Such as," Brent clarified, "until the film is out and going strong, you won't take any role that goes against his values-based entertainment."

"Well, it's not like I'm drowning in offers over here," Celia said.

Jerry added, "And you'll give your word that if the project is a go long-term, you'll agree to consider signing on."

"That's it?"

"Bobby puts a lot of store in giving his word," Jerry said.

Celia and Candace exchanged a long look. Candace asked, "You believe this?"

"The guy sure isn't Hollywood," Celia said.

"No," Brent agreed. "He's not."

"The question is," Celia said, "can he deliver on the screen?"

Brent stood up. "That's why we're here."

The duo crossed the emerald lawn and climbed back into Brent's rental car. Jerry looked over the car, back at the house, where Manuela smiled and waved at them before shutting the door. Then he took a long glance at the almost-empty road before sliding into the car and saying, "She thinks the world of you."

"Manuela had trouble getting legal status." Brent started the car and pulled from the curb. "I had my lawyer help her. She took care of me through the worst of it. She came to see me in the city lockup. I asked her to stay with Celia."

Jerry rolled down his window and adjusted the side mirror. "I wasn't talking about the maid."

Brent pulled up to the stop sign and looked hard at his passenger. "Now I know you're talking about Candace Chen."

"Her too. Sure."

"Sorry, Sport. Celia Breach loathes the sight of me."

Jerry kept fiddling with his mirror. "Drive on."

"What's the matter?"

"I've seen that guy before."

"What guy?"

"Keep driving." Jerry leaned back in his seat. "The guy in the car behind us. I saw him before. Twice for certain. Maybe more."

Brent locked his eyes on the road ahead. "Where?"

"Outside Bobby's office in Nashville. He was arguing with a cop after parking in front of a fire hydrant. Then I saw him again when you picked me up at the airport. I recognized his car as soon as we came out of the house."

"It might be just a similar car."

"I'm not wrong about the guy following us." Jerry glanced over. "And I'm not wrong about Celia Breach."

tanley Allcott climbed into Liz Courtney's car. "Remind me again where it is we're going."

"I'm not too sure about that myself. Which is why I asked you along as backup."

The former pastor settled himself more deeply into the car's plush confines. There was room enough even for his massive frame. "I'd have offered to drive us. But I doubt you'd find my pickup as comfortable. What kind of car is this?"

"Infiniti. Top of the line." She glanced over. "What, you men are the only ones allowed to enjoy your toys?"

Stanley waited until she was on the eastbound highway headed to Houston. "So there's this group of rich guys who get together and pray."

"That's what I heard."

"In Houston."

"All over." She drove like a man, gunning the supercharged engine, muscling smoothly into the fast lane. "The reason I decided on making this trip is because I want to make sure the backers of the project are as real as Bobby Dupree. He said they're doing this as a collective. He's been made chairman. Over thirty investors are involved. Everything he told me, I liked. If it's real." When traffic eased beyond the city limits, Liz punched harder still until she settled on a steady eighty-five. In the wasteland between Texas cities, speed limits were posted for tourists.

The meeting took place in one of the steel and glass skyscrapers that dominated the Houston skyline. Liz parked in a downtown lot. They walked the pedestrian tunnel system that laced together the business district and came up the escalator to find a young man standing by the guard station. "Are you Mrs. Courtney?"

"That's right. This is Reverend Stanley Allcott. I hope it's all right that I brought an escort."

He led them to the bank of elevators. "The folks upstairs don't run a closed shop, ma'am. Some meetings are private, but mostly they're just . . . well, you'll see."

The floor was high enough for the boardroom windows to reveal a backdrop of sunset and tankers and harbor lights. A distinguished gentleman Liz recognized from the cover of business magazines introduced her around the table. They found places. The host asked, "Who's in charge tonight?"

"I believe that would be you, Harry."

"Can't be. I was in the hot seat last week."

"Try six months ago."

The woman seated next to Liz was richly Hispanic in coloring and Caribbean in accent. She explained, "Harry doesn't like leading because he can't make us behave."

"Be quiet, Consuela."

The lady smiled at Liz. "See?"

Harry gave them a brief formal welcome, calling Liz and Stanley by name, mentioning that Bobby Dupree was their sponsor. "Okay, let's open with a prayer. Who's got issues and needs?"

The stuff was standard. Spouses, business, children, friends. The friends list was perhaps longer than normal. People from all over. People in missions. People in distant lands. But still pretty much what Liz heard every time believers got together. She openly studied the people as they talked. They numbered perhaps forty in all. Half sat around the long table, the other half around the walls. Some wore suits, others were more casual. Liz nodded to several she recognized from meetings, conferences, or television talk shows. There was one marked difference. Each time a need was mentioned, there was a pause. Then one person made a note in his or her Bible and said, "I'll pray for them." If it was in response to someone in the room, that person inevitably said thanks. Finally the woman next to Liz leaned over and explained, "They're committing to pray about this issue every day for a month."

Liz glanced across the table. Stanley had heard the woman. He mouthed the word *Wow*.

Harry finally asked, "Anybody else?"

Then Liz surprised herself.

"Actually, I've got a prayer need, if that's okay."

"That's why we're here."

"One of my very dearest friends is why I'm here tonight. His name is Brent Stark. Some of you might know his story. Bobby Dupree wants him to direct a film. Brent is terrified of failing Bobby, failing himself, and failing God. I'd like to ask for prayer support."

Harry made a note. "Bobby's on my list already. I'll pray for Brent as well."

She swallowed hard. "Thank you, Harry. That means more than I can say."

They stood then and clasped hands and prayed. When they were done, they remained standing, their heads bowed. Someone started singing "In the Sweet By and By."

The singing was fine. The feeling was far better. When they began the first chorus, "We shall meet on that beautiful shore," the people to either side of Liz released her hands so they could raise theirs upward. The next round of the chorus, Stanley began singing a harmony line with "the sweet by and by," his bass echoing in balance to the others. "The glorious gift of His love, and the blessings that hallow our days." Liz stopped so she could just stand and let the sound resonate in her heart. "We shall meet on that beautiful shore."

When they were seated, Harry said to Liz, "This year, we're studying Matthew."

Stanley caught her eye once more and mouthed, *This year.*

"Our aim is not to progress at any particular speed. Each week, the leader takes as long a passage as he or she wants. He talks for a while, and then others chime in." Harry found his place in the Book and said, "Tonight's passage is one verse long. Chapter four, verse one. 'Then Jesus was led by the Spirit into the wilderness to be tempted by the devil.'

"I'd planned on doing the entire desert story tonight," Harry went on. "I've always had problems with this passage. I skip over it every chance I get. Studying for tonight has made me look not just at the words, but myself. I guess that's what's intended. But it's been very hard on me."

Harry swiped off his reading glasses. "Y'all know what Doris and I have been going through. I got elevated to the driver's seat and the first thing I learn is my predecessor falsified three quarters of earnings. Overnight our company loses half its book value. Two of my board members are indicted. And then after four months of courtroom hell, my son . . ."

Harry stopped. Just stopped. The woman next to Liz wrote one word. *Leukemia.*

The boardroom waited with him. No pressure. Nobody was going anywhere. Harry's voice was roughened when he finally continued. "Most of my life, faith was something I left at the door to the golf club bar. Doris and I've been through our hard times, sure, but like a lot of couples we just soldiered on. We figured it was about par for what we had and how we lived our lives. Then four years back, we had our own little epiphany. I won't go into that. You're here. You know what I'm talking about. The Spirit began working in our lives and our marriage. I got involved with you fine folks. Hope became a word with a completely different meaning. And joy. And life."

He stopped and looked around. "I'm telling this all out of order."

The woman next to Liz said, "You're doing fine, Harry."

"If one of my aides gave me a report this mangled, I'd send him back to the mailroom."

"We're your friends," the woman replied. "And you tell it any way you like."

A man further down the table said, "Long as your heart comes through in the message, you're taking the right course."

Harry went on, "Look at the verses just before the one I read you. Jesus is baptized. The Spirit arrives in the form of a dove. God's living presence descends from heaven and resides among us again. This is what we've all been craving, am I right? To feel that incredible high of God's empowerment. But what happens? I'm not talking about six years down the line. This is what happens *the very next moment*. How does God reward this young man He's just called His own beloved son? He sends him out to be tortured!"

Harry glared around the table. "You know how that makes me feel? It makes me furious! I'm so angry at God I can't get to the next line! I've been stuck here all week! So here I am, supposed to be leading you folks closer to God, and all I can say is, Enough! I'm done! I've been tortured enough!"

He wheezed hard. Not a cough. A whispery breath of knife-edge pain. The woman next to Liz said, "Harry?"

"I'm all right." He reached for his glasses. "Let's move on."

The entire room watched this captain of industry unable to fit his glasses back on his nose. His hands trembled too hard.

"Harry." The woman reached across and took his hand. "Look at me, Harry. It's all right. We're here for you, brother. Just relax now."

Across from Liz, Stanley cleared his throat. "I'm the stranger to this room. But I'm feeling God punching me in the heart, and I'd like to tell you why."

A woman in the far corner said, "Say it."

"I spent nineteen months in prison for gambling and drinking away my church's building fund. Among other things. This passage was one of those I spent a lot of time running from. And I tell you the truth. I don't know what Paul found in prison. For me, it was not a time of answers. It was a time of *asking*. What meant the most to me, what I've taken from that time in the bowels of hell on earth, was learning which questions were important enough to keep asking until I was pretty certain of the answer. May I?"

Stanley reached over and slid Harry's Bible in front of him. But he did not read anything. Instead, he set both of his hands upon the open page. "Here's a question I thought was important enough to pray over. Did Jesus *know*? And here's the other. Did Jesus know *why*?

"Was the Son of Man sent out there to be tested? That's what the pastors tell you. He was to know the temptations of mankind. He was to be tried and, like you say, tortured. But did He know this? Did he have advance knowledge? Because if He did, to my mind He went into this thing with the battle already half won. The worst part of my own dark nights has always been how unexpected they are. How totally and utterly helpless this lack of foreknowledge leaves us. We have no chance to prepare! We have no way to get ready! Or do we?

"So that's one question. And the other, now. Did Jesus know *why*? Do we? How many of us here know why we're tried by life until it's over and the pain is removed? And if Jesus did not know, could it be that He went into this with another reason entirely? Something *more* than temptation and thirst and loneliness and burning heat and hunger. Something *beyond* the torment."

Stanley caressed the pages, big roughened hands tracing

words like a blind man reading Braille. "I think He was at His most human here. I think He didn't have a clue. And I think there *was* a purpose beyond the temptation, the one He did not know until after. And that was a question. The one each of us must ask at some point or another. The question is this: Who am I, and why am I here?

"The reason I can even suggest this is what comes after this passage. 'From that time on Jesus began to preach. . . . ' Not before, when the Spirit came. *After* He came back. Why is this timing important? We have no answers to these questions except through prayer. And I prayed on this for months as I lay in my prison bed and listened to the prison clamor. Why *after* His desert experience? Because in His time of testing, Jesus was broken. This made His experience out there the *most human* of His time on earth. Why? Because Jesus learned what it meant to become crushed into the earth. Through this, it became a time of His revelation. He in His divine nature looked beyond the death of thirst and famine and pain and temptation, and saw His role in eternity. To live and die for us."

Stanley shut the Bible and slid it back over to Harry. "That's one ex-con's opinion, for what it's worth."

Liz could not reach the entire way across the table. But she slid her hand as far as it would reach across the cool polished surface. Not just closing the distance. Humbling herself. She said to Stanley, "I'm going to tell them."

Stanley just nodded.

Liz remained in that position, staring at him as she said, "Stanley was my pastor. I was on the board of elders. I discovered the missing funds. I testified against my own pastor in court. I listened to his sentencing. I stood and watched them drag him away in chains. Four months later, I lost my husband to a massive coronary. That was over four years ago. I still have nights when I lie in my lonely bed and wonder if God was punishing me for what I did."

"No, Liz," Stanley said. "No."

"I'm so sorry, Stanley."

"You did what you had to do." He settled his bulk upon the table to reach her hand. "You did *right*."

"After what I just heard you say, I think maybe I can lay that old ghost to rest."

———•———

At the meeting's close, Harry gave Liz a brotherly embrace. "You and your friend are welcome back here any time."

"I want that," Liz replied. "I want that a *lot*."

———•———

The drive back from Houston took place in the silence of friends needing time to digest. Liz only spoke when they hit the Austin city limits. "Where should I drop you?"

"I left my truck at the church. Liz . . ."

"Yes?"

"Nothing."

"Go ahead and say it." When he remained mute, Liz said, "We're friends, aren't we?"

"Absolutely."

"Good. So tell."

"I lost my wife eight years back. My kids were both gone. One lives in Boston. We don't talk, though I've tried hard as I know how. The other is my best friend, but she's married to a neurosurgeon in Denver. When Cindy passed . . ."

Liz said softly, "I know."

"I'm not making excuses. There are a lot of empty nesters who lose a spouse and they don't descend into the nightmare of booze and gambling and theft. It was all my fault. I pretended I could handle the loss of my true love, and I ended up a hollow shell. A pastor on the outside, and inside, nothing." He shifted in the seat. "The reason I bring this up, I didn't know what you were thinking in your own dark hours."

"How could you? I've never mentioned it to anyone before tonight."

Stanley shifted around so he could look at her full on. "That was real back there, wasn't it?"

Liz pulled into the church lot and parked. "It sure seemed that way to me."

He reached over and touched her hand. A surprisingly gentle contact for such a big man. "I caused a lot of people pain. You included. You had a sick husband. You were trying to cope with new responsibilities at the bank. You discovered a crime I had committed and went through the agony of deciding to go public. You did what you thought was right, and then you felt punished for your deeds. It's my fault. I want to tell you how sorry I am. You're a good woman, Liz. The best. You deserve a lot better than what you got."

She swallowed hard. "I don't know what to say."

"I tell the folks I mentor that a simple acceptance of the apology is enough."

"They're lucky to have you. Your protégés, I mean."

"Thank you, Liz."

"I accept your apology, Stanley."

He released a breath neither knew he had been holding. "Thank you."

They sat in the dark lot, friends. Stanley said, "I better go."

"Thanks for coming tonight."

"It was one of the nicest things I've experienced in a very long time."

"You want to do it again next Thursday?"

"Any time, Liz. I mean that."

andace Chen stayed at Celia's far longer than the four hours measured out on the clock. She remained long enough to borrow one of Celia's swimsuits and go for a paddle while Celia made notes on her script. Long enough to walk into the kitchen and chat with Manuela about her secret chili recipe and watch the Guatemalan shape her special pan-baked bread. Long enough to slip from the sofa onto the floor, so she could slide her legs under the coffee table and start making notes of her own.

Long enough to have the characters on her pages waken from their six-year slumber. Long enough to taste that long-forgotten spice, the flavor that burned and hurt and created more hunger than it satisfied.

Celia was sprawled on her back, two of the sofa cushions elevating her head, her painted toenails twiddling on the sofa back. She slapped the script shut, rubbed her eyes, and said, "Now tell me what you're thinking."

"I thought that was what I've been doing since the guys split."

Celia kept her hand over her eyes. "I mean, tell me what you've been working out, down at the level below your words.

I'm only asking because I can't figure out what my own inner voices are saying."

Candace slipped up and onto the sofa. She curled her feet under her. Gripped her ankles. And wondered at her willingness to trust this woman. An actor of the female variety. The same specimen that had shredded her the last time she dared enter the cave of cinematic shadows.

"When I went back to Hawaii, I left behind a lot more than my first script and my money. I didn't know it at the time, of course. I figured I'd get up there on my mountaintop and write my magnum opus." Candace gripped her ankles so hard her feet tingled from lack of circulation. "In all this time, I've only made it to page three."

Celia dropped her arm. She stared up at the ceiling. She did not speak.

Candace took a breath. Let it out. Tried again. "I'm thinking I could trust you."

Celia swung her feet to the floor. She reached for the gold box now surrounded by script pages and sticky notes. "I shouldn't smoke. It makes my scarring worse. I've been to five plastic surgeons and they all say the same thing."

"They don't have to wear your skin, though, do they."

Celia lit her cigarette, blew hard, said, "I made a deal with myself. I only smoke two cigarettes a day."

"How many does that one make?"

"Seven. No. Eight."

"It's Brent, isn't it."

Celia rose to her feet and walked to the sliding doors. She stared out at the jacaranda tree, now illuminated by the soft pool lights. "Since he's gotten out, he's been popping up every now and then. Usually it's a phone call. But he wrote me four letters. And he's come by twice before this time."

"You still have the letters?"

The cigarette crackled in the quiet room. "I wasn't going to let him in. I don't know why I did. No, that's not true."

"You kept the letters, didn't you," Candace said. "All four of them."

"I dreamed about him. Brent."

"When?"

"The night before he showed up." Celia told her about the dream. "Why would that make me cry?"

"You tell me, girl. It's your dream."

"You're religious too, aren't you."

"I was. I'm trying to be that way again."

"What happened?"

"Sam Menzes."

Celia dragged deeper still. "Oh. Him."

"I felt like God let me down so bad I must have missed something major in the fine print." Candace could have stopped there. But it was just the two of them. And the night. "I thought I'd gotten over being angry with Him for letting me down so bad. Maybe I did. But when Brent showed up and he started talking, what I felt most was ashamed. All the days washed away and lost forever."

Celia walked back over and stabbed out her cigarette. Hard.

From the kitchen came the sound of singing in Spanish. Soft. Lyrical. Candace heard one word she recognized. Over and over. *Jesu.* "I forgot she was here."

Celia stared at the open kitchen door. "I've never heard her sing before."

"You did, didn't you. Keep his letters." When Celia walked back over to the sliding glass doors, she pressed, "Did you tie them together with a pink ribbon?"

"Pu-leese. A rubber band."

"Where are they?"

"In a box on my bedroom mantel."

"What did he say?"

"I only opened the first one." She hugged herself. "I wasn't going to let him make me cry again."

"But you kept them. I've got shivers."

Celia began rocking back and forth. "I don't want him to hurt me again."

"You want my opinion, Brent Stark will do everything in his power to make sure *nobody* hurts you."

Celia stood and rocked a little longer. "What about you?"

"Oh, sure. Me too."

"No." She turned around. "I mean, are you in?"

Candace felt her face stretch and remembered to call it a smile. "Girl, that man had me before he climbed off his bike."

r. Dupree? Brent Stark. Hope it's all right to call this late."

"Jerry probably told you I'm not much interested in sleep. Besides which, if I don't want to talk I don't need to answer. What's up?"

"Jerry thinks we're being followed. I'm beginning to agree. I wanted to make sure the guy isn't one of yours."

"Jerry is my only eyes and ears on this gig. I wouldn't be doing a decent job of building trust if I had other folks on your tail."

"Another tracker probably means one of the studios is sniffing around your project."

"Now, why would they do such a thing?"

"It's standard practice in Hollywood if they have a project chasing the same market. My money's on Sam Menzes. I spoke with Candace Chen before calling you. In their last meeting, Sam said he was going to develop a script of his own and bury her."

"Those folks don't mess around, do they."

"If it's Menzes, you haven't seen anything yet. We need to know if Menzes has a project in development that has anything to do with Daniel Boone."

"Let me see what I can find out."

"Mr. Dupree, there's another favor I'd like to ask."

"You can keep calling me *mister* as long as you like. But if I had my druthers, you'd call me Bobby and drop the sir."

Brent explained what he was after. Bobby gave it a moment's silence, then said, "That's a good idea. No. It's better than that. It makes me feel like we're gonna make this thing work."

"That means a lot, Bobby."

"Let me make a couple of calls. My number one lady, Fiona, will be in touch." There came a pause, then, "Things working out between you and Jerry?"

"Too early to tell."

"So give me what you can."

Brent waved at Jerry, who was pointing at the LAX departures board, which now flashed *boarding* for their flight. "I told Jerry you probably hired a consultant who's been in this business a long time. And they probably said Jerry has serious potential. But moving from handling a college crew and a single camera set doesn't make him able to handle what you have in mind."

"What exactly is it you think I've got in mind?"

"Going nonunion means the top specialists will all be shut out from you. The director's job will be that much harder. But if you want a top-drawer film—"

"Which I do."

"You're still looking at a budget of somewhere around twenty million dollars. Two location teams, three film crews. Sixty-five staff behind the camera. Maybe a hundred days of shooting time. This film will require a serious coordination effort, made worse by a relatively untested team. The person you consulted said you needed a senior director. But working on a nonunion film would basically ruin them for life in Hollywood. So you'd have to find somebody who had been banished. Which brought you to me."

"Actually, your name came up later. But otherwise you're right on the money. And if you're this smart, you've also realized

I need you and Jerry to work as my team. Got any ideas on that one?"

"As a matter of fact, I do." Brent sketched out what he had in mind.

"You know what? The more I get to know you, the more I like what I find." Bobby Dupree's voice hardened a notch. "Now I got one last question for you, then we both got to get back to our other dance partners. Are you in or are you out?"

———•———

They took the last flight from Los Angeles to Denver and spent the night at the new airport hotel. Brent did not pretend to want to spend his dinner seated across from a silent Jerry. The man's sullenness was gone. But the distance remained. The restaurant was noisy without being full due to two tables of homeward-bound skiers. Brent asked for a table by the glass-fronted fire and worked on his lists. When Jerry entered the restaurant, Brent nodded but made no movement to clear away his work or invite the man to join him. He knew Jerry kept glancing over. But a little suspense worked as well in business as it did on the screen.

The next morning Brent was awakened by the phone. Bobby Dupree gave him the information Brent had requested and hung up, leaving Brent more energized than he'd ever been from coffee. He and Jerry took the nonstop to Norfolk and drove to Brenton University's main campus. Named after their chief benefactor and fast-food king, Brenton U had grown from concept to full-blown university in just nine years. Unlike most other Christian centers of higher education, Brenton was rich. The Brenton trust had been founded with just one objective in mind: turn a patch of green outside Norfolk into a world-class institute, and do so fast.

The red-brick Fine Arts building had the raw look of fresh construction. The early March sky was a brittle gray, the wind salt-laced and very cold. They parked in a visitor's slot and entered by the main doors. They were directed down corridors filled with students until they reached a sound stage door. The light overhead was off, so Brent knocked and entered.

Several of the departing students recognized him. Brent saw the shock register, heard the whispers rise behind him. Brent felt a poignant stab at the sight of Trevor standing with one hand draped over the camera dolly. On set, Trevor rarely released hold of what he called his most trusted friend.

"As I live and breathe. Brent Stark in the flesh." Trevor offered his hand. "How are you, dear boy? All right?"

"I'd like you to meet Jerry Orbain."

"I love your work, sir."

"A fan. How nice." Trevor had an Englishman's ability to smile with nothing but his eyes. "Speaking of which, I believe you have caused several of my charges to froth at the mouth."

An attractive young woman asked, "Can I have your autograph, Mr. Stark?"

The former cinematographer waved his student away. "No, you most certainly may not. Mr. Stark here has agreed to give a special lecture at two. I suggest you hurry back to your chambers and watch one of his films. *Torn Curtain* was always a personal favorite, though the Hitchcock original was better still."

Brent waited until they were alone to say, "A lecture?"

"Oh, did I fail to mention that? I do apologize. But they are ever so eager. It's quite rare that a real live Hollywood star makes it to the wilds of Norfolk."

"I haven't talked to a group in six years. And I'm hardly a star anymore."

"Ah, but this is your ideal audience. They grew up watching your films on cable. And they're too young to recall the scandal." Trevor's eyes were a luminescent gray, gentle as an English rain. "You really didn't expect me to sit through your pitch without extracting a pound of flesh in return."

Trevor Wright insisted on taking them back to his cluttered

office and making them tea. He puttered about in his shapeless jacket, fussing over a tin of biscuits that his students kept full. Brent observed, "You really are happy here."

"Other than a loathing for faculty meetings, yes, I suppose I am. Will you take sugar, Mr. Orbain?"

"I'm good, thanks."

Trevor directed his words to Jerry. "I grew tired of listening to my fellow believers complain about the state of Hollywood entertainment. I decided to take matters into my own hands. Do my part, as it were. Try and elevate the quality of young believers destined for the film trade."

Jerry said, "I've worked with students from Biola University."

Trevor nodded slowly. "That's where I've heard of you. Of course. You directed the series for Hope."

"You saw it?"

"I watched several segments. For a limited budget and untested actors in starring roles, you did yourself proud, young man."

Jerry almost kept himself from glancing at Brent. "That's right. I did."

Trevor's eyebrows lifted a notch. "Do I detect friction around a genuine project?"

Brent replied, "Financing, green light, stars, the works."

"Oh dear. You're putting me on the spot, are you. I rather thought this meeting would be more off-the-cuff."

"We wouldn't fly three thousand miles to see Norfolk in March."

"Quite." Trevor tasted his tea. "Scripts, I have to say, don't interest me much these days. Which was why I accepted Brenton's offer when they came calling. And the only thing I like less than the scripts are the people fashioning the story."

"You already know the project. You liked it."

"Dare I ask which one?"

"*Long Hunter.*"

"Oh, I say." Trevor set his cup aside. "Candace Chen's script."

"None other."

"You're starring?"

"And directing. Celia Breach will costar."

"You and Miss Breach in the Chen story. That will certainly set tongues to wagging." Trevor played at a distinct lack of interest. He straightened the crease of his rumpled trousers. Crossed his legs. Flicked at dust on his cuff. "Dare I offer a bit of advice?"

"Always."

"Directors who are also actors fail more often than they succeed. Put simply, the director can't take off his actor's hat. The film never achieves proper balance."

"What's your answer?"

"We're speaking theoretically, mind."

"If you want."

"For every shot that includes the director-actor, he may not study the monitor. He risks focusing too tightly upon his own role and ignoring the scene's broader scope."

"Sounds reasonable."

"I'm not nearly done. For all such shots, the director must hand over control of the scene to another."

"Meaning you, as DP."

"Now, now." Trevor wagged his finger. "We are speaking theoretically."

"But that's what you meant, wasn't it. The director of photography would control the shot. What if I wanted to share this responsibility between two people?"

"And who might that other individual be?"

"My assistant director."

Trevor blinked slowly. "The concept is certainly novel, but not without merit. Sharing the responsibility would also mean the director could maintain a greater sense of overall control."

The assistant director was supposedly the number two on the set. But with a dominating director, the role was often reduced to that of a glorified slave. "I don't need a gofer," Brent said. "I'm after balance. A second set of eyes. A person I can trust to take over the second unit."

"Did you have someone in mind?"

"Are we still talking hypothetically?"

Trevor rose and collected their cups, walked to the sink by the rear window and rinsed out the pot. "I may love teaching. But I'm far from wed to this alone. Were you to agree to my terms, and if the script is as good as I remember . . ."

"It's better."

Trevor wiped his hands on the dishtowel. "You wouldn't object if I made up my own mind over that?"

"I'll leave you a copy."

"When do you need to know?"

"I can give you two weeks. But I'll need you on location at the end of that time."

"We are moving swiftly, aren't we." To his credit, Trevor Wright did not offer superfluous objections about classes and the like. To a pro, shooting schedules took precedence over everything. And Trevor Wright was, above all else, a pro. "I suppose I could arrange a substitute for the remainder of the term."

"If you need anything between now and then, contact Jerry. I'll be out of touch for a while." He rose and offered Trevor his hand. "Thanks for seeing us, Trevor. I'll be back in time for the lecture."

"The students will be agog." The gaze was no less keen for its mellow aura. "One final question. That bit of news I heard about you finding faith after they sent you away."

"All true."

"Yes. Soon as I saw you, I gathered as much. Staying sober, are we?"

"Since the night of the accident."

"So glad to hear it." He settled his other hand atop theirs. "My dear boy. You've had a rather trying time of it. But from what I see before me today, Christ has worked His miracle yet again. Your dross has been turned to gold." He smiled them a farewell. "See you in the lecture hall at two."

———•———

Back at the car, Brent pulled a fresh script from his valise and handed it to Jerry. "You may want to spend a few minutes in there with him alone. Establish a rapport." He handed over the car keys. "You take this one. I spotted taxis by the Admin building. I need to rent another car before coming back to do the lecture."

"Where are you going?"

"Bobby's arranged for me to get some help with my role." Brent handed over his three lists, which now totaled more than twenty pages. "While I'm gone, I'd like you to get started with these."

"What are they?"

"Lists of critical elements we have to get lined up before moving into production. They're divided into location and studio sets, roughed-out shooting schedule, and general problem areas. If I were you, I'd show that second list to Trevor. Say you want his advice. But what you're really after is him to take it from you and start work on it today."

"Why are you doing this? So you can go back to Bobby and blame me when it's wrong?"

"No, Jerry. So I have the ammo I need to ask Bobby to make you my AD." Brent snapped his suitcase shut. "This is what you wanted, isn't it? To run the show? So run."

rent's call caught them just as Liz pulled into the Houston lot the following Thursday. Liz put the call on her car phone system so Stanley could hear and said, "You're late."

"I've been fighting traffic for five hours," Brent replied.

"Where are you?"

"In a truck stop off I-85. I'm headed for the southern tip of the Appalachians, down Georgia way. Bobby Dupree has set me up with a real-live frontier tracker. The man does not own a phone. As in, no contact whatsoever with the outside world."

"Why would Bobby do that to you?"

"Because I asked him to. Is Stanley there with you?"

Liz glanced at the bearlike man hulking in the passenger seat. She wanted to answer, sort of. Stanley was not merely silent. He was scarcely present at all. "Yes, but we're due upstairs now. You're not the only one who's been fighting traffic."

"I could call back later, but to be honest, I'm so tired I doubt I'll be awake. And I'm due to meet Bobby's mountain man at five-thirty tomorrow morning. I'll be gone twelve days. I'd like to leave packing your answers."

Liz could have used a few answers of her own. As in, what

had she done to turn her former pastor to sullen stone. And why Brent was going to be out of contact for two weeks. "I don't suppose we'll be the first folks to show up late."

Brent launched straight in. "After my first meeting with Bobby, I set out a fleece before God. Two of them. A pair of ladies with every reason in the world never to speak with me again. I've had two separate phone calls on today's drive west. Both ladies have officially signed on."

"That's a good thing, right?"

"It would be," Brent said slowly. "Except for one thing. It's left me needing to commit."

Stanley might have coughed. He uncrossed his arms and started to look in Liz's direction. But he caught himself just in time. Instead he stared at the radio's screen, where Brent's phone number was spelled out in backlit blue. Liz gave the pastor beside her more than ample time to respond, then said, "You can't expect all those fears to disappear overnight."

"It's more than that." The Bose sound system in Liz's car gave Brent's voice the resonance of the silver screen. "I want this thing. It's a craving in my gut. Strong as breath."

She was listening to Brent but watching Stanley. The man stared at the car's receiver with his mouth slightly ajar.

Brent breathed soft and strong over the speakers, then added hoarsely, "Strong as drink."

Stanley covered his eyes.

"What is *wrong* with you?" Liz asked.

"Excuse me?"

"Not you, Brent." She poked Stanley in the arm. "This man needs your help."

Stanley did not lower his hand. "You're doing fine."

Liz had been around strong men all her life. A rancher for a father, six older brothers, her dear husband. She knew bone-deep hurt when she saw it. Liz said, "Well, Stanley here seems to be all out of answers."

Stanley muttered, "You got that right."

"But if you want my two cents' worth, you're welcome to it."

"Please."

"Brent, the only thing you've ever wanted in your entire life is to perform. It's your *gift*."

"But it's also what destroyed me."

"Because you did it alone, and for all the wrong reasons. Now listen to me, because I'm talking to you from the experience of one who's climbed out of her own dark well. You're going to have some hard times ahead. That's what happens when you're willing to take chances. And there are going to be times when you're desperate to crawl back into your cave. But this time around, there's a difference. And you know what that is?"

"Yes."

"Sure you do. You know who you are now. You know why you're here. You know who you serve. You know where your strength comes from. You know . . ." She hesitated. Stanley dropped his hand and stared at her with such a wounded gaze she could look straight through that lesion, down into the man's hurting soul.

"Liz?"

"You know your purpose, Brent. You won't be making the same mistakes again, because this time around you're not doing it for yourself."

Brent's voice lowered an entire octave. "You see a lot more good in me than I do."

Stanley gave another wracking cough. But his eyes did not leave her own. Desperate eyes. Yearning to hear what she had to say. "Honey, you're focused on your past and your failures. I'm focused on your *future*."

He breathed in, and out, and in. "Thank you, Liz. A lot."

"Trust me, Brent. You're more than a good man. You're *ready*."

She cut the connection, gave it a minute, then said, "You

want to tell me what's going on here?"

But Stanley was already reaching for his door. "We're late."

Liz held her peace through a Bible lesson she scarcely heard. Stanley remained hunched over in his seat. Because they had come in late, all the places around the table were full. Her chair was closest to the door, set hard against the outer wall. Stanley was nudged into the corner by the floor-to-ceiling windows and the night skyline beyond. All she could really see of him was his muscular back and the top of his head, where the close-cut gray hair revealed a bare spot darkened by the Texas sun.

Liz waited until the lesson was done to say across the room, "Stanley. Look at me."

Slowly the big man rose from his crouch.

"If you won't tell me, tell them."

He blinked, drawn back to the present in reluctant stages.

"For your sake as much as mine. Please."

The boardroom chairs swiveled around until all eyes were on him.

"I'm a stranger here."

The man leading tonight's session was a port operator whose bulk rivaled Stanley's. "If you are, brother, it's our fault as much as yours."

Stanley spoke across the distance to Liz, "This afternoon I was offered a senior pastorate. I didn't even know I was being considered or I would have told them I wasn't available. But they've been coming in and listening to my Wednesday night sermons. And they've had talks with the other pastors about my outreach program. All of the church's deacons came in together. They've been praying about it and they feel like God has made the decision for them. I'm the only pastor they're approaching."

The collective silence held until Liz asked, "Which church is it?"

Even before he spoke, she knew. Nine years earlier, a dynamic young pastor had taken a slumbering neighborhood church and transformed it into a mega-explosion. The church had grown so fast, not even having six services a weekend could meet the needs. So they purchased a farm on the interstate between Austin and the Texas hill country and built a sprawling new campus. Two weeks after blessing the new sanctuary, their pastor had a massive heart attack and died.

Stanley said, "New Hope Church."

The gathering rustled. Somebody gave off a low whistle. They all knew the place.

Liz felt a sudden trembling, as though her heart were being touched by unseen fingers, prodding her into a higher form of wakefulness. "So what Brent talked about downstairs . . ."

"His worries might as well have come from my own mouth."

"You want this."

Stanley dropped his head again. "So much."

The Spirit filled the room. She knew this with the same degree of certainty that she could name the color of her own blouse. And just as vividly, she knew what she was being asked to do.

Liz twisted the wedding band on her left finger. She thought of all the friends in her church. The funeral of her beloved man. The support she had received in those dark hours. The ties. The memories.

She raised her head. "Take the job, Stanley."

He tore the words to shreds. "What if I fail God again?"

"I'll go with you."

The offer took a moment to sink in. He looked at her. Blinked slowly. "What?"

"I'll come, too. Be your advisor. Keep you accountable. Sit in your office before the Sabbath service and pray for the strength and direction I know God is waiting to give you." She felt her trembling fade with the power's departure and knew it was the right move. "If that's what you want."

erhaps it was the afternoon sunlight. Any actor with serious camera time knew a five-degree change in the light's angle made the difference between a smash and a dud. Or maybe it was simply that during Shari's second personal meeting with Sam Menzes, the adrenaline rush did not blind her quite so badly as it had before. Whatever the reason, this time she noticed the scar on his neck. She knew he had gotten it seven years back, when he and his latest mistress had been trapped in a New York hotel fire. Sam was reported to have saved as many as two dozen lives by racing up and down the hallway, waking people and breaking down doors to make sure no one was inside.

He refused to discuss the incident. In fact he made it a habit never to give interviews of any kind. Ever. It was part of the Menzes legend.

This was, of course, long before her time. Shari Khan knew the story because she had spent the previous two weeks discovering everything she could about her new boss. Since Menzes ran Galaxy Studios, she had always answered ultimately to him. But now she worked *with* him. All the difference in the world.

Menzes greeted her with, "How's Bud?"

"Progressing more slowly than he'd like, Mr. Menzes. It looks like he'll be in traction for another week."

Shari's boss had been so furious at hearing how she'd scooped him, he had fired her from his hospital bed. Shari had phoned the news in to Sam's secretary. Something had happened. Something big, because ten minutes later her erstwhile boss had called back, subdued to the point of meekness, and blamed his outburst on the pain. That night, according to the nurse who despised Bud and loved dishing out the dirt to Shari in their now-nightly phone calls, the guy had actually freed himself from his support system, climbed out of bed, and done his leg further damage. But if Menzes wanted to pretend that little drama had never happened, fine. Shari said, "He sends you his best."

"Keep me posted." Menzes pointed to the man seated across from her. "You know Derek."

"Only by reputation." Derek Steen was Galaxy's chief counsel. Those who had negotiated against him claimed he was the world's first vampire lizard. "A pleasure, Mr. Steen."

"Okay, Shari," Menzes said. "Tell me why we're here."

Shari Khan opened the leather portfolio from Aquascutum, a gift from her grandmother. She passed over single-sheet printouts. Sam Menzes was notorious for ignoring any print that went over two pages. The idea of coating her report in plastic had come to her in the middle of the night. Producers and directors often did this with story pitches, called leave-behinds. They plasticized the leave-behind and stamped a copyright seal on the cover to make it tougher for some in-house leach to steal their idea and paycheck.

Shari had been at the printer when it had opened at six. Instead of the copyright seal, the bottom right corner was stamped with the Galaxy logo. She thought it was a nice touch. Shari was not normally such a perfectionist. But she had waited all her life for the chance to sit at the table with Sam Menzes. She handed a second copy to Derek Steen. "Bobby Dupree."

Sam Menzes opened a lacquered case and withdrew a set of Cartier reading glasses. "I know that name."

"Probably from the cover article *Forbes* ran on him last year. The photo they used is on the back."

Both men flipped over the sheet. Bobby Dupree leaned on a polished truck bumper. To his left, a Mack bulldog snarled in direct contrast to his own boyish grin.

"Bobby Dupree is forty-three years old. He got his start in trucking and currently owns fourteen companies outright and controlling shares in two dozen more. All his operations are centered east of the Mississippi. Four years ago he acquired the largest producer of Nashville-based music videos. Mostly C&W and inspirational."

Steen spoke for the first time. "That last term is new to me."

"Inspirational. It means religious. Christian music."

"Like in church?"

"I wondered the same thing, Mr. Steen." She drew another sheet from her folder. "Inspirational music is one of the fastest growing sectors of the music business."

"Says who?"

"My information comes from *Billboard* magazine. Revenue from CD and video sales last year topped a billion and a half dollars."

"Dupree is religious?" Menzes asked.

"The word is, seriously."

"He successful?"

"If he made the cover of *Forbes*," Steen said, "he has to be doing something right."

"I meant in what interests us."

"Very," Shari replied. "If you'll look on the bottom right of the front page, you'll see in the four years he's controlled this music video group, he's effectively doubled their turnover. A good deal of this has come from branching out into other related businesses. Dupree's company is now the largest independent maker of theater-directed advertisements outside New York and LA."

Steen said, "Big leap, from sixty-second ads and three-minute videos to a feature film."

"But it's a natural progression." Menzes did not look up from the sheet. "What are these other names here?"

"Dupree's other investors. Those I've managed to identify, anyway."

"He has nineteen other backers?"

"I'm sure there are more, Mr. Menzes."

"How much are they ponying up?"

"Two million is the minimum I've found so far."

The two men exchanged glances. Steen said, "The guy must be some salesman."

"He's got a war chest of forty million dollars?"

"My guess is, a great deal more."

"What about their Boone film?"

Shari extracted a third page. "The project is definitely a go. I don't have a budget estimate, but I'm working on that. Their director, Brent Stark, has disappeared. The last sighting was nine days ago, when he met with a retired cinematographer now teaching at Brenton University."

"Where?"

"It's a Christian college in Norfolk. After that, he vanished. My people haven't been able to find him."

Steen laughed, a coppery disused sound. "The guy is back on the bottle."

Shari decided now was the time to say, "I checked him out when he was here in LA." She briefly recounted her attending the AA meeting in East Hollywood. "He was sober at the time."

Sam Menzes asked, "What was your impression of Stark?"

Shari had a fleeting memory of the eyes that followed her from the room. "He might be down and out. But he's still got something about him."

Menzes nodded agreement. "A star's aura."

"He's a once-was," Steen countered. "You know what they say. A reformed drunk is just one step away from his next barstool."

Menzes gave his attorney a thoughtful look, then asked Shari, "What else do you have?"

"The cinematographer is now at the former Angelini studio in Wilmington, North Carolina, working with an aide to Bobby Dupree named Jerry Orbain. Orbain has directed two low-budget series for Hope-TV."

"I don't get it," Steen told his boss. "You're worried about a project fronted by a drunk, a religious nut, a retired camera geek, and a guy who did soaps for a network that went bust?"

Shari looked up. It was the first time she had heard that her boss was genuinely concerned.

"I've got a lot personally riding on our film." Menzes jutted his chin in Shari's direction. "So they're in Wilmington."

"Set design is underway. I've got photos if you're interested. They're using Dupree's plane to scope out locations in western North Carolina. They've signed Celia Breach to costar."

"She's good," Menzes said.

"She's another has-been," Steen asserted. "So their project is a go. So what? It's like a guppy going up against a shark."

Shari personally agreed. But this being her reason for sitting there at all, she was not going to be the one to say it out loud.

Menzes asked, "What should we do about it?"

Steen snorted but did not protest further.

"I've got an idea," Shari said.

"Let's have it."

"We go public with our project. Have the stars and the director at a gala event. Take over a major venue. In the middle of the sound and lights, I drop it to one of the trades how there's this other no-name group doing a nonunion project out in the back of beyond. Feed them some of what I've found. Let them do a high-damage profile. Something we can show to the distributors when the time comes."

"I like it." Menzes traced his logo imprinted in the plastic. "This is good work."

"Thank you, Mr. Menzes."

"How much are we paying you?"

She blinked. "Not nearly enough."

He flipped the sheet back across his desk to her. "Write yourself a new contract."

Shari was unable to mask her total amazement. "Thank you, Mr. Menzes!"

"Have it on Derek's desk tomorrow morning. Oh, and Shari."

"Sir?"

"You know the most important detail you haven't included here?"

She wasn't sure her legs would support her across the room. But she knew the answer to that one. "Their release date. I'm working on it, Mr. Menzes."

Sam Menzes tightened his lips enough to almost have Shari call it a smile. "Of course you are."

———◆———

When the door closed behind the departing woman, Derek Steen said, "'Write yourself a new contract'? What kind of nonsense is that?"

"I've got a feeling about this one."

"Are we talking about the competition or the woman?"

Menzes rose and walked to the rear window. He watched the studio traffic for a while and said, "Her idea is good."

"Maybe. It better be. Since tomorrow she'll have written herself into a Bentley and a back lot cottage."

"A bill says you're wrong."

"She's all of what, twenty-five?"

"Twenty-seven. I had Gilda check."

"Twenty-seven years old. Seriously good looking, if you like your women exotic." Steen started to ask if Menzes was promoting the woman into a position as his next paramour. But Menzes could be very touchy about his private life. "She's spent a couple of years being stomped on by her boss. She'll write herself into a star-size fortune. Sure, I'll be happy to take a thousand dollars of your money."

"You just be sure and have your check on my desk by lunchtime tomorrow."

"What if I'm right?"

"Then you can have the pleasure of firing her." Menzes returned to his desk. "But I'm not wrong."

hari arrived home that evening just after nine. Most of the young aides she knew lived jammed together in sardine conditions. Either they took a cramped room overlooking a West Hollywood freeway, or they found a partner higher up the food chain and pretended at love. But Shari's grandmother lived in one of the apartment towers lining Santa Monica Boulevard in Brentwood. As far as the movers and shakers were concerned, Brentwood held all the appeal of a Kansas City suburb. Brentwood was staid. Brentwood was old money. Brentwood was a haven of Republicanism in the sea of West Coast Democrats. Shari couldn't care less about politics, except of course for the vital affairs of state that ruled the studio system.

What Brentwood was for Shari was safe. And safety in the midst of the carnivores trolling the Hollywood waters was a rare commodity.

"Gran, I'm home."

"Hello, darling."

Shari set her keys in the ceramic bowl and her purse on the hook in the foyer closet. Shari was not a guest. She was home here. Her grandmother had a six-day-per-week housekeeper and expected Shari to live by her rules. As in, the public rooms were to be kept hotel-lobby immaculate.

Shari leaned on the wall and pried off her heels. She padded down the hallway to her room. If the military had designed a grenade that could totally blow order out the window without damaging anything, the result would look like Shari's room. The maid refused to even glance inside. Shari hung up her work clothes, pulled a SoCal sweatshirt and stylishly torn jeans from their respective piles, and padded barefoot back to the living room.

She bent over and kissed her grandmother's offered cheek. Lizu Khan was as flawless as her apartment. She was not going out. She was expecting no visitors. Yet her makeup was ready for a closeup, her nails manicured, her hair as perfectly coiffed as her twice-weekly beautician could make it. She wore pearls and a diamond-studded bracelet, nylons, and a Dior suit knit from pashmina clouds.

Her grandmother smiled at the exposed knee and asked, "How was your day?"

Shari's normal response was, so-so. She usually plopped into the sofa by the rear window, scrubbed her scalp hard enough to erase the day's frustrations, and opened the chest where she kept her nightly reads—scripts, corporate doggerel, various trades. If it was a particularly awful day, Shari took a drink and a pile of what she called her flip-throughs out onto the balcony. The apartment faced away from the traffic and was high enough to watch the sun set over Santa Monica. Shari would sit and dream that her ship had finally arrived in the smog-ridden glint of water on the horizon. Her grandmother was neither one to pry nor cling. If Shari wanted to talk, her grandmother was available. Otherwise, they were comfortable with silences that often lasted from hello to good-night.

Friends.

Tonight, however, Shari replied, "Today was actually great."

"Well, finally." Shari's grandmother set aside her book. "Maria left your dinner in the oven. Go have your dinner and then we'll talk."

Instead, Shari fixed herself a tray and brought it back into the living room. She appreciated her grandmother's interest in her job, especially since her own mother was mortally ashamed of her daughter working in Hollywood. Between bites, she told her grandmother what had happened over the past few weeks. The skiing accident that had claimed her boss. The maneuvering. The news she'd learned from a friend about the new Nashville-based production company. How she'd phoned the detective agency her boss used and claimed authority to set up surveillance. She took it through today's meeting with Sam Menzes and Derek Steen.

Her grandmother's only response was to toy with her pearls. She was truly a queen, this woman. A dowager who had been preserved in the essence of power. Her sofa was a makeshift ivory throne, the apartment her only kingdom. But she emanated the heartless wisdom of one who had once ruled a fiefdom with a velvet voice and absolute authority.

Shari's memories of her grandfather were hazy, mostly of a smiling old gentleman whose snow-white mustache she loved to pull. Her father had been born in Islamabad while her grandfather had been Iran's ambassador to Pakistan. When they returned to Tehran, it had been for her grandfather to become a minister in the shah's inner circle. The ministers controlled access. And to the multitude of companies that wanted to do business in Iran, access was everything. Money poured in a constant deluge. During those days of endless wealth, the Brentwood apartment had been the smallest of six family residences, purchased so her father would have someplace to live while he studied engineering at UCLA. Shari's bedroom had once housed her father's live-in butler.

Her grandfather had been one of the wise ones, or perhaps

merely lucky. When Iran had descended into chaos, Shari's grand-father had spirited his family away. He had promised he would either follow them if things grew worse or bring them back once order was restored. Instead, Shari's grandfather had disappeared into the bedlam that followed the revolution. They never learned what had happened to him. Shari's grandmother still tried.

The Brentwood apartment and a small annuity were all that remained from those fabled days of wealth and power almost beyond imagination. Even so, Shari knew just how lucky they were. Every now and then she returned home to find her grand-mother hosting friends who greeted Shari almost slavishly. Shari's grandmother would introduce them as a former general or prince. They would be carefully groomed in a manner that only heightened the strain of poverty. They spoke together in Farsi, which Shari had stubbornly refused to learn, but she did not need to understand the language to know her grandmother politely served tea to desperate beggars.

Her grandmother had learned English at an Oxfordshire boarding school that had also housed three of the Shah's family. "I'm always telling you, whatever you decide to do in this life, go into it with your eyes wide open."

"I'm fully aware of the risks."

"Oh, piffle. You know nothing." Lizu Khan even criticized with elegance. "Your adolescent blindness is so complete you take pride in ignorance."

Shari flushed. "Stop talking down to me, old woman."

Her grandmother's eyes widened. "The tone you take with your elders."

"Then show me a little respect." Shari shifted her tray to the coffee table, setting it down hard enough to punctuate her anger with clatter. "I'll tell you the risks I know. I know you're not talk-ing about this one chance but the whole Hollywood tribe. I know the women who make it to the top here have nothing *except* their job. They're all divorced. They're all lonely. They all live for nothing except making the next film."

"This is the life you want?"

"Of course not. Stop asking silly questions. But that's what you said, wasn't it. Know the *risks*. I'm telling you, I want this job. I hope I can escape the other women's fate. But I'm going in with my eyes wide open."

"I'm sorry I upset you."

"It's all right."

"No, no. Forgive me. Somehow your grandfather's spirit skipped a generation, but you have it in full, I'm happy to say. Now tell me the rest."

Shari recounted how today's meeting had ended.

"He told you to write your own contract? This is normal?"

"Of course not."

"One can never tell. So much is alien here. Very well. Then this gentleman has handed you a test. You see that, of course."

"Yes."

"He will expect you to concentrate on yourself. More money. More expenses. More travel. Perhaps a car. You will do none of this."

"I'm tired of crumbs."

"Listen to me, darling. I am not wrong. You will ask for *power*. You will ask for *responsibility*. You will ask for *access*."

"I need the money too."

"You will leave that blank, do you hear me? You will name the position, describe it in careful detail. Then you will march in and ask *him* to pay you what you deserve."

Shari mulled that over. "You're right."

"Of course I am. You think your grandfather rose to the top of the kingdom alone? I was a mistress of power."

"You still are."

"So. We remain friends. That is good." The smile descended into worried creases. "But I am most concerned about this opposition you face."

"What, the Nashville group? They're nowhere. They don't stand a chance."

"Which is exactly what the shah and his advisors said about the rabble screaming in the souks. They are religious, this group, yes?"

"The man in charge is. I don't know about the others."

She wagged an arthritic finger. "I remember their missionaries. So quiet, so very polite. But they ate at the people's minds. Suddenly there were secret churches everywhere. The imams were terrified over losing their authority. But the shah's hands were tied; the American authorities ordered him to let the missionaries in. And his advisors, they sneered at these missionaries—they were just peasants from silly little towns in Texas. Phah. What did they know, these princes who never left Tehran except to ski in Gstaad or summer in St. Tropez? These missionaries talked the language of the people. They enraged the imams to the point that the imams threatened to take matters into their own hands. Which they did, inflaming the people who chafed under the shah. And down the house of cards fell. Costing us everything. Even your grandfather."

"I never knew that was what happened."

"And now you do." The jewels on her wrist winked a warning glimmer. "Mark my words. This is not rabble. Never mistake them for smoke. They are the enemy. They must be dealt with mercilessly."

hari Khan stood to the right of the studio limos, hidden behind her oversized Max Mara shades. She glanced down at the concrete, just making sure her feet were still in contact with the ground.

The studio PR brass clustered between the limos and the runway. A hot Santa Ana wind blew her dark hair across her face. Shari tossed her head to clear her eyes, and caught sight of the studio brass glancing her way. They had no idea who she was, and it bothered them. She smiled, ever so slightly. Let them wonder.

Six o'clock in the morning, the day after her meeting with Sam Menzes, she had been the first to arrive in the studio's central offices. As ordered, she had left her new contract on Derek Steen's desk.

When Steen ordered her to appear, Shari was so drenched in adrenaline sweat she felt like she squished with each step. "You wanted to see me?"

"Shut the door and come sit down." Steen's office was directly opposite Sam Menzes' suite. It was marginally smaller than Menzes', and his desk was executive standard. But the air of power was the same.

Sam Menzes was an anomaly within the Hollywood trade. He had come up through the ranks of distributors. He started off in the late sixties, inheriting a chain of New England movie theaters. Menzes built the first megaplexes outside the major metropolitan centers, predicting that if the public was offered high-quality digital sound and huge screens and rocking-chair seats, the ongoing decline in ticket sales could be reversed. Menzes was proved spectacularly correct. In twelve years, Menzes built a chain of a hundred and fifty theaters. When a Hollywood distributor tried to buy him out, Menzes arranged a hostile takeover of the Los Angeles company. The trades called it a real-life case of the minnow swallowing the whale.

Menzes continued to grow and to acquire. When Galaxy's former owner, the largest distiller in North America, put the studio up for sale, Menzes acquired both the production company and the studio's impressive library of films. He then purchased a cable company, which granted him a means of paying himself rent for airing old movies.

Menzes ran his conglomerate like the film giants of old. He hired good people but never gave them free reign. Derek Steen was the power behind the throne. When Sam Menzes ordered an execution, Derek Steen wielded the knife.

Steen said, "You cost me a thousand dollars."

"Excuse me?"

"I bet Sam you'd come back with a list of demands big enough to choke an agent."

Shari heard herself speak from a disembodied distance. "I'm sorry you opted to wager against me, Mr. Steen."

He lifted her contract by thumb and forefinger. "This has also cost me the pleasure of firing you. I am very good at that particular portion of my job, Ms. Khan. Do you read me?"

"Loud and clear, Mr. Steen."

He flipped the contract to page two. "You want a managerial position in Admin. Are you sure you have what it takes?"

"It's the chance I've been dreaming of," she replied.

Sam Menzes and his executive team occupied the top two floors of the Galaxy administrative building, which anchored the northeast corner of the vast lot fronting Pico Boulevard. The next three floors were given over to producers and directors under contract to Galaxy. Directly below them were Accounts and Legal. Menzes liked to say it was his way of sandwiching in the talent. The floor below was Sales. Then came Film Editing and Archives. Ground floor and the two above that housed Galaxy's massive PR complex, considered by many to be the best in the business. Shari's former boss was one of Galaxy's four vice-presidents of Public Relations. Like all Hollywood studios, Galaxy sprouted more VPs than LA grew oranges.

Between PR and the film library was the mystery floor. It housed what was officially known simply as Admin. Galaxy's stable of talent knew the building's fourth floor by a different name. They called it the snake pit.

Every Hollywood studio had such a group. Often it was kept at arm's length, run through a trusted attorney's office so deniability was an option. Menzes, however, had no intention of letting that much power remain outside his direct control.

Admin had one basic function; to ensure that every Galaxy film made as much money as possible, by whatever means necessary. The Admin sector contained a rogue's gallery of former agents, forensic accountants, and courtroom-hardened attorneys. They were all ruthless. They were hungry. And they were utterly without scruples.

Steen said, "We don't have managers in Admin."

Shari nodded but did not speak. She knew it. But she could not bring herself to write in the alternative. She had gone back and forth over it, then finally gone to her grandmother, who had totally agreed. Use the insipid word, her grandmother had insisted. Let him bestow upon you the crown.

Which was exactly what Steen proceeded to do. He unscrewed

his pen and scratched out the word *manager*. He then proceeded to scrawl in a dream come true. "Your official title will be Assistant Producer. Which means absolutely nothing unless you make it work. Are we clear on this?"

"Totally, Mr. Steen. I won't let you down."

"You'll answer directly to me. Admin is my own personal domain." He flipped to the back pages, the ones she had left blank, and scribbled busily. "Sam sees something in you, Ms. Khan. I personally have my doubts."

Shari resisted the urge to scream, dance, race around the desk and hug this man who claimed to dislike her and want her gone.

"Hand this to Madeline on your way out." He initialed the bottom of the last page and passed over the completed contract, then gave her a full two seconds of his lead-colored gaze. "If you want to have a job this time next month, Ms. Khan, you will continue to prove me wrong."

———•———

The John Wayne Airport was on the wrong side of LA and in Shari's opinion an odd place to land a private jet full of stars. Shari made no attempt to approach the studio's PR group clustered on the tarmac. Her grandmother had given Shari only two bits of advice after reviewing Shari's new contract. "You will remain hidden until you are certain both of the timing and the direction of your strike."

"I'm not after drawing blood here. I'm after making a great film."

"Phah." A finely lacquered nail tapped the pages. "You have been hired because you are a great filmmaker, yes? A woman with a reputation for creating great stories?"

Shari felt her face flush. "Of course not."

"So don't talk nonsense and listen. The people who are also not story makers, they will see you as a threat. Which you are.

So you will remain silent and keep your dagger hidden. They will study you. They will ask around. They will receive nothing from you. Nobody was ever defeated by words they did not speak or actions they never took. Soon, they will begin to ignore you. Perhaps even forget. Then, when it is time." Her grandmother slapped the papers. "You strike."

Shari wanted to take back the contract trapped beneath her grandmother's hands. But something told her that was exactly what her grandmother expected her to do. "You said there were two parts to your advice."

Her grandmother leaned back in her chair, but her hands remained where they were on the contract. "You are listening. Excellent. So here is the second portion. Seek out others like you."

Shari smiled. "This contract says there isn't anybody like me."

Her grandmother not only smiled but reached across and patted her hand. "You not only have your grandfather's spirit but his conceit as well. Which is good. You will see. What I mean is this. Search for others with hidden strengths. People who are overlooked by the peons who cluster around the throne and scrabble for crumbs of power. Find them, and make them your allies. No. More than that."

Her grandmother leaned across the dining room table, so close Shari could see the chandelier reflected in those coal-dark eyes. "You will make them your friends."

Which was why, when she heard the male voice behind her say, "You're missing all the excitement, standing over here with the outcasts," Shari did not snub him by moving farther away.

Instead, she turned and saw a man with the muscular frame of a stunt guy leaning against the fender of the last limo. He wore his suit like other guys might dream of fitting into Speedos, bulging about the shoulders and neck, slimming down to narrow hips. His neck was large enough to demand a tailored dress shirt. The afternoon sun glinted off a gold Rolex and wraparound shades. His salt-and-pepper hair was LA perfect.

Shari watched as a woman made her way back across the tarmac carrying a pair of Styrofoam cups. "You believe this place? They don't even have a Starbucks."

The guy accepted the cup with, "I asked for this?"

"Hey, a gentleman never lets a lady drink alone." The newcomer peeled off the top, blew, and sipped. "I go half an hour with no caffeine, I'm ready for rehab."

"It's hot as a hair dryer out here and you want me to drink coffee?"

"Just hold it for me, then. I'll get to you momentarily." Her Ray-Bans glinted as she shifted her gaze to Shari. "Who's this?"

"She hasn't said. My money's on the mystery lady we've been hearing about."

"The new kid Steen's taken on board?"

"The same." The guy called over, "What, you're the latest Menzes flame?"

Shari bit back her angry retort. She walked up and said, "If that's his motive, he's about to be seriously disappointed."

"Ooh, character. That's a new slant."

The woman elbowed the guy. "Be nice. We might even be in the presence of a lady."

"Nah, Border Patrol stops those kind in Van Nuys." But he shifted the cup and offered his hand. "Leo Patillo."

"Nice to meet you, Leo. I'm Shari Khan."

"This is Emily Arsene."

Shari cocked her head and studied the woman who appeared about a decade older than herself. "I've heard of you. Wait, sure, you're Sam's chief reader."

A simple adage of Hollywood was that producers didn't read anything longer than the zeros on their paychecks. Some, in fact, were almost illiterate. All, however, were deluged with pitches and stories and scripts and books and magazine articles. All this fodder was desperately shoveled their way by agents and writers and directors, who frantically searched for the next green light. A reader was someone whose taste the producer trusted. They were the funnel. Or in the case of some producers, the locked door. The reader studied the material, distilled it down to a few terse sentences, and gave a verdict. The closest most would-be screenwriters ever came to Hollywood credit was a *pass* from a major producer's reader.

The simple act of turning his head accented the cords of muscles on Leo's tanned neck. "What do you know, Emily. A fan."

"Don't mind Leo. He overdosed on Muscle Beach steroids when he was eleven."

"Sharr-ee . . ." Leo exaggerated the unusual pronunciation. "That's what kinda name, Mexican?"

"Persian," Shari said.

Leo shrugged. "Same thing."

"Leo. Please," Emily said. "Your ignorance muscle is bulging again."

Shari asked, "So what brings you out here in the heat?"

"Leo is Sam's minder. I'm here to make sure Leo behaves."

"Like you could stop me, I get on a tear."

"Leo used to be a cop," Emily explained. "Sometimes he gets carried away, thinks he can still hide behind his badge."

He did a fair imitation of a famous action star. "I never hit nobody who didn't ask for it."

"See what I mean?" Emily finished her coffee, looked for a wastebasket.

"Here, I'll take care of that." Shari took the cup and carried it to the trash bin by the nearest hangar. Crossing the concrete was like walking on a superheated mirror. Leo and Emily watched her intently as she returned.

Emily said, "You believe that?"

"No wonder Menzes is after putting her in his private corral," Leo said.

"I told you," Shari said. "That is not happening."

"Stop with the trash talk," Emily said. "We're in the presence of class as well as smarts."

Shari said, "I'm still not clear on what Menzes thinks needs minding here."

Emily Arsene pointed to where a jet whined its way toward them. "Maybe nothing."

Leo had to shout to be heard. "Oh. Right. Like anything ever went smooth in this town."

The PR cartel was moving before the jet braked and the engines whined down. By the time the pilot opened the door and unfolded the stairs, they were clustered in an expectant semicircle.

But nothing, no advance notice of any kind, could have prepared Shari for what happened next.

Raul Solish, who had managed to win Oscars both for screenwriting and directing, the man *Variety* called an understated genius on both page and screen, appeared in the jet's doorway wearing a flight attendant's jacket replete with silver flying wings. He also wore leather chaps, riding boots, spurs, and a sombrero. He held a half-gallon magnum of Dom Perignon in one hand and a neon-green giraffe in the other. His sunglasses were missing one lens, but Shari doubted the director noticed. He was kept from tumbling headlong down the stairs by a hand that reached out from behind and gripped the flight attendant's jacket, which fit Solish like the undersized uniform of a dancing monkey. Solish tried to shrug off the hand and managed to drop his giraffe.

He stared down at where the stuffed animal lay on the tarmac and wailed a note of utter bereavement.

"Is that actually a sombrero?" Leo asked nobody in particular. "They came from Budapest by way of Cancun?"

Emily said, "Maybe the pilot had a touch too much of Solish's lunch and got lost."

— A second head appeared by the director. Shari recognized Colin Chapman, a true Hollywood legend, a child star who had managed to not only hold on to fame as he grew, but become a bigger star in the process. Lasting power was the rarest of talents in the Hollywood spectrum.

But Shari doubted that Colin Chapman's millions of fans would recognize the actor just then.

Chapman wore what Shari assumed was a sozzled version of the national Hungarian costume. A round leather hat hung from his neck by a braid. An embroidered white shirt the size of a sail. And a gypsy vest of rainbow hues.

It was good that the shirt was so large, because the star wore no pants.

Raul's grief over the lost giraffe was cut off by the former child star saying, "We can't disappoint our fans."

"We can't?"

Chapman remained upright because of the two-armed lock he had taken of the director's shoulders. "Nooooo! They want an encore!"

The two men then launched into what Shari could only describe as a unique rendition of "Cabaret."

Leo crossed the tarmac, pushed aside the gaping PR clones, and called up, "Gentlemen! Mr. Menzes sends you his regards." The studio boss's name had a calming effect. "You can come quiet or you can come loud. It's your call."

Emily and Shari watched as Leo ushered the pair into two separate limos and confiscated a camera being surreptitiously wielded by a PR flunky. Only when the parade pulled away did Emily say, "That's our cue."

Emily and Shari climbed into the plane. The co-pilot greeted them with the stone silence of a man seriously in need of another dose of patience. Emily took a look around the demolished interior and said to him, "Mr. Menzes says for you gentlemen to add the appropriate sum to your bill."

"Don't worry, we will."

"Where's Billie?"

The pilot pointed to the back of the jet. "She locked herself in at takeoff and hasn't come out."

"Can you get the door?"

"No problem." The pilot led them to the back. He knocked on the burl walnut, tried the handle, said, "Ms. Rondelle?" When there was no answer he fished a key from his pocket and unlocked the door, knocked again, then opened it and stepped away. "All yours."

Emily stepped inside. "Billie?"

The impossibly beautiful young woman who had fed the dreams of a billion young men pushed aside the yellow silk sheets, peeled off her eye mask, and said plaintively, "They stole my giraffe."

"Sam worked out a five-picture deal with the Hungarian government," Emily told her. "It was a typical Menzes move. He flew over with Steen and an accountant. No creative types to mess up the works. Menzes told the prime minister he could guarantee years of work, tons of good publicity, hundreds of new jobs, yada, yada."

Shari tried to concentrate on what Emily was telling her, but the scene beyond the smoked glass cried out for her attention. She had driven down this very stretch of road a hundred times and more. But never in the back of a limo. The tourists crowding the sidewalks stood out like they had been backlit, because only a visitor from the sticks would give a stretch limo in Hollywood a second glance. If the passengers were anybody worth watching, a local knew the windows would be as dark as their Ray-Bans.

Emily went on, "When Menzes had the minister and his staff ready to break out the brandy or whatever it is they drink, he left. Derek stayed." Emily glanced over. "You've met Derek."

"Twice."

"Then you know. Derek and the accountant lock the minister and his staff in a double vise and squeeze. They get everything they want. Cash, hotels, caterers, free location shoots, even time inside the prime minister's office for a story they haven't written yet."

They passed the fire escape where Julia Roberts had climbed away from her landlord in *Pretty Woman*. They turned onto Hollywood Boulevard and passed the Egyptian Theatre, which premiered the original *Robin Hood* in 1922. Next came the much more famous Chinese Theatre, which Sid Grauman completed in 1927. As usual, the buses blocked Shari's view of the tourists shooting pictures of their favorite stars' handprints. Next came the Roosevelt Hotel, where the first Academy Awards were held—the ceremony took a grand total of sixteen minutes.

"The downside is obvious," Emily went on. "For this current frontier project, they found a section of Transylvania that defines primeval wilderness. But the only place for the cast and crew to sleep is a state-owned castle. Half the showers don't work, and there's never enough hot water. There are no paved roads in the entire province. The nearest decent restaurant is in Budapest. They're basically locked in at night. Wolves. Or maybe vampires, I forget."

Elizabeth Rondelle, renamed Billie by the studio marketing gurus, had until now been happy to alternate between braiding her green giraffe's forelock and staring out the side window. Now she turned and whined, "Hello! Am I, like, invisible here?"

"Sorry, Billie," Emily soothed.

"I'm a person too, you know."

"Of course you are."

Shari leaned forward, not because she had the slightest

interest in what the star had to say. Rather, she wanted another glimpse of the woman's astonishing beauty. Billie Rondelle defined physical perfection. Her face was flawless. Her eyes huge and emerald.

Billie whined, "I've got feelings too."

"You certainly do." Emily fished in her voluminous purse and came up with a plastic folder. "I have some lines for you to study."

"We're doing a Boone scene in West Hollywood?"

"It's for tonight's event, Billie. You'll be talking to the press, remember?"

"Oh. Right. Okay."

Billie Rondelle shifted the giraffe so the green animal could read the lines with her. Shari wondered what it was like, possessing a viscerally magnetic beauty and the mind of a nine-year-old.

Billie said to the folder, "I hope you told Charles to come do my hair."

"He's waiting for you in your suite."

"It better not be one of his little peons either. Only Charles knows what to do with my hair. Nobody else cares."

"I care, Billie."

"Yeah, sure, okay. But you tell Sam everything."

"Not all of it. You know that. Only the good bits." She patted the woman-child's knee. "We're here."

The hotel's security guard had the barrier up in advance of their arrival. The limo swept through the mob of photo journalists clustered by the front gates. Tucked into a lush enclave overlooking the Sunset Strip was the Chateau Marmont. The hotel had been famously decadent for eighty years. The staff was professionally adept at handling trouble. Harry Cohn, the founder of Columbia Pictures, had often warned his stars that if they were going to seriously misbehave, they were to make sure they did it at the Marmont. For Oscar week, the castle was booked five years in advance. Marilyn Monroe partied there between husbands. John Belushi died there. Jean Harlow cheated with Clark Gable there—while on her honeymoon. Chateau Marmont was where the bodies and secrets came to be buried.

One of the PR types Shari had last seen at the airport scurried down the front stairs, shooed away the valet, and waved frantically for them to stop. When the window rolled down, he had to pause for breath before gasping, "Take her round back."

Emily leaned over Shari and said, "Trouble?"

He wrung his hands. "The press are already doing a live feed!"

Emily leaned back in her seat. "Driver, you know what to do?"

"On my way."

As they pulled toward the rear loading dock, Emily retrieved the script from Billie's hands. The ingenue complained, "But I haven't learned the lines yet."

Emily shared a smile with Shari. "Something tells me it won't matter a whole lot."

obby Dupree told himself he was not going to be overwhelmed. About ten thousand times. He also said it to his wife that morning. His wife just smiled at him and said, "Oh, go ahead and let yourself be twelve years old again."

"I'm a big boy now."

"Sure you are, honey."

"I'm president of companies."

"You say frog and people croak."

"Hey, you're not helping things here."

Darlene kissed him. "You just run along and remember everything so you can tell me about it tonight."

"Huh. Like I'm gonna forget meeting Celia Breach." Bobby fished his keys from the bowl on the front table, then fitted his cell phone into the belt holster and the remote into his ear. "Why don't you come with me?"

"This is your fantasy, not mine."

"I thought I was doing this for God."

Darlene no longer bothered to hide her smile. "Last I checked, God never said you couldn't have a good time."

Bobby kissed her a second time, then said, "Some wives would be worried, their husband going off to meet a Hollywood star."

She laughed out loud. "Call me when it's done."

Bobby did what he did every morning as he left the home life behind and settled into his game face. He checked his watch, climbed into the Escalade, turned on his phone, hit the speed dial, backed from the drive, and said to Fiona, "The office building burn down?"

"Not that I've noticed."

"The banks call about that overdue loan?"

"You don't have any."

"Guess I managed to slip one by you as well. Okay, what's up?"

"You know what's up. Their plane is on time."

"Whose plane would that be?"

Fiona's laugh sounded remarkably like his wife's. "Yeah, right."

"Who do I need to talk to now?"

Fiona went through a customary list of urgents and finished with, "Jerry Orbain phoned last night after you left."

"Put him through first."

"He didn't say it was urgent, and it's two hours earlier there."

"I know. But let's get him done now."

Jerry was up and running, as Bobby knew he would be. "Jerry, do you ever actually lay down and sleep?"

"Sure. Sometime last year. I remember it distinctly. My Evereadies went flat."

Jerry's ability to go without sleep was one of the reasons Bobby had decided to give him a try. It was good to hear the younger man not sounding morose. "What's up with you?"

"Brent Stark arrived back last night."

"He tell you how it went?"

"He said it was the hardest thing he ever did in his entire life."

Jerry paused, then added, "He also told me I've done a good job."

"See? All that worry over nothing."

"How did you know?"

"Because I trust the man. Just like you should. What are you guys up to today?"

"We're meeting with actors the casting agent has rounded up. Trevor Wright, our director of photography, has lined up his crew. I'm flying back to Wilmington with them tonight. We start rehearsals tomorrow. Brent's spending tomorrow going over the storyboards and the shooting schedule with Trevor. They come in two days—the same day Celia arrives."

Bobby smiled at the little zing he got over hearing the star's name. *His* star. In *his* film. He had to work hard to keep the lilt from his voice. "How are things going on the sets?"

"Trevor checked them before he flew out. He says the crews are doing great things. I've been busy out here for the past five days, so I can't—"

"If Brent says we should trust the man, that's good enough for me."

There was a pause, and Bobby shook his head over the hesitation. Jerry was doing his mental routine again, as in, if you trust Brent why can't you trust me? The guy had a serious load of shoulder chips. But hey, not even God found twelve perfect men, and He had His Son on the hunt. "Jerry, you there?"

"I'm here."

"Have Brent call me when he's conscious." Bobby cut the connection, which put him immediately back to his secretary. Her office console resembled NASA's control system, and his cell phone bill rivaled the space shuttle for altitude. Bobby said, "Find me somebody who's got a remedy for bad attitude. I want to buy their company."

"There's nothing the matter with Jerry Orbain that a little success won't heal." Fiona considered Jerry one of her personal favorites. "Ready for the next round?"

By the time he made it downtown, Bobby had worked through most of the overnight problems. He stopped by the fourth floor and had a word with his music video staff, the only group in his entire company that rivaled him for energy. Bobby had taken bids for this new work from four different groups. The music video team had done what he had hoped, which was slave over the challenge night and day until they had a concept that knocked his socks off. He stopped by that morning to tell them so.

Their reaction to his announcement—that they had won the right to handle promotion and marketing for his new film project, *and* that a genuine star would be stopping by later to see their work—brought to mind igniting a dump truck full of plastic explosives.

He was still grinning when he got off the elevator on the top floor. Fiona asked, "What's got you so happy?"

"Ain't nothing finer in this whole world than giving young people exactly what they want."

"Oh. I thought maybe you were just excited over today's guest." She rang his office phone. "Brent Stark on line two."

Bobby switched the little gizmo by his office phone over, so his headset now responded to both machines. When they'd started, the phone company had said it wasn't possible, he'd just have to switch headsets when he came into the office, to which Bobby said, obviously they'd designed their phone systems for folks who were in love with chairs. He'd brought in his own wizards, who'd fashioned him something that did the trick but looked like his desk had grown a tumor, until Darlene found a Chinese lacquered box at an antique store and had the same technicians hollow it out. The phone system had cost him more than a new Lexus, but it meant he could move from office to car to basement to roof and never be out of range. "Brent, what's the haps?"

"You don't ever need to eat coon, Bobby."

Bobby did not try to hide his laugh. Every time he spoke to this guy, he liked him more. "Explain to me why it is my company has paid for you to go play in the forest for a week and a half."

"I told you before. I need to fit myself into this role. I've got to tell you, making it in frontier times was harder than anything I could ever have imagined."

"I have trouble remembering how I survived before Starbucks. That wilderness fellow knew his stuff?"

"He didn't say much, and what he did say I'm not sure I understood. His accent was pure twang. But he wore me plumb out. Where did you find him?"

"You know how it is. I made a couple of calls, is all."

"I'd like to bring him up to our first location, have him do a weekend training for the whole team. He says his wife will do the same for the womenfolk."

"It's your band, Brent. You call the tunes." Bobby gave it a moment, then said, "Tell me about Jerry."

"He did good work. Accomplished more than I would have thought possible. We're actually ahead of schedule, thanks to him."

"That's real good. Now tell me about Jerry."

Brent sighed. "We won't know for certain until he gets into trouble. If he can admit it and ask for help, then we're good to go."

"You still want to make him your, what did you call it?"

"AD. Assistant director. And yes. I do."

Bobby liked the absence of hesitation enough to say, "Go for it."

"Thanks, Bobby."

"Got the word back from them folks I hired out Hollywood way. Galaxy is into principal shooting of their *Iron Feather* project."

"Yeah, Jerry gave me the news soon as I got back. We've

decided to drop a week of rehearsal time and push hard."

"I'm fretting about the films being too similar."

"Don't worry, theirs won't be the same."

"But they're doing our story."

"No, Bobby. Sam Menzes is doing his story. And it won't be ours. Not by a mile." Brent was silent a moment, then said, "We need to find out what their wrap date is. And the planned release date. If we can, we need to beat them. They'll throw a ton of money at their marketing. If they come out first they'll capture all the PR thunder."

"I'm with you."

When he hung up the phone, Bobby's secretary was in the doorway, grinning like a Christmas elf. "They're five minutes out."

Bobby was used to the things only big money could bring. He'd been invited to the White House. He'd had lunch with six governors of four different states. He'd sat on stages and even given a speech or two.

But nothing, not even shaking the president's hand, had prepared him for the rush of knowing a star was on her way up to his office. "What am I supposed to do? Meet her at the elevator?"

Fiona shared his wife's pleasure in watching him dance. "I doubt there's ever been a rule book written for this one."

Fiona's console was always lit up like a Christmas tree. No matter how early Bobby got in, at least one light was blinking. But there was a separate line, one that had a special alarm chime. Bobby's wife had that number. His mother and brother. A very few close friends. Two people with sick kin he and Darlene were praying for daily.

Both of them tensed when the chime went off. Fiona stepped to her desk, then called over, "Jim Evans."

"Shut my door. Show the folks into my conference room." Jim was the man who had brought him into the prayer group and remained his principal contact. Bobby hit the button. "Jim? How are you, brother?"

"Bobby, I've got Stan Saucer on the line. You remember Stan."

"You kidding?" Saucer ran Global Oil out of Houston. He was also one of the hold-out investors in Bobby's film project. "What's up, gentlemen?"

"Go ahead, Stan."

"Bobby, we've been hosting a couple of new folks at our Thursday meetings. I believe you know them. Liz Courtney and Stanley Allcott."

"I've met Liz. I'm sure they're both fine folk."

"That they are. I know you're a busy man, so I won't go into details. But they've impacted me in a major way. I mean, moved me like few things ever do. As much by how they are as anything they've said."

"You don't need to try and explain that, brother. I felt the exact same way."

"Back when you first told me about God pushing you into the film business, I was interested, but worried." He had an oil-man's voice, equal parts gravel and raw-boned muscle. "Real worried. I figured you had a good chance of pouring your money down an armadillo hole."

"I know exactly what you mean."

"I can't tell you what I felt back then. Whether God spoke to me or not. It's easy to walk away from that silent voice. You understand what I'm saying?"

"All too well."

"But these people, they've struck me hard. And every time we meet, they ask that we pray for you and for that director fellow, Brent Stark. Did it again this week. And this time, I heard God in a different way. Like He was standing next to me. And I'm calling to tell you, I'm in. Where do I send my check?"

They talked for a while longer, in the manner of men feeling their way into a new relationship. Then they prayed. When they were done, Bobby set down the phone and sat there. Hands folded on the desk. Eyes shut. Not saying much. Just dwelling in the moment. So intent on giving quiet thanks he wasn't even aware Fiona was in the doorway until he lifted his gaze.

"You all right?" his secretary asked.

"Fine." He headed for the side door. "You hear about God's timing so much, you don't give it any thought until the next miracle sneaks over and smacks you upside the head."

hateau Marmont's ground floor was one huge open space, which was how members of Led Zeppelin had turned the hotel lobby into their own personal motorcycle drag circuit. Shari stood by a cart of soiled laundry as Emily and Billie, accompanied by an utterly unfazed front-desk manager, slipped into the servants' elevator. Shari stopped by the ladies' room to freshen up, then entered the main hall.

Shari had been on her share of sets. She loved the flavor, the compressed electric frisson, the clock that ticked in all the behind-the-camera voices. And this was what the Marmont's front rooms reminded her of, a set waiting for the stars to appear.

A young pianist who had recently graced the front cover of *Teen People* played a variety of hits from Galaxy films. She and the band were almost lost behind the potted fronds that formed a mock wall between the bar and the restaurant. Several hundred people milled about, pretending not to watch as a half-dozen lollipops, Hollywood's name for cable TV reporters, did their start-up pieces for the cameras. To an outsider, it might look like the party was in full swing. But Shari knew better.

Leo Patillo, the former cop, appeared at her elbow. For such a huge man, he moved with surprising stealth. "You think the cable networks include *brain dead* in their lollipop job descriptions?"

Shari was not sure about this guy. He reminded her of a loyal bulldog, one that at the snap of a single command would go from calm to vicious. Even so, she recalled her grandmother's edict and said, "Any idea when they start the main act?"

"Not long now." He touched his finger to a miniature earpiece. "Menzes' limo is two minutes out."

"You were really a cop?"

"Protect and serve, baby." He had eyes like a bulldog as well, and they stared at her now with the moral blankness of colored glass. "They're laying odds as to what Menzes has in mind for you. As in how long it takes you to move from the snake pit to the chairman's bedroom."

She gave a Hollywood smile, all lips and neither teeth nor humor. "I assume we're speaking about the PR cluster holding up the bar."

"Them and the assistant director types who can't decide if you're a threat or a temporary hassle."

"Let them guess," Shari said. "Why spoil their fun?"

Leo's reply was halted by a shrill scream one octave above frantic. Two waitresses tossed their silver platters of crab claws and pâté toward the ceiling and fled. Behind them came a roaring Colin Chapman. The heartthrob to a hundred million teenagers managed to both wear a tuxedo and be scarcely dressed. He raced a wheelchair.

"The wheelchair is how they got him into the hotel," Leo told her. "Guess the shower woke him up some."

The television lights swung in remarkable unison. The cable lollipops smiled like a chorus line and hopped around, struggling to keep in view of the cameras without blocking the star. Chapman did a wheelie, spun through a three-sixty, did another wheelie, then spied the bar. The crowd parted like the Red Sea.

"He's actually not bad with that thing," Leo observed. "Probably been practicing for that final trip to the OD corral."

A roar from high overhead was the only warning the crowd had before Raul Solish, the director, came flying down the polished curved banister. Over his tux Solish wore a bed sheet as a cape. He launched himself off the end and did a full gainer into the shrieking PR cluster.

Leo's teeth were small and chopped at the ends like he had ground them down to miniature dominoes. "Just another day in Hollywoodland."

The star and director slid onto the bench to either side of the pianist, who at their insistence launched into a rendition of "You Can't Always Get What You Want" between swigs from the director's bottle of champagne. Juiced as they were, the pair actually made a not-bad duet.

"This is unbelievable."

"Hey, they're just letting off a little steam. After being trapped in Albania for a couple of months, who's to wonder?"

"Actually, they're filming in Hungary, and it's only been three weeks."

"I'm sure I don't care. They're here and they've still got most of their clothes on. This will play for months. PR couldn't buy this much publicity with a dump truck of dollars." Leo pointed up the stairs. "Wait. Here comes our leading lady."

Billie Rondelle did not descend the stairway. She floated, held to the mundane earth by Sam Menzes, who kept a dead solid lock on her elbow. Billie was dressed in a sequined gown the color of pearl smoke, high necked and gathered at three points—right shoulder, right waist and high up her right thigh. Each folding of the fabric was fastened with a diamond brooch. It was a knockout dress, something from a thirties black-and-white drama where the ladies dressed like queens. Billie's smile and poise were equally regal.

Menzes' capped teeth were the only portion of him that

captured any attention, for they possessed an otherworldly gleam. All lights, all eyes, all attention were held by Billie Rondelle. Menzes hit the bottom stair and slipped away with the grace of Fred Astaire, leaving Billie to face the flashing camera strobes and the sudden cluster of cable lollipops. Emily Arsene appeared as by magic. Somehow, in a forest of crystal stemware and caviar, Emily held an insulated coffee mug. With ironclad politeness, Emily kept the interviewers from clawing at Billie and each other.

Menzes came to stand by Shari. Leo instantly vanished. Menzes glanced over to where his male lead and director were still singing and swigging at the piano. His smile remained firmly in place, but his eyes glinted scalpel sharp.

Shari felt an icy quiver in her gut, in anticipation of the chairman's verbal blade. Instead Menzes said, "I've got to congratulate you, Ms. Khan. For your first time at bat, you've done solid work here."

One of the network anchors overheard the studio chief. Instantly the woman circled one finger in the air, which was all her cameraman needed to shift his focus from Rondelle to Menzes. There was a world of difference between network and cable entertainment coverage. Network anchors shifted between news and morning shows and entertainment prime time, developing a general method of punching all of America's viewing buttons.

"Mr. Menzes, I'm Carey McGraw with NBC's *Evening Entertainment*. Would you have a word for us?"

"You know I don't give interviews, Ms. McGraw."

The anchor flashed a coquettish smile. "Can't shoot a girl for trying."

For the first time that evening, the chief's smile was genuine. "Why don't you talk to my chief aide on this film, Ms. Khan."

The anchor's antennae were up and sniffing. "Can I keep you in the picture as well, Mr. Menzes?"

"Long as you focus on Ms. Khan here, most certainly."

It was only at this point that Shari realized her jaw was still hanging loose. Her teeth clipped inside her head as she snapped her mouth shut. And just in time, for the cameraman swung his focus and said, "Ready."

"What is your first name, Ms. Khan?"

"Shari."

"On me, three, two, one. I am here at the infamous Chateau Marmont, haven to stars and star-size scandals. Only tonight we're celebrating the newest megahit from Galaxy Studios, *Iron Feather*, starring Colin Chapman and Billie Rondelle, directed by Raul Solish, whose voice I believe you can hear in the background, singing 'Let's Face the Music and Dance.' With me now is Shari Khan, one of Sam Menzes' growing stable of young producers. Thank you for taking a moment to speak with us."

Shari took a firm grip on her quivering frame and tried to match the anchor's smile. "A pleasure to be here, Carey."

"This is quite a shift, a period piece coming from the studio whose latest releases were *Bloodwork* and *StarShip Warrior*."

"America has been waiting a long time for this story." Shari took enormous lift from the steadiness of her voice and how the words were there waiting for her. "There has not been a successful frontier drama since *Last of the Mohicans*. It's time, and we have the story."

There was a glimmer of something else in the anchor's gaze, a sharp probing, a cutting edge. "You're forgetting *The Patriot*."

"I'm not forgetting a thing," Shari lied, and wrested her voice free from the sudden quiver of fear. "That was Mel Gibson at the height of his popularity. He could have danced the lead in *Sugarplum Fairies* wearing a leotard and a pink tutu and still topped the weekend charts."

The anchor's glint turned to respect. "Of course there have been several megadisasters that dealt with America's early days."

"They don't apply here. The audience is ready for the right

story. And we have it in spades. *Iron Feather* is the story of Daniel Boone, but told from the Indians' perspective. Boone the invader. Boone the point man for the European's rape of the continent. This film is directed at the young audience that has become jaded by the false hype and fake heroism they're fed in school. They want the truth, and that's what we are delivering. Truth with a star-driven edge. This is hot, and this is now."

Carey McGraw waited for the leading man and director to finish their high note and the ensuing applause. "Is it true that Colin Chapman shed real tears when they cut the Gucci tag out of his fringe leather jacket?"

Shari Khan actually laughed out loud. "Where do you people dig up this drivel?"

"Well, that's all the time we have. Ms. Khan, thank you for speaking with us." She faced the camera. "This is Carey McGraw, and you heard it first on *Evening Entertainment*."

Menzes guided Shari away from the cluster at the foot of the stairs. He waved to someone Shari could not be bothered to see. "Once again, you have handled yourself exceedingly well."

Now that the lights were gone, Shari could not stop shaking. "Thank you, Mr. Menzes."

He saw her nerves, and approved. "You know what they call somebody who can face the gun and stay calm and say the right thing in television-sized bullets?"

"A lady with a job?"

His smile turned genuine for the second time that night. "Close. A woman with a future." He nodded once. "Good to see I was right about you."

ecause of the phone call and prayer time with his newest investor, Bobby Dupree was able to open the doors connecting his office to the boardroom, walk in, and say as smooth as his wife's finest silk, "Celia Breach, as I live and breathe. Bobby Dupree."

"How do you do, Mr. Dupree."

Normally he would go into his aw-shucks routine, insisting she call him Bobby. But there was something in that drop-dead gaze. A seen-it-all wariness. And a depth of sorrow he had not expected.

He wanted to stand there and gawk. But he was two men just then—the teen who was watching a dream from the screen come to life, and a man who had just seen God at work. What he did was turn and walk to the second woman. Candace Chen was deeply bronzed and high-cheekboned, a woman of singular strength. But she wore the same wounded borehole in her eyes as the actress. "An honor to meet you Ms. Chen. I loved your script."

"You read it?"

"Cover to cover. Which is saying a lot, on account of I never got into the reading habit. Not for pleasure, anyway. A balance sheet can work wonders for me, and there's a lot of myth in the worst of them. But I treated your work like I did a blueprint, something I needed to slog through and wrestle with and understand. I didn't get as tight a grip as I'd like. But I tried."

"Not many producers will read an entire script."

"I suppose I can understand that. I wouldn't know a good one if I saw one. But I talked to people I trusted. I hired me a script consultant—I think that's what they're called. Actually took the gentleman off a DreamWorks project. They all tell me this is hot. And my folks downstairs said the same thing."

"Downstairs?" Celia Breach asked.

"I'll get to that in a minute. You ladies like to relocate to my office?"

"We're fine here, thanks."

Celia Breach had either chosen the head spot at the conference table or Fiona had placed her there. Candace Chen was at the seat to her left. Fiona had set up a silver coffee service and little finger sandwiches between them. The two ladies were not unfriendly. Just guarded. Bobby took a seat two places down, far enough away not to crowd. The leading lady's magnetism was unlike anything he had ever seen or known before. She was not simply a beautiful woman. She had a quality that drew him around and commanded his attention.

"It's interesting that you used the word *blueprint*," Candace Chen said. "That's how a lot of behind-the-camera people see a working script."

"I'd like to claim that wisdom as my own, but I can't. It was one of the things the consultant I hired described to me. He told me to look beyond the script and see how it would be up there on the big screen. And I couldn't do that. I don't have that gift."

Celia Breach turned to Candace and said, "This honesty business is as novel an approach in a producer as it is in a director."

Bobby started to ask what she was talking about but was struck by a thought. So he got up and went over and made himself a cup of coffee he didn't want, just so he could have a minute to digest what had just hit him.

Which was, this woman had all the experience in the world at people fawning and gaping and barking and running around at her feet. And that was what she expected from him.

And before that telephone call, it was exactly what Bobby Dupree would have given her.

But during the prayer spoken by that Texas oilman and Bobby's mentor, Bobby had felt that same undeniable force he had last known when God had told him to get into this project in the first place. The impossible made real. Calm and thrilling all at once.

Which granted enough distance for Bobby to sit there and sip his coffee and realize that the one thing this woman had probably never been offered, at least not from someone in his position, was the sort of bonding he'd just been offered on the phone.

There was no way he could say it. Celia Breach had heard it all. And been told it by people with a lot more polish than he had.

So he'd just have to show her.

Bobby had the feeling that was the real reason for the phone call. Not for the money. For the reminder of why they were here.

He said, "I didn't have an agenda for today. I just wanted to give you folks a chance to have a look at me. To ask what you needed to put your minds at ease."

Celia and Candace exchanged a glance. The writer said, "You first."

"What's the budget for this film?" the actress asked.

"We're all feeling our way here. I've got some estimates. But I'm not going to hammer nails into the numbers."

"Ballpark."

"Eighteen million. That's production. Another whatever for marketing."

"You can do that?"

He fiddled with his cup. "I usually keep finances close to my chest. That's one of the nice things about running a private company. But the biggest thing I was hoping to get out of this meeting was trust. So I'm gonna break my own rules here and lay it out for you. I've got financing in place for four films. If we lose it all, I'm done. If not, everything I earn is going back into the company."

Bobby Dupree couldn't talk numbers and sit still. He resisted the urge to bound to his feet and made do jerking his chair through tight little turns. "I'm aiming to offer the same thing to everybody on the projects. They're not *my* projects. They're *ours*. I do the same with all my companies. The only folks able to buy in are people who work with me. So once this first project is out there, if it goes, we're gonna sit down with the accountants and try and figure out what the real worth is. Then anybody who wants can buy in at the ground level. All I ask is the same as what Jerry says he's already told you. That folks who sign on for the long haul don't get involved in projects that run counter to our aims."

Candace Chen said, "You trust Brent Stark to work on an unlimited budget?"

"Nobody said nothing about no limits. I've got two accountants who're down there costing everything out to the dime. But I told them not to crowd the man. Long as Brent stays true to his word, they're there to *help* him. But to answer your question, yes, ma'am. The more I get to know him, the more I think I've found myself a winner."

"So do I," Candace said. But she didn't say it to Bobby. She said it to Celia.

Celia studiously avoided the writer's gaze. "You've heard about the Galaxy film *Iron Feather*?"

"Oh yeah, we're all over that one. Which is why we're pushing forward the start date. I understand you're comfortable with losing a week of rehearsals?"

"Rehearsals are a wonderful thing, Mr. Dupree. But timing is everything in this business."

He grinned. "That's the nice thing about working with pros, Ms. Breach. They don't shed tears over the difference between perfection and nitty-gritty."

Celia studied him. "You're not what I expected."

He resisted the urge to squint. He could have sworn her eyes just changed color. "Why's that?"

Candace said, "Your secretary said you were so nervous she doubted you'd be much use to anybody."

He found it hard to pry his gaze away from Celia Breach, but he did. "Tell the truth, I was nervous as a kitten in a rainstorm. But a friend called just before you arrived, and when he spoke to me, it felt like I was hearing God's voice at the same time."

Celia studied him some more but did not say anything. Instead, Candace Chen asked, "Do you see many films?"

"You mean in the theater? Two or three a year. I buy some. Mostly the older ones."

"You're not addicted to the theater. You're not driven by ego to own a studio. By your own admission you don't read all that much. I'm just curious. Why are you getting involved here?"

Celia added, "Most outsiders who invest in films get badly burned."

"You know the old Hollywood adage," Candace said. "The best way to have ten million dollars is to invest a hundred million in a Hollywood film."

Celia said, "Not that we're not grateful to be here."

"We're just curious, is all."

Bobby let his grin show through. He loved the interchange and what lay behind it. Two very smart ladies who were being open about their doubts. And growing tight with one another, despite what Bobby had heard about Candace Chen's dreams being fried by another Hollywood star of the female variety.

Definitely a God thing.

He bounded to his feet. "Would you ladies like to take a little walk?"

———◦———

There was something to be said for strolling through his office building beside Celia Breach. The reception area beyond Fiona's station was one notch below jammed. They got a lot of smiles, plenty of quiet whispers. A number of comments popped into Bobby's head, as usual. But he decided to just walk along, see how a star handled this. And the answer was, calmly. Celia wore dressy casual, a silvery-white off-the-shoulder sweater long enough to be a short skirt, gathered at the waist by a woven leather belt a shade lighter than the sweater, designer jeans, and boots that matched the belt. The sweater's sleeves were bunched up around her elbows. She had a platinum and diamond bracelet on one wrist, a matching watch on the other. Bobby's wife might play at not caring, but she'd eat these little details with a spoon.

Candace Chen walked a half step behind them, clearly comfortable with being outside the spotlight. Her dark complexion and strong features formed a striking mix. Not beautiful, but unique. Bobby was certain many folks found her intimidating.

Bobby punched the elevator button and said, "Mind if I get your take on something about Brent?"

He felt more than saw the sudden change in Celia Breach. "I suppose."

There was something between them, he realized. Not in the past. He knew all about the accident and the court case. Something now. He filed that away for future reflection. "Y'all know about him spending the past week and a half with the country boy. I was just wondering, you know, we're pushing hard on this new timeline. Even so, he dumped a load of gotta-get-dones in Jerry's lap and took off."

Celia stepped into the elevator. "He's learning the ropes."

"Do all actors do this?"

"Brent Stark is not all actors," Candace Chen said.

"The good ones do," Celia said. "I will. He's found a ladies' group that keeps the frontier traditions alive. I intend to work closely with them."

Candace said, "Like the men have war enactment groups, or back in Hawaii we have groups that keep the old traditions alive."

Celia touched the hair gathered tightly away from her forehead. It was only then that Bobby noticed the scar. He found it added to the woman's appeal, this touch of human fragility in an otherwise perfect image.

"It's not about learning frontier life," Celia told him. "Not directly, anyway. What Brent is doing is preparing the role. He wants to become comfortable with the forest and the rifle and the knife."

"And the hatchet," Candace said. "The frontiersmen adopted the Cherokee throwing hatchets."

"Brent's goal will be to *own* these items. The clothes, the weapons, the environment. He wants to arrive at a place where he can slip into his character every time his hand touches one of those items."

Bobby said, "Sounds to me like there's a lot more to this acting gig than it appears."

"That's right," Candace said. "There is."

They stepped from the elevator. Beyond the doors with the music video company's logo etched into the glass, Bobby saw his team ready to spring. He held up one hand at the young people. *Wait.*

"Four years back I bought the town's largest music video production company. I got them involved in doing some TV and theater ads. They've been real successful. When they outgrew their place on the outskirts of town, I put the production group in one place and gave Admin and Editing and Sound Stage this entire floor. Folks think I keep them locked up here so the zoo animals don't run wild. I just love having all that energy down here where I can slip in and feed off it. The oldest person you're about to meet looks like she's shy of her thirteenth birthday. I'd have told them to dress up for today, but all they'd do is put on a clean T-shirt. And no, none of them have ever worked on a film project before. But they're just about the best I've ever met at what they do. And I'm proud of them. So all I'm asking is that you give them a chance."

Celia gave him another of those careful inspections. This time Bobby was certain the color of her eyes actually did shift along the blue gray scale. "It's nice to hear you talk about your people like this."

Candace nodded. "Hollywood is full of parasites who suck away the credit due to other people."

"That's not my way," Bobby said. "And in case you missed it, we're a long way from LA."

Taking Celia Breach through his music video group's headquarters caused a very quiet riot. It was a lot for these young people to absorb in one morning, hearing they'd been tagged to do the promo work for a feature film, then having a star arrive to see their work. Bobby thought they handled themselves pretty well, all things considered. It was hard to say what Celia thought of them. She remained poised, calm, distant. Offering very little. Which was probably why the team managed to keep from shooting off like a barrel full of bottle rockets.

Celia clearly knew her way around sound studios and film-editing rooms. She listened to their explanation of what it meant to go digital and asked intelligent questions. Bobby held back and let the team take over. Which gave him a chance to study the two ladies openly.

He saw a pair of strong women who had been beaten hard and come up stronger still. Stronger, in fact, than they realized themselves. That was Bobby's impression. He knew neither of them had worked in years. And it had bothered him at first, the thought that he was tacking all his hopes on a bunch of has-beens. But now, with the clarity of prayer still lingering, he saw the whole thing was knitting together in a truly amazing way.

Their destination was a rear windowless room. The team had done what he'd asked, which was to clear away the old pizza and drinks, but not even the building's AC on full could erase the smell of popcorn. Bobby settled them into the sofa that appeared the least stained and said, "I expect you're used to a lot nicer viewing rooms."

Celia said, "This is the most comfortable I've been since touching down."

Candace agreed, "You ought to see some of the working studios out in LA."

"The equipment is first rate," Celia said, "and your people talk a good line."

Bobby nodded his appreciation. "I contacted the three best ad companies in town—they've all worked on art house films. I told the group here they didn't have much chance, but they could give it a try if they wanted. Y'all heard what the Hollywood trade magazines said about us and our little project?"

Celia's voice turned copper hard. "We've heard."

"We assumed it was a line fed to them by Galaxy," added Candace.

"I can't confirm that yet, but I'm working on it."

"A shoestring operation," Celia said. "That's what they called you."

Bobby nodded with his whole body. "Like being careful with money is a failing."

"A lot of people think it is in the movie business," said Candace.

Celia sighed. "I'd bet you anything you'd care to wager, that concept came from somebody in Galaxy."

"Wherever it started, I'd sure like to prove the whole bunch of them wrong," Bobby said. "Then I got to thinking and decided Shoestring might make a nice name for our little project."

The two ladies shared a look and a grin. "I like it," Candace said.

"Shoestring Films," Celia agreed. "It will stick like a thorn in their side."

"That was my thinking too. So I went to those outside ad agencies and my own video team and I gave them the same challenge. Take that shoestring idea and make something positive of it."

Bobby turned in his chair. At his insistence, only the team leader was in the room with them. "Show them."

The lights dimmed. Music swelled from a dozen speakers, an orchestral wash. The wall-size screen came to brilliant life.

All they saw was a man's hands and work-stained trouser legs. The hands were massive and old and curled by a lifetime of hard work. The man hoisted an open Bible onto his legs. The Bible was as ancient and scarred as the man. The pages were yellowed and frayed and were coming loose from the binding. The Book was open to the first chapter of John's gospel. A light shimmered around three words of text: *In the beginning*.

Gingerly the work-scarred hands lifted the Bible's front cover and shut the Book. The unseen man took a length of twine and bound the Book together. The camera tightened upon the knot he made.

The knot turned into a cross of fire.

The cross became the *t* in the word that rose from the twine to fill the screen.

Shoestring.

The word shifted up and to the left, still written as though made from the twine.

The music swelled to a crashing wave of inspiration. Bobby had heard it a dozen times now and still got chills.

The screen continued to form twine-shaped words with that single fiery letter, the one like a misshapen cross. *Shoestring Productions presents* . . .

The visual faded with the music, until only a softly thunderous drumbeat remained and the screen drifted with gray smoke. The smoke sharpened into a fog-wrapped forest. The drumbeat became a man's pumping breath. The man was just a silhouette racing through the forest. He ran at an impossible speed, such that the fog swirled behind him, as if his footsteps generated smoke.

The fog coalesced into a title of gray steel, formed in an ancient script.

Long Hunter.

The film ended.

Fifty-seven seconds from beginning to end.

Bobby glanced at the women. And had to grin. These two hardened pros refused to look away from the empty screen.

"I'll tell you what I think," Bobby said. "All of a sudden, the dreaming and the scheming and the prayers and the sense of calling, it's been turned into something *real.*"

Candace took a shaky breath.

"You think we could see that again?" Celia asked.

Bobby turned to his team leader. The kid looked ready to weep. "Oh, I reckon we could manage that."

our days after the Chateau Marmont party, Shari emerged from her bedroom two hours later than normal. She poured herself a cup of coffee and shuffled into the living room to find her grandmother seated in the sofa reading *Variety*.

Lizu Khan smiled at her granddaughter and said, "You came in late."

"We didn't get the stars and crew off to Budapest until four in the morning."

"Vulgar animals," her grandmother sniffed.

Shari retreated into her cup. Throughout that grueling week, so long as they had been in view of the cameras, the director and male lead had behaved themselves reasonably well. Which had been good, because the PR crew had put together a three-ring circus of journalists and personal interviews and an appearance on *Saturday Night Live*. But as soon as the lights went off, the pair went wild. Shari had never known just what the word could mean until that week. She had played handler along with Leo Patillo, and in the process gotten to know the LA club scene. The upside was considerable. After making the bookings and then climbing from limos with Colin Chapman and Raul Solish, Shari could now hit any of the West Coast's hottest places and walk straight to the front of the line.

That morning, however, with her head still thumping from the music and the limo's cloying smoke, she was not sure how much that actually meant. Shari rose and refreshed her coffee mug. She needed some way to take the coffee intravenously if she was ever going to wake up.

At least that was how she felt until her grandmother said, "I heard some interesting news this morning."

Which probably meant some minor scandal involving the local Persian community. "I'm really not in the mood right now."

"Oh really." Her grandmother held out that day's *Variety*, one of filmdom's leading journals. "Mr. Rapello in 7D greeted me in the elevator this morning with the news that my granddaughter is on page two."

Shari would have thought it completely impossible to wake up that fast. "What?"

"See for yourself."

The article was entitled "New Star in the Galaxy Firmament?" Then she saw her name in the second sentence. Beside which was a *Wall Street Journal*-style line drawing of herself. And had to stop. And get over a full-on heart attack.

So her grandmother took back the journal and read, "'Galaxy has always bucked the current trend to tack executive producer titles on everyone from the second coffee girl to the greenlight guy's niece. Which made all the more interesting Sam Menzes' confirmation, when approached by this author after Shari Khan's appearance on *Evening Entertainment*, that the striking young woman would have an assistant exec producer credit on their latest expected megahit *Iron Feather*. Shari Khan has been seen all over town this week, playing hostess and troubleshooter while Colin Chapman and Raul Solish, back from location work in Hungary, cut a fire line down Sunset Strip. Such hands-on work is normally restricted to Sam Menzes' most trusted lieutenants. Does this mean Shari Khan is a power on the rise? Watch this space.'"

Her grandmother dropped the journal. "I can only wish your grandfather were alive to see this day."

———◆———

Like story concepts and shooting venues, words came into fashion and then fled from the mouths of Hollywood insiders. For a while, the word was *prince*. A prince was someone—male or female—who cut a deal and lived by the agreement. Last week, a prince had held the power to put a story into play. Today, however, *prince* was used by every zero on the street who wanted to pretend he could play the film game. Recently the guy who stitched a tear in Shari's boot called her a prince for offering a tip. Nowadays, prince was just another synonym for putz.

Today's term was *the read*. This was a recent import from Washington, where the read was what the powers did every time a new book on politics hit the market. Those with clout, or those who wished they had it, found an out-of-the-way shop where they could safely heft the new book and check the back index. The inclusion of a person's name with a citation was a clear signal of importance in the rapidly changing Washington waters.

As usual, Hollywood had its own spin, even on an imported term. No book on LA mattered to insiders, since by the time anything was bound in hardback, the films, and the players, would already be archived.

The read was what people did with the trades, as in *Variety, Hollywood Reporter*, the *LA Times* film section, and a very few top-ranked blogs like Defamer. The read was a noun, as in, I caught you in the read this morning.

Shari felt a thousand eyes follow her every move when she entered the studio lot that morning. She heard doors open. She heard talk stop. She heard footsteps scramble as people shifted over to the windows and watched her walk briskly down the studio's central lane carrying a large wrapped box.

Shari Khan. Mentioned by name in the read.

Emily Arsene's office was in the sprawling office structure called Building 2. The office complex was separated from Galaxy's headquarters by a mock Lower Manhattan street, two sound stages, a row of director and star bungalows, and a billion miles. Building 2 was actually nicer in many respects than the rabbit warren in the older headquarters building. The lighting was muted, the air-conditioning didn't rattle the overhead grill like it did in Shari's office, and the halls were lined with framed posters from decades of Galaxy hits. None of this mattered, of course. To those lucky enough to possess a cubicle in headquarters, Building 2 was known as the Tombs.

Shari balanced her load on one hip and knocked on the open door. "You in?"

"Who wants to know?" Emily Arsene swiveled from her computer screen. "Well, well, a visit from royalty. What have you got there?"

"A present."

"In case you didn't realize, we peons relegated to the back lot don't deserve such attention."

"You want to give a gal a little room?"

Emily rose to her feet and shifted a pile of scripts. She remained standing as Shari set the box on the edge of her desk. Shari motioned to the wrapping paper. "Have a look."

"Hey, you're on a roll. I'll let you do the honors."

"Whatever you say." Shari plucked off the bow and set it on the top rim of Emily's computer screen. She slipped one hand under the wrapping paper and peeled it back. "I got to thinking."

"Risky move, thinking in this business."

"If I were Sam Menzes, I would find me someone whose loyalty was so strong she would let me relegate her to the Tombs."

"Those of us stuck in the back of beyond don't take kindly to that name."

Shari pried open the top of the box. "I'd ask them to be my eyes and ears back here."

"Where on earth did you come up with this?"

"In the limo with the boys from Budapest. Listening to them razz the people in the Tombs, the folks working hundred-hour weeks to make their film a hit. It occurred to me that the Tombs is a perfect place for a studio to spring dangerous leaks. I'd make it a point to have somebody in here who could let me know of any serious problems long before they arose. Whatever it cost, whatever I had to promise or pay on the sly, it would be well worth the investment."

Emily Arsene kept her eyes on the bubble-packed implement slowly rising from the box. "If that were the case, and I'm not saying it is. But if it were, that person would be totally required to deny any knowledge of anything like what you're suggesting."

"Absolutely."

"Long as we understand one another."

"Oh, I think we do." Shari elbowed the empty box onto the floor. She unwrapped the bubble pack to reveal a coffee maker.

"Oh my," Emily said as she touched the silver-plated Thermos.

Shari had found it in the Rodeo Drive shop for kitchenware. In the window. The machine was Italian designed and Swiss manufactured. It looked like an art deco sculpture. It had cost a bomb.

Shari handed Emily the plug. "Water."

Emily found an unopened bottle of Evian. Shari filled the tank and fished out a bag of Mrs. Gooch's finest from her purse. She poured the beans into the top. Hit the button. The grinder gave off a sibilant rush, like cymbals beat by brushes.

"My kitty makes more noise purring," Emily said.

Shari smiled. "You like cats?"

"Doesn't everyone?"

"Almost everyone who matters."

They waited for it to brew, then poured two cups, seated themselves, and savored.

Emily did not speak until her cup was drained. "More?"

"You kidding? I'm thinking I need another raise so I can buy myself one."

"You're welcome back here any time, honey."

The endearment did not go unnoticed. "I need some help."

Emily took her time settling into her second cup. "Shoot."

"Did you ever read the script? Not ours. The other one."

"*Long Hunter*. Sure. It was one of the first Sam handed me after I started answering directly to him." She rolled over to her computer and typed. The printer whirred. Emily glanced at the two pages, then handed them over. "There's my analysis."

"Thanks." Shari stowed them in her purse. "What was your take?"

"Most of the scripts landing on my desk are basically what I call fatburgers. Great tasting, solid commerciality, and no leave-behind. You understand what I mean by that?"

"I think so, but tell me anyway."

"The audience comes in, they warm their seats, they eat their faces greasy, they get up, they go home. By the time they pull in the drive, they've forgotten what they saw and they're hungry for the next go-round. Fatburgers. Fast food and friendly, but when it comes to vitamins, a vacuum."

"You're saying *Long Hunter* was different."

"Very fifties. The big hero, the big theme. Man against nature and an enemy and himself. Suggesting that if it was possible then, it's still possible today. That's what made it different. This wasn't just a historical drama. It suggested the challenges aren't so different today as then, in terms of ethics and principles and life itself." Emily smiled. "The critics would have poured gasoline all over it and set it alight."

"Even so, you suggested Galaxy film it?"

"I liked it. I thought it would do well in the heartland."

"What about the script for our new film, *Iron Feather*?"

Emily tasted her words as carefully as her coffee. "The critics will eat it with a spoon. Daniel Boone fed into the blender of deconstructive history. The stars should play well with the Generation X and Y'ers."

Shari tried to read what Emily was not saying. The result had her feeling the same chill in her gut she'd known when her grandmother had warned her. "You think we might have some serious trouble from the upstart studio project, don't you."

"Not if you do your job." Emily slipped several files into her case and rose from her desk. "I've got an appointment with our mutual god. Care to come along?"

Another word on the rise in Hollywood insider circles was *aristocrat*. Cool. Authoritative. Stylish. Understated. If anyone on the Galaxy lot defined aristocrat for Shari, it was Sam Menzes. Menzes possessed an aristocrat's casual ruthlessness. He felt no emotion whatsoever over applying the knife. A skillful slice and his competition was filleted, and Menzes could go back to his latte.

Shari Khan did not want to work for him. She wanted to *be* him.

When Menzes saw the pair of them enter together, all he said was, "What have we here?"

Emily Arsene seated herself and said, "I'd like you to meet my new friend."

Menzes gave one of his patented smiles, a brief tightening along the edges of his mouth and eyes. "Well, well."

If Shari had any doubt of who Emily Arsene really was, it was

dispelled by the way she waltzed through the six script summaries—five passes and one definite buy—then leaned back in
her chair and said, "Shari here has some concerns about the quality of our *Iron Feather* competition."

"Did you feed her that line?"

"No, this was all on her lonesome." Emily smiled across the
conference table extending from the chief's desk. "Girl's got a
good nose."

"If she came to you with this, then I agree." Menzes asked
Shari, "What do you want to do about it?"

"I'd like to come out with both barrels firing. Tell our journalist allies how an upstart is working on an old concept and
trying to play the parasite and feed off our publicity. A second-
rate story being worked by a third-rate studio, and stealing our
thunder in the process."

"*Variety* called them a shoestring operation," Emily recalled.
"Did they get that idea from you?"

"Sort of."

"How?"

"I have a friend who is assistant to their chief editor. I might
have mentioned the term."

"Might have mentioned," Emily said, smiling approval.
"Naughty girl."

"It's a good idea and a better tactic," Menzes said. "Work it."

"I don't want to personally shoot the bullets. I want to
remain a positive face who talks only about what a great place
Galaxy is, the quality films we're producing, and what a great
role we've carved for ourselves in American entertainment."

Menzes studied her. "You're afraid of wielding the knife?"

"Not at all. I just don't want to do it publicly."

"Where did you come up with that one?"

The truth was, her grandmother. Shari had taken to discussing
tactics over coffee. Her grandmother normally just listened, which
made her a perfect sounding board. Her grandmother loved being

in the know and accepted that what her granddaughter needed most of all was the chance to practice. Occasionally, however, Lizu Khan spoke up. And when she did, it was with ironclad certainty. This had been one of those times.

But what Shari said was, "Watching you, Mr. Menzes. You stand above the fray. If you speak publicly, which is rare in the extreme, you never have anything bad to say about anyone. That doesn't keep you from declaring Armageddon when it suits you."

"Armageddon, I like that."

"Too late," Emily said. "It's already been used as a title."

"Still, it's got a weight about it. Maybe we should have the snake pit guys fit out a special list of tactics. File them under Armageddon."

"I'll see to it," Emily said, and made a note.

Menzes turned back to Shari. "What you need is one of our tame street-meats."

"Excuse me?"

Emily answered for him. "He means a talking head."

"Somebody with clout," Menzes said. "Somebody who'll throw a serious punch at our command."

"They're mostly second-level pundits," Emily said. "Consultants, professors, activists, actors, journalists, bloggers, opinionated dentists. They're all desperate for a chance to shine on their own commentator spot. They would sell their Porsches and mortgage their daughters for a chance to sing our tune."

Menzes said to Emily, "Have one of Derek's snakes set her up."

"Happy to."

"Anything else?"

They took that as their cue. Shari rose with Emily, who said, "Always a pleasure, boss."

They made it to the door before Menzes said, "Ms. Khan."

"Sir?"

"Speak with Gilda on your way out. Have her set you up with your own line."

A line. As in a line of credit. Otherwise known as an expense account. Shari felt slightly giddy. "Thank you, Mr. Menzes."

"Tell her I said for you to get usage of our table at The Grill and the Polo Lounge." He made a process of circular filing the five analyses for the scripts they were passing on. Making sure Shari saw him drop them into the wastebasket. "For the duration."

Emily waited for her at the elevator. When the doors slid shut, she asked, "Where's your former boss?"

"Still in traction." Shari's voice sounded weak.

"Fair summary of his job security. He won't be missed, especially by the folks he stole credit from." Emily leaned against the wall. "I don't need to warn you not to let this go to your head, do I?"

"No." A breath and the word were enough to refocus the world. "You don't."

"That's what I thought."

"Who else knows? I mean, about you."

"Leo is my contact in the snake pit. And Derek Steen handles all the really major stuff." The doors slid open. "But you know what I'm going to say now, don't you."

"There is nothing whatsoever for anybody to know," Shari confirmed.

Emily had a smile as tight and hard as their boss's. "I always did like a fast learner."

iz Courtney and Stanley Allcott carried their argument onto the tarmac.

"I'm telling you, I couldn't spend nine hundred dollars on a suit and ever put the thing on."

"That is just so like a man."

"Not to mention the fact that you've got me buying four of them."

"Oh, just get on the plane, Stanley."

She knew he had intentionally dressed down that morning. Determined to show her he wasn't about to put on airs. Not even for Bobby Dupree, who had sent his own private jet to pick them up. Stanley's denims were fashionably pale, but only because he'd washed them about five hundred times. He wore a cowboy shirt as faded as his jeans, and ancient boots whose heels clicked up the metal stairs.

"My *truck* didn't cost me nine hundred dollars."

"Why do you think I've insisted on driving us every Thursday?" She prodded him into one of the plush leather seats. "Sit down and buckle up. You're so big you rob the plane of air."

"I still don't understand what we're doing."

"I declare, I've wrestled broncos that made for more pleasant company. Now just hush up and say hello to the nice man."

Stanley realized the pilot was watching them and harrumphed. "Hello."

Liz said to the pilot, "All sweetness and light, that man."

"Nice to see you again, Ms. Courtney. We'll be wheels up in about ten minutes. Flying time to Boone is just under three hours."

"Where?" Stanley asked.

"Stanley. Please." To the pilot, she said, "At least one of us is very grateful, sir."

"We stocked up on some fresh sandwiches and the coffee is brewing. You folks help yourselves."

When the cabin door shut, Liz said, "You were saying?"

"You never wrestled a bronco."

"Caught, wrestled, branded, broke. My daddy was a lover of the west country. He taught me because I wanted to learn."

The private jet taxied and whooshed into the air with a sports car's zoom. Stanley's eyes widened at the experience. "This sure ain't Delta."

"Are you going to play nice?"

"I would if you'd get off my back about those suits."

"Stanley, I want you to be still for just a second and pay attention. You think it's a fancy banker talking to you. You think I'm suggesting you put on airs. And that's not it at all. You're going to be a pastor again, Stanley. Of a church with twelve thousand members."

"At least I will be until they discover who it is they've actually hired." He sounded like a bearish nine-year-old.

She surprised them both by reaching over. "Give me your hand."

His eyes grew suspicious. "Why?"

"Because you're a dear sweet man and I want to hold it."

He did as he was told. And sat looking at the fingers suddenly intertwined with his own. "How am I supposed to argue with you now?"

"Stanley, I'm not trying to build a lie, and that's what's scaring you. You're afraid of becoming the fraud you made yourself into the last time you took the pulpit. Tell me I'm wrong."

"No. You're right."

"But those deacons who hired you know what I know, Stanley. You've grown beyond that. I remember how you were before. You always dressed nice for Sundays. You said it was honoring the place and the people."

"You said it yourself. I'm different now."

"That doesn't mean you can't take the good from your past. What worked well. What made you such an engaging minister."

"I don't dress for Wednesdays, and I'm at the pulpit then."

"And you don't have to there. But Sundays are different." She studied the man, the craggy features, the strength, the miracles. "You could use a haircut too."

"Don't press your luck."

"And a facial."

He started to bark again, until he caught her smile. "You had me going there."

"I know a fabulous nail specialist. She could do up your pinkie in sequins."

Stanley took a firmer grip on her hand. "I never thanked you, Liz. Giving up the church you've been a member at since . . ."

"Only church I've ever known. My husband and I met because our parents were founding members."

"I didn't know that. Or maybe I did and forgot." He reached over so he could add his second hand to the mix. "I would have never done this without you."

Her response was cut off by the pilot opening the door. He caught sight of how they were seated and said to the co-pilot, "I guess it's okay to take off the Kevlar now." He went on to Liz, "Mr. Dupree is on the line, ma'am. He'd like to have a word."

"Do I come forward?"

"Handset is in your armrest."

She pulled out the phone and said, "Bobby?"

"Howdy, Liz. They taking good care of you?"

She smiled at Stanley. "Everything is fine."

"Looks like I won't be able to join you after all. Wildfires breaking out everywhere. The reverend with you?"

"Right beside me."

"I know you're going because Brent asked you to come. But he did it because I asked him to. Here's what I'd like to see happen. There are nine Shoestring investors from the Houston and Dallas prayer groups. They'd appreciate hearing what you folks discover while you're down there."

"I don't know the first thing about making a film."

"I know that and so do they. I've got my accountants ready to sit down with you tomorrow morning and walk you through the numbers. But what's more important is just to get your impressions and share them with the group."

"They haven't known us long enough to accept our impressions."

Bobby's smile came through at thirty thousand feet. "Sorry, Liz. But that's where you're wrong."

"You wanted to see me?"

"Come on in, Trevor. Shut the door, will you?"

"Certainly." Brent Stark, director and star, was "in the chair," as they said in Hollywood. The chair being the padded stool placed before the three-sided makeup mirror. They had managed to bring in a top-flight artist, Rachel Drewe, another of those drawn from the long list of unwilling early retirees. Hollywood was like the rest of America, as far as Trevor was concerned, much too willing to cast experience on the refuse heap and embrace the youth, the latest, the fad.

Trevor remained mildly astonished at the team they had pulled together in such a short time. If he had any complaint, it was how the crew was either grayheads like himself or so young they looked scarcely able to drive, much less handle the rigors of a feature shoot. Yet even here the chemistry was already working. Those aged and experienced, burned by LA life, were balanced nicely against the fresh-faced hyperactive young hopefuls, many of whom were believers. The elders were kept from clustering and turning cynical. The youth were reined in from dangerous excesses.

Trevor was, to say the very least, astonished.

"I'm worried," Brent said.

Trevor leaned against the doorjamb. Crossed his arms. And did his best to hide how pleased he was to be taken into the boss's confidence. "I take that as a good sign."

Brent asked the makeup lady, "How much longer will you be?"

"A few minutes still." For some unfathomable reason, Rachel Drewe had died her dark hair a shade that reminded Trevor of a polished two-penny coin. Somewhere between red and copper, so metallic he could almost catch his reflection. She wore it short and determinedly curled. Rachel dabbed at Brent's chin, inspected her work in the mirror, then wiped it off. "This is your first scene, first take. It's not a day to skimp on time. We want to get this shade exactly right. You'll be wearing it for the next eighteen weeks."

Trevor said, "Anything you want to say won't go any further."

Rachel agreed. "Makeup artists who can't keep secrets tend not to be hired again."

"I'm good with actors," Brent said. "I'm good with scripts. But I'm worried about my ability to choose shots."

"We're going with the right one here, mate."

"It's kept me up all night. Starting with this big of a scene. Maybe it'd be better if we held off, just for a few days, and shot something tight and easy."

"First of all, no shot is easy. Second, we're not shooting for the cameras."

"An interesting take on things, seeing as how it's coming from my DP."

"That's what you hired me for, mate. And here's a lifetime behind the lens distilled into one take. You want everybody on board. Not for the day. For the season. So you start with a bang. Maybe the sound is a little muffled. Maybe the light isn't perfect. Maybe you look back in ten weeks' time and wish you'd done something about the shoot entirely different. That's not what's important here."

Trevor walked over. Moved in tight enough to fill the director's vision. "You want a big scene at the top. You want people to go away tonight thinking and talking and all saying the same thing. You're after a wow. You want your crew to *believe*. Believe in you, believe in the story, believe they're working on a hit. When your gaffers join in and sing your chorus, you know you've got a winner."

Rachel dabbed his forehead and said, "He's right, you know."

Brent stared at his reflection and said nothing.

"You've rehearsed this take for what, five days?"

"Four. Maybe we should go one more."

"No, mate. No. I said five only because the days have been so long." Trevor hesitated, then gave a mental shrug. In for a penny, in for the whole ride, his dear old mum liked to say. "I'm sticking my neck out here, saying things before we've shot our first scene. But now's as good a time as next week. I've been in this business a long time. Started as a lighting drone on a pot-boiler called *Panama Jack*."

"I saw that movie. I was ten. It was pretty awful."

"Pay attention to the here and now. What I meant to say was, in all my days, I've never had a director show such respect to the DP, and *listen*. I insisted on being the judge of quality whenever you were in front of the camera. You agreed not to go near the monitor. I suggested you limit the amount of basic rehearsal and move to working on the set."

"You were right. We've got a high-action film, which means it's camera driven and set driven, not script driven."

"I wish you could hear yourself. Telling a DP he's right. Directors don't do that."

"This one does."

"That's right, mate. You do. And so believe me when I tell you, it's not just me who is noticing the difference. This crew is looking for a reason to believe in you and in this project. So go out there and shoot the big bang."

Brent waited while the makeup lady set the plastic cone around his face and sprayed his hair. Then, "Bobby wants me to start with a group prayer time."

"I'd go one better. I think you should stand up there and give them a little devotional. Those who don't share our faith know what they're working on and who our backers are."

"I feel like I'd be living a lie."

"No, mate. I'm sorry, but you're wrong there. You'd be lying if you masked where you've been and who you are as a result. But if you stand and give them honest, why, who knows what might happen."

Brent looked at him then. And let his naked fear show through.

Trevor was far too much the reserved Brit to give in to his first impulse, which was to walk over and embrace the man. So he made do with, "My first DP, the man who gave me a leg up in this trade, used to say, 'First you shoot the schedule, then the script, and if there's any time left you shoot the art.' I'm sticking my neck out here, but my gut tells me we might turn that adage on its ear. It's touch and go to be making predictions before the cameras roll. But I'm thinking we just might shoot more than a picture here. I'm hoping and praying that we'll make history."

he changes kept coming fast and furious to Shari's life. Perks sprouted like desert blooms after an unexpected rain. Her third-floor office was shifted to a corner spot. The old occupant vanished along with his name off the door, guillotine-clean. Shari shared a secretary now with the forensic accountant assigned to *Iron Feather*, but since he was off counting rubles or whatever the Hungarian currency was, Shari possessed her very own lackey. The woman's name was Natalie. Shari did not like her. Natalie's otherwise blank expression was marred by a barely veiled contempt. Shari kept her around for two reasons. First, Shari was not entrenched enough to begin shifting personnel. Second, she liked the reminder in Natalie's eyes, the warning that one false step and this would be her fate, resigned to the rubble heap of broken dreams, fetching coffee and hunting down street-meat for a younger, luckier person climbing the slippery ladder.

Another change was her phone.

Shari had given her cell phone number to maybe ten friends. On a normal day, or what passed for normal until the previous week, she might have two messages. Now the message box was constantly blinking full. She emptied it every morning and by noon it could accept nothing more. She was getting pitched story ideas by the truckload.

And being invited everywhere. By people she had never heard of before.

Another change was the pink slips.

There was a certain irony to Sam Menzes' choice of color for his handwritten interoffice notes. He wrote them on the same pad Derek Steen used for firings. The first one had arrived the afternoon following her meeting with Menzes and Emily. Shari would have wailed aloud had she been able to find the breath.

Then she read the scrawled message. *Handle this.* It was attached to a printout of an email from an angry New England distributor whose copy of Galaxy's latest hit had arrived scrambled, with one incorrectly labeled reel, which they had only discovered in the middle of a packed showing on opening night. Shari had arranged for air shipment of a new edition, then personally spoken with the man and comped him and his family for a weekend bungalow at the Beverly Hills Hotel. She waited for something, a query or comment or anything, from Menzes, but heard nothing more. Except another such memo. And another. And another.

She was handling another crisis when her secretary's head popped into her office and said, "There's an agency limo at the gates asking for you."

Shari cupped her hand over the receiver. "CAA sent their tame commentator by limo? I didn't agree to cover that."

"You want me to check?"

"No. Tell them I'll be right down." Shari rang off, gathered two scripts and a contract all bearing the terse pink queries, and grabbed her purse. As she passed Natalie's desk, she said, "I don't know when and I don't know where."

Natalie responded with a snide little, "Whatever."

Shari popped out the front door, then stopped in midstride. A thought caused her to veer right and head for the Tombs.

She marched into Emily's office and waited while Emily lightly basted a sweating techie from their computer-effects division.

When the kid fled, Emily said, "They were given a thirty-second gap in our latest Pixar-style film and turned it into a month-long assignment that's currently costed at ninety-one thousand dollars."

"How do you keep your low profile and still manage to rip them apart?"

"All he knows is I'm helping him keep his job. Which is true. The problem with firing the current generation of geeks is the next one is no better." She sighed. "Have a seat."

"Can't. Got a limo at the gates." Shari grinned. "I can't believe I just said that."

Emily smiled back. "It's a rough gig, but hey, somebody's got to keep the drivers busy."

Shari handed over the contract Menzes had sent down that morning. "You seen this?"

Emily took it and flipped through the pages. "No."

"It's a CAA star."

"I'm not sure Sam would want this being shown around."

"I'm not showing it around. I'm showing it to you."

"You sure know the way to this girl's heart." Emily handed the contract back. "So what's the issue?"

"We're shooting the talking head this morning. He's handled by CAA. At first I thought the agency was just padding his expenses, sending him in a limo. But now I'm wondering."

"That's the way you keep your head in this town."

"But they haven't seen this." Shari shook the contract. "How would they know I'm handling it?"

"Maybe they're just guessing. Or maybe . . ."

"They've got a mole," Shari finished. "In Sam's office."

"Or on your floor. Who brought you the contract?"

"No idea. It was on my desk this morning. . . ." Shari snapped her fingers. "Natalie."

"Who?"

"My secretary."

"Ah." Emily nodded. "It's all becoming clear. Natalie was in PR. She mishandled a big one, and in a very big way."

"Derek probably assigned her to me as a warning."

Emily thought a moment. "Let me see the contract again." She flipped the pages, then said, "Okay. The agent in charge is one Zubin Mikels. I know him."

Emily picked up the phone and dialed. "Front gate? Let me speak to Jules. Jules, hey, it's Emily. Yeah, not bad. You? Great. Look. There's a limo waiting . . . yeah, that one. Do me a favor, hon. Go out and say Ms. Khan has been held up a moment by Mr. Menzes, she just wanted to let them know she's coming as soon as the boss finishes up. Yeah, that'll cool them off. No, wait, there's something else. Take a look in the back of the limo. See if there's a round little slimeball in a ten-thousand-dollar suit with shoes the size of ballerina slippers back there. Yeah, I'll wait."

She drummed her fingers for a second, then, "Is that so. Okay, dearie. I owe you. No, I don't owe you that much." Emily hung up the phone. "Bingo."

"What do I do?" Shari asked.

When they had worked their way through the contract, Shari rose and said, "What was it you said to the guard? I owe you."

"You better believe it."

She started for the door, hesitated, then turned back. "Why me? It should be you going for the brass ring."

In that moment, Emily aged fifteen years. "I broke one of the cardinal rules in this town. I fell in love with the wrong man."

"An actor?"

"No, honey. A guy who didn't stay invincible. He's sick and he's going to stay sick and we need a stable paycheck more than I need a chance to go for the gold."

"I'm sorry, Emily."

Her smile was twisted with old pain. "It's all smoke and mirrors anyway, right?"

———•———

There were three men in the back of the limo, but Shari knew instantly which one was Zubin. The agent had a smarmy expression, dead fish eyes, olive complexion, and dark oily hair.

"Shari Khan. Always a pleasure to be kept waiting by a lovely lady. Isn't that what I was telling you, Harv?"

"Sure, Zubin," the younger man agreed. "That's what you said."

"Meet my associate, Harv. Harv, say hello to the newest star in the Galaxy, isn't that what *Variety* claimed?" He had tight, even teeth and feet the size of an infant's. His legs were too short to reach the limo's padded carpet, so they stuck out slightly, their diminutive size accented by hand-stitched Italian lace-ups polished to a midnight shine. He patted the seat next to him. "Come make an old man happy. Let me read your fortune."

"I'll accept the seat, Mr. Mikels. But Sam Menzes is my destiny maker."

"Call me Zubin. I'm sure there must be something that could lure you away from Galaxy." He motioned to the distinguished-looking gentleman seated next to Harv on the limo's rear-facing seat. "Of course you know our distinguished expert."

She nodded a greeting to the talking head and replied, "Thanks, Mr. Mikels. I'm happy where I am."

"Loyalty. How quaint." He said to his associate, "Why are we still here?"

"Sorry, Zubin." The junior associate knocked on the black partition glass. When it rolled down, he said, "Let's move."

Zubin Mikels had a voice far too resonant for his body. "So, my dear. I have been hearing some very fine things about you. We have an opening on our senior team, and I'm here to see if you might be what we're looking for."

"Why don't you give Natalie a look," Shari shot back. "I hear she's soon to be hunting for a job."

There was a flicker of something deep in those dead black eyes. "Sorry, that name doesn't ring a bell."

Shari smiled and did not respond.

"You're sure you want to turn me down before you even know what it is I'm offering?"

As though on cue, the pundit for hire and Harv, his agent, began a conversation of their own. Shari leaned closer and said, "That's not why you're here, Mr. Mikels."

"Is it not."

"You're hitting on me because I'm handling the contract for that loser of a project you're trying to shop to Galaxy."

"You obviously are mistaken. I don't handle losers."

"*Snowbound*," Shari replied. She was close enough to smell the pomade he used in his hair. "A stinker in leather with a gold embossed cover is still a stinker, Mr. Mikels."

He did not move save to lace his fingers across his belly, which along with his voice was the only part of him that might be called oversized. "Khan. That's a Pashtun name, is it not?"

"In my case, it's Iranian, or Persian, as my grandmother prefers to say."

"Persian, Pashtun. My own family is from the frontier region between Iraq and Turkey. From this distance, it makes us almost cousins." The smile was more calculated. "Where we come from, Ms. Khan, a handshake and a verbal agreement are still highly valued. Men of honor do not go back on their word. And that is what Sam Menzes gave me on this project. His word."

"Sam Menzes is the most honorable person in this business." She was hot over his male arrogance. Men of honor. Huh. "Present company not excluded."

Back in her office, Emily had warned Shari that agents of

Zubin's caliber seldom made mistakes. But his eastern European pride was pierced by what Shari said, and he made one then. "Obviously Sam was thinking with some other portion of his body than his brain when he hired you."

Shari discovered something about herself then. She had inherited a trait directly from her grandmother, another little item that had skipped a generation entirely. When her father grew irate, his voice rose until it was higher than his American wife's. Shari's grandmother, however, became calm. Quiet. Reserved. And deadly. Shari did not know how her grandfather had been when he was irate, as she had never seen him lose his temper. Or perhaps she had simply been too young to recognize the secret signs. Shari had always been adept at volume and tantrums. Now she realized it was only because she had never been this angry.

Her voice grew so soft she could have sung the words to a sleeping infant. Her entire body was washed in an icy calm. But something clearly came through, because Zubin slid a notch away from her, moving back from the carefully contained explosion.

"Zubin." She smiled as she said his first name for the first time. "I want you to listen carefully. Sam Menzes agreed to your project in its original form. Which was before Moore Madden, your director, fired a screenwriter with three Oscars under his belt and proceeded to rewrite the story. Now Madden's nineteen-year-old nymphet of a girlfriend is the heroine, instead of Colin Chapman, the box-office marvel who agreed to the story and now has backed out."

The young agent said, "Excuse me, Zubin."

"I'm busy."

"We're here, sir."

"So go."

"Sir, we're on air in less—"

"Remind me, Harv. Why is it that you're here? To handle things, yes? So go handle." When the pair slid from the door held by the driver, Mikels said, "My client, the director Moore Madden, is one of the hottest names in the business."

"If that's the case, I'm sure you won't have any problem schlepping this across town."

He toyed with his jacket's middle button. "There has been no mention of casting the female lead."

"Come on, Zubin. Men of honor don't lie to one another. Isn't that what you just told me?"

His expression hardened. "So what's on offer?"

"Galaxy insists on final script approval. The director drops any intention of co-writing credits. He also drops his lady from any role in this project."

"I can perhaps work out something on the former. But his lady stays."

"Not even in the lunchroom, Zubin. She's out. If she wants to make her mark, she'll do it legitimately and not on Mr. Menzes' dime." Shari gave Zubin a moment to object, then went on, "And one more thing. The original screenwriter is back on the project. And it's your job to resell the project to Colin Chapman."

"He's filming somewhere. Rome, I think."

"Actually, it's Hungary. I hear it's lovely this time of year. Who knows, maybe you'll take a few days off, travel farther east, go see the clan."

"We've got a better name in mind for your project's starring role."

"Let's get this straight, Zubin. Right now there *is* no project. Menzes has Chapman's production company on long-term contract. Chapman wanted the original script as his next vehicle. So it was green-lighted. Then your Moore Madden began his rewrite, and the whole thing unwound. If you want this thing to move, you have to get us the original script and the original star. And no ladyfriend. She is gone. Finished. Buried."

Zubin's gaze had gone slit-thin. "Young lady, there is an

important lesson you've not managed to learn in your meteoric rise. You don't make enemies in this town. Too often, they're the allies you need on the next go-round."

Shari opened her door. "I guess that's one memo your inter-office spy forgot to copy me on."

———✦———

Shari was still steaming as she entered the television studio's lobby. The place was jammed with casting agents and starlets applying for a job on a hospital soap opera, the company's latest hit. Shari rammed her way through, exuding such force the crowd parted ten feet in advance of her passage. Harv, the junior agent, blanched at whatever he found in her face.

Shari demanded, "Where is our guy?"

"He's in makeup."

"Don't *tell* me, Harv. *Move.*"

"Sure. Right." He gave her the same sort of look she had just garnered from Zubin. As in, who is this woman? At any other time, she might have actually enjoyed it.

Harv knocked on the makeup room door. Shari, however, did not wait. She pushed in. The makeup guy said, "You mind?"

"I need a minute."

"We're on in three and I'm still—"

"I need a minute *now*." She stepped forward, then turned around and gave a viper's smile. "Help us out and guard that door, Harv. From the outside."

Shari turned back. Maybe in time she'd learn to compartmentalize. Right then, however, she did not see a distinguished expert on film trends, impeccably dressed and groomed. Instead, she saw just another man who stood between her and her goals. "I need to go over a couple of items with you."

He had recently become famous introducing cinematic hits from the fifties on the Menzes archive-film channel, and doing occasional spots on entertainment shows about by-gone celebrities. He was a man on the rise, and he knew it. He probably did not mean to come across as patronizing as he patted his silver-gray hair and said, "Oh, I'm sure you'll do fine just leaving that to me. I've got several great ideas about what I'll—"

He stopped because Shari had taken hold of the napkin tucked into his shirt collar. She had to do something, and it was either crumple the napkin or take hold of his neck and squeeze. But the tone of her voice never changed. A soft, melodic rush. "Listen very carefully. I want you to go out there and hammer two points." She rolled the napkin into a tighter and tighter ball, the effort straining the muscles from her wrist to her jaw. "One, that their take on Daniel Boone is the same line of heroic rubbish that we've been spoon-fed by romantic historical junkies for decades. But America has moved beyond that. We're after a new history. The one that talks about Indians as a noble race that was decimated and left to rot. Now do you have that or do I need to go over it again?"

"I had rather thought—"

Shari got in very close.

So close, in fact, she could hear the rise and fall of his swallow. "And here is the other point *you must make*. This other production company is so raw they don't even have a name. *Variety* recently ran an article suggesting this upstart runs on a shoestring budget. That's by far the most important thing you can say right now. They're a nothing group and they're working on a shoestring. They're nobody. Now tell me you have that."

Another swallow, then, "Yes."

Shari took a step back. "Good. Now go out there and bury them with all the polish you can manage."

andace Chen had flown into Asheville, North Carolina, the evening before. After spending the night at an airport hotel, she had driven four hours west. Arriving on location, she met the director of photography on the path leading to Brent's trailer. The DP's face was pink from the outdoor work he'd been doing the past few weeks. His features were also mobile in a distinctly English way.

"Candace Chen, as I live and breathe," he greeted her.

"Mr. Wright, I've admired your work for years."

"Now, now, I'm much too old for you to be wasting your charm on me."

"It's true, though."

"Far be it from me to turn down an honest compliment." He took her proffered hand in both of his. "It's not often I have the chance to shake the hand of a true Hollywood legend. The only woman in living memory to wrest a script away from Sam Menzes."

"It cost me everything."

"If you'll forgive me for correcting you, Ms. Chen. I'm sorry, but you're wrong. Honor, my dear lady. It's a priceless quality. One you can't buy, or build, or steal." He seemed genuinely reluctant to let go of her hand. "May I say, Ms. Chen, I'm looking forward to having a right old time turning this fine work of yours into an even finer film."

"Thank you." She hefted the script she held in her other hand. "I've just this morning finished the final changes requested by Celia and Brent."

Trevor Wright's attitude went through a distinct change. "Brent must be looking forward to getting hold of them, so I won't keep you. But do look me up and let's have ourselves a chat, will you? There are a number of points I'd love to cover with you at my elbow."

Candace tried to tell herself there wasn't a warning in the man's final look. Climbing the stairs to Brent's trailer, she heard the generators thrumming on the other side of the pines. As though they echoed a rising sense of fear.

She stepped inside and was greeted by Brent's reflection in a three-sided mirror. "Candace, good, I was just going to send somebody to find you."

She exchanged brief smiles with the makeup artist with metallic curls. "Jerry asked me to tell you the crew will be ready in ten. Oh, and your two friends have arrived."

"Do me a favor, will you, Candace? When we're done, go introduce yourself to Stanley and Liz and bring them to the gathering point. I won't have a chance to speak with them until later."

"No problem." She set the script on the makeup table. "We're good to go. At least I think we are. The green plastic tabs mark the rewritten scenes."

"I'm sure your work is excellent." He waited until the makeup lady with the amazing helmet of hair pulled the napkin from his neck. "Thanks, Rachel."

"You are more than welcome." She patted his shoulder. "Trevor was right, you know. About everything."

"We'll see." Brent waited until Rachel had left and shut the door, then slid a slim folder to rest beside Candace's script. "Take as much time as you like. But if you're going to stay here on the set, you're going to have to sign the document."

She felt the liquid fear congeal. "What?"

"There's a reason why directors don't generally allow a screenwriter on the set. It's because they can't let go of their work. But what we're trying to do here is buck a lot of trends. I'm willing to go against this one as well. But only if you sign that document." He tapped the folder. "It says you are turning over all decisions to me. That we have a shooting script and you are no longer in control of what happens. From this point on, the script is mine. Control is mine. Decisions as to what gets changed are mine and mine alone."

Candace felt herself split into two people. One of them shrieked a silent panic note. All the nightmare fears had been taken from the dark of her volcanic nights and compressed into a slender manila folder.

The other, however, whispered that she could trust this man.

Candace wanted to tell the quieter side of herself that it was impossible. But she had spent the past few weeks learning the same thing about a woman named Celia Breach. That all actors were not created with equal measures of slimy deceit. If she could trust an actress, why not a director?

No, her other voice screamed. *Never. Not this.*

She looked from the folder to the man. Brent wore a deerskin shirt and trousers. His frontier boots rose from leather soles to supple leggings that were lashed to his ankles and shins. He might be dressed like an actor on location. But he was every inch a director. Calm. Resolute. In total control.

She licked her lips. "I-If I sign?"

"Celia has offered to share her trailer with you. You'll be either here or back at the Wilmington soundstage, wherever we feel scenes need more work. You'll be welcome to speak with me about any changes I'm considering. But you must agree not to discuss any such decision with anyone else, and once the decision is made, you won't discuss it at all."

He gave her half a beat, then said, "Pray on it, why don't you. But if it takes you longer than tonight to decide, I'll have to ask you to come no closer than the motel."

⸻ ⬩ ⸻

Liz Courtney stood on a trailer porch that smelled of freshly sawn wood. Everything had a raw, bustling look. Stanley leaned on the railing and squinted into the sunlight. The winter appeared over. Birdsong drifted upon a softly perfumed breeze.

The production encampment was in a field connected to the highway by a newly graveled road. Somewhere to Liz's left, behind a hedge of towering pines, drummed a battalion of generators. The field now housed a dozen massive trailers and piles of equipment.

Landing Bobby's plane had required every inch of the runway in Boone, North Carolina. They had traveled west from there, across the Tennessee state line, into tight-rimmed valleys with jagged ridgelines and rocky clefts. The low-altitude hardwood forests were just beginning to show a minty trace of spring. The ridgelines were dominated by towering pines, some of the biggest she had ever seen.

Jerry Orbain, whom she had last seen doing his investigative work in Austin, had been there to greet them. The diminutive man had only responded to direct questions, and then as tersely as possible. Liz had gathered he was present because Bobby Dupree had ordered it, and saw the duty as beneath him. She learned they were traveling into Cumberland frontier territory. They were south of a national forest, north and west of an American Indian reservation. Twice she saw deer grazing beside the road.

The woman who now approached their trailer was not lean so much as taut. Her dark hair was caught in a bundle at the nape of her neck, her checked shirt rolled away from strong hands. "Ms. Courtney? I'm Candace Chen."

"How do you do. May I introduce Reverend Allcott."

"Stanley," he corrected. "An honor, Ms. Chen. Brent has talked very highly of you and your work."

Liz might be surrounded by a world of strangeness, but she knew a troubled woman when she saw one. "Is everything all right, Ms. Chen?"

"Call me Candace. Fine. Why?"

"I'm sorry. I didn't mean to pry. It's just . . ."

Stanley took up the slack. "You look troubled, is all. And the young man who met us at the airport."

"Jerry Orbain."

"Right. He seemed to share your expression."

"Jerry is Jerry." She clearly did not like being compared to the young man. "I'm sorry it shows. Brent asked me to take you over to the gathering. Not unload on you."

"Liz and I have a lot of experience being there for others, Candace."

Liz asked, "Is there any way we might help?"

Candace Chen appeared blasted by elements stronger than most people ever endured. Liz had seen the same taut expression in cowhands and oilmen, folks accustomed to handling imposs-ible situations in worse weather. She recalled what Brent had described of her background, living on the edge of lava land, and said, "There is nothing harder for a strong person than admitting they need a helping hand."

Candace rapidly blinked her dark eyes and held determinedly to control. "Thanks for your concern. But I'll manage."

"Of course you will." Liz risked a brisk pat on the woman's shoulder. "But just know, if there's anything we can do, feel free."

"Thanks. Please come this way." They walked from the trailer that acted as a front office and staging room to the set. "Who are you anyway?"

"Friends of Brent. Stanley runs his AA program back in Austin. I was partner in his business."

"The lawn care company, right?"

"Liz is president of a bank," Stanley supplied. "She did the lawn thing to help out a man in need."

Candace came to a complete halt. "You trust him."

"Who, Brent? With my life." Liz stepped in close. "Why don't you tell me? At the very least, we'll know what to pray for."

Candace related the problem in the midst of a very tight sigh. She finished with, "Sam Menzes took control of my first story, my baby, and turned it into a twisted, deformed, stunted, evil . . ."

"Brent Stark will not do that," Liz said.

"My heart tells me you're right. My head . . ."

Liz asked, "Is it normal to have the screenwriter around while they're filming?"

"It almost never happens."

"Why hand this choice to you today? Why not last week?"

"I just got in from Los Angeles this morning with the final changes."

Stanley had a big man's ability to gentle his way through the most impossible of statements. "It sounds to me like Brent already has control. What he's saying is you need to recognize that."

Candace did not move, did not breathe, did not look up from the rocky trail.

"Brent wanted to make sure you understood the reality of this situation. He is the director. He has to have final say of, what did you call it?"

When Candace did not speak, Liz supplied, "The shooting script."

"Right. He's told you that if you agree to trust him implicitly, even when you disagree with him, he will give you the freedom to stay around and be a part of this creation. Trust," Stanley repeated gently. "It's a hard thing he's asked from you."

Candace glanced at her wrist, though she was not wearing a watch. "We need to be going."

Liz touched the woman's shoulder a second time and let her hand linger as they walked. "I will be praying for you."

Cables as wide as her ankles ran along either side of the trail they now took. Liz thought of it as a trail because it left the pasture and entered a forest so thick the sunlight dimmed to cool emerald shades. But the trail was graveled and freshly packed, hard and smooth and as broad as a two-lane road. Somewhere to their right a river ran in full spring rush, but the trees were too dense for her to spot the water.

The trail joined several others, and they were joined by an astonishing variety of people. A trio of hulking bikers in beards and leather and tattoos joked with two young women in buckskin and tie-up moccasins. The lady who looked most like a genuine American Indian studied a script and smoked a cigarette and walked without looking at the trail. Construction workers mingled with what Liz could only call nerds, right down to their plastic pocket guards. There were hunters and more Indians and British soldiers in crimson uniforms and a trio of young girls in tattered homespun.

Stanley said, "I keep spotting people I think are probably famous."

They rounded a final bend and entered a meadow bordered on one side by the river and on three others by forested hills. The meadow contained an Indian encampment. Rounded huts of branches and bark and deer hides were clustered into three distinct units. Between the forest and the encampment was a battery of equipment.

"No tepees?" Stanley asked.

"Shawnee didn't use them so much in Kentucky and Tennessee," Candace replied. "They called these dwellings *wegiwa*, which is where we got the name wigwam. That larger structure in the center is the *msikamekwi*, or council house."

They joined a gathering of perhaps forty people. A chuck wagon had been drawn up to the meadow's opposite side from the encampment. Folding chairs dotted the grass. Candace asked, "You folks want anything?"

"Absolutely," Stanley said. "I'd like to know what it is I'm seeing."

Liz knew Candace wanted to refuse the request to explain. That talking shop would only make it harder to work through the jumble in her head. But the scriptwriter said, "Boone took his family on his third trek through the Cumberland Gap. Boone had used funds supplied by a Colonel Henderson to purchase fifty thousand acres in a land the Indians called *Caintuk*. Boone called it New Canaan, the promised land. He actually had visions . . ."

Candace stopped talking because a woman Liz recognized walked over and said, "Mind if I join you?"

"Sure. These are two friends of Brent. I'm sorry, I've forgotten—"

Liz reached across the screenwriter. "Liz Courtney, Ms. Breach. A pleasure. This is Stanley Allcott."

For once, Stanley was beyond words.

Candace said to Celia, "You're not on today."

"I thought I'd see our fearless leader address the troops."

Candace turned back to Liz and asked, "Where was I?"

"Visions."

"Boone envisioned a land of rich farmsteads and horse pastures. Which was in direct contrast to the life they'd had in Carolina, relegated to rocky highlands and indebted to the colonial merchants. But by the time Boone moved his family out, the Revolutionary War had started and the British had formed an alliance with the Shawnees. The Indians saw this as a chance to renege on their land deal. They kidnapped Boone's two daughters and another young woman and threatened dire torments unless the Boones and the other settlers packed up and left." Candace pointed to the settlement. "The first scene we'll be filming is Boone rescuing his children."

Stanley managed to find his voice. "I thought Brent said you'd be rehearsing for another couple of weeks."

"Plans changed. Trevor Wright, our DP, suggested we could use the time better on location. Trevor also suggested we start with this major action sequence."

"He may well be right," Celia said thoughtfully.

"It's a risk," Candace fretted.

"So is this whole project," Celia said.

"But to take a raw crew and start on a major shoot."

Celia shook her head. "I agree with Trevor. Going straight to set gives everybody a chance to acclimatize. Just like when Brent was off doing his frontier thing."

"And the other actors. I heard four of them were ready to quit before the weekend was over."

Stanley said, "I never did feel comfortable listening to words I'm supposed to know and not understanding a thing."

Candace explained, "Instead of rehearsing the script, they have slotted in more advance work for the big action sequences."

Celia leaned forward so she could look around both the writer and Liz. "Rehearsals mean sitting around in a room and practicing your lines. Brent is treating everybody on the set as pros. Which is a risk, but I think he's right to do so."

"I'm not so sure," Candace said.

"Action sequences like this are camera dominated," Celia went on. "Brent wants to get as much as possible in uninterrupted shots. Which means this isn't just about hitting their mark and saying their line. This is run and shoot and run some more. The cameras and the lighting have to be in direct and constant sequence."

"You trust him to get this right?" Candace asked.

Celia smiled. "That's right. I do." Her hair was almost white in the sun and pulled back tight from her face. Liz spotted the scars on her temple, a trio of shadow lines revealed by the afternoon light. She felt a tug deep inside her at the suffering the scars represented. Perhaps it was the absence of makeup, but Celia looked both fragile and immensely strong.

"This is some role reversal," Candace said.

"You don't trust him anymore?"

Candace opened her mouth to reply, then said, "Here he comes."

The crowd quieted as the man appeared from the trailhead and strode purposefully toward the wooden deck. The raw-wood platform held a camera and what to Liz looked like a television draped in a white plastic tent stenciled with the words *Director Only*.

Stanley asked uncertainly, "Should I go to him?"

Liz wondered the same thing. For here was both a man she knew and a man she had never seen before. And it was not merely the longer hair or the frontier clothing. A definite change had come to Brent Stark.

Celia said, "Maybe you should let him be the director now. When he's done, he can come over and be your friend."

A gray-haired man climbed the steps behind Brent. Candace said, "That's Trevor Wright, our cinematographer. Also known as DP, director of photography. He's responsible for all lighting and cameras. Trevor also pinch-hits when the sound man is away, which he is."

Trevor fit Brent with a mike and battery pack, said, "Test, test. Larry, can you confirm they can hear us in Wilmington?"

"They're piping this to the studio?" Celia asked.

Candace shrugged. "News to me."

A voice at the back said, "Good to go, Trevor."

But when the Englishman started to depart, Brent said, "While you're up here, why don't you lead us in an opening prayer. Folks, for those of you who haven't had the pleasure, I'd like to introduce Trevor Wright, our resident wise man."

Trevor's British accent added a certain formality to a benediction that covered the film, the story, the backers, the workers, the set, the action, the day. When he was done and the group had intoned an amen, he started to leave, only to turn back a second time. He embraced Brent and said, "I thank God for the day you called me to this duty," which the body mike picked up.

A voice from somewhere in the crowd intoned, "Amen."

Brent stood and watched the Englishman clamber down the stairs and seat himself on the front row. Liz studied this man she thought she knew so well and wondered how she had missed noticing the incredibly potent force that now surrounded him. Brent's vulnerability and wounded spirit were still evident. But his aura of power, this she did not recognize. She felt as much as saw how Candace Chen shivered slightly, and nodded agreement. There was something remarkable about this moment, so vital an augury she did not need to name it to be affected.

"You all know why we are here," Brent started. "We intend to honor a great man, a founder of our nation. Daniel Boone was the most famous of the early American scouts, a legend before he reached middle age. A score of books were written about him while he still lived, some of which even contained a morsel of truth. Lord Byron even wrote a poem in his honor.

"Boone was born and raised a Quaker, and with simple humility believed that God had granted him a divine mission—to lead his nation westward. But neither his faith nor his strength nor even God's mission kept Boone from knowing one enormous failure after another. Those of you who have read Candace Chen's remarkable script know we intend to honor both his successes and his setbacks. Because it is in the balance of both that we come to know this man as the hero he was."

Brent paused so long Liz wondered if he was done. Even in this silent repose, the man radiated a commanding presence. When he spoke, she realized he had not hesitated; he merely gathered himself for what was now to come.

"You all know why I am here. A film set thrives on back story, and I have supplied more than my share. You know about my drinking and my drugs. You know about the accident and the imprisonment and the hurt I caused so many others."

He paused then, for his gaze had found Celia in the crowd. Liz saw the physical effort it took to tear his eyes away. She felt a lump grow in her throat, swallowed hard, and listened harder.

"How could it happen, that I would transform my early success into such a massive failure? The answer began at age five, when my father packed his bags and took off. Just another family argument, just another kid without a dad. I'm not offering excuses. I'm telling you because I want you to understand who I am today. And to do that, you need to know where I've come from.

"My five-year-old brain decided my dad had left because I was a bad kid. This became the core truth that I built my life around. I spent the next twenty-three years living up to that fact. I decided nobody would ever see me again. I would hide the secret me, the bad kid that drove his daddy away.

"I became such a good actor because I'd already spent my life building a false face. My life off the set became just another way of masking the evil little kid who chased me everywhere. My success only fueled this certainty. If people knew who I really was, I'd be shunned. A failure. They would drop-kick me out of the game.

"The car I drove, the women I dated, the booze I drank, the coke I snorted, were all parts of the armor I built around myself. The house in Malibu, the prizes, the public scenes. Shields, one and all.

"I never really enjoyed my success. Even so, fear drove me higher and faster. The fear's name changed, but the need to drive myself stayed the same. Without success, without all these lies that masked the true me, I had no place. No value. I was worthless. Down deep where it mattered, nothing changed.

"I watched myself win the Oscar for best-supporting actor through the wire-mesh cage that held the prison television. In that moment, all my shields fell away. I was left completely and utterly broken. Two months later, I found the only way to change *everything.*"

Stanley's amen was so unexpected Liz jumped in her seat.

Brent looked over, started to say something, only to be interrupted by applause from a group of roadies and a pair of Indians. He waited for silence, then went on. "Some other time, if you're interested, I'll share with you the road back. Right now, this is what's most important. I am here to do a job for Jesus. I have been called back, and I hope to be of service to God. This responsibility is not just to the film. It extends to each and every one of you. If there is any way we can help you, pray for you, reach out to you, believers and nonbelievers alike, I am here for you. This is the atmosphere I would like to foster within the crew at large. That we are all part of God's family, bound to a higher service than profit or even just one film."

This time, the amens resounded throughout the gathering.

"God willing, and with your help, we are going to make a sixty-million-dollar film for eighteen million dollars. I know there's a lot of talk about our changing the way Hollywood looks at entertainment. I can't see that far ahead. All I have room for is my responsibility, to the film and to you. My crew. My family for the shoot. I hope and pray we will find this a period of great growth and astonishing miracles. When it comes time to pack our bags and leave, I hope we will, each of us, feel that we have accomplished two things in the time we share here.

"First, that we have produced the finest work each of us is capable of doing.

"And second, that we have, as a team and as individuals, grown closer to God."

Out of the corner of her eye, Liz saw the two ladies seated to her left, Candace Chen and Celia Breach, both wipe their faces with shaky hands. And this time it was she, the banker in her city suit, who called the first amen.

Brent said, "Jerry Orbain, did you make it here in time? Great. Everybody knows Jerry, my AD. Jerry, would you come up here and lead us in the closing prayer?"

The man moved with head bowed so low his back was hunched over. He climbed the stairs very slowly. When he reached the top, he whispered something.

"Wait a second," Brent said.

The director fumbled with his mike and finally unplugged the battery pack. No one heard what was said. But they all saw the two men, director and assistant, embrace.

iz and Stanley found themselves in the solitary company of a star after Candace rose without a comment and made a beeline for the platform. Brent now stood on the bottom stair, one hand on Jerry Orbain's shoulder. He spoke with Trevor and a pair of roadies. To Liz's eye, Jerry still looked seriously bent out of shape.

Stanley said to no one in particular, "Wonder what's going on up there."

Liz replied, "Looks to me like that young man got hit by more than Brent's words."

"Those words weren't bad."

"That's not what I said. Jerry's had a problem since we saw him in Austin. Remember we thought he was a fed? He was uptight and angry back then. He was like that when he met us today. This change wasn't Brent's work."

"Would you look at that," Stanley said as Candace ignored the two men to either side of Brent and said something that left Brent smiling and reaching for her as well. "Guess somebody's found an answer to her prayers."

Celia turned and gave them a hard look. "Just exactly why are you here?"

"We're not certain," Liz replied.

"Bobby called and sent his plane," Stanley said. "We thought it was to give Brent support on his first day of filming."

Liz added, "But Bobby seemed to think we could report back on this to investors down in Texas."

"What possible information we can give to folks with money is beyond us," Stanley said. "I couldn't be any more lost than if I was up there in those woods."

Celia looked from one to the other. "What is this, an honesty convention?"

"I could think of worse places to be," Stanley said.

"Why does that bother you?" Liz asked.

The star shifted in her seat. "I need a coffee."

Stanley was already up and moving. "I'll get it. How do you take it?"

"One Sweet'n Low."

"Liz?"

"Please."

Celia followed him with her gaze. "He moves like a dancer."

"Stanley boxed in his younger years. Won a couple of regional titles as an amateur heavyweight."

"Are you two an item?"

Liz started to backpedal herself out of that. But before the denial could form, she stopped. And rubbed the place over her heart.

"Never mind," Celia said.

"I sent Stanley to prison."

Celia was the one who rocked back in her seat. "Whoa."

"Brent's not the only man who came back from the pit armed with a different mindset. Stanley ran Brent's AA group until he was named head pastor of one of the largest churches in Texas."

Celia ran a hand down one cheek, leaving a wet streak. "I hate how you people can tear me apart."

Liz snagged the woman's hand. "What's the matter, honey?"

"Nothing."

Liz made her grip feather light. "My heart tells me you're not a woman to give in to pressure, dear, so I'll only say this once. It's not my nature to pry where I'm not welcome. I will never press. But if you want to talk, folks have told me I'm hard to shock."

Stanley surprised her by appearing at her other side. "She's the best listener I've ever met, and even better at praying."

Liz reached with her free hand without looking over. "Give us a minute."

"No problem." He set the second cup on the empty seat beside her.

Liz handed the actor her coffee. Without lifting her gaze, she saw how they were part of a crowd, yet left in an island of solitude. A celebrity's right, and her curse.

Celia Breach saw nothing but the grass by her feet. "I can't let him destroy me again."

There was no question in Liz's mind who the star meant. "Has he said anything to you? I mean, of a personal nature."

"No." Celia's sigh was a ragged shiver. "I've been down this road before. Emotions run fast and furious on a set. You arrive, you dive in, you wrap, you hug, you leave. Only I can't do that with him."

"Celia, honey." Liz did what came natural. Which was to smile. "I've carried a mystery for quite a while. And it's only now, this very minute, that I've finally found the answer."

"I'm not going to like what you want to tell me. I can feel it."

"You and I can probably agree on at least one thing. That Brent Stark defines the word hunk. Which makes his behavior down Austin way a tad strange. You see, since he got out of prison, the man has not dated. I mean, not even once. I had women in my bank and friends from town offer me some serious bribes for an introduction. I tried to set him up with ladies from church. But I've stopped trying. The man was always nice. Soon as he could, though, he'd disconnect and walk away. You know how it is in a theater group. People talk. And if they don't know the facts, they make do with myth. I think most folks figured he'd had something happen in prison. I admit, I was worried. But he's never talked about it. Not to me, nor to Stanley, and we know him as well as anyone."

Celia Breach hid herself from the crowd by taking back her hand and covering her face. She bent over until her face and hands met her knees.

"I didn't know anything about what went on with you two, except the accident, of course. The whole world knows about that. And Brent won't talk about that either. And now I see."

Celia might have told her to stop. But this time Liz decided if she did say it, she didn't mean it. Liz stroked the white blond hair beside the scar on Celia's temple. "I might be totally wrong. But I don't think so. It's not just guilt over the accident. It's love. I think he's trying to make himself into a man who deserves you."

The young woman rocked in her seat. A few people turned their way, then looked off. Anywhere except at a woman who was coming completely undone.

"Can I ask you something? In your other location romances, have you ever had a man go out of his way to leave you alone?"

Celia shook her head on her knees. Back and forth. No.

"Well, you're a big girl. You can do what you want here. But I know this new man, and believe you me, he is new. Changed from the inside out. And I think one reason he's never said anything to you is, if you decide not to let him into your life, it could very well destroy him. So my advice is, if you choose not to love him, let him down just as gently as you possibly can."

he closer they came to sunset, the tenser the crew became and the more frenetic their movements. Stanley found Liz standing well back from the fray. She chatted with a young woman with a clipboard and neon-green eyeglasses. Stanley asked, "Everything all right?"

Liz gave him a look he had never seen before. One that carried something so potent he felt it down in his boots. "Everything is fine."

All the questions he had carried over with him, about the star who was standing with Candace now, neither woman speaking, and both of them watching Brent with hollowed eyes. About how everybody kept looking from the pair of them to Brent and back, and not approaching either. About how Brent was studying the encampment through a portable lens, talking with Trevor Wright, talking into a walkie-talkie and then studying some more. It all just went away. Her look was that strong.

Stanley said, "Well, okay then."

"This is Lisa," Liz said, indicating the young woman with funky glasses. "Lisa is studying film. Trevor is her professor."

"Mr. Wright is the best," Lisa said.

"Lisa is interning as what they call a script girl. She was sent over by Brent to keep us company and tell us what is going on."

"I couldn't think of anything I'd like more than to understand what's happening," Stanley said fervently.

Something in the smile Liz gave him suggested she understood more than he expected. But it was Lisa who said, "They've chosen a super tricky shoot for their first go, like, they've been rehearsing for four days, which is amazing, I mean, four days on location with all the cameras and lights and everybody, and now they're going to blow the whole thing up, we're talking some serious pyrotechnics, and like, wow, I mean, really, if they don't get it right, we're one day into filming and already a week behind schedule, that would be so totally not good."

"Well, that sure cleared everything up for me," Stanley said.

Liz said, "Run that blow-up business by me one more time."

But a voice yelled, "Quiet on set!"

Lisa gave a huge grin and finger wave and bounced away.

The last sliver of sun disappeared behind the forested slopes. Trevor Wright worked as many as two dozen technicians handling lights and filters and reflectors. A trio of bullish men strapped into tanks began walking around the encampment, blowing out a blanket of mist.

Candace Chen had approached unnoticed. "Inert gas. Heavier than air. Since there's no wind, this will help maintain a constancy of lighting and extend the semblance of a single minute in time. And hide the burn. They've got three sets of residences, and they'll rebuild for three full takes. The gas hides the ashes and the burn marks."

"There you go again," Stanley said, "talking words I ought to understand."

She pointed to where the cinematographer, assistant director, and Brent were clustered by the camera stand. A stocky man equipped with a second massive portable camera stood a few feet away. "They intend to shoot this three times, and each go-round sweep through the entire scene. We're looking at maybe nine minutes of film time. The risk is huge."

Celia spoke up from Stanley's other side, "Feature-film location work averages three minutes of film a day. Instead of shooting this nine-minute sequence over three days, they have taken four days to rehearse. The trick is to make the cameras sweep along with the actors and have everybody work in such tandem that they don't have to cut and paste. In film parlance, they're shooting an entire action sequence in one continuous take. The result on screen will be a sensation of stepping inside the action."

"If it works," Candace added.

"I still don't understand," Stanley said, "but I'm nervous."

Jerry Orbain accepted the headphones from Brent, punched him on the shoulder, and watched him walk away. The makeup lady worked on his face for a moment, then sent him off with a nervous smile. Brent walked to the edge of the forest. He turned around. A man with one of the blowers moved up beside him, layering the ground.

Brent lifted the flintlock musket and the hatchet to the crew. Then he backed into the forest. And vanished.

"I've got chills," Candace said.

"Wait," Celia said.

"Boone came home from a hunting trek to discover his children had been kidnapped," Candace went on to explain. "He has been tracking his children's captors for two days. He's actually run away from the five men who started off with him. He attacks at sunset. Alone. Against an entire Shawnee settlement and a small squad of British soldiers."

Jerry called, "Sound!"

"Check!"

"Lights!"

"Ready!"

"Cameras!"

"Camera one, rolling!"

"Two, check!"

"Clipboard!"

A young man stepped in front of Trevor with an electronic board. "Scene twenty-seven, take one."

"Action!"

For a tight endless instant, nothing happened. Then Boone loped from the trees.

Not Brent.

Daniel Boone.

The man moved in incredible stealth. The only sign of his approach was the shifting ebbing swirling fog. One minute all was quiet—Indians by several campfires, British soldiers shaving in the stream, just another approaching night.

Then mayhem.

Boone was everywhere. His actions swept him through the first cluster of braves so fast they did not even have time to reach for their weapons. He took down three with one sweep of his flintlock, clubbing them into the mist. He flitted into one Shawnee dwelling, then another and a third.

The alarm had still not been raised.

A shout then rose from the British. Boone did not run directly toward them. Instead, he headed *parallel* to the riverbank. The hatchet fell to a thong on his wrist as he raised the musket. Two of the soldiers hurried their shots and missed. Boone, however, waited until he had lined up the soldiers. Lined them up in tandem.

His single shot punched through all three men.

"Priscilla!"

His roar was the first time the man had spoken on set. Stanley's brain, overloaded by the speed, the sheer shocking *force* of a warrior on the attack, managed just one thought.

He had just heard Daniel Boone speak.

"Priscilla! Madeline!"

A child called back, *"Father!"*

Boone dropped his musket and hefted two firebrands. They

became his weapons now. They and the fire he left in his wake. He spun and he flew and he fought. There was no force on earth that could hold him off. Not with his children in danger.

The light played upon Daniel Boone's features. Stanley shivered. He could not help it. In his younger days, he had faced killers in the ring, felons who were kept in check only because they had this legal means of expressing their rage. He knew the look.

Daniel Boone was in full warrior mode. He bulled through the last remaining braves blocking him from his daughters. The hatchet gleamed in the rising firelight as he chopped through the children's bonds. He swept them up and fled.

When he bounded back into the forest, Jerry shouted, "Cut!"

The entire crew erupted in applause.

Liz liked to think she saw the change in the moment of its conception. A gentle wave coursed through the crew, starting before the applause began and ending long after. They were no longer members of a disparate group, drawn together by one man supposedly hearing the voice of God. They were a team. They were making a movie. A film they *believed* in.

And it was all the doing of one man.

They rebuilt the Shawnee encampment in no time flat, or so it seemed to Liz. But by then, all concept of time had vanished. She could not believe Boone's fight through the village had actually lasted nine minutes. It felt as though she held her breath through the entire take.

If anything, the second take was more intense than the first. She knew what was coming and where to look. She knew the muscular young man running behind Boone was a Steadicam operator. She understood that even the slightest shift in the actor's movements or angles was crucial, the timing of each blow to each opponent, the spot from where he took his shot all set with exactitude by the placement of the lights and the man on the Steadicam. Which made the speed and precision even more incredible.

The third take was equally mesmerizing. While they rebuilt the set that final time, Celia became the one to get them coffee from the chuck wagon and drape her arm on Liz's shoulder and explain things. Celia talked of how the lighting had to be restructured between each shot to maintain the exact same point in the day's clock. She pointed to the new klieg light positioned high in the western hill, the one with the silver-orange tint, suggesting dusk's final rays. She talked about how the soldiers and Shawnee had to practice fighting and falling so the cadence was maintained throughout, even down to where they hit the ground and how they lay.

Liz tried hard to pay attention. But what she mostly took in was how this man she knew and liked so well, how he could transform himself into a complete and utter stranger. One who carried her into a myth that became more real than the surrounding night. Even as they reenacted the scene for a third time.

After the third take, as Trevor and Jerry called it a night and thanked the crew, and Brent collapsed into the makeup chair and toweled off his dripping face, Liz finally glanced at her watch. She was astonished to find it was a quarter to three.

In the morning.

The last thought she had before her head hit the pillow was she had no doubt in her mind what she would say to those investors back in Texas.

This project was a go.

very other Sunday, Shari and the gang met at some Hollywood focal point and hung out for hours. Their Sunday gang numbered anywhere from twelve to twenty. They watched the trades and they chose their destinations carefully. They had to. They spent a major portion of their meager salaries on the indulgence. And no matter how they couched the gathering in excuses, it remained just that. A total extravagance, one they looked forward to with the carefree hope of children.

They emailed back and forth with avid fantasy and ragged humor, borne on eating crumbs and claiming to be almost satisfied. They were all employed in one segment of entertainment or another, and all somewhere near the bottom rung. Their Sunday meeting points were chosen with the same desperate intensity they applied to all their so-called free time. Other days, they scrounged tickets to screenings, when warm bodies were needed to fill the seats and impress the critics. They met for coffee in known locales and chattered intelligently about European trends or hot spots in Cannes. Hoping to be noticed. Sharpening their tactics for the ninety-second chance they desperately craved.

Their meetings every other Sunday were the same, only more

so. They shared rumors about places where major players were to gather, for all of them were invisible enough in their jobs to overhear conversations about where directors and producers were going to brunch. They bribed waiters for tables close enough to be noticed. Maybe. Even if their faces were remembered and they had a chance to sip cocktails another night, and the power guy or gal started seeing them around and assumed they were somebody, then maybe . . .

Their lives were built on a mountain of maybes and a myth of chances just around the next corner.

This Sunday's brunch was at Shutters on the Beach, a major-player spot in Santa Monica. Shutters was located where Pico Boulevard actually ran into the sand, one of the few buildings that did not have the road between it and the sea. Rooms at Shutters began at nine hundred dollars a night. The hotel had two restaurants. One was a diner with a sun-drenched patio. The other, called One Pico, was impossibly expensive. So they bribed their way to a table closest to the main restaurant's entrance. The glass-rimmed patio was packed, though only the tourists paid any attention to the cinematographic backdrop of ocean and sand. Shari sat with eighteen cronies crammed into a table meant for twelve. The patio could not be booked, and though they had waited almost two hours, this was the largest table the restaurant was willing to give them. There was no need to worry about finding somebody worth being seen by. Not here, not on a Sunday afternoon. The place was that hot.

There had been a little chatter about Shari's *Variety* mention at the outset, but she played it down. A mistake, she called it, and laughed. She hadn't known how she was going to handle it until that moment. But the table went super quiet when her closest friend, Tiffany, mentioned it. Shari went with her first instinct, which was to pooh-pooh the whole thing. She did not know why until after, when she felt the sudden barrier dissolve. Shari spent a lot of time crammed into the corner, laughing in tandem with the others at things she scarcely heard, glancing repeatedly at the almost-invisible glass walls separating them from the street and the beach. These were her friends.

Tiffany was seated to Shari's left, a guy named Alf who worked as a junior contracts lawyer in the town's leading entertainment firm to her right. Shari tried hard to put aside the sense of a divide separating her from the rest of the table. She slipped her chair back a notch so she was not touching shoulders and elbows on both sides and asked the waiter for another espresso.

Tiffany, however, sidled even closer and said, "Okay. The real scoop now. What's it like?"

"What are we talking about?"

"Your date with Brad Pitt. Come on, this is *me*. I've got to get a call from Alf to know you're in the read?"

"Because it was all a mistake, I'm sorry to say. You know I'd tell you if it was anything."

"I wonder."

"What's that supposed to mean?"

"Hey, you don't have to get sharp. I'm just saying if it'd been me mentioned on page two, you'd hear the scream at Zuma Beach."

"I didn't have the energy. I was up until four that morning playing babysitter to Colin Chapman."

"Oh. Him."

"Don't get that way. It was another gofer duty. Only with champagne."

That satisfied her friend, at least partly. Tiffany was pretty enough and blond enough to be taken as just another vacuum head. But the sweet Arkansas exterior hid a young woman with the drive and the smarts to make it. If only. "Still. Colin Chapman."

Shari pretended not to notice that the rest of the table was listening again. "Believe me. You see the guy pass out three times in four nights, need the bouncer and the driver to pour him back into the limo, a lot of the glitter wears off."

Alf supplied, "My boss does Chapman's personal work. I know when he's been out with Chapman on account of how he can't take off his shades for a week."

Shari could have kissed him. "He and Solish spent the entire time so stoned I doubt they remember anything, much less a grommet sent by head office."

"Let's see, that would be Raul Solish, the world-famous director?" But Tiffany was smiling now.

"I've done that once," said a ravishing redhead schlepping deal memos at Paramount's subsidiary rights division. "Played minder to a visiting producer. He wanted to unwrap me like ice cream on a stick."

"I always liked ice cream," Alf said.

"You wish," the redhead said and suddenly the attention was bouncing around the table with the conversation, and Shari was able to breathe easy again.

At least until Tiffany said, "There's a whole universe of power people around here. Moore Madden just turned and smirked at me."

"Sorry, hon," the redhead said. "That was me. I know on account of the waiter just slipped me a note, Madden asking for my phone number."

Tiffany shot back, "Sorry yourself. I thought you were smart enough to know the waiter used Madden's name to get your info for himself."

The redhead sniffed. "There's one table in the front room big as ours, must be six green-lit films just begging for somebody like me to make things happen."

Alf said, "All I need is one of those guys in the other room to let me handle his work, I'd have my place in limo land."

The redhead complained, "Why are we out here sweating when the power guys are all in the shade? I thought the patio was the happening place."

"It was," Tiffany said, "until certain parties who weren't actually invited showed up and bounced them inside."

Shari waited until the talk swung away to ask Tiffany, "Madden is here? You're sure?"

"Just inside the front room. Turn around and get an eyeful for yourself, and it was me he smiled at." Then she saw the change. "What's the matter?"

"Nothing. I just . . ."

She stopped because the table went totally silent, and a shadow fell on her place.

"Let me see if I got this straight," a voice said. "Some nowhere chick from donkey land hitches a ride in my agent's limo and thinks that gives her wheels to say my script won't fly? Where do you get off?"

Shari took her time turning around. "And you are?"

"Honey, if you don't know, you got no business in this town. Wait, what am I saying? We already knew that."

The table was frozen. The day demolished. Her dream of a few hours with friends, away from the confusion of a week she still had not digested, all gone. Shari kept herself from rising to her feet. That was something a clone did, a mailroom gofer. Not the woman she was now, the lady instructed by Sam Menzes to handle this guy. She shifted her chair around.

"I get a call from my agent," Madden sneered. "You remember my agent, right? Zubin Mikels. Head of CAA. A *real* player in this business. Zubin tells me there's this new brain-dead reader or whatever it is Sam Menzes calls his lackeys these days. She gets her name in the trades and suddenly she thinks she *belongs*."

It wasn't the director's rudeness that turned her body to ice. It wasn't her grandmother's silent voice that kept her calm. It was the sadness of knowing she had turned the corner. And whatever she said, however she responded, Shari knew the instant she opened her mouth she'd bid farewell to her only friends in the Hollywood jungle.

Moore Madden the director cocked his fists on his hips. With the sun behind him he looked like a double-barreled pistol with both triggers in firing position. "Here's what's going to happen, Khan. Tomorrow my agent is going to arrange a meet with Menzes. Zubin Mikels is going to make this deal happen like I want. Then he's going to have Menzes send you back to Kabul."

Shari shook her head, ostensibly to clear her dark hair from her eyes, but really to let the director's words fall away like water. She said calmly, "I'm sorry to hear you take that option, Mr. Madden."

"Oh hey. Wait. Let me take my pulse, see how much that bothers me. Not. At. All."

"You see, Mr. Madden, I am one of your biggest fans. I've seen *Broken Angel* a dozen times and more. Your power behind the camera is second to none. And that's what I told Menzes when he sent me the pink slip telling me to ax your project."

One of the cocked triggers fell off his hip. "What?"

"Yes, sir. You see, that's why I made Zubin wait so long. Zubin must have mentioned that, how I kept his limo by the front gates for over half an hour. I planted myself in Mr. Menzes' office and basically tackled him as he came out of a meeting with Mr. Steen. You know Mr. Steen. He's the man who wrote the cancellation clause into your original contract. The one that says you owe Galaxy the four-and-a-half mil they fronted you for development funds?"

The other arm trigger uncocked. "I won't pay those bums a dime."

"I admire you, Mr. Madden. If it were me, I'd pay with my own blood not to have Mr. Steen and his snake pit guys go after me."

Madden crossed his arms. He appeared completely blind to the fact that the entire patio now listened in rapt attention. "There's a padded cell with Steen's name on it."

"You don't have to work with the guy on a daily basis." Shari gave a delicate tremor. She deserved two Oscars for this day's performance. One for calming Madden. The other for pretending it didn't hurt to watch her friends gradually fade into the background. "Menzes saw your original script as a perfect vehicle for a star he basically owns."

"Colin Chapman."

"None other. When Chapman refused to work with your rewritten script, which I thought was brilliant, by the way, just brilliant. But not Chapman. And so not Menzes. When he heard from Chapman's agent that he was off the project, Menzes sent me the note. Two words, Mr. Madden. Offer retracted."

"He can't do that."

"Menzes thinks he can, and he has Steen to back his play."

"Okay, okay, I'll have Zubin give them a call." Madden ran his hands through his hair. "You in tomorrow?"

"For you, Mr. Madden, I would be in any day of the week."

"Let's do lunch." He headed for the exit. "The Grill at noon."

A few beats of heavy silence hung over the patio. Finally Tiffany spoke up. "So that's how it's done."

— ◆ —

There was little of the normal banter at the conclusion of that afternoon's brunch. Instead, they all seemed to just drift apart, blown by the realization that one of their own had actually made it. Shari Khan had entered the realm of dreams come true.

Shari listened to them talk about where they were going next, a couple across the street for a towel on the beach and some rays, three off to some beachside volleyball tournament, four others to a local café for yet more caffeine-fueled chatter. The glances said that the talk would mostly be about her. Shari wanted to say she'd join any who would have her. And she knew they all would make room, but only as the newest outsider they had to schmooze. The glass barrier surrounding the patio glinted in the strong California light, and she knew it would follow her wherever she went.

"Shari, you mind if I ask you something?"

She raised a hand as though to shield herself from sunlight off the glass, and pressed something out of her eye. "Sure, Alf."

The guy she had laughed with, caroused with, even contemplated a little fling with at one time, was suddenly as nervous as if he were seated in his boss's outer office, and not waiting for the junior accountant at the table's other end to calculate their share of the bill. "I've got a pal, he's been working on this screenplay. It's really something. He's even had McConnell over at USC do a read-through. The guy said if he was still at DreamWorks he'd green-light the thing tomorrow. But you know how hard it is to get face time in this town."

Her heart thudded like it had been transformed to a lead-lined gong. "All too well."

"I was just wondering, and it's okay if you can't, you know, do it. But I just thought maybe, if you had a minute . . ."

"Me reading the thing would be about as helpful as giving it to the waiter." But her joke fell flat and she saw how he took it as a turndown. Just another refusal in the land of closed doors. "I know Emily Arsene, she's Menzes' principal reader. I could ask if maybe she'd take a look."

Alf stared at her like the heavens had suddenly opened. "For real?"

"All I can do is ask. And I got to tell you, she is one tough cookie."

"Hey, who isn't in this town? The way you handled Madden, I'm amazed he could walk away on his own steam."

"All I did was pass on a message."

"Sure. A message from Sam Menzes." Tiffany laughed with equal parts of silver and lemon. "Like the rest of us wouldn't give away our firstborn for the chance to say those words."

"Come on, Tiffany, lay off."

"What are you talking about, girl? This is awesome. You've made it."

"Right. And my limo is waiting outside the door."

"Maybe not now. But tomorrow. The same day you tear the page with my address out of your Day-Timer."

"Now you're talking total—"

"Ms. Khan?"

How the guy managed to sneak up on them was a complete mystery. He was drop-dead gorgeous, in a town where looks were about as unique as white bread on a minimart's shelf. "Yes?"

"Jason Garrone. I represent Colin Chapman."

This time she was on her feet before she could tell herself it wasn't done. "It's an honor, Mr. Garrone."

And the guy was tall. Tall enough to smile down at her. Hair a shade darker than russet. Eyes like an emerald sea. Great smile. Not just the teeth but the lips . . . oh stop. This wasn't happening.

"I have to tell you, Ms. Khan, the way you handled Moore Madden was a stellar performance."

"You obviously mistake me for somebody worth buttering up."

His laugh was as rich as the rest of him. A white polo shirt turned special by the patchwork silk lining the collar. Cerruti, probably. Brioni jeans, she knew because the name was sewn into the front pocket. Alligator belt. Deck shoes with the discreet Ferragamo label. Anywhere but Hollywood, the man would have to be gay. But ever since the weekly cable show where gay guys dissed some unfortunate victim over his clothes sense, refined dressing was in.

"I was wondering if I might have a word."

"Sure. Grab a chair."

Alf did a jackrabbit out of his chair. "Right here, Mr. Garrone. I'm Alf Waters, with Stone and Kimball."

"So nice to meet you, Alf. Please keep your seat." The man actually had manners to match his looks. "I played golf with Rich last week. He used me to polish the eighteenth green."

Alf's laugh had a manic edge. Shari knew Richard Stone, the firm's senior partner, had never even shaken Alf's hand. "Yeah, that sounds like Rich."

Jason Garrone said to Shari, "I'd love to join you, but unfortunately I'm hosting Shirley O'Hane and her sixth husband. Or maybe it's her seventh. I lose count and I'm her manager." He motioned to the back room. "If your friends could possibly spare you, I'd love to introduce you and have a word about this *Snowbound* project. Colin really would like to participate, if you can handle Madden and convince him to return to the original script."

If *she* could handle *Moore Madden*. Shari should have been singing the words. If she could *handle* a top-tier director. "Lead the way."

As she followed the agent inside, she glanced back. Tiffany tried to give her a smile to match the thumbs-up but couldn't. Alf made the universal sign for *I'll phone*. The others just watched her pass through the door barred to them.

Shari could have wept.

am? It's Derek. Thought you'd want to know. Zubin called me. *Snowbound* is back on track again."

"This is Zubin talking smoke, or has Madden actually agreed?"

"Zubin just got off the phone with Madden before he phoned me. I also spoke with Shari Khan. She met Madden."

"When, today? Sunday?"

"Apparently so. And she had lunch with Garrone. Who has agreed to lower Chapman's scale for the film."

"She told you that?"

"Actually, I spoke with Garrone himself. While he was still at the table with Khan. And Shirley O'Hane, who apparently has expressed an interest in seeing the script as well."

Menzes laughed. It was a rare sound. "Looks like you owe me double."

"I got to tell you. The girl had me fooled."

Menzes laughed again. "Move her into that vacant office on our floor."

"Isn't this a little fast?"

"I don't want her learning the snake pit tactics. Put her in charge of this *Snowbound* deal."

"She's not ready, Sam."

"She got them to sing from the same page."

"Emily was feeding her the lines."

"Correction. Emily gave her the background. She handled Zubin all by herself. And now Madden. Not to mention the fact that Garrone is no pushover."

Steen did not respond.

"Let Shari run with this thing."

"If you say so."

"Where's the secretary they think fed the inside scoop to Zubin . . . what's her name?"

"Natalie. I believe she's looking for a job in Guam."

"Good. Watch Khan, Derek. Watch her close."

Derek hung up the phone, not saying what he was thinking, which was, if he knew his boss at all, he'd say Sam Menzes was setting Khan up to fail. Which made no sense at all.

er grandmother entered the studio lot with the assurance of a queen.

The limo cruised to a halt by the front gates. Shari had made a point of introducing herself to the main guard, who grinned as the smoked window came down.

"How we doing today, Ms. Khan?"

"Fine, thanks, Herb. Could I please get a day pass for my grandmother?"

"No problem. Always a pleasure to see a pretty lady in the back of a studio limo." He tore the sheet from his pad and slipped it through the window. "Make that two pretty ladies."

"How extraordinary," her grandmother purred, "that they would think to place a gentleman in such a position of responsibility."

Herb laughed with genuine pleasure. "Hey, you obviously got me mixed up with the folks I pass through these gates."

"On the contrary. You are the studio's public face. My granddaughter told me about you, but I thought, no, this is not the Hollywood I know, to take such concern over vital details." She slipped her hand through the window. "I am Lizu."

"Great to meet you, Lizu. That's a swell name."

"Thank you, Herb. It was my own grandmother's name. It is very old. From Persian royalty."

"Which is why it suits you so well." He actually saluted. "You pretty ladies have a swell day."

Shari rolled up the window and said, "Next time you want somebody to try and shift the earth a few degrees for you, you know who to ask."

"I saw how he looked at you, who he smiled at first. You have learned the lessons well."

Shari let her grandmother set the pace. Lizu Khan wore a discreetly expensive St. John outfit, a coarse weave silk suit in three shades that all matched her pearls. Lizu Khan had a softly elegant word for the receptionist, another for the two aides they passed in the lobby. She even made the three snake pit fiends in starched shirts and suspenders they met in the elevator stand up straight and speak with respect. Something they would not do for anybody.

When they came out of the elevator on the twelfth floor, Shari pointed down the main foyer and said, "The king and his chief of staff are down that way. Us peons are kept penned over here."

"Lesser nobility, perhaps," Lizu Khan corrected, "but look at where you are."

"Yeah, who would believe it."

"I still don't understand why you made me wait until today to see where it is you work, my dear."

"I had my reasons." The hall's narrowness was masked somewhat by the decoration, which caused Lizu Khan to walk more slowly still. Original Galaxy movie posters from the thirties and forties alternated with signed portraits of the stars and glass shelves containing duplicates of the Oscars they'd won. "This is my secretary, Kitty Sheen. Kitty, this is my grandmother, Lizu Khan."

"A real pleasure, Ms. Khan." Kitty was an ample woman with playful eyes.

"The honor is all mine, Ms. Sheen. Is that an Irish lilt I hear?"

"I left the bog a wee lass," she said, heightening the brogue, "and here I am, a century and six children later, still singing the old-country tune."

"I have always admired someone who is able to claim their heritage with pride and beauty."

"Why, Ms. Khan, you talk like somebody who belongs in this business."

"I am happy to live this through my granddaughter, thank you. She speaks very highly of you and your friend."

Shari said, "She means Emily."

"I know who she means. And you look like a woman who values truth, Ms. Khan, so I'll share a tidbit with you. The only reason Emily Arsene has helped your granddaughter is because Shari here deserves it."

Lizu Khan smiled at her granddaughter. "I see you have chosen your front office ally wisely."

Shari shared a look with her secretary, then took her grandmother by the arm. "This way."

Kitty scurried to the office door. "Allow me."

Lizu started to enter the office, then froze.

Shari did not try to hide her pleasure. "You know it, don't you."

For once, Lizu Khan's legendary aplomb was lost to her. "Oh my."

"When I got here the first day, the room was empty. Emily explained I could decorate the office however I wanted, long as I used things from the studio warehouse. I asked, they delivered." Shari swept an arm around. "Simple as that."

"Well, not quite, my dearie. Oh my, no." Kitty stood just outside the doorway and explained, "Your granddaughter took it upon herself to charm the studio's chief archivist out of her ample stores, which was no mean feat, I don't mind telling you. The lady and Shari here spent the better part of a day searching dusty boxes until they found the items. Which is amazing if you happened to know this lady, which to my great sorrow I do, all too well, for it's from this dire fate your granddaughter rescued me and lofted me up into these far reaches of heaven." Kitty smiled sweetly. "There now, I believe that's enough blarney for the moment. I'll just leave you two to have a wee chat."

Lizu probably did not hear her, as her attention had been captured by the sofa. Or rather, the sofa and the signed black-and-white photo that hung above it. And the movie poster that was beside that. All of which were from the palace set of *Istanbul Affairs*, one of the biggest hits of the forties. The film garnered nine Oscars, reignited the fading career of one of Galaxy's leading men, and introduced him to a twenty-year-old vixen with bedroom eyes and pouting lips who, in both the photo and the poster, turned the sofa into a sultry playground. The on-location romance made headlines around the world. The two stars subsequently married and made history by staying married, despite the thirty-three-year difference in their ages.

All this was of relative unimportance when compared to the fact that *Istanbul Affairs* was her grandmother's all-time favorite film.

"Everything except my office chair came from the sets," Shari said. "The desk was from the sultan's palace, remember, Grandma? And the coffee table and the other chairs were all packed into the same box as the sofa, so I thought, why not?"

Lizu glanced over, nodded, then returned her attention to the striped-silk divan. "May I?"

"Of course."

She settled herself down, spine straight, poised even when living an unexpected dream. "You shouldn't have done this for me, my dear."

"I didn't. Well, not entirely." Shari could not stop smiling. "Hey. A girl's got to have a desk, right?"

Lizu Khan ran a hand over the silk damask, then patted the seat beside her. "Join me."

"Sure." But her progress around the coffee table was interrupted by a knock on the door.

"Sorry to interrupt, ladies," Kitty said. "But a certain Mr. Garrone would like to have a word."

"Garrone," Lizu Khan said. "Isn't that your young gentleman?"

"He's not my anything," Shari said, wishing she could hide the sudden blush.

Kitty lowered her voice. "I could think of several anythings I'd love to make of this one. Though my dear sweet husband, whose name I'm certain to remember before too long, might have a thing to say about it. Shall I show the gentleman in?"

"Okay. Sure. Have him join us."

Jason Garrone is just an agent. Just an agent . . . But even as Shari fed herself the mental line, her heart sang a different tune. Their lunch at The Grill with Moore Madden had been followed by a private dinner at Spago. He had called her twice. Supposedly about business. But each time there was the off comment, the sly referral, the witty aside that had her laughing long after she hung up. He did not push. He did not make the constant error of most Hollywood males, which was to *expect*. Especially the handsome ones and those with power, who treated a conference call with any woman as all the foreplay she ought to require.

But not Shari Khan. Which was why she spent so many nights alone.

Which apparently was something Jason Garrone had picked up on without her having said a thing. Maybe it was osmosis. Maybe it was his very own mating dance. Whatever the reason, her entire body hummed. She wished she knew what to do with her hands. She felt like a teenager waiting for the prom king.

"Shari, how nice of you to make time . . ." Jason stopped a

pace beyond the doorway. "I am so very sorry. I am interrupting."

"Jason, may I introduce my grandmother, Lizu Khan. This is Jason Garrone."

"Mrs. Khan, what an honor."

"Thank you, Mr. Garrone." Her grandmother permitted the young man to take her hand. Jason did not give it the standard American shake. Instead, he did a slight half bow, holding only the fingertips. A very European act. "Won't you join us?"

"Are you certain I'm not disturbing, Shari?"

Lizu said, "My granddaughter was simply indulging me, Mr. Garrone. Are you an agent?"

"The proper term is manager, Mrs. Khan, but in many respects, yes, I serve many of my clients as an agent would. Some, like Colin Chapman, have done away with his agent entirely."

Lizu Khan clearly liked how he did not denigrate the moment with condescension. "What is the difference?"

"Legally, an agent is not permitted to package a project. Managers can. A packager brings together screenwriter and stars and director, and shops the entire product to a studio. In these cases, we serve as coproducer with the studio's in-house people. *Snowbound* is different. That is the project Shari and I are discussing."

"I thought Shari was working on *Iron Feather*."

"That is the studio's current project, yes, ma'am. But people in our trade work two and sometimes three or four films in advance."

Shari said, "We're planning to go over to the commissary for lunch."

"Excellent. I remember my first time in the Galaxy executive chamber. I had John Boyfield at one table and Lionel Strangemore at the other. I grew up wanting to be one or the other, depending on what was playing that weekend at the local cinema." Jason started to seat himself, then froze. "I know that photograph."

He rose back to his feet. Shari watched closely. She was becoming adept at reading Hollywood hype. And what Jason showed seemed to be utterly genuine.

He almost whispered his question. "Is this for real?"

"Not just the sofa," Shari said. "Every stick of furniture in the whole room, except my chair. Can't do without my ergonomic support."

Jason stepped around the coffee table and asked Lizu Khan, "May I?"

"By all means."

He seated himself on the sofa, his gaze never leaving the photograph. "I was fourteen the first time I saw that film on TV. I spent the entire next year dreaming I was the one sharing this sofa with that lady." He rubbed his hand over the damask, the same place Lizu had. "She might have married *him*, but I knew it was only because we didn't meet in time. Her heart was always mine to claim."

Lizu actually smiled. "You were too young to appreciate her."

"That's the joy of movies, Mrs. Khan. They never grow old. They never let you down." His gaze kept wandering back to the photograph. "I worshipped her."

"I am sure my granddaughter would be delighted if you joined us for lunch, Mr. Garrone."

He treated that as the boon it was. "I am honored you would think to invite me. Unfortunately, I am due across town in less than an hour. I just stopped by to tell your granddaughter something, if you don't mind my mentioning a little business in your company?"

Lizu Khan gave a regal wave. "My husband, may he rest in peace, never saw the logic in separating business from the rest of life."

"Thank you." He said to Shari. "I've just gotten off the phone with Colin. The last sticking points in what Derek offered have been cleared up."

"The points?" Shari asked. Points were the share of profits to be granted the actor.

"All worked out." Jason smiled. "I had to meet with Sam about something else this morning. He has signed off on the film. *Snowbound* is a go, Shari. And it's all your doing. I asked Sam if I could be the one to tell you."

"Congratulations," Lizu said. "I'm so pleased for you both."

"Shari Khan," Jason said. "Executive producer of the new Galaxy megahit starring Colin Chapman, directed by Moore Madden. The PR feed goes out tomorrow. Will you take a bit of advice?"

"Of course."

"They will hit you with several other producers. Colin has a woman he uses; the lady lead will have another. Don't make a fuss. Just make sure your own name goes up alone on the screen. Don't insist on position, before or after this name or that—you're not seasoned enough. Just so long as your name appears on its own. The world will remember that."

"You mean, the powers in Hollywood."

Jason smiled, and instantly the seriousness vanished. "What other world is there?"

"None," she said, glad for a reason to smile with him. "None at all."

He rose to his feet, straightened his tie, rebuttoned his jacket, then turned and bowed a second time over Lizu Khan. "If you would please excuse me for saying, Mrs. Khan, I have always admired your granddaughter's Modigliani eyes. You know, the artist."

"I know Modigliani, sir."

"Of course. What I meant was, Shari has eyes as unique as his models. And now I see why."

Shari could not stop smiling. "I'll show you out."

When Jason passed Kitty Sheen's desk, the secretary used the FedEx envelope she was opening to fan herself. Shari took hold of his arm to keep him from glancing back and said, "My grand-mother likes you."

"She is an amazing woman."

"Yes. She is."

"Can I speak to you about a bit more business?"

She knew the jump back and forth between business and personal was typical Hollywood. And with anyone else it might not be so extremely difficult. "Sure."

"Have you given a thought to who would costar with Colin in *Snowbound*?"

"To be honest, I'm so green I didn't even know this was part of the gig." She actually shivered. "I can't believe this is happening, much less I'm supposed to talk about *stars*."

"That's Hollywood. They light the rocket and your job is to hang on." His smile was the best part about him, and the rest of the package wasn't bad. Not at all. "Would you like some advice?"

"Are you kidding? It's the only way I'll survive."

"Hearing you admit that makes me fairly certain you're going to be around for a very long time, Shari."

She shivered again. "So give."

"I have several people in mind. Some are our clients, others not. What I'd suggest is you and I get together for dinner. I will lay them out and describe the role and what I see them doing with it. I won't tell you which ones are our clients, and I won't push them over the others. I'll just give you my input on casting that will take the film to a whole new level."

"You should be the producer, not me."

"I wasn't the one who brought Madden to his senses. And I'm not the one Sam Menzes listens to."

"I would be honored to dine with you, Mr. Garrone."

"Thank you, Ms. Khan. I'll have my people phone your people." He pushed the elevator button. And turned serious again. "I'm going to trust you with something. But you can't ever tell anyone this came from me. Not even Menzes."

The intimacy drained away. "I understand."

"Yes. I believe you. Which is why I'm going to do what I said I wouldn't." He glanced around, then slipped his hand into his pocket and handed over a sealed envelope. "This is an article that will be appearing in tomorrow's *Hollywood Reporter*."

"It's bad, isn't it. I've goofed and I don't even know enough to know what I've done wrong."

"No, Shari. If it were murder and mayhem, you'd see the vultures circling." He tapped the sheet. "But you need to be aware, and you need to prepare."

The doors slipped open. "I owe you, Jason. A lot."

He gave her the deepest look he had shown yet. And whispered to the sound of the closing doors, "Good."

When Shari returned to her office, the first thing her grandmother said was, "He is right about Modigliani's models."

"I take it you like him."

"Like is not a proper term for a prince of Hollywood."

"Hollywood doesn't have princes anymore," Shari said, pretending at a light tone. "They're aristocrats now."

Her grandmother sniffed. "The flakes in this town may think they can move the world by using a different term. But fact is fact. Your young man reminds me of a Florentine courtier. All of a package. He is not merely handsome. He is intelligent. He has learned to use the rapier. Your grandfather would have said he murders with skill."

The remarks suffused Shari with such a conflict of emotions she could not be certain whether she wanted to hear more. It was rare that her grandmother would be so effusive. But lurking within the silk was the Persian dagger, the one with the poisoned blade. Shari knew that if she asked her grandmother what she meant, she might not like the answer. "I'm not sure I agree with you."

Her grandmother sniffed. "Shall we go have lunch?"

"Sure." Shari hesitated, then slipped the envelope from Jason into her purse unopened. It could wait a half hour. It had to. Her grandmother's observations disturbed her too much to permit anything else just then.

The Galaxy commissary was divided into two distinct segments. The general-staff side had cafeteria-style service and open seating. By unspoken rule, the large circular tables by the front window were reserved for wannabes, who clustered and lusted as the more senior staff headed for the second room. The executive chamber was much smaller and had no name. There was no sign on the door. But the waiters knew who was welcome and who they had to politely turn around.

Shari was still uncomfortable passing the window between her and the tables where, until so very recently, she had been imprisoned with her tofu and sprouts. She felt the eyes, but a little less with each passing day. Her grandmother strolled along the glass wall with the demure elegance of one whose birthright was never to *consider* eating anywhere but in the exclusive room. It was another reason why Shari had not invited her grandmother to the studio lot until now, when she could push through the padded leather doors and enter the chamber with its six Isfahan carpets over light-oak flooring. With the three power tables in the darker corners. And the elegant buffet line, and the leather-backed menus for those with enough time to order, and the chef ready to make whatever else the diner might care to have, from lobster bisque to milk-fed New Zealand lamb.

After they ordered their salads and wild tilapia flown in that morning from the Louisiana gulf, her grandmother said, "It bothered you, what I said about your gentleman."

"I don't like violence."

"Most civilized." Lizu Khan did not scorn. But she also did

not back off. "Answer me this, my dear one. How does a young man . . . How old is he, thirty? Thirty-one?"

"Thirty-three."

"Extremely young, wouldn't you say, for someone with so much power?"

"It's a young person's game."

"Perhaps. Yes. It is a young person's world, the speed and the changing words and the flash of emotions on the screen, there and gone in an instant. Yes, I agree with you. But still. He is a prince in the realm of light and shadow, yes? So tell me. How does a man rise so far, so fast? Charm?"

"He says it was a series of lucky breaks, a lot like mine. He helped Colin Chapman when Chapman's former agent was stiffing him on a deal. He did not ask for anything in return, and got the world."

"Modest and charming. Very good. But I think if you were to look more deeply you would find there are a number of people in this realm of yours who bear scars from this young man's rapier." She smiled as the waiter delivered their beverages. When they were alone, she added, "I am fairly certain he is Jewish."

"With a name like Garrone? Get out."

"Ask him. My guess is, Sephardi. I knew many like him in Tehran. They have been through twenty centuries of living under masters who tolerated them because they were the finest at their craft. Only the paramount survive. So intelligent, so polished, so intimate with power. They learn this young and well, the Sephardim."

"You don't mind?"

"Why should I mind? He is what he is." She tolerated the arrival of their food, ignoring the waiter and commanding Shari's complete attention. "Do you recall what I said the day you started in this work?"

"I remember everything you tell me."

"My dear child. You do my heart such good, honoring the

opinions of a crone in an era and a land where the old are tossed aside like refuse." She reached across and took Shari's hand. "Remind me of my advice."

"Stay aware of what I'm getting into." Shari stared at the hand holding her own. The diamond and emerald ring and the matching bracelet, the age spots, the finely lacquered nails, the strength. "Know the price."

"The price, yes. The *price*." She did not smile. In fact, it was hard to see just precisely how it was her face changed as much as it did. But suddenly Lizu Khan was fully and utterly Asian. The eyes that would glitter as they sentenced another to torment and death. The gaze that had seen everything and tasted more than Shari could ever fathom. "Loving such a man as Jason Garrone will require a price. This is not Cinderella land. He will rise to become a master in this realm. He will accept you only if you too are willing to fit the role of queen."

Shari wanted to cling to the words that meant the most. Loving the man. But her grandmother's eyes had tilted somehow, as though redrawn by an unseen hand, one that could stretch the skin out until they angled as sharp as the rapier blade she claimed this man carried unseen. Dark eyes, shimmering with the world's knowledge.

Shari realized then why her mother detested her grandmother. Her mother had never said as much. Her mother loved her father, and her father honored Lizu Khan in the manner of one born to the Orient and the respect of one's forbearers. But Shari knew her mother well enough to understand what her father had chosen to ignore, that her mother loathed her grandmother, and this was one reason her mother was so eager for Shari, her only child, to leave Los Angeles forever—the fear that her mother-in-law would reshape Shari in her own image.

It was to her grandmother's fearsome awareness that Shari responded. "This also isn't Persia, Grandma."

The old woman nodded in the manner of one who had

expected nothing less. "You are young. You think you have re-invented the world. You think everything happens for the first time when it happens to you. Listen to me, my beloved daughter I never had, the one I hold most dear in this world. *There is nothing new.* Your young man, if he is as real as we both think he is, has two sides. The polish and the handsome looks and the glamour. And the shadow. Inside him, where his secret heart softly beats, he knows the power of the knife and the poison and the manacles deep in a hidden dungeon. And you, my dear, if you are to be his equal, must learn these lessons as well."

Shari tried to pull away but could not. Her grandmother leaned closer still, her voice an ice razor. "The price, my dear. Remember the price."

Their talk turned polite, two women of culture lunching in public. They spoke of the weather and films, both current and in the past. They spoke of people they knew. But in truth, neither of them moved very far from what her grandmother had said. It rested over the dining table like a shadowy benediction. When they were finished, the pungent tinge of sulfur followed Shari past the bowing waiter and back out into the California afternoon. Not even the brilliant LA sunshine could completely erase the veil that drifted between Shari's eyes and the light.

They passed an astonishingly realistic cyclorama of a Hawaii beach and crashing surf. Shari paused because her grandmother did. She smiled a greeting to someone who spoke her name. When her grandmother was ready, they continued up a street from a defunct Western, past a soundstage filming a hit reality show, another doing scenes for a major cablevision gangster weekly. The respectful granddaughter hosting her matron and mentor. Nothing wrong. Nothing changed. All the world open before her.

The three parking spaces closest to the front entrance were restricted to the studio limos. Two drivers lolled and smoked on the grass nearby. Shari recognized one. "Paul, hi, are you busy?"

"Just holding up my bit of the sky, Ms. Khan. What's up?"

"I was wondering if it was okay to ask you to take my grandmother home. I don't think it's really official, but I don't know who to ask."

"Hey, Ms. Khan, you ask me, you could have me pick up your dirty laundry and nobody's gonna say a thing."

The other driver agreed, "Your name's on the roster, Ms. Khan. You say drive, we drive."

"Sure thing. Where does your grandmother live?"

"Santa Monica Boulevard in Brentwood."

"No problem. I'll just go sign out. You ladies prefer to wait in the back, I could turn on the AC."

"Grandma?"

"I'm fine, thank you, Paul. It's so wonderful to see you gentlemen be so nice to my granddaughter. She appreciates it as much as I do."

"I got to tell you, ma'am. Your daughter—"

"Granddaughter," the other driver said.

"Hard to believe, a lady of your age has got a granddaughter. What I'm saying, though, it's a pleasure to drive a real lady for a change." He dumped his cigarette in the clay urn. "Back in a flash."

"Such a nice gentleman," her grandmother said, playing for the other driver.

Shari realized she still carried Jason's envelope. "Excuse me." She stepped away, slit it open, unfolded the paper, and screamed, "Who are they *kidding*?"

"What's wrong, dear?"

"This is *insane*!" She crumpled the page with such force she felt her forehead knot. "I am going to *kill* them! Kill them *stone dead*!"

The second driver took a pair of steps away. "Glad it's not me, whoever they are."

But her grandmother's response was merely to smile and say, "Do you know, I believe Jason Garrone has chosen wisely indeed."

———•———

Sam Menzes angry was a fearsome sight.

"Are you sure about this?" he demanded.

"I trust my source," Shari replied.

Derek Steen gave her that look, the one where he cocked his head slightly to one side and inspected her through tight lids. Wondering anew who she truly was.

But Shari could not focus on Steen. It would be like watching a cobra while an angry tiger paced and readied himself to pounce. Shari went on, "He had no other reason to give me the article than to help us out."

The *Hollywood Reporter* article was written with genuine respect for the Shoestring Productions demo ad and snide humor over how Galaxy's comments came back to bite them. The journalist's tone made for snippy reading. The article described how, when it came time to tape an on-air story criticizing the Shoestring project, the so-called film expert had arrived for the show with Galaxy's newest exec producer in tow, one Shari Khan, who according to one unnamed source did everything but tattoo the lines on the expert's forehead. The article dripped with LA humor, bright and acidic.

Steen asked, "Was it that manager of Colin's who fed you this article?"

Shari kept her focus on Menzes.

Sam Menzes tapped a gold Dupont pen on the article. "They haven't called and requested a response?"

"I checked with PR before coming up," Shari told him.

"There's been no call from anybody."

"They're laughing at me." Sam Menzes looked like he had suffered a botched plastic surgery. His face had become drum-tight and was blotted with pale coin-sized blemishes where the blood simply could not force its way through. "I will *crush* them."

"Careful," Steen muttered.

"I'll give them careful." His drumming increased in fury until he stabbed holes in the paper. "I'll give them every reason in the world to be careful."

Shari said, "I have an idea."

The hand holding the pen froze. "Go on."

"Actually, three. First, we take out a double-page ad for *Iron Feather* in *Variety*. We do it every day for two weeks."

"A double tombstone would cost us a quarter mil," Steen protested.

"That's right," Shari agreed. "Two hundred and fifty thousand dollars to the *Hollywood Reporter's* competition."

Menzes leaned back in his chair. "Do it."

"Second," Shari said, "we have no official response. Nothing at all from anyone in the studio. Derek issues a directive to that effect. Anyone in the snake pit or PR who is caught feeding anything to the press is sacked. Instead, we get someone in the unions to talk about this Shoestring Productions. About how the studio's move to North Carolina and its nonunion attitude means a loss of decent-waged jobs. How this indie studio's owners are laughing all the way to the bank. How they're robbing the employees and feeding their own bank accounts. How this is a perfect example of why there are unions in the first place, to keep a balance between the owners and the people who really do the work."

The two men were silent for a moment. Then Sam Menzes asked his lawyer, "Can we plant this to run tomorrow?"

"No problem." Steen's gaze did not leave Shari. "This is solid."

Menzes asked, "What else?"

"We follow this up with another identical comment from the governor's film commission. The commission agrees with the unions but goes back to the original point, that this Shoestring group is trying to parasite off our marketing efforts. They complain how this is a double whammy, stealing union jobs and stealing our marketing dollars. Both of these go to *Variety*. The *Reporter* will be clamoring by now for something. Let them get it from the competition."

Sam was nodding now. "Pass the word to PR. The next few scoops all go to *Variety* and the *LA Times*."

Shari knew they thought she was done. "Actually, that was just two different parts to the second tactic."

She reveled in both men's surprise. Steen asked, "There's more?"

"That's up to you." Shari focused her attention on Derek. "I'm not sure you want to hear this."

"As of this moment, Derek is no longer here," Sam said. "Talk."

Shari outlined her idea. When she was done, neither man spoke. It was Menzes who finally said, "I am shocked you would even suggest such a thing."

"Shocked," Steen repeated.

"If this had come from an experienced aide on the second floor, I'd have her fired on the spot."

"Drop-kicked out of LA County."

Shari replied carefully, "I am sorry for having brought it up."

"You should be. It's a scandalous idea. If anything like this ever happened, it would be a tragic loss to the film community."

Derek scrawled something on his notepad. He slipped it across the table far enough for Shari to read, *Talk to Leo*. He withdrew the pad, tore off the page, and slipped it into his pocket.

"You can go now," Sam said.

———◆———

Leo Patillo's office occupied the corner position directly below Menzes. The view was nothing special. But Shari walked over to have a look anyway, something she would never have dreamed of doing in the chairman's office. Leo did not say anything. But the glitter to his dark eyes said he knew precisely what she was doing.

Shari saw another blank-faced limo pulling up to the studio's front gates. Beyond that were six lanes of congealed traffic. To her left, a window washer was belted to a creaky cage. She asked the polished window, "Where are you from?"

"Philly. But the family's from Torre Del Greco."

She returned to her seat. "Italy, right?"

"Bay of Naples. Famous for carved coral and gangsters. The made guys, they'd go do their business, then have their pasta at restaurants on the slopes of Vesuvius and return to their villas overlooking Capri." Leo gave her a humorless smile. "They had the game pretty well sewed up, according to my pop. Philly wasn't much better, far as I could see."

"So you migrated west."

He waved at the view she had just given up. "Look at me now."

"The power behind the throne."

"Where it's at." He picked up a stiletto letter opener. "You don't have to be there."

"Yes I do."

"I didn't offer because I'm after stealing your glory."

"I'm putting this into motion. I don't hide behind you or anybody. I want them to see me, and I want to know who they are."

Leo rewarded her with tight approval. "Then let's do this thing."

They took a cab to a biker bar across from the comedy club on Sunset. At midafternoon the place was tomblike and smelled of stale ashes and disinfectant. Shari had heard the same rumors as everybody else who tried to stay up on what was going down in LA. The bar was supposed to be the latest gathering point for the city's methamphetamine trade. It was a natural fit. The place resembled a massive warehouse down to the concrete floor, industrial lighting, and raw steel pillars. The bar was a metal slab riveted to pillars of hubcaps. By midnight the street was lined with thousands of custom bikes and the music pounded passing cars with acid-rock fists. Bikers traveled from all over the nation, drawn by a place so potent and dangerous that cops would never dare make an arrest inside. It was called simply The Cave.

The three men who approached their table were as close to deadly as Shari ever cared to come. They were carved from the same piece of fleshy stone. Scraggly beards, muscles, gut, leather, boots, chains, tattoos, lumpish welts on their wrists and knuckles. Horrible smell.

One of them asked, "You Leo?"

"That depends," he said, "on who sent you."

"All I know is a man in a café across town said do this thing or don't make another trade in this town."

"Yeah, that sounds like our guy." Leo made a grand wave, which opened his jacket and revealed the holstered gun and the minibadge given to all cops upon retirement. "Take a load off, why don't you. Beer?"

If the biker saw the gun, he gave no sign. He used two fingers to flip a chair around. He straddled it and the other two stood behind him. "We won't be here that long. Cops give me hives."

"Know what you mean." Leo indicated Shari with a jutting chin. "Lady's in charge of the details."

Three sets of reptilian eyes crawled over her. Shari reached into her pocket and came out with a slip of paper. "This is the address of a new movie studio. One that is operating strictly non-union."

The seated biker made no move for the paper. "This means something to me?"

"The guy who sent you," Leo supplied, "the one who likes a twist of lemon peel in his espresso. He's not happy about this."

"Okay, so we got a problem." The biker twisted his head around. "Wilmington."

"As in, North Carolina."

"Long way."

"We need this done quick."

"Sorry. I got business over here. Maybe next month."

One of the bikers standing behind their spokesman reached for the sheet of paper. He put it to his nose and snorted. His eyes crawled over Shari a second time. "Nice."

Shari ignored him. "Maybe we should take a little trip across town. Try the man's method of taking coffee."

The biker said, "Guess I could make a phone call. Cost you twenty."

Twenty thousand was only half of what Leo had in the trunk of his car. But Shari replied, "The union man said nothing about payment."

"I don't know nothing about no unions, baby." His yellow teeth were almost lost to the scraggly beard. "But you want me to make the call, you gotta invest the dime."

The man standing behind him licked the page. This time Shari could not completely hide the shudder. "Ten now. Ten when it's done. And only if it's done by this time tomorrow."

"You ain't even told us what you want doing."

"That should be clear enough even to you." Shari was on her feet. "I want them gone."

iz was so deeply asleep she dreamed she answered the phone and slipped back to sleep, all without actually waking up.

The ringing stopped when the answering machine came on. Then it started again.

Liz finally woke up enough to fumble for the receiver. "What?"

"It's Stanley, Liz."

She moaned. "I didn't leave the bank until after midnight. Can it wait?"

"I'm coming by with coffee. You need to get up or we'll miss the plane."

The words refused to connect. She rubbed her face. "Am I traveling today?"

"Liz, listen to me. Something's happened. Brent needs us."

That got her motor running. "What is it?"

"Get up and get ready. Bobby's plane is landing in twenty minutes."

Liz thought they made quite a nice crowd, considering they were gathered around a funeral pyre. Which it appeared to be, as far as the faces around her suggested. A pile of ashes and cremated dreams.

The former Angelini Studios had been built on land reclaimed from the Wilmington harbor. Carlo Angelini had migrated east after a massive fallout with his former Hollywood studio, vowing to never have anything to do with the production side of LA again. Angelini had made his mark with a series of midbudget gangster films, and almost made a go of his East Coast project. But six self-financed flops in a row had left him desperate for a face-saving measure and a ticket west. Bobby Dupree's offer must have seemed like a gift from benevolent beings. Not God, of course, who Carlo Angelini had spent a lifetime scorning. But someone.

Bobby had related the news on the flight east. They had landed briefly and gathered up as many from the location shoot as the jet could hold. They stood at the studio site now, seventeen morose souls, Brent and Celia among them. They were joined by a fire chief and somebody from the sheriff's department, along with the head of the state's film office. Several hundred onlookers milled behind the fire cordon—locals, news people, former employees. Cold ashes and a damp sea breeze blew in their faces.

There was nothing left. The studio was burned to a wet and blackened mantle. The harbor lapped on three sides of the nine-acre site, scattering wind-blown froth across the ashes. The parking lot was filled with fire engines and news vans. A score of television cameras recorded the crowd's stunned dismay. Liz might have been a novice at such things. But she had no doubt that the image of them standing there, a pair of Hollywood stars, a new studio president, the governor's representative, and acres of ashes, would play for weeks.

The fire chief said to Bobby, "There's no question this was arson. The only question is who."

Bobby said, "I got a call yesterday from some union joker, had a northern accent you could cut like smelly cheese. Said I oughta tuck my tail between my legs and scuttle back to hicksville."

"Did you get a name?"

"Even better. I got the whole conversation on tape." Bobby patted his pocket. "Brought it with me."

"I'd like to run that by the feds," the sheriff said.

"Fine with me."

The state film director said, "The governor asked me to convey his personal guarantee that we will do everything in our power to help you rebuild."

The unspoken question, whether Bobby actually intended to start over at all, hung in the air like oily smoke. "You tell the governor I'm much obliged," Bobby said. "We could use all the help we can get."

Liz saw the flicker of hope gleam in Brent's gaze, though the man still looked hollowed. "You're going ahead?"

Bobby looked at him, clearly astonished by the question. "What, you thought I'd let scum like that run me off?"

"Tell the truth, I didn't know what to think."

"Son, you don't know me well." Bobby jammed his hands deeper in his pockets. "I'm no quitter."

The governor's representative looked ready to leap for joy. "This is the biggest production studio east of the Mississippi."

"I like the way you say that," Bobby replied. "Not was. Is."

"We wanted to use this as a beacon to draw in other production companies fed up with the Hollywood way of doing business."

"There you go again," Bobby said. "Singing my song."

Trevor cleared his throat. "Sorry to be the one to throw cold water on this moment. But there's just a tiny problem we need to be addressing."

"It's not tiny," Brent said.

"The issue," Trevor said, "is timing."

Jerry took up the worry. "Wardrobe is gone. Our people have been working 24-7, getting the frontier and British and American soldier outfits ready."

"Not to mention the sets," Trevor said. "Even if we had immediate access to a warehouse that was made to order, we would need three weeks to get up and running again."

Bobby nodded. "That long."

Celia Breach spoke for the first time. "Maybe we should talk about putting off the project for a release cycle."

"Is that what you think?" Bobby asked.

"It would be the logical course," Trevor said. "The pressure we were under to beat Galaxy's release date was already enormous."

"No question there," Bobby agreed.

"Not to mention whether we could even locate a proper space to begin rebuilding," Trevor added. "Given the shots we envision, I need at least forty feet of ceiling height to string the camera platforms."

Bobby looked from one face to the other. "Are y'all about done?"

"Here it comes," Stanley said.

"I don't want to be starting until y'all have gotten all the worry out in the open," Bobby said.

"Tell them, brother," Stanley encouraged.

"All right. I will." Bobby pointed to the ashes. "You know what I see there? I see a *sign*. If we weren't doing God's will, you think they'd be bothering with us? No, they wouldn't."

Stanley drummed deep in his throat, something between a tune and a chuckle.

"This entire business is *impossible*. It's *impossible* that I would be standing here, between a world-class actor and a director and an Oscar-winning photographer."

"Cinematographer," Stanley corrected.

"It's *impossible* that I would have brought together a major list of investors by calling around a prayer chain. It's *impossible* that I've gotten a dozen calls since I got word of the fire, and didn't tell a soul myself, everybody phoning in to ask how they could help. It's *impossible* not one of those investor folks would pull out. It's *impossible* the only thing they've told me is they're praying hard as they know how."

Bobby stabbed his finger at the ashes. "A sign I said and a sign I meant. Now here's what we're going to do. We're going to join hands and we're going to pray. And we're going to ask God to be just what He is. A *great* God. A God of *miracles*. We're going to *thank* Him. You know why? Because right there, we have a chance to watch our Lord *perform*."

29

I am utterly against it," Trevor said.

"We don't have much choice," Brent pointed out.

They had returned from the coast late the previous night. They had shown up at their shooting location to find a trio of pastors waiting for them. The filming of Daniel Boone was apparently big news throughout the region. Reports of the fire played on the local nightly news. The pastors had arrived with North Carolina's film representative in tow, bringing with them an offer of help.

Trevor said, "We could postpone the release date. I fail to see how we must remain bound by a calendar designed around Sam Menzes and Galaxy Films."

They were crammed into the trailer Brent used as an office—Bobby Dupree, Celia Breach, Jerry Orbain, the chief set designer, the chief gaffer, and Candace Chen. The assembly left the cinematographer with very little room to pace. But he gave it his best.

Bobby had taken Brent's chair from behind the desk and jammed it into the far corner. Even so, he continued to swivel in time to Trevor's movements, causing the back of the chair to thump the walls. "I got to tell you, it's tempting. Except for one thing. Every time I pray about this, I feel like I'm being pressed to keep going."

Brent said to his chief cameraman, "Explain to us again why this is a bad idea."

Trevor pointed beyond the closed door leading to the cramped foyer and out to the burgeoning spring day. Through the trailer's front window, Brent saw the crew mill about the graveled lot, where a pair of church buses were now parked.

"What you have out there are *enthusiasts*." Trevor turned the word into a disease. "They are dreadful to work with. A walking horror. They will second-guess your every step. They have spent years researching the minutiae of the era and the dress and the food and the guns. They consider themselves experts on Boone, the Revolutionary War, the Yanks, the Brits—you name it, they know everything. And there is one thing they love above all else. And that is, to argue. They will *drown* you in disputes. They will annoy you to death."

Trevor bent over and began pinching the back of his arm. His face screwed up in a miserable little scowl. "Oh, you can't put the bowl on the fire like *that*. No, no, no, the British soldiers couldn't *possibly* be in the water. Wait, now, the children were captured in the *autumn*, and here you have it the *spring*."

Brent glanced at his chief set designer. "How long do you need to rebuild?"

The art director was a smallish, delicate individual with the unlikely name of Roy Crabbe, for he was eternally cheerful. Not even seeing the sets he had spent weeks designing and building turn to rubble had diminished his easy smile. "Find me a decent structure that doesn't require refitting, get me all the equipment I need and an army of seamstresses, four weeks."

Trevor kept worrying his arm. "Pick, pick, pick, pick."

Brent had his chair up on two legs, leaning against the wall opposite Bobby. He asked his AD, "Jerry?"

Jerry Orbain leaned against the windowsill next to the chief gaffer. The two men could not have been any more different. The assistant director looked churchgoing formal, his clothes carefully pressed, his hair trimmed and neat. The gaffer was a bearded giant with a torn black T-shirt and tattoos. Jerry said, "You say go, I'm gone."

The gaffer had a voice that was born in a cement mixer. "I'll give that a big amen."

"Explain," Bobby said.

"I talked to the crew," the gaffer told him. "They're ready. You point, we shoot."

Trevor stopped picking at his arm and looked up.

"That how you feel, Jerry?" Bobby asked.

The AD jammed his hands deep in his pockets. "I've spent too long being the whiner on this crew. The day we shot the first scene, what you said up there on the shooting platform . . ."

Candace Chen said, "It convicted me."

Bobby Dupree leaned back and crossed his arms behind his head. "Looks to me like you've got yourself a team, sport."

Brent asked Candace, "You'd be willing to rewrite your script to fit what we can use for backdrops?"

"Like the man said, you're the boss. Wind me up and let me go."

Bobby said, "We've heard everybody's opinion but yours, Brent."

He was tired. He could still smell the smoke, though he'd scrubbed his skin raw. But he also felt easy enough with himself to reply, "There is no logical way we could possibly make this happen. But if God is offering us a miracle, we need to grab hold with both hands."

Bobby thunked his chair to the floor, got to his feet, and walked over and opened the door. He said to the pastors and governor's rep gathered on the front porch, "You folks want to join us in here? I reckon there ain't much more for us to do but pray and go have a look at what's on offer."

The entire crew went basically because they were invited. The church bus seat dug at Brent's back, and the seat in front jammed hard against his knees. But he did not complain because no one else did, not even the massive roadies. The journey took just over two hours and covered some seventy miles of twisting two-lane roads. When they finally pulled up, they discovered themselves surrounded by astonishments.

Trevor descended the steps behind Brent. He blinked in the noonday light and asked, "Where precisely are we?"

"Chatham County, North Carolina," Brent replied. "Wherever that is."

"I thought perhaps we had traveled back in time."

The county seat was a village carved from a bygone era. The building directly in front of them was a stodgy relic of the colonial era, with a broad front veranda and a Georgian cupola that gleamed in the sun.

The state's film representative stepped up beside them. "The valleys prospered at the turn of the nineteenth century when they discovered a vein of marble that folks claimed was as fine as anything from Italy. They shipped the stuff as far as San Francisco."

"Farther," one of the pastors corrected. "I hear tell they got palaces in Mexico City with walls from our little valley. Not to mention the state house in Hawaii and some big building in Rio."

The art director said, "But this entire square is distinctly colonial."

"Fake as my granny's teeth," the pastor said. "They got plans from the Smithsonian in Washington, scaled down the buildings, and built a fantasy. Washington as it should have been."

"It's magnificent," the set designer exulted. "What about the interiors?"

"Three big chambers are museums, left pretty much as they were. The mayor's that fellow in the general's uniform. His county council is all officers with horses. They say, long as you can put things back like they were, you're free to dress them rooms up like you want."

"There are no wires," Trevor commented.

"Yeah, we buried everything a while back. Seemed like a waste of good money at the time. But I got to admit, it prettified the place."

Trevor walked back and forth, examining the shots. Now and then he cast glances back over his shoulder at the opposite side of the square, where several hundred townspeople were gathered around trestle tables. All the people were dressed in colonial garb. Every single one. Right down to the children.

The art director was ecstatic. "We can haul in dirt, hide the streets and the sidewalks, and have you ready to do the exteriors while we go to work on the interior chambers."

The pastors were grinning now. "One thing we got plenty of around here is dirt."

The governor's film man said, "There's more."

"More?" Trevor asked weakly.

"I've been on the horn to my counterparts in Tennessee and Kentucky. Word from them is the same as here. We're ready to pull out the stops and do what we can to keep you folks up and running." He opened a file. "What you see here is just a sample they've put together over the past day and a half. I downloaded these and printed them off in the church office, so you'll have to excuse the quality. There are two outdoor museums—one is a fort and the other a colonial settlement." He flipped through the photographs. "Trading post, general store, jail, here's the fort, and a pair of colonial encampments. You can use what you want for free."

"Excuse me?" Bobby said.

"We meant what we said, Mr. Dupree. We can't rebuild your studio. But we're here to offer a helping hand."

"Y'all are gonna give us the sets for free?" Bobby said.

"If you want 'em, they're yours for the duration."

One of the pastors said, "We got folks walking away from their jobs, claiming vacation time or sick leave, whatever works."

The state film rep said, "Got a call from some feller outside Chattanooga. Says to tell you the Tennessee volunteers are ready to ride. He's got almost a thousand men, a third of them dressed and drilled as a battalion of Redcoats."

Candace said, "I could get busy and write you some super crowd-and-battle scenes."

"I've got an idea," Brent said to Bobby.

———————

Brent helped Candace climb onto the table, then took a step back. On one side stood Trevor, the look of quiet astonishment having completely erased his earlier skepticism. On his other side stood Jerry Orbain.

Brent resisted the urge to embrace them both.

"Hi, folks. If I could have your attention please."

Two of the pastors shouted for silence.

Jerry said, "You could do worse than using the reverends as crowd control."

Brent whispered, "Make it happen."

"Me?"

"You're hereby in charge of all extras. And the second camera crew. And coordinating Candace's new scenes into the shooting schedule."

"What about you?"

Brent let his smile emerge. "I'm gonna be busy making a film."

The lady on the table said, "My name is Candace Chen, and I'm the writer of *Long Hunter*. Down here is Brent Stark, the film's director. Hold your applause, please, or we'll be here all afternoon. Thank you. And over here is Celia Breach—good to know you're fans. Okay. And Jerry Orbain, our assistant director. Raise your hand, Jerry. And Trevor Wright, director of photography. Bobby Dupree is over there. Bobby is the producer and chairman of Shoestring Productions. And we're all friends. I guess that's as good a place as any to start. We're friends, and we're here because we need you."

Trevor murmured, "I take my hat off to the lady."

"She's good," Jerry agreed. "Maybe you should offer her a job."

Candace went on, "But this will only work, ladies and gentlemen, if you can work with us *on our terms*. Let me explain what that means. I spent three years researching Daniel Boone. He was a hero from my childhood, and I became passionate about the man and his era. But when it came time to write my story, I spent a year and three drafts *unlearning* much of what I had learned. Because in the process I discovered something very important about myself. I did not live in that time, and no matter how much I study, I will never belong to that era. And neither does our audience. They do not come to the movies for a history lesson. They come to be entertained. They will *accept* history only so long as they enjoy the show. And that is our first challenge. To keep as much as we can about the essence of the truth while not becoming enslaved by the facts."

"Oh, I say," Trevor murmured.

"There can only be one decision-maker on the set. And that person is Brent Stark, our director. Not me. I wrote the script, and now I have passed it into his hands. I trust Brent with a work that I have struggled with for . . . well, let's see." She faltered and looked down at Brent. "Has it really been eleven years?"

He nodded and called up to her, "You're doing just fine."

Candace gathered herself. "All I'm saying is, if you're here because you expect us to make things exactly as you have envisioned them, then you will do us all a great favor if you'll just pack up and go home. Because we don't need you. But if you are willing to help us do our best to bring my hero back to life again, then please stay and help. But only on our terms. And the first of these terms is simply this: no questions. We can't cope with a hundred different people thinking they've got something vital to either ask or say. To help us, you have to accept that you are extras. You listen carefully. You go where you're told. You do what you're asked. And you trust Brent to make it all right in the end." She looked down at him again. "Just like I do. Trust him, I mean. Because I know this for a fact. He will do everything in his power to make us all immensely proud."

The Bald Mountain Resort had a landing strip long enough to take Bobby's jet. Brent drove him over at sunset. Celia Breach was in the backseat basically because she had insisted on coming along. And Bobby wasn't about to tell a star to stay behind.

Brent drove the rented minivan up to the plane and cut the motor. "When will I see you again?"

"You holler, I'll come. But otherwise I'm leaving this whole shebang in your hands."

"You think that's wise?"

"I'll tell you what I think. I think signing you on was just about the finest deal I've ever pulled out of my hat." Bobby opened his door. "I've gotten a couple of phone calls today from folks in my music-video group. Seems one of the country singers they worked with has heard about our troubles and wants to help. They say he's a big star. You got any idea what you want to do for a soundtrack?"

"A film's music director is usually selected by the producer."

"Yeah, well, that might work okay in Hollywood. But I'm just another lost soul in need of a pilot."

Celia spoke for the first time since they had left the gathering. "If your singer is willing to give us original recordings, you could put together a money-spinner of a soundtrack."

"Now you're talking." Bobby slid from the van. "I'll bring the folks together, see what they got in mind."

"You're the boss."

Bobby grinned through the open door. "Naw, son, that's where you're wrong."

he late afternoon was balmy enough for Brent to roll down his window. Springtime flavors laced the early evening air. There was a distinct spectacle to the Carolina spring, one he had never seen before. The humid air was packed to overflowing. Brent drove the winding road and reveled in the surrounding rebirth.

Celia lowered her window and propped her head on the seat back's corner, far enough over to revel in the warm air. "I was beginning to believe I would never have any time alone with you."

Brent glanced over. Celia's eyes were mere slits against the wind. "Are you hungry?"

"I don't want to share you right now, not even with a restaurant full of strangers."

The matter-of-fact way she spoke only heightened the impact of her words. Brent stopped at a roadside grill and bought a couple of burgers with fixings. Celia remained in the car. He drove in silence as the road climbed the rise separating them from the shoot. At the pinnacle was the pull-off he had spotted on the way out, a narrow parking area fronting a pair of picnic tables and their sheltering pines.

Celia opened her door and walked to the drop-off while Brent unpacked their meal. Their peak was surrounded by the minty shades of new life. Directly below them, a pasture was ringed by blooming trees, shimmering like tethered clouds in the evening light. She asked, "What are those, cherry trees?"

"More likely wild dogwood. That and tulip poplar."

She grinned. "Font of all knowledge."

"One of the pastors at the gathering told me."

They ate in the comfortable silence of old friends. A pair of jays complained over having to share their hilltop. Three sparrows arrived to beg for crumbs. The occasional car passed in a quiet whoosh, there and gone. Otherwise the dusk was theirs.

Celia scrunched up the waste paper and carried it to the trash can. Above it was a sign that warned in bold letters to refasten the lid and not feed the bears. When she returned, she slipped onto the bench beside him. She used both hands to free her hair from its tightly bound ponytail. She swept the hair down over her left shoulder, a gesture that tugged hard at Brent. This was how she had always worn it. Before.

She said to the westering sun, "We need to talk."

Brent felt his heart kick into a gear he did not recognize.

"We're paid to be temporary," Celia said. "There ought to be a clause in every actor's contract that warns them that their star will soon fade. People want to escape, they want to live vicariously, they want safe adventure, they want forbidden fruit. And when they're done, they walk away and leave us with the empty popcorn containers. The attendants come and they sweep us up and dump us out. We're paid to shine and then disappear."

"That's hard," Brent managed.

"I've had five years of sitting in my living room listening to the phone not ring." She stroked her hair where it spilled over her shoulder. "Don't talk to me about hard."

The sun touched the ridgeline, and all their world became rimmed in gold. The scar on Celia's temple was the only dark shadow on an otherwise perfect day. "I've said it a hundred thousand times. To you, to God, to anybody who'll listen. I'm so sorry, Celia. So very, very sorry for the pain I caused."

She sat and stroked her hair and studied the gold-green valley. "I need you to be honest with me, Brent. I can take a lot of things. I'm a big girl. But I can't handle this uncertainty. Liz thinks you're in love with me. I want to know if it's true. I'm not sure I can handle that either. But before I even consider . . . I need to know. That's all."

Brent felt his heart swell so big he had to give himself a while just to find breath. "You're the reason I got so blind I parked my car in somebody's front room. Don't get me wrong. I'm not blaming you. But I knew down deep that I was undone by how I felt about you. All the shields I'd built to hide behind couldn't stay in place. I wanted you to know who I really was. But I knew, Celia. Down in my gut I knew that if you saw the real me you wouldn't love me anymore. So I tried to end it all. Not consciously. Down deep, where the little kid screamed at me in total panic every time I was around you."

The hand touching her hair rose up to stroke her temple. The golden girl probed her wound, her memories. The gesture left him choking on the acid of old sorrow.

She asked in a voice one notch off idle, "Is it true what Liz told me? You're living alone, not dating, not seeing anybody?"

"The last time I went out with anybody was the night of our accident." He let that linger in the still air for a time. Then, "I was afraid to even think the thoughts. Afraid to hope . . ."

The sun disappeared, leaving behind a crown of arching light and a sea of shadows below. "Hope what, exactly?"

"That I might make myself good enough to have you love me. And if not love me, be my friend. And if not that, then maybe just forgive me."

31

NN carried a snippet. The LA station that gave the most coverage to the film world played it hourly. A would-be challenger to the Hollywood system stood in front of a charred expanse of rubble. Farther out, the windswept waters of some unnamed bay glinted blue-green. The man, a producer with no soundstage, an investor in carnage, stood defiantly and asked the people watching to pray for a miracle. The reporter asked if he thought there was any credence to the rumors that the film unions were behind the fire. The man with the decidedly southern name of Bobby Dupree, and with an accent to match, simply repeated his confident request. People who shared his dream were asked to pray with him and give thanks for the miracle he knew was about to unfold. All the while, oily ashes swirled in the stiff breeze and made a mockery of his defiance.

Shari wanted to laugh. She would have, in fact, had it not been for her grandmother. Lizu Khan insisted upon watching the news piece a second time. And then a third.

Shari tried hard not to glance at her watch. Again. "Grandma, there's something I need to tell you."

Her grandmother shook her head at the television. "I know this man."

"You've met him?"

"His kind. You think just because you stomp upon the snake's head he is gone. Joined to the dust. Never to bother you again." She flipped the channels. "Wait. Here it is again."

Shari wanted to brush it aside. Today of all days. "It's exactly the same thirty-second spot."

"Yes, but do you not see?" Her accent, always carefully hidden away, was becoming more pronounced. "He is *everywhere*!"

This time she could not completely repress the sigh. "Grandma. Jason is picking me up in ten minutes."

"Yes. Of course. That is most excellent. Speak to your gentleman. He will tell you what needs doing."

"That's not . . ." Shari reached over, took the remote from her grandmother, and shut off the TV.

"I was watching."

"I'll be gone and then you can watch this guy all day. Listen to me, Grandma. Jason is taking me sailing."

She turned crossly from the television. "Yes? This is your big news?"

"I've done some checking. He has a boat, but it's kept under his attorney's name. It's his secret hideaway. Jason never mentions this to anyone."

Finally, finally, she had her grandmother's full attention. "You wait to tell me five minutes before the gentleman arrives?"

"I wanted to tell you last night. Actually, I've been putting it off for the past three days. Since he asked me."

Lizu Khan was astute as always. "So. Your gentleman and you are about to become an item."

Shari twisted her hands in her lap. "I think he's going to ask me to move in with him."

"And you are going to say yes."

"I . . ." Her fingers were a tight knot. "I think that's what I want."

"Of course it is. So you have lost sleep over telling your grandmother she is about to live alone again. Is that it?" Lizu's back straightened even further. "I shall not lie and say that I won't miss you."

The doorbell rang. Shari said miserably, "I wish I knew what to do."

"You know *precisely* what you are doing." Lizu Khan patted her granddaughter's hand. "You simply wish it were easy."

The Los Angeles River basin was a charmless concrete funnel. When it rained hard, which happened more often than Angelenos liked to admit, the city's runoff colored the Pacific from Zuma to north San Diego County. The Los Angeles harbor's reputation for being refuse-filled was based upon such days. But outside the periods of torrential floods, the harbor was beautiful and, for a city of this size, relatively empty. Which was exactly how the locals wanted it to remain. Let the tourists clog the roads to Malibu.

This much Jason told her as they motored out of the boat slip. Shari wore shorts, a sleeveless sweatshirt from Commes des Garçons, and boat shoes she had bought for this excursion. Jason had welcomed her on board with the gift of a yellow Specialist slicker, fleece lined and hooded. A desert wind blew in from the east, but even in the harbor Shari could feel the Pacific chill rising from the water.

She knew it was a test. That he was watching her carefully.

"Have you done much sailing?" Jason asked.

"None at all. I've been water skiing on the lakes up north a couple of times. Otherwise I have no experience with boats at all."

Jason was as serious as she had ever seen. "Are you frightened?"

"Should I be?"

"I will keep you safe and bring you home at the end of the day." He talked as though outlining a new contract, spelling each item out with somber exactitude. "Or earlier if you ask."

"Why would I want to come home early?"

"You may be seasick."

"What do I do then?"

"There's not much you can do. If it gets really bad, I'll bring you in. But if you can, it's best to endure. With some people it just goes away."

"How long does it take?"

"Couple of hours is about the average. Sometimes longer. But they can be very long hours." He was clearly very worried. "Sometimes it never leaves."

He wore the same white knit shirt she had seen on him the day they met. Navy shorts, no belt. Boat shoes, but his were worn to the consistency of battered moccasins. Ray-Ban Wayfarers were slung from a woven leather leash around his neck. A white cotton sweater and a yellow windbreaker to match her own lay on the pilot's seat. He stood so he could watch their progress across the harbor and observe her seated in the opposite chair. He rested one hand on the massive wheel, the other on his seat back. Shari had never seen his legs before. They were tanned and very muscular. He looked utterly at home. Completely in charge. And so very concerned.

Shari slipped from her seat and crossed the teak deck. She ran her fingers lightly over his wrist, up to the dark hair sprouting from the back of his forearm. "Well, in case I'm soon incapacitated, I want to say how much it means that you would invite me out today."

Jason did not move. "I've never invited anybody before. I mean, not from business."

"I know."

"I don't mean to say this is a business thing."

"I know that."

"That's not it at all. I never talk about this with anybody. It's my one place where I can go and leave the world behind."

"Jason."

"What."

She wrapped her arms around his neck and kissed him. "Thank you."

—◆—

The swell began building as soon as he made the first turning and headed for the harbor mouth. The water rushed in a sibilant hush against the hull, spilling in a constant musical stream. The stone barrier fronting the harbor entrance was topped by a whitewashed lighthouse, and it by a wind vane. The blades whirled to a pale blur. She heard them squeak over the motor's rumble.

"Are you okay?"

She smiled at him. "So far."

"You want a Coke or anything, the galley's right at the base of the stairs."

"I'll wait." She remained so close to him that the boat's motion joined them in a slow dance. "Tell me about your ship."

"You generally don't call anything this small a ship. It's a vessel, or just a boat."

"I might not know anything about sailing. But I know this isn't just a boat."

He seemed to like that a lot. "It's a thirty-six-foot sloop of Finnish design. I flew to Helsinki twice. First to see its keel laid. Then to work on the outfitting. It's designed for single sailing, and I can guarantee you it works, because I sailed it back."

"Alone?"

"Yes, alone. Didn't you hear me say I don't bring people down here?"

"Just checking."

"It was real, what I told you, Shari."

The feeling of intimacy was so strong she kept her silence, and when the next wave pressed her to his chest, she held herself there with one arm around his waist.

"You feeling ill?"

"No, Jason."

"Really?"

"This is wonderful," she replied, and meant it.

She was grateful for the closeness, because it meant she could feel the shiver of response that coursed through his muscular form.

The waves continued to build until the ship slipped down the rear face like it was surfing. The bow pushed up the next face, careened through the frothy peaks, and plunged again. The first few times Shari feared for everything—her balance, the boat, her footing, the possibility of becoming extremely ill. Gradually she drew into the rhythm, copying Jason's balanced sway. Even when a pair of larger waves broke and spilled across the bow, he was unconcerned. Either she trusted him or she didn't. Shari relaxed further.

"You're really okay?"

"Are you kidding?" She felt like singing. "This is the greatest thing I've ever done!"

He laughed, the most genuine sound she had ever heard him make. "The forecast was for three to four feet and a ten-mile-per-hour wind. If I'd known it was going to be like this, I would never have taken you out."

"Then I'm glad you didn't know. Is this really rough?"

"'Is this . . .'" He laughed again. "Shari, you are *amazing*."

He helped her into the slicker and showed her how it also served as an inflatable life vest. He walked her through the various components of the vest—mini GPS, dual lights, even a pouch containing two energy bars. She asked, "How much did this cost?"

"You don't want to know."

"Tell me."

"I could have bought you a Valentino fur and come out better."

She gripped the front of his jacket and pulled him in for another kiss. He smelled of some spicy male scent and tasted of salt and coffee and a perfect day.

When he released her, it was to grab a wire cable. "I'm going to tie you up."

"You say the sweetest things."

"Think you can handle the ship?"

"Don't call it a ship. It's a sailboat or a vessel."

Jason had laughed any number of times. But this sound was something entirely new. "Can you?"

"I'd love to try."

"Okay." He showed her how to line up the bow for the incoming wave, not fighting against the flow, just holding it easy and allowing the ship to correct itself once the downward rush was gone. He stood beside her, one hand by hers on the wheel, the other around her shoulders. Three waves later he said, "I think you've got it."

"You sound surprised."

"Are you kidding? I'm absolutely staggered."

"Is that good?"

"Yes, Shari. That is extremely good. That is the goodest thing I could possibly have imagined."

Before she could respond, he was gone.

"Wait!"

His head popped back into view. "What?"

"You can't just leave me here!"

"Lady, you have the helm."

Three minutes and two waves later, he emerged from a square

opening far forward. He unzipped canvas coverings first from the jib and then the mainsail—she learned the words because he shouted back what he was doing. Shari watched the way he moved with ease, despite the increasingly rough seas, and knew she was seeing the secret man.

The sense of intimate power was superb.

"Shari, do you see the button marked Jib? Press it."

At her command, the forward sail slipped up the front wire. Jason kept a hand on the guide rope, making sure everything ran smoothly. "Now the mainsail."

The larger sail sang up the mast above her head. The world became framed by snapping, billowing canvas. Jason slipped down beside her and steered them ten degrees further off the wind. The sails snapped once more and went taut. Jason inspected both carefully, then hit the red button marked Mains. The engine died.

She had never known anything so amazing as the silence that followed. It was intensely quiet, yet filled with sound. The wind whistled, the ropes banged against the mast, the waves broke and tumbled, the bow cut a splashing valley through each crest. And yet it was so powerfully *silent*.

The galvanized wheel was four feet across and rimmed with a softly abrasive finish. The compass was set in the middle of the dash and was gimbaled so that its globular face always looked directly up at the helmsman. There were all sorts of other dials and a pair of radar screens to either side of the compass. Jason checked them occasionally, a habit so ingrained he appeared to do it without thinking.

"What is it?" he asked.

"Nothing. I'm fine."

"No. The way you were looking at me."

"I was just wondering what it would be like to sail this across the ocean. How it would feel to become so attached that the vessel almost becomes an extension of you."

He looked at her for a time, then reached into a side hold and pulled out a cap. "Want to get the sun out of your eyes and the hair off your face?"

"Please."

He fit the cap into place. "Would you like to find out?"

She met his gaze and question with equal frankness. "I think I would."

He nodded once. Then disappeared into the galley.

The solitude seemed to have been waiting for just that moment. She knew all she had to do was call his name and he would return. For the first time, she felt genuine fear. The waves were huge, almost as tall as the mast. When she crested each wave, there was nothing else. Just more waves and the wind and the sun. On and on forever. Her ship was tiny.

She shivered again. *Her* ship.

The fear vanished as swiftly as it had appeared.

After a time, Jason returned bearing two steaming mugs and a plate of sandwiches. "Hungry?"

"Suddenly I'm starving."

"The sea will do that to you." He set the plate on the dash by the compass, returned below, then came up with a plastic map. He pointed at a spot in the blue and said, "We're somewhere about here."

"If you say so."

He tapped a speck of green in the sea. "I thought maybe we'd sail around Catalina Island."

"Why stop there? Why not Hawaii?"

He rewarded her with another secret laugh. "Permission to kiss the helmsman."

They returned home in a roundabout fashion, coming into view of land well south of the harbor. Shari had dozed off, warmed by the late afternoon sun, sprawled on the cushioned bench that framed the stern deck. Twice Jason had suggested she go below. But she had no intention of missing any moment of the day. Even when asleep. She knew it did not make any sense, but Jason understood enough to laugh. Shari carried the sound into slumber.

She did not sleep so much as travel the waves on a different level. The sun finally tickled her salt-brushed nose. She sneezed and sat up.

"I was just about to wake you."

She rose and stretched. "That was a delicious sleep."

He smiled, understanding. "Sometimes I sneak out here and bunk on the boat just so I can wake up to the sound of the water, even if it's just the harbor."

She moved over beside him. "Where are we?"

"Coming up on Marina del Rey."

The crashing surf created a rim of smoky white. Above it rose the ochre hills and waving palms. The houses of the rich and famous beckoned from the hillsides, their windows turned to defiant shields by the westering sun.

He reached for her hand and drew her close. Jason wrapped the arm not holding the wheel around her neck and pointed to the highest of the hills. It rose like a steep cone, crowned by a steel and glass sculpture to success. "That's my home."

"All of that?" The day was too fine to hide her astonishment. "It looks like an apartment building."

"It's big and it's beautiful," he conceded. "But it's also lonely."

Her heart went from barely awake to overdrive. "Oh, come on."

"You're too careful not to have checked. You know I don't play the Hollywood field."

"I know you've had a string of models and stars."

"I've tried with a few," he agreed. "Somehow it hasn't worked like I'd hoped. I'd almost given up. For the past sixteen months, Valerie has been my mistress."

"Who?"

He patted the wheel. "The one lady I have never shared with anyone before today. This was as far as I hoped to make it. Down from the marina and back again. Instead . . ." His arm drew her tighter still. "I know this might feel rushed, but . . . Move in with me, Shari. Make that lonely hilltop our haven."

———————

Jason's unanswered invitation loomed between them as they returned to the city. Shari did not hold back her response because she was tempted to refuse. She did it simply to savor the moment. Draw it out in a way that she could only describe as her feminine right.

Jason drove an oversized Land Rover, the back stuffed with sailing gear. She laid her head on the leather headrest and breathed the tangy sea air that remained only in her head. From time to time she glanced over at this man, strong enough to not press her for an answer. She thought of all the men she had been with before, all the mistakes that had seemed so right at the moment. She shut her eyes to the memories. They both had secrets that would only eat like worms at the day's specialness.

They were on the freeway when he glanced at his watch and asked, "Mind if I turn on my phone?"

"As a matter of fact, I do."

"I had no idea we would be out this long. And I'm supposed to be available for a deal breaker of a call."

She knew the moment had to end sometime. But now that the time had come, she felt a hollow sorrow. "Go ahead."

The instant he hit the switch, the message bell chimed. He fitted the Bluetooth earpiece into place, held the phone by the wheel, and coded the Message button.

It was ridiculous to think the day's splendor could vanish in the space of a sigh. But that was exactly how it seemed. Jason shifted from sea-bound freedom to the chains of business in one breath. He snapped the phone shut and said, "I need to do this, Shari."

"So go."

He reopened the phone, dialed the number, and spoke in a voice she hardly recognized. "Make it fast."

Shari turned her head to the window and pretended to watch the zipping cars, tattered houses, and businesses that topped the concrete walls. She kept her head turned away when he finally cut the connection and tossed both phone and earpiece into the center console. "Sorry, sorry."

"Jason, please."

"Today of all days."

His regret was palpable, so strong she found it possible to ease herself around and say, "I have a problem. At least, my grandmother thinks so."

"About us?"

"No. Business."

He grinned at her. "You had me worried there."

She told him about the morning's newscast and the coverage given Bobby Dupree and the burned studio. Jason's nodding rocked his upper body. "I saw it. Twice, as a matter of fact."

She waited for him to ask if she'd had anything to do with it, and liked immensely that the question, even if just thought, did not register on his features. "Grandmother thinks they are still a threat."

"They've lost their sound stage, probably their wardrobe."

"That's what I told her."

"Even if they were working in Culver City and had a whole industry to call on, I doubt they could make up the lost time."

She caught the hesitation because she was listening for it. "So give me the other half."

"Your grandmother is one amazing lady."

"I'm glad you think so."

"It couldn't hurt to check it out. Do you have eyes on the ground?"

"I could."

"If it were me, I'd go to Menzes and Steen both. Tell them you're not worried. Nothing that strong."

"Just want to make sure."

"That's it. And I'd have a backup plan ready in case they ask What if?"

She nodded slowly. "My grandmother thinks you're Jewish."

Jason laughed, and once more the day's delight returned. "What a dame."

"Are you?"

"Half. My mom. Pop was just a Baltimore portside mongrel—part gypsy, part pirate, if you want to believe my mom. He split when I was eleven. I don't even know if he's still alive."

"She said you were Sephardi."

"Wow."

"Are you?"

"I have no idea. I'll call Mom and ask." He pulled up in front of her apartment building. "You know what I'd like?"

"Tell me."

"If your grandmother joined us for dinner on a regular basis. We make it Lizu's night, part of our weekly routine. Take her out to someplace special. We sit and we walk through the week. Yours and mine. We get her take on this world. I bet we'd learn some incredible things, Shari."

She leaned over and kissed the point where his jawline met his hair. "I'll go up and pack an overnight bag. We can come back tomorrow for the rest of my things."

32

Shari held vivid memories of what it was like to do the work and receive no credit. So the first words out of her mouth were, "Leo has come through again."

"Let's hear it."

Their morning meetings were not daily events. But they were becoming such common practice that Menzes' secretary no longer even asked if she had an appointment. She simply nodded Shari through. Gilda was typical of senior executive secretaries, protective of their bosses and jealous of their position. She responded to Shari with barely veiled hostility and made a habit of sniffing at some point in almost every conversation. Shari assumed it was because she represented opportunities Gilda either never had or failed to capitalize on. So she spent a moment when she could, discussing items that were not confidential or explaining precisely the purpose behind the meeting. Gilda would never be an ally. But she also never kept her waiting unnecessarily.

Derek Steen was off fighting battles in other lands, so Shari met that morning with Sam Menzes and his new assistant, a young woman named Beatrice or Elizabeth or something. It was hard to believe this bright-eyed young thing was only a year or so younger than Shari. She watched Shari from the corner beside Sam's desk with an expression akin to awe.

"Shoestring is going for it," Shari told him.

"You can't be serious."

"Leo was so shocked by the news he flew out himself. He thought the people he'd referred to me were just extending their paycheck. He phoned last night. They're not only filming. They're editing as they go."

Menzes did not take the news well. "They're intending to beat our release date."

"I'm afraid so."

"Can we move ours up?"

"Not with Solish as director." Raul Solish was a phenomenon within the industry, known for drawing the best work from his actors and milking mood from the Gobi Desert of scripts. But he was also a perfectionist, which in the past had caused horrendous delays. Menzes had hired him only after Solish agreed to a contract stating any extra days of filming would be taken from Solish's final paycheck. The director's agent claimed his claw marks were still visible in Menzes' carpet, as he was dragged kicking and screaming into the deal.

"Talk to Solish," Menzes said. "Explain the situation."

"Should I go through his agent?"

"No, I want you to tell him personally."

"Solish is in Hungary."

"That's right. Tell him about the Shoestring situation. The guy is a lot of things, but dumb is not one of them. Explain that the timing has become crucial."

Shari blinked. "I'd like to set some things in motion here first."

"Such as?"

Her response was slow in coming. Flying her over to discuss a timing issue with a world-class director meant a definite change. What precisely the change was, she could not say. But Sam Menzes did not like to be kept waiting, so she hustled together her thoughts. "I'd like to use some of the guard dogs penned downstairs. Have them contact their allies in the system and send out a dire warning. How a Shoestring success would cost them all."

"Imagine a world where our system doesn't function," Menzes agreed. "Where the star they represent doesn't rule. Where pay scales are slashed to the bone."

"Where they can't play like they want," Shari added. "Or live like they want. Where they're judged by their behavior as well as their work on the screen."

"I like it. Have them put out the warning in the strongest possible terms. Say it comes directly from me. But since it's the snake pit we're talking about, you need to stress that we don't want any direct attacks. No smoking gun that can be traced back to us. There's too great a risk that the troubles they've had recently will be dumped in our laps. We clear on that?"

"Perfectly." Shari knew a dismissal when she heard one. But she remained where she was, held by a sudden thought.

"Yes?"

"I'd like to have Emily come with me. To Hungary."

Sam had not been expecting this. "Explain."

"I could tell you it's so we can discuss the new *Snowbound* script with Colin. And we might as well, if we're going to be there. But the truth is, I owe her."

Sam's eyes tightened in that momentary smile. "You play it straight with me."

"Always."

"I like that. Okay. Make it happen."

"Thank you, Sam." It was the first time she had ever used his first name. "A lot."

His voice tracked her across the office. "Tell your team to make it clear the warning comes straight from me. Anybody who promotes this Shoestring picture, they'll never again set foot on our studio lot. They even say the word *shoestring* and they're toast."

Once again the unexpected drew her to a halt. "My team?"

He liked the fact that she had caught it the first time. She could tell. "Tell Leo I said to assign you some people. Do you want an intern?"

She gripped the knob to hold herself steady. "I don't have enough to keep my secretary busy."

"I expect that to change."

The moment's intensity clarified the nightmare whispers that had repeatedly robbed her of sleep. "What happens if they make it happen? Shoestring, I mean. What if, despite everything, they come up with a finished product, and on time?"

There was no trace of his former good humor. "That's why I want your team in place. And ready. To deal with that very threat."

———— ·•· ————

There was only one word to describe their trip to Hungary. Stunning.

For a while, it looked like Jason might be able to join them. But an unforeseen disaster with one of his clients, a hyper young woman who responded to being dropped from Hollywood's A-list by shoplifting almost forty thousand dollars worth of furs and jewels from Saks, left him commuting from the Beverly Hills courts to the jail in LA County.

Shari missed him, but she was not altogether sorry that he had not come along. This way, she was the star. Not the star in front of the camera, with a billion pairs of eyes watching her every move. But a star just the same.

Budapest was a jewel box filled with old Europe treasures. If there was a better place to travel on a Hollywood-size budget,

Shari could not imagine it. She and Emily shared a two-bedroom suite in a former royal palace that was now the latest prize in the Mandarin Hotel chain. The concierge downstairs in the lobby was for peons. They had their own butler. All Shari needed was to express the first word of a wish, and it was done. Poof. The prime minister's box at the opera. The finest table in a restaurant booked years in advance. For their treks through the city, they had a vintage Rolls that had once belonged to the British embassy and used to ferry visiting dignitaries, including Churchill.

For their forays into the countryside, they had a chopper.

What was more, the film folks treated it as normal.

She was out there doing business for Sam Menzes. Of course she was given the best of everything. After all, before they wrapped, *Iron Feather* would cost the studio ninety-seven million dollars. All this money had to be spent in less than eight months. Speed was everything. Of course she had a chopper.

For his location headquarters, Raul Solish had taken over what in France would have been called a manse. Shari had no idea what the farm enclave would be called in Hungary. But the ancient stone chateau was presently filled to overflowing with frenetic Hollywood energy. They sat in what, according to Solish, had once had been a count's library, the central table blanketed with equipment and cables.

Solish responded to the prospect of an upstart company stealing his film's thunder like a pro. He watched Shari tie up her dealings with her snake pit team via satellite phone—cell phones had not made it this far into the eastern European countryside— and accepted the threat as both real and *now*.

Solish liked to rough-cut as he shot, which gave him a chance to reshoot anything that did not fit precisely with his vision. The downside was obvious; any change in direction meant extra shots and huge overruns, not to mention the threat of his becoming absorbed in his editing and losing a day. Or a week.

He showed them rough cuts of three scenes, all of which took Shari's breath away.

"We took out the British soldiers," Solish said when they were done. Nine of them were in a semicircle before the flatscreen monitor, seated in chairs the size of thrones. "They were getting in the way of *our* story."

Shari stared at the empty screen and felt the electricity exploding in her gut. She was not making a film. She was creating an image that would dominate the culture and reshape thinking. "That scene of the Indian village on the move, that was incredible."

"The Shawnee didn't live like that, of course. We stole it from the Navajo. The Shawnee were domesticated. Which means they knew perfectly well what they were doing when they sold Boone that land." Raul Solish waved that aside. "What's important here is that Boone and his men arrived and stole away the Indians' way of life, using the white man's more sophisticated weapons."

The AD piped up, "The British had armed the Indians by then. Which was why they had to go."

"Absolutely," Solish agreed. "If the Brits were in, it was white against white. And we lose the drama."

"You did right," Shari agreed.

"Okay, so here." He slipped her a trio of DVDs. "I burned these last night. Four scenes. Show them to the trades."

"This is exactly what I need," Shari said.

"I know."

Shari let herself be shepherded back to the front door. As soon as she stepped outside, the chopper's rotor began spinning. "About the timing issue—"

Solish shouted to be heard over the revving chopper. "Tell Sam he can count on me. No group of religious wackos is going to upstage a Raul Solish production."

rom Chatham County, Brent and his crew traveled to a tiny hamlet called Fairhaven. They then shifted to an outdoor museum in Lincolnville. After that they worked in a river valley containing a genuine frontier settlement. They spent three days filming at each location. Then they packed up and moved again. Their days started before the first rays of dawn. They shot for hours and hours and hours. They stopped when the arc lights created silver echoes of the stars overhead. Roadies worked until they were ready to drop, laying out the next day's shoot. The pace was grueling. But they got it done.

The second camera crew, led by Jerry Orbain, was normally one day ahead of them. The set designer and his building crew struggled to remain one scene ahead of Jerry. Their meetings, either by video link or in person, started when the day's shooting and building were halted by exhaustion or lack of light or both. Bobby hired a chopper to ferry them back and forth. No one asked him. Brent and he spoke several times a week, usually in ninety-second bursts.

The most amazing thing was the people.

Not the people on the set. People in general.

Their portable headquarters and the actors' trailers and the camera rigs and the scaffolding and the buses of extras formed a moving cavalcade. They gave no notice of the next shift because they seldom knew when they'd be finished. Even so, people were there to see them off and there to greet them when they arrived. Small towns poured out to wave them through. By the time the gaffers stepped from the vans, people appeared and offered to help unload. Occasionally Brent caught wind of local announcers telling radio audiences of their progress. Local news teams showed up unannounced. Bobby sent over some of his PR staff, and Brent lassoed them into handling the extras.

The extras just kept showing up. Candace wrote the scenes larger, then had to write them larger still.

Brent gave no interviews and spoke to no one outside his team. He had no idea how the peripherals were being handled—just trusted those he knew to handle what he could not.

The shooting schedule was the beast he fought each and every day. He stared at it the last thing each night. He studied it over the rim of his morning coffee. The pace demanded of them was impossible.

Somehow, someway, they stayed on time.

———————

On Sunday, Brent was enjoying a rare bit of downtime when a shadow darkened the doorway of his trailer. "Mr. Stark, you got a minute?"

Brent had the *no* loaded onto his tongue. But before he could fire it off, he saw who stood on the threshold. "Sure thing."

"Appreciate it." The trademark Stetson walked in a foot or so ahead of the man. And the man himself was both big and hugely impressive. "Tim Crawford."

It was not all that often Brent had to look up to another man. Especially a star of stage and screen. "I love your music."

"That makes my visit a whole lot easier." He eased himself down into the sofa and propped one lizard skin boot on the scarred table. "That coffee I smell?"

"Four hour dregs. My first morning off in years and I still couldn't sleep past dawn."

"Yeah, I know all about being on the road and wishing I could find my old buddy sleep."

"You like, I could put on a fresh pot."

"I've drunk old coffee before, Mr. Stark."

"Call me Brent. How do you take it?"

"You can't get it too sweet for me."

When Brent returned, he found the Stetson on the sofa beside the singer. A crease rimmed his forehead and hairline. Tim Crawford nodded his thanks for the lukewarm mug and studied the page of Scriptures where Brent's Bible was opened. "Don't reckon there's anything much nicer than a well-worn Word."

Brent lowered himself back into his seat. "Sounds like the makings of a good song."

Tim Crawford, leading male country vocalist for over a decade, twelve platinum albums and a whole roster of Grammys to his name, spoke to the dark brew in his mug. "Bobby Dupree said it was time to come down here and sound you out. Here's the thing. I want to do your score. I ain't never scored a movie before. And if you say no, I'll still give you a song or two. More, if you'll have 'em. But I haven't been able to get this thing outta my head since I first heard what you folks were up to."

Crawford set down his mug, rose from the sofa, and crossed to the wall holding the shooting schedule. "I heard tales about where you've been and what you've been through. I guess you mighta heard I plowed my own furrow in that rocky soil."

"I remember when you did that concert at the prison outside Chicago, what you said on the stage. It was about six months after I came to faith. Your statement meant a lot."

"The only reason I wasn't where you were, was I never got

caught." He jammed his hands into the rear pockets of his jeans. "My granny was from just outside Booneville in the Kentucky flatlands. She played the zither. Nothing but gospel. Couldn't sing a note. But she could make that old music box stand on its hind legs and howl."

He turned back to scowl at Brent. So tense, so hungry he looked furious. "I want to score this thing with all the music we let slip through our fingers. Good old gospel, done with country choirs and the specialists we got hidden in these here hills. I want to bring in friends I got in this business, let them sing what they want, long as their songs are based on the old hymns. String that together with music that'd make my granny smile. I want to give a spirit to your film, sir. I want it in my craw."

Celia had grown so accustomed to the quiet tapping of Candace's keys she could fall asleep to it, then wake up to darkness and wonder how the dreamed sound of typing could bring peace to her soul. The Hawaiian woman carried a chieftain's strength in her lean form and leathery skin. Even when she wore the same plum-colored smudges beneath her eyes they had all grown. The door to their shared RV was open to the day and the birdsong. The weather had stayed with them, raining only four times since filming had begun, and never for more than a few hours at a stretch. It had rained again the previous night, and the breeze drifting through their doorway smelled of awakening earth and the surrounding pines.

For once, Candace's computer was off, the folders of notes stowed away, the note cards stacked neatly, the printer cold. When Celia left the larger of the RV's two bedrooms, she found Candace seated on the padded bench, her bare feet stretched out in front of her. A mug and a nibbled bagel rested on the fold-down dining table. A Bible was open on her lap.

Celia said, "I thought we were supposed to be on deadline around here."

"The deadline got the day off."

"You read that in the Book you're holding?"

"As a matter of fact." Candace set the Bible on the table. "How'd you sleep?"

"Fine, except for the nightmare about flubbing my lines."

"Sounds like my night, except for the part about how I erased the entire script and nobody bothered to keep a copy."

Celia poured herself a mug and slid into the banquette across from the writer. "What's on for this morning?"

"Brent is going to give us another talk. He didn't want to. But the roadies who weigh more than the semi they drive ganged up on him. It was either talk or show up early at the heavenly gates."

Celia did not smile. "Brent has been avoiding me."

Candace had eyes the color of polished onyx, and just as unreadable. "You two have a fight?"

"Actually, it was the exact opposite. He said he loved me."

"Oh. That."

"You don't sound surprised."

"No, Celia."

"Does everybody know?"

"There might be a blind-deaf-mentally challenged extra who just arrived on set this morning who is still clueless. Other than that, yeah, I'd say everybody pretty much knows Brent has a crush on his leading lady."

"He's got a strange way of showing it."

Candace gave her a searching look, clearly taking her measure.

"What?"

"I was just wondering whether you really wanted to hear what I'm thinking."

Celia did her best to hide in her mug. "Go ahead."

"It's not like I'm lifetime friends with the man. But what I've seen . . ." Candace pushed her bagel and coffee and Book to one side, and leaned her elbows on the table. "You can punt it out of the park if you want. But what I think is this isn't just about love. It's about you joining him in his faith."

"Puleese."

"Just give me a minute. Brent loves three things. You, his work, and God. He's made a mess of the first two and found a lot more than salvation by bringing the Lord into focus. God is the center of his existence now. You can laugh about it, you can disbelieve it. But the truth is, Brent lives for Jesus. He shames me with how intent he is on getting it right."

"How can he ask such a thing of me?"

"He can't. Why do you think he's not talking?"

"Did he put you up to this?" The instant the question was formed, Celia wanted to take it back. "Sorry. Forget I said it."

"That's okay."

"No it's not. It's terrible. It's typical Hollywood trash. Suspecting everybody of talking behind their backs, scheming, conniving, stabbing."

"All the things we both love so much about the town and our craft," Candace said wryly.

Celia reached across the table and took the remnants of Candace's bagel. She began nibbling at the edges. "You're telling me he won't love me unless I convert?"

"Wouldn't life be easy if all the corners matched. No, Celia. He loves you now. He loves you desperately. But he's hoping you might come to join him."

"So why doesn't he talk to me about it?"

Candace smiled. "Because he can't."

"You know how much sense that makes? Zero. Zip. Nada."

"Stop arguing with a guy who isn't in the room and think about it, girl. If he talks to you and you do it, are you doing it because you love him or because of God? If it's for Brent, the

action is worse than wrong—it's a lie, and he's the man responsible."

"Who said anything about me loving Brent?"

"Let's focus on the eternal for a second, okay? Brent isn't
talking because he's hoping for *two* impossibles. One, that you'll
love him back. Two, that you'll join him at the altar, and do it
for God."

———•———

Celia walked down the path leading away from what had
become an RV park. Camper paradise. It reminded her of home.
What a joke that word was. As if the dry-scrabble wasteland of
broken lives and beat-up mobile homes outside Reno could ever
honestly be called a home. Celia had two sisters. One was raising
three kids from two different men and living alone in a trailer
and a life cloned from their shared beginnings. The other was
tight and angry and fiercely alone, calling herself a winner
because she had made it through dental technician school, was
earning a decent wage plus benefits, and had never let anybody
close enough to do to her what had happened to her mother and
her older sister.

And then there was Celia. The golden girl. The one who had
hid a determination of titanium and fury behind a very practiced
smile. The one who had sworn to do whatever it took to make it
to the top. And she had.

God had no place in this life.

Nor, truth be told, did love.

The clearing they had made into a temporary headquarters
was a parking lot for another outdoor museum. Celia was fairly
certain they were in Kentucky, but she had no idea of the place's
name. Beyond their RV settlement rose a fort, where the Shawnee
and British were going to attack. They had been rehearsing the
scene for two days and were scheduled to begin shooting after

sundown. Celia kept her head down, gripping the loose sweater tight across her middle as other people joined her on the trail. No one approached her. She realized she had never been bothered as seldom or as gently as on this project. At first, she had simply assumed it was part of her star being on the wane. Now, however, she knew differently. Wherever they went, Candace's instructions were passed on by the extras and the pastors who shepherded them. The rules might be strange, but these folks respected them anyway.

She emerged from the forest trail and gasped.

The clearing was a sea of people.

The roadies had been busy. They had set up a makeshift soundstage with the fort as a backdrop. Old-time gospel poured from speakers piled to either side of the stage. To her left, trestle tables ran in continuous lines from the chuck wagon to the river, almost lost beneath their load of platters and serving dishes. Washtubs of soft drinks dotted the spaces between tables.

So many people.

"Ms. Breach?" a gentle voice beckoned. "We'd count it an honor if you'd take this seat here."

She smiled and offered a quiet thanks, and nodded to comments from a man and woman, neither of whom she truly saw. They got the message and left her alone. There was none of the fawning pursuit she normally attracted. Celia sat in a sea of people, utterly alone.

The same way she had gone through so much of life.

A murmur rose from the crowd. The woman next to her said, "That's him, ain't it?"

"You been working for Mr. Stark for five days and you don't know him yet?"

"Not Brent Stark, you ninny. Him. That singer feller. The one Ida claimed she saw."

"Well, I'll be."

"Oh, oh, I seen him a dozen times on TV. What's his name?"

Celia lifted her head in time to see Brent and Jerry and Trevor take seats at the back of the stage, and Tim Crawford settle the guitar strap around his neck and let the roadies fiddle with his lead and mikes. He strummed a chord, and the woman next to her said, "I got chills."

"Hush, now. This is church."

"That don't matter. Tim Crawford. You wait till our Becky hears about this. She's gonna be sick she missed it."

"Welcome in the name of our Lord," Tim said. "I thought I'd play us a couple of songs just to get things moving in the right direction. Any of you folks who feel like it, y'all join in."

"The Old Rugged Cross" got them all on their feet. "Amazing Grace" resulted in a choir that caused the pines to tremble. After that, Jerry rose and approached the mike and gave them a prayer. Three more songs, and Tim started into "I Surrender All." After the first two lines, he swung his guitar out of the way, then backed away from the mike. Just letting the people carry the song. *I surrender all.*

Celia felt as though she were the only one in a crowd a thousand strong who did not sing.

Tim leaned into the mike just long enough to give the first few words of the next verse. Then backed away. Letting the crowd move on their own accord. He raised Brent with a gesture. The two men embraced and switched positions.

When the singing ended and the people settled, Brent said, "The book of Acts is built on two solid foundations: Jesus Christ and personal testimony. That's what I intend to do today. Tell you a little of how I got to be here, and do my best to love my Lord and Savior for the freedom He has given me.

"A few weeks back I shared with the crew how I wound up in the internal state that got me into trouble. I imagine most of you know about the accident. I was tried in federal court on two counts. I had crossed a state line with a whole mountain of cocaine, so I was convicted of interstate trafficking. And I had a pistol in my glove box that had been used in a crime in Texas. To this day, I have no idea how the gun got there or whose it was. I could well have bought it myself. That's how wrecked I was. And I'm not talking about the accident. Or even my physical state that one night. Wrecked. A life in total ruin."

A different man. The thought rose unbidden in Celia's mind and heart. Not merely changed. Completely different. Brent wore the skin of the man she had been drawn to with a passion so wild she would climb into his car when they were both so blind on booze and drugs she could scarcely find the door handle.

Brent was the same, yet totally singular. This was not merely a man who had suffered through loss and public humiliation and prison. He stood there in a strength and a certainty that shamed her. He had taken the tragedy and grown into a giant. A hero.

And he loved her.

Brent went on, "Like everybody entering the system, I was sent to the county jail until a slot in a federal pen opened up for me. Everything you've heard bad about being inside exists inside the walls of county jails. That and more. It's dangerously over-crowded. I was put in a cell meant for two and housing five—a murderer, a poor joke of a student with thirty outstanding traffic warrants, a bipolar nut case going off his meds, a drug runner who spoke no English, and me. The movie star."

Love. It was a word to be spoken with a special inflection. A moment to be captured on film where she shone with the softest and most alluring light. The word to be used as part of a verb, as in, to *make* love. Celia found herself flooded with images from her past. Of moments when she had mocked the concept of love with her actions. She bowed her head to her knees, clenched her entire body like a fist. The images kept pounding at her.

"Once inside the federal prison, I learned there were three dif-ferent ways to do time. Many inmates fed on rage and focused on getting out. Their whole life became dominated by one single laser-strong determination. Get out, and do a better crime. And never, ever let the cops catch him again. They put blinders on. None of this was actually happening. And when reality managed to slip under their defenses, they responded with a rampant frenzy."

The truth was, she could *not* love. It was impossible. The concept mocked her. To give herself freely to a man? To *this* man? The man who had wrecked her face and her career, left her stranded in a hospital bed, surrounded by the baying hounds of entertainment news? Love him? She had spent months wanting to kill him. Yet even then, she had ached with longing for what she knew he had never offered. How was it possible to be so blind? She had wanted him desperately, dreamed of him, hungered to lock him up and possess him, make a prison of her longing and her so-called love. She was, after all, a star. Who could deny her anything? Then he had robbed her of the only thing she held as important. The only thing that mattered. The reason she lived. Love this man? Trust him? She wanted to stand on her seat and scream curses at him. Shout at him in rage and pain and hurt and fear.

Yes, fear.

Because down deep, down where he said his little wounded child lived, she had a secret voice all her own. One that said, *Love this man and never let him go.*

If only she could.

"Most nonviolent offenders took the second approach," Brent was saying. "They focused on one small item and blew it into the single dominating factor of their daily existence. Dominoes, chess, gym, TV. It could be anything. So long as they were shielded from the horrors of prison life and from the threat of dealing with themselves. Their goal was to avoid the moment. For these guys, when they get out, prison remains a pungent odor. He swears he'll never go in again. He struggles hard to go straight. But he's not done anything about what got him inside the first time. And that, brothers and sisters, is why the recidivism rate in this country stands at seventy-eight percent. Four out of five men who are doing time today will be arrested again and sent back to prison. Four out of five."

The truth was crippling. Celia felt her breath tearing in and out of her constricted throat, passing through her clenched teeth. She yearned to love him. It was not the accident that held her back. It was her. She did not even know what love was. Love him? Be *real* with him? How on earth was she supposed to do that when she had no idea who she was?

"When I got to the federal pen," Brent said, "I did what everybody said I should, which was, step one, take a chill pill. Step two, find me a car. A car is the inmate term for the group that is going to watch your back, keep you alive. There are a lot of cars—the Aryans, the Mexican Mafia, the Crips, the Bloods. Me, I chose the car known to the other inmates as the Hypers. As in, hyper-Christians. I figured, why not? They seemed the least likely to stab me in my sleep or beat me to a pulp. How hard could it be?"

Something in what he'd said, or something in the crowd, or some whisper murmured far below the level of her hearing. Something reached down and pulled Celia up straight. She blinked away the fog over her eyes. And she fastened upon the man at the microphone. The stranger she knew so well.

"I wasn't the first guy who entered the believers' group with a lie on my lips and in my heart. They knew, and they accepted me anyway. They talked to me about the third way of doing time. And that was changing my life from the inside out. They kept on until I finally came face-to-face with the truth that broke me down. The truth we all know here, don't we. That there was no way on earth I could change myself. Not ever. I was trapped. I was imprisoned by a lot more than the bars on my cell."

The crowd was so rapt, so silent that the man who roared made them jump—even the ones who stood along the edges. "Amen!" the man cried, his throat strangled. Celia felt the pressure of that cry squeeze tears from her eyes. She jumped again as the woman seated beside her reached over and put a hand on her shoulder. *Don't touch me*, she wanted to scream. *I'm a star*. The words that remained unspoken only caused her to weep harder.

"It was not the accident that broke me. Not the conviction that cost me my career. Not the sentence, not the county jail, not the federal pen. It was a black man named Amos who was doing thirty to life. A man with a light in his eyes and wisdom in his voice. Who told me what I had already come to realize. That I could *not* change. But Jesus was waiting to change me. Do it for me. Forgive me, teach me, heal me, and make me whole."

Brent looked down at the front row of seats and said, "You brothers want to join me?"

He waited while a group of roadies came to stand at the foot of the stage, then said, "If there's anybody out there who's hurting today, anyone who doesn't know Jesus and is ready to come kneel with us at the Cross, my brothers and I are ready to pray with you. Jerry is going to come forward and offer us another fine prayer. Tim, why don't you come up when he's done and lead us through 'I Surrender All' one more time."

She was up and moving before Jerry came anywhere near the amen. Stumbling in terror that if she looked up she would see the people watching, afraid her shame would force her to turn away. Afraid of herself, afraid of being wrong, afraid there was nothing up there but humiliation and weakness. But she walked anyway, so blinded by tears she could not really see where she was going. Her sweater flopped out around her because she had to keep her arms outstretched to maintain her balance.

Then the man by the stage started toward her. And though she could not really see him, she knew who it was. And she ran.

tanley entered his office after the third and final Sunday morning service. He looked as though he had aged ten years. He asked his visitor, "Shouldn't you be at lunch or something?"

"I'm right where I need to be," Liz replied.

"Give me a minute." He disappeared into the bathroom. Liz heard the water running. She recalled a pastor from her teenage years who claimed to lose five pounds in sweat every Sunday. Stanley's approach was somewhat quieter than that old Texas revivalist's. But the exertion required to carry three back-to-back services was telling.

Especially today.

Stanley emerged wearing a fresh shirt and a sweater-vest, his customary office garb. He combed his hair and said, "I didn't sleep a wink last night."

"Of course you didn't."

"I was chased around Austin by all the bad times." He slumped into the chair next to Liz. "I don't guess I realized until last night just how much I want this job."

"Stanley, the job is yours."

"Come on, Liz. There are two biddies on the board who

would like nothing better than to show me the street." He rubbed his face, the skin turned rubbery by exhaustion.

A thump from the conference room directly overhead lifted both their heads. The church elders were gathered to vote on Stanley. He showed her the terror gnawing at his gut. "What if they cast me loose?"

"That's not going to happen. But even if it did, your course is set. Another church will take you in a heartbeat."

"How can you be so sure?"

"Because I've heard what people are saying about you. The congregation loves you, Stanley."

"Not all of them."

"You'll never carry everyone. In a church of two, one has to be a dissenter. It's human nature." She smiled warmly. "Can I talk to you about something else?"

"I can't promise I'll hear you, but fire away."

"I spoke to Bobby last night. The unions have requested an injunction to shut down their filming. Something about using nonunion labor on location."

"This is the same group that burned down his studio?"

"Bobby thinks so."

"Is he lawyered up?"

"He says he is."

"I don't see how we can do much more for him than pray."

"That's why he called. I've already spoken to our friends in the group." She studied this man whose brute force was in direct contrast to the dress shirt and sweater-vest, the office's oiled cabinetry, the fine leather furniture.

"You're looking at me that way again, Liz."

"What way is that?"

He actually blushed. "I don't know how to call it."

"Stanley."

"What?"

"Let's go out. Have dinner. Maybe take in a movie."

"You mean a date?"

"I've spent weeks waiting for you to ask me. Obviously that's not going to work."

"I haven't been on a date since . . . oh my." He leaned his head on the seat back. "I married Cindy when she was nineteen and I was in my last year at seminary. Call it thirty-five years, give or take an ice age."

"There have to be rules covering this. I'll have one of my staff do some research, write up a memo, and messenger it over."

"Liz, a pastor doesn't just date."

"I know that."

"I mean, especially one of his own congregation. It'd be like lighting a Roman candle in the chicken coop. The only way a pastor could possibly be seen with a single woman is if, well . . ."

She reached across and took his hand. "I know what I'm asking, Stanley."

he sunset dragged on in perfect cinematic style. Beverly Hills glittered with people living the high life. The streets were packed, the bars and cafes teemed—only the sidewalks were empty. Off Rodeo Drive and a very few other spots, only tourists walked. If a local was on foot, he was either jogging or walking his beast.

Shari drove Jason's Land Rover. The thing was only slightly smaller than a Hummer but drove like a cloud on steroids. She loved being this high off the street. She felt like she could look down on the universe. Jason had given her a set of keys and begged her to use it. During the week he went everywhere by company limo. Shari had a full pass to the Galaxy limo service but still felt uncomfortable being shepherded around town. She also hated the way people slowed whenever the limo halted, then looked disappointed when they didn't recognize her.

She pulled up in front of The Ivy. Jason had heard from allies along the food chain that several celebrities were dining here tonight. That had clinched the deal. Shari's grandmother loved being treated regally by staff who were desperate to please Jason, while being observed by stars whom Lizu pretended to ignore. Their weekly dinners with Shari's grandmother were always unique occasions. The fact that Jason went to such trouble for Lizu, and did so week in and week out, was another reason Shari felt increasingly close to the man.

But that was not why tonight was so special.

Despite the fact that the evening was crucial, Shari arrived both late and on the phone. She paused to pull a bill from her purse's side pocket. Jason had advised her to change a hundred into singles at the start of each week. Put them somewhere she would not have to stop and hunt to locate, or risk slipping out a fifty by mistake. She had laughed at the time. But already her days had accelerated to where Shari was needing to replenish the supply by Thursday.

The Ivy's concierge was a pro, which meant he accepted Shari's keys and the bill without saying a word. He had two jacketed employees doing nothing but keeping the paparazzi away from the front walk and out of the street, which meant the celebrities were already inside. The Hollywood posse had an amazing nose for public sightings, especially when there was a chance of photos that could be sold to the gossip sheets. Shari slipped through the forest of cameras and tripods, climbed the brick stairs, and walked onto the restaurant's extended front porch. She said into her phone, "No, Zubin. Absolutely not."

The diminutive agent was at his most oily. "My dear Shari, I seem to recall a recent conversation in the backseat of a limo. I suggested that you not tighten the screws too hard, because sooner or later we would be back doing business again. Does that ring a bell?"

The maître d' said quietly, "Your guests have arrived, Ms. Khan."

She nodded, angry that she could neither hang up nor accelerate the agent's pace. "Zubin, ten million dollars is double what Tracy Alwin earned on her last picture. Which was a complete and utter disaster."

"Not her fault, Shari. The film was a stinker and directed by a moron."

Jason had celebrated their first week's anniversary of living together by giving Shari the lightest and most fashionable Bluetooth earpiece. The entire apparatus was the size of a large earring and was so light she often forgot she was wearing it. The device had crystal-clear reception and possessed a battery that would not die even on a day like today, when she used it ten hours between charges. The system had two drawbacks. First, it cost almost two thousand dollars. Second, the mike was back by her jaw, so there was no way to use it and whisper.

Which meant every person on the restaurant's front deck heard her say, "I will go six million and not a cent higher."

The maître d' bowed and ushered her inside.

The front room of The Ivy was the size of a modest parlor. Despite the films that showed actors seated on the terrace, only the tourists dined outdoors these days. The paparazzi had forced the stars indoors. As a result, The Ivy's front room had become one of the hardest places in Los Angeles to book a table.

The number of tables varied depending upon how many guests were seated at each. Tonight there were just five. One contained Shari's grandmother. And her mother and father. Shari's mother, never very comfortable around Lizu, was somewhat mollified by the fact that seated at the next table was Disney's latest find and the hottest child star in the world. But that was not why Shari had arranged for this evening's meal.

By the corner window, appropriately shaded against flash photographs, was a British actress by the name of Samantha Vaughan, who played a southern vamp on a television sitcom and sounded like she had been born and raised in the Louisiana bayou country. The television show currently occupied the nation's top slot, and Samantha's picture graced the cover of this month's *Vanity Fair*. The previous week, she had also headlined a small feature released by Fox Spotlight, and the film had crashed through the weekend opposition like a battering ram.

Shari's mother might fret over her daughter becoming imbedded in a world she called trashy, but she was as amenable as anyone to this much star power.

As Shari hugged her parents and grandmother, Zubin said on the phone, "There is no way I could take such a paltry offer to my star."

Shari covered the mike with her entire fist and said to her family, "I'm really sorry. But I have got to finish this thing. I have a meeting with my boss tomorrow at seven."

Her mother frowned. "Seven in the *morning*?"

Her father said, "It's fine, darling."

Her grandmother said, "Does she not look magnificent?"

The maître d' managed to bow and hold her chair at the same time. "Mr. Garrone has rung the restaurant three times, madam. He says your phone has been tied up and he wanted you to know that he has been delayed but is underway."

"Her Jason has the manners of a courtier," her grandmother said.

Her mother sniffed.

"I'm really sorry, but I have *got* to finish this call." Shari uncovered the mike and hardened her voice. "Listen carefully, Zubin. I'll only say this once. Six and a half million dollars is my last and final offer."

Her mother gasped audibly.

"That is laughable," Zubin said.

"I'll tell you what's a joke, Zubin. Your request for twenty-five thousand dollars a week expense money on location. Just so you are aware, Tracy Alwin is not Liz Taylor."

Her father said, "Is she talking about Tracy Alwin the actress?"

Her mother said, "Twenty five thousand dollars a *week*?"

The fact that her evening was being stolen by the discussion made Shari angrier still. "Forget the masseuse and the hairdresser and the astrologer. Where does she get off thinking we'd ever pay for a full-time vet for her *cat*?"

"I'm sure there is a little room for discussion on that point. But not the sum for her participation. Nine and a half is as low as I can possibly—"

"Then I hereby withdraw Galaxy's offer, Zubin."

"May I remind you, Colin Chapman has insisted that Tracy be his costar."

"Colin Chapman is not writing the check. Sam Menzes is."

Her mother said, "Colin Chapman?"

Her grandmother leaned back and smiled.

Zubin said, "Perhaps I should take this up directly with Sam. I'm sure he will see reason."

"I'm sure he will," she shot back. Her face was flaming hot. "I'm meeting him about this tomorrow for breakfast. He told me to wrap this thing today or go elsewhere. I'll let him deliver the news that we are no longer interested in working with your client. Not now, not at any time in the future."

"Not so fast—"

"This conversation is so totally over, it's incredible." Shari ripped out the earpiece, pressed the Off button, and jammed it into her purse. "I hate that thing."

"No you don't," her grandmother said. "You hate the moment."

She said to her parents, "I'm really sorry."

"My dear young lady," her grandmother replied, "I was just telling my son and daughter-in-law that only something of critical importance would have detained you. One look at your face is enough to know this was not of your making."

Shari realized the entire front room, including the waiters, was watching them. She felt her face go redder still. "No. Absolutely not."

Her mother said, "You were talking with Tracy Alwin, the movie star?"

"Her agent. Zubin Mikels." She said to her grandmother, "I'd like to wring his fat little Kurdish-Armenian neck."

"Such language," her mother chided.

"No doubt well deserved," Lizu said.

"He was supposed to meet with me at two this afternoon. He put me off until I was leaving the office. Knowing Zubin, he probably heard I had dinner plans and was meeting Sam tomorrow."

"Sam Menzes," her grandmother interpreted. "The chairman of Galaxy and Shari's new boss."

"Well, Sam's not new. But my position is."

Her mother asked, "And already you're calling this man Sam?"

"Hollywood is a pretty casual place," Shari replied.

"Casual is not always a good thing," her mother said.

Her grandmother frowned but held her peace.

Shari's father asked, "This agent would know of your movements and use it against you?"

Her grandmother smiled. "It sounds positively Persian, does it not?"

Jason did not actually burst into the room. But he did enter so fast he beat the maître d' to the table. "I am so tremendously sorry. Of all the nights to get trapped by a crisis."

"Tell me," Shari said. She kissed him lightly, feeling all the room's eyes on them once again, most especially her mother. "Mom, Pop, I'd like you to meet Jason Garrone. Jason, these are my parents."

"Mr. and Mrs. Khan, what an honor this is. I've been looking forward to this for so long. And then to arrive late." He leaned over and kissed Lizu's proffered cheek. "I can't tell you how sorry I am."

Shari said, "I just got here as well."

He studied her face. "Trouble?"

"Maybe we should leave it for later."

"Why later?" Her grandmother spoke with quiet authority. "Your parents have not driven all this way for you to play nice. They are here to learn about your new man and your new life."

Her father said, "I am certain I would find it fascinating."

This was the point at which her mother would normally have either offered a snide rebuke or sniffed loudly. But the combination of Jason's looks, the celebrities sharing their room, and their daughter just having played hardball over a six-million-dollar movie contract left her numb.

Not, Shari decided, altogether a bad thing.

So she told them about the two interrelated projects. *Iron Feather* they knew about, particularly as their daughter had recently flown to Budapest. What they did not know was how intimately she had become involved in the new film scheduled to begin shooting three months after *Iron Feather* wrapped.

"Shari Khan, executive producer of *Snowbound*." Her grandmother purred the words. "Aren't you proud of her?"

"Very," her father and Jason said together.

That was all it took. The two men and Shari's grandmother all laughed, and in an instant the table's mood changed.

Shari loved her mother very much. But her mother sought solid stability in every aspect of her existence. She would have liked nothing more for her daughter than a proper marriage to a doctor or lawyer and a few well-mannered children. Stable. Normal. As far from what Shari wanted for herself as Pluto. Shari saw in her mother's silence a recognition that Shari was going her own direction. No matter what she might think of her daughter's chosen course, it was happening. Her mother's silent resignation added a special flavor to the moment, a sharp poignancy that bordered on pain.

She felt Jason enfold her hand in his own. "All right?"

Shari forced herself to smile. "Fine. Well, not fine. But getting there." She joined her other hand to his. "Thanks to you."

Everyone at the table saw the exchange. Her grandmother

and father shared a smile. Her mother did not speak. Shari wished she could convince herself that two out of three was not bad.

While they were having coffee, the English star's table broke up. Samantha Vaughan smiled her guests on ahead and slowed as she passed their table. "Mr. Garrone? I don't know if you recall, but we were introduced at the De Niro fund-raiser."

Her boyfriend instantly became a manager. "Of course, Ms. Vaughan, what an honor."

"I do hope I'm not disturbing. You must be Ms. Khan. I've heard such nice things about you recently."

Shari found herself disconcerted on two levels. First, that the star would shine so brilliantly on her behalf. And second, that the woman she had only seen speaking in a sultry bayou-laced voice was now addressing her with a tony British accent. "Thank you. These are my parents, and my grandmother."

"How very nice. I do apologize for barging in like this."

Her mother allowed, "I enjoy your show."

"Oh, thank you so much. That means more than I can say." The woman's illuminating force shifted back to Shari. "Forgive me for being so bold. But were you by any chance speaking about *Snowbound*?"

Shari did her best not to gape. "How did you know?"

"It so happens that the original writer is a dear friend. He was devastated when Moore Madden redrafted his script. He's been over the moon since you and the studio insisted upon his reinstatement. I managed to sneak a look at the script, and I must tell you, I would give my eyeteeth for the chance at that role." She laughed delightedly. "I assure you, Ms. Khan, there would be no such nonsense over cost or expenses with *my* agent."

Shari found herself at a loss for words. "I'll convey that to Sam."

"Oh, *thank* you. You don't know how much that would mean." She reached in her purse and handed Shari an embossed card. "My producer is having a few people over for a screening of my latest film next Tuesday. I don't suppose you might possibly be free to join us for dinner? I'm sure he would be delighted."

Shari looked at Jason. Help.

Jason, who had far more experience with such moments, said, "We'd be honored."

"Oh, splendid. I'm *so* pleased." She returned her smile to the seated trio. "Well, I mustn't keep you any longer. What a delight this is. I'm so grateful for your time, Ms. Khan."

Shari lowered herself back into her chair, aware of her grandmother's knowing smile.

"At certain levels," Jason said, "Hollywood is a very small town."

Her grandmother actually chuckled. "At certain levels."

Her mother said nothing at all.

he Beverly Hills courthouse system could exist nowhere else than the center of Hollywood wealth. It flanked Santa Monica Boulevard in a four-acre enclave of palm-studded lawns. If the set designer from *Casablanca* had been given a blank check, the result would have been the new city hall and courthouse. No jail, of course. The city paid the county jail a fortune so they could schlep the detritus beyond the emerald city's borders.

The previous night, Shari's long days had culminated in a genuine Hollywood coup. Carey McGraw, on-screen personality of *Evening Entertainment*, had headlined the film *Iron Feather*.

They were seated in the rear of the studio's largest limo, a white stretch Esplanade that was usually reserved for the flavor of the month. Today, however, it contained Derek Steen, Shari, Leo Patillo, and a courtroom bulldog named Roger Lang. Although the court case was being brought by the collective unions, Roger was being paid by the studio. Nobody outside the limo knew that.

The reason they were all so somber was heightened by Derek saying, "Play it again, Shari."

"Change the name," Leo said, "speak a little lower, and I'd swear I was listening to Bogie."

Shari used the remote to turn on the DVD and feed the signal to all three screens. A trio of brightly eager Carey McGraws launched into her wind-up. She described *Iron Feather*'s progress from the long-held dream of Sam Menzes to reality. She then segued to a brief introduction of the second Boone film, being shot by a company whose only work to date had been country music videos, and ended with a shot of the smoldering remains of the Wilmington studio. When the camera returned to the studio, an uncomfortable Bobby Dupree was seated around the curved dais from Carey. As far from the television personality as he could possibly get without falling off the stage.

"Mr. Dupree, you are here in Los Angeles to answer charges brought by the film unions that you are not adequately compensating your employees."

Bobby Dupree had a double-fisted clench on the chair's arms. "Maybe you can tell me something. Where's that Menzes fellow shooting his picture, Outer Mongolia?"

"I believe the location work is being done in Hungary. But—"

"Hungary, Mongolia, Upper Elbonia. You mean to tell me Menzes is paying them fellows union rates?"

The bulldog lawyer said, "Ouch."

"I don't believe the Menzes film has been mentioned in the court proceedings, so how—"

"That is the problem in a nutshell, Ms. McGraw. You *don't* believe. You don't *believe*."

Carey McGraw had not risen to the position she held by being a shrinking violet. "Let's get back on the subject, shall we?"

"I never left it."

"Would you care to respond to the charges leveled against you?"

Bobby shrugged. "Those goons across town burned us out, but that didn't stop us. So now they're gonna try and use the courts. I don't know how to put it any simpler than that."

"Are you implying that Galaxy Studios is behind the attack on your facility in North Carolina?"

"You'd sure like it if I did say that, wouldn't you?"

"Is that a yes?"

"It's my telling you I know what your game is."

Carey swiveled around without thanking her studio guest. The camera moved in for a closeup on McGraw. Good-bye, Bobby Dupree. "And now we have an *Evening Entertainment* exclusive, the first look at Galaxy's upcoming release, *Iron Feather*. Directed by Raul Solish. Starring my own personal heartthrob, Colin Chapman."

Their in-house team had slaved over the rough cuts, refashioning them into a ninety-second trailer. They had laid on the music director's first run at a film soundtrack. The result was dramatic, vivid, potent.

"Plays well," Derek conceded.

Carey McGraw's face returned to the screen. "We invited Bobby Dupree to share a cut of his own film, entitled *Long Hunter*. Mr. Dupree's response was, 'When I'm good and ready.'"

Carey McGraw's tight smile showed precisely what she thought of that. The bulldog laughed out loud.

"The list of also-rans that have tried to piggyback on larger studio releases is endless. The tactic does not grow any nicer with time. It is this reporter's opinion that even if *Long Hunter* does manage to overcome the court injunction and its recent trial by fire, its only hope for any audience at all will be by beating *Iron Feather*'s release date. Because as soon as *Long Hunter* comes out, it will be left in the dust. That is, if the film does not go straight to DVD. This is Carey McGraw for *Evening Entertainment*."

Steen declared, "It couldn't have played better if we had scripted the thing ourselves. We didn't, did we?"

Shari replied, "I arranged for Sam Menzes to invite Carey and her actor husband to one of his dinners and private screenings. But the program is all her doing."

"So why the long face?"

She nodded to Leo. "Tell them."

Leo didn't mince words. "They're ahead of schedule."

"That's impossible."

"Maybe so. But it's also happening."

Steen's face resumed its customary scowl. "You're telling me we've thrown everything we can at this thing and can't make it go away?"

"Not only is the filming on target. The Nashville music crowd has pulled out all the stops. Tim Crawford is doing the score. He's got eleven different acts putting time into the soundtrack. All original works."

Shari said, "We need to assume they're going to be ready with a finished project ahead of us."

Derek reached out a hand and traced a finger across the slick surface of the nearest screen. "I still have trouble seeing them as a bona fide threat. You saw the trailer. Our dailies are fantastic. Solish has done a superb job. You've just seen our opposition. There's nothing coming out of Carolina but a bad attitude. Even CBS is calling this a straight-to-video clunker."

Shari desperately wanted to agree. But the conversation she'd had with her grandmother the previous evening, after watching the *Evening Entertainment* piece together, still lingered. "If I'm wrong, we'll put it down to giving me some experience and a case of first-time nerves. I'll personally apologize to Sam for wasting his money."

"That won't be necessary," Derek said. "When it comes to protecting his investment, Sam always was a suspender and belts guy." He studied her. "But you don't think that's what is happening, do you."

"I want to. I really do. But the risk, Derek. What if they have a halfway decent film and it's ready before ours?"

"We can't let that happen." He turned to Lang. "What're our chances you can stop the Shoestring film in court today?"

"Slim to none."

"Then why are we paying you?"

"I told Ms. Khan the same thing the day she waltzed into my office." He shrugged with the easy manner of a man too powerful to be shoved around. "We've given it our best shot. At least we've gotten a hearing. But do I think the judge will rule in our favor? Probably not."

Derek took aim at Shari. "What are you going to do about it?"

"Post production is going well. I've spoken with Solish. He agrees with you, that I'm probably hyper because it's my first film. But he's also agreed to a release date five weeks early, which would put us two weekends ahead of the Shoestring flick."

"It's a huge effort and probably not necessary," Derek mused. "But when it comes to crushing the opposition, Sam Menzes has always had a taste for overkill. Okay. I'll take the release-date change to the boss. What else?"

Shari addressed Lang and Leo, "You mind giving us a moment?"

"No problem," the lawyer said as he opened the door. "See you in court."

When Leo and the lawyer stood under the same palm tree as their driver, Derek said, "I'm listening."

Shari outlined her idea in quick Derek-sized bites.

He chewed on it for a while, then said, "This conversation never took place."

"Why do you think we're talking about it in the back of a limo?"

He nodded. Once. "Make it happen."

Shari hoped she appeared as calm as the others. In fact, she had only been in a courtroom once before, and that had been a county court for an unpaid traffic violation. This was totally different. She sat between Derek and Leo, two pros positioned by the rear doors. Even so, the shabbily dressed attorney seated next to Bobby Dupree turned and smirked, then spoke to his client. Bobby turned and scalded them with a piercing look.

Shari held his gaze. But it was hard. Why, she could not say. Particularly as she was learning to handle the diamond-hard glares of some of Hollywood's biggest players. But there was something about this man. He looked like a kid, right down to the freckles. But there was nothing whatsoever childlike about his gaze. He did not merely study her. He reached across the distance and bored down deep.

Derek muttered, "Who's the clown in the bad suit?"

From her other side, Leo replied, "Some legal schmuck from Riverside. His biggest client until today has been a church."

Derek leaned forward. "This is a joke, right?"

"Am I laughing?"

Derek leaned back in his seat. Crossed his arms. Expelled a long breath. "This is a total waste of company time and money."

"I hope you're right," Leo said.

Derek leaned forward again. "Don't tell me she's got you worried too."

"Her, him, the fact that they've taken everything we've thrown at them and kept going. Something."

Derek examined the former cop. "You heard something you haven't told me?"

"You know that's not my game." Leo hesitated. "But my gut won't let me go."

"Your gut."

"A cop learns to trust his gut, Derek. Sometimes that's the only thing between you and the bullet."

Derek looked like he was about to say something more. But

the bailiff said, "All rise. Fourth district court of Beverly Hills. Judge Ridgeway presiding."

The judge was a woman in her sixties, greyhound lean and California tanned. "Be seated." She took the first file from her day's pile, checked the computer screen to her left, then said, "I have before me a request for an injunction against Shoestring Productions by the Teamsters, Local 612. Who represents the union?"

"I do, Your Honor. Roger Lang."

"All right. And for . . . Shoestring, that's the name of the company?"

"Indeed so, Your Honor." The lawyer's lumbering form and wrinkled state only accented Lang's polished exterior. "I represent Shoestring Productions."

"And you are?"

"Larry Hessler, Your Honor."

"I don't recall seeing you in my courtroom before."

"I practice out of Riverside."

"And who is this with you?"

"Bobby Dupree, Your Honor. Chairman and chief executive of Shoestring Productions."

"Very well." She motioned to Lang. "You may proceed."

Shari pretended to listen as Lang outlined his writ. But as she had been behind the complaint's formation, she had ample time to study the back of Bobby Dupree's head and again recalled her grandmother's comments of the previous night. They had been seated in her grandmother's living room. Shari had gone there after an endless day of meetings. Jason was in Hawaii on business, trying to wrap up representation of a bestselling author. Despite the four thousand miles between them, Shari and her grandmother had watched Carey McGraw's program with Jason. He phoned just before it came on and watched with his phone in his ear.

When Carey McGraw moved to the next segment of her

show, Jason's first comment was, "I could land you an exec role at any studio in town."

Shari hit the Mute button on her TV. "I'm not looking for another job. Besides which, my name's not mentioned anywhere."

"Rule one in this town, you're always looking, Shari. Always open to offers."

"Are you?"

"If a studio offered me a firm five-film production contract, sure, I'd jump. But this isn't me tonight. This is you. And the fact that your name isn't on the deal makes it even more incredible. A woman who can wield this much influence and not need to be in the spotlight. That's rare."

"More like a deer in the headlights," Shari joked.

"This is serious, Shari."

Her grandmother said, "What is he saying?"

Shari related Jason's side of the conversation. Her grandmother said, "Your gentleman is correct. But you both are missing the crucial point."

"Which is?"

Lizu Khan motioned to the screen. "The man you cannot see anymore. You think he is dead and gone. So does the announcer lady. But I know better."

Jason asked, "Shari, are you there?"

Shari passed on her grandmother's comments.

"How does she know?" he asked.

Lizu replied, "I know what I know."

To Shari's surprise, Jason did not scoff at the response. Instead, he said, "I confess this is a new one. But your grandmother never ceases to amaze me."

When Shari was leaving that night, her grandmother allowed Shari to kiss her immaculate cheek and then said, "Mark my words. This man, he is still a threat. You must find a way to destroy him. And do so mercilessly."

Lang took half an hour to lay out his writ. The principles, however, were simple. Back in the thirties, the federal courts declared the studio system monopolistic. It had been disbanded. And here Shoestring was doing it again.

The judge interrupted the union's lawyer only once, and that was to ask, "What is your client's interest in this?"

"We fought against the studio's hold on power then, and we're doing it now, Your Honor. What makes this worse is how this upstart company is striking at our workers with a double-whammy, by filming with nonunionized employees."

"Which makes them not 'our' employees, does it not?"

Lang faltered. "Excuse me?"

"If they are not unionized, they cannot be represented by you."

"Your Honor, I represent the workers whose jobs are at stake here."

She flipped to the last page of the writ. "And your desire is what, exactly?"

"That should be self-evident, Your Honor. We want them stopped. We want an injunction against their operation, and a cease-and-desist on their filming until contracts are renegotiated under proper terms."

"Very well. Mr. Hessler?"

The burly attorney rose to his feet. He indicated a massive leather satchel on the side of the table. "Your honor, I have here copies of the contracts signed by all Shoestring employees. I'd like to introduce them as evidence."

"What, all of them?"

"Yes, Your Honor. It's the only way we could think of to stop this nonsense dead in its tracks."

The judge worked at keeping a straight face. "Do they vary greatly?"

"Not much at all, Your Honor. The same structure was used by everybody, from the cameramen to the stars."

Derek and Leo exchanged astonished looks.

"Do you have a sample?" the judge asked.

"Permission to approach the bench?"

"Proceed."

Hessler handed one to the judge and another to Lang. "I also have a list of the exact items that were ruled unlawful by the US Supreme Court in the original case. To each I have responded with the position taken by Shoestring Productions. I would like this introduced as evidence."

The judge reached across the bench. "May I?"

Hessler made a second trek to the front of the courtroom. "Shoestring Productions has taken the same contractual structure used by hundreds of thousands of companies. In truth, the only real exception these days is companies in the entertainment industry. The contract stipulates that so long as their employees work for Shoestring, they cannot be employed by a competitor without Shoestring's express permission. Shoestring will continue to pay them a monthly salary whether or not they are actually filming. And Shoestring will only reject their working on other projects when or if the project conflicts timewise with a Shoestring film or when the project conflicts with the objectives of this company. Shoestring seeks to establish a moral high ground in entertainment and wants its employees to represent this position so long as they are under contract."

"Mr. Lang, would you care to respond?"

"Your Honor, this entire proceeding is ludicrous. We are in the entertainment business. Actors in particular are hired by the project."

"Mr. Hessler?"

"There's no law stating this is the sole way to conduct business, Your Honor. And speaking of which, I am still not clear why a Tennessee company filming in North Carolina, Tennessee, and Kentucky is being forced to respond to an injunction leveled by a Beverly Hills court."

"I completely agree." The judge slapped the file shut. "Case dismissed. Plaintiffs are hereby ordered to pay all costs." She leveled a finger at Lang, or seemed to, although the direction of her ire seemed equally focused at the rear of her courtroom. "I remind everyone in this courtroom that the studio monopoly system was struck down because it stifled fair competition. Any other injunctions of this kind will be considered frivolous and the plaintiffs will be held strictly accountable. Court adjourned."

------◆------

Shari was halted on the courthouse's top stair by the pinging of her phone. When she heard the voice of Gilda, Sam Menzes' secretary, she waved the others on. Gilda put Sam on, and Shari gave her boss a brief summary of the events, making no attempt to gild the bad news. Sam Menzes preferred his reports hard-boiled.

When she clipped the phone shut, a southern voice behind her said, "Ms. Khan, do I have that right?"

Shari turned and felt her gut freeze. "Mr. Dupree."

Up close, the man held none of Sam Menzes' aristocratic cool. Instead, he appeared unable to let go of the little boy he once had been. But he was surrounded by an aura of intense power.

Or maybe it was Shari's own nerves.

"I've been trying to figure out whether God had some special reason for me to make this trip. Especially since it landed right smack in the middle of the busiest time I've known in years."

Shari started to back away. "If you'll excuse me, I've got to get back—"

"Oh, I know all about how you Hollywood folks measure

time by a different clock. I don't aim on keeping you but a minute."

Only one thing kept Shari from turning and walking away. She happened to catch sight of Bobby Dupree's rumpled lawyer standing at the base of the courthouse stairs, not even trying to hide his smirk. Shari crossed her arms and showed him her grandmother's style of cool resolve. "I'm listening."

"I'm glad to hear it." Bobby Dupree reached into his pocket. "Only it ain't me you need to be listening to."

"Excuse me?"

"Here. I'm thinking this might be meant for you."

Shari took a step back. "If you want to serve a writ, Mr. Dupree, it should be to the studio's attorneys."

"Don't that sound just like Hollywood? I'm not after dueling lawyers, Ms. Khan. That's your game." He showed her what appeared to be an oversized business card. "Does this look like a legal document to you?"

"The unions came after you, Mr. Dupree. Not me."

"Now, don't you be tainting these waters with such talk. Here, this won't bite you. It's a gift."

When Shari hesitated further, Bobby Dupree reached over and placed the paper between her fingers. "There are nine Bible passages printed there, sort of leading you through the need for salvation. And three more, talking about what you should do if you want to pray."

Shari started to protest the way he had invaded her personal space, then decided, "I have nothing whatsoever to say to you."

As she turned and walked away, Bobby called after her, "It ain't me you need to be talking with, Ms. Khan."

Shari strode the sandstone walkway to the taxi stand. As she opened the first taxi's rear door, she spied a waste bin beside a nearby bench. Shari walked back and dumped the card in the can. She slipped into the taxi and said, "Galaxy Studios on Pico."

As the taxi pulled away, Shari glanced back but could not

spot either the strange boyish man from Nashville or his attorney. Her fingers tingled strangely, as though they had been infected. Her grandmother was right. She wiped her hand on her skirt, willing herself to put aside the man and his twang and his strange burning gaze.

he first thing Bobby saw when he approached his boardroom was a miracle in progress.

Jerry Orbain was seated in the chair by the window. He was surrounded by the other team leaders. They all focused on the assistant director, whose hostile attitude had initially threatened to derail the project. Now, however, his head was down over his notepad, writing as hard as he could and nodding in time to what the others were saying. Bobby stopped just outside the open door so he could watch. They were so intent on their discussion they did not notice him.

The entire crew looked exhausted. Stretched thin, worn to nubs. Despite the outdoor tans, they seemed pale. Almost translucent.

But they also looked happy. Calm and immensely comfortable with one another.

Brent was saying, "Most actors only have three takes in them. Four at the most."

Celia said, "A star will talk to people she trusts who have worked with the director. She'll go in knowing the director's habits. If a star knows this director goes for seven or ten takes, she'll give him twenty percent less."

Trevor scoffed. "Try fifty percent."

"Obviously you have worked with a lower grade of actor," Celia said.

Trevor's fur stiffened. "I'll have you know I have worked with the tippy-top."

"Nobody says tippy-top anymore."

"She's pulling your chain, Trevor," Brent said.

"Was she? Shame on you, Celia. I advise you to exercise more caution, else I will give Brent the closeup of your spots."

Celia bridled. "I don't have spots."

Trevor smiled. "Got you."

Jerry impatiently drew them back to the matter at hand. "What about the less experienced actors? Don't they need the extra takes?"

"Some do," Brent conceded.

"Not many," Celia said. "It mostly breeds bad attitudes. They start to doubt themselves. Especially if the director says, go this way, then no, let's do it totally different. They're afraid the director doesn't know what to do with them or the story."

"My second film, I worked for a guy who's gone now," Brent said. "A great man. He held to a set of pretty firm objectives, and they've served me well. Film every take. Give the script two goes. As in, hold the actors strictly to the book for two takes. After that, give them some room to play with it. But only after they've talked the changes over with the director."

Candace said, "The writer has an objection against that last part."

"No she doesn't," Celia said.

Brent went on, "Two takes with these actor-led digressions. Three at the most. Then wrap, unless there's some serious issues to be dealt with."

Jerry continued his note taking. "Anything else?"

"If I might insert my two-pence worth," Trevor said. "Build a reputation for buying the first take."

"Excuse me?"

Celia explained, "If a director is known to treat the first take or two as add-on rehearsals, the whole crew goes slack. They build slowly. But your star might shine the brightest in the first take. If the lighting's off or the other actors don't play the scene for keeps, you've lost your best chance at a hit."

Jerry rubbed his eyes. "I did that in the television project. I was afraid of not having a handle on the scene. So I ran everybody through and tried to fix things in my head. But by the time I was ready, one of my leads was pretty much done."

"It happens," Celia said.

"I saw it then," Jerry agreed. "But I didn't know what to do about it until now."

"You'll get it better next time," Celia told him.

"Forget next anything." Brent said. "You've hit the mark *this* time. Your work with the second team is superb."

Jerry looked up from his notebook. "Really?"

"The word our editor used was *seamless*."

Bobby took a step back. A second. Then he turned and walked away.

His secretary watched his retreat. "Aren't you going in?"

He had to force the words around the lump in his throat. "Not just yet."

"Liz? Bobby Dupree. I know I've brought you outta something important; I just heard your secretary fussing at me when she thought her Mute button was on."

"Never mind her. You're on my put-straight-through list."

"I could sure use a little of your time."

"Wait just one second, Bobby." Liz walked to the door and said to her secretary, "Tell Jeffrey this is going to require a few minutes. Have him take over the meeting for me."

She shut the door and pulled off her earring as she walked back to her desk. She shut her eyes and pushed away the day's business as best she could. Then she lifted the receiver. "All right. I'm back."

"I know what it means to steal minutes from an overpacked day. So I'll come straight to the point." Bobby huffed a hard breath. "I just got back from Los Angeles last night. I hired myself one of these super-duper consultants to get us a distributor. In the film business, you take on one of these distributor companies and they handle getting the film into cinemas. And after that, out on DVD and then onto the cable channels. Because we're an unknown, I hired the most expensive consultant I could lay my hands on to grease the way."

Knowledge of what was coming sank her into the chair. "They've shut you out."

"My fellow started at the top and worked his way down to the bottom rungs. Couldn't get a single one of them to even sit down and talk."

"Oh, Bobby."

"Galaxy has hit us with a knock-out punch, Liz. Whacked us right out of the ring."

She searched for something to say, some small kernel of hope, and came up blank. "I'm so very, very sorry."

"Reason I called, I was walking into the boardroom where I've got my team. And what I saw . . ." He stopped and huffed again. "Your man Brent has taken a group that wanted to murder each other and turned them into a team. A family. He sits there, this strong humble man, and they follow his lead even when he's silent. I couldn't be prouder if I'd invented the guy. And now I'm supposed to go in there and tell them I've failed."

"You haven't failed anybody."

"I've let them all down, Liz. They've done some great work. I haven't seen more than snippets of the film, and I don't need to. No matter how the finished product winds up playing, this group of mine, they're a living, breathing miracle."

She took a long breath. "It sounds to me like that's what we need right now."

"Come again?"

"I'm supposed to be the hard-driving businesswoman. But at night, when I lie in my lonely bed and wonder how I'm supposed to make it all work, I cling to God, Bobby. I clutch at His promises with both hands. So here's what I think you should do. Go in there and tell them the truth. Be the bruised and shaken man. Pray together. I'll get busy and pass the word along the prayer chain. And Bobby?"

"I'm here."

"Don't underestimate Brent. The man is strong. Stronger than I hope I'll ever need to be."

They took the news like a team.

Bobby laid it out in more detail than he had to Liz. But the telephone conversation granted him the strength to be both raw and, as she had instructed, fully broken. The man who had prayed his way through LA and come up empty-handed. The man who had never felt such a sense of defeat as he did not once, but twice. First, when he got back on his fancy jet for the return flight to Nashville. And second, when he stood in the doorway and saw just how badly he had let down his team.

His friends.

They sat and waited. Not for some shred of hope from Bobby. No. For Brent to speak. Their leader needed to respond for them all. They would take their direction from him.

Brent said, "There are certain lessons I feel have become branded on my soul. One is, I am a product of the fall of man. This is not something that changes with a momentary success, or a chance to take on a bigger job. No matter how grand the day might be, this simple fact remains. And this is truly liberating knowledge. It gives me the permission to fail. I am human, I have flaws. Hard as I strive to follow my Lord's call to discipleship and all the lessons of perfection, still I know. On my own I can do nothing. My salvation depends upon His eternal gift alone."

Brent leaned back in his chair. "There are certain elemental promises I will do my best to remain true to. I pray for the strength to remain absolutely free of booze and drugs. I pray God will grant me the wisdom never to let the world put me back on the lonely pedestal. If fame comes again, I pray to acknowledge it for God's glory. Not mine. Never mine. And above all else, I pray that I won't fail at holding on to God."

He leaned forward and leveled an iron-hard gaze at Bobby. "Any day I can look back and see that these prayers have been answered is a success."

Bobby felt the words groan out of his chest, "I let you folks down."

"Have you, Bobby? Have you?"

"You gave me your best. I went out there to find—"

"No, Bobby. Excuse me. You went out there to *serve the Lord*. What else happens is in His hands." Brent waited long enough to be sure Bobby did not want to come back at him. "Let's just say for the sake of argument that something you did or didn't do had a hand in this not working out like we wanted. Which, by the way, I don't think is the case. But let's say it did. Failure is not an indictment of you in eternity's eyes. You did not fail your friends' trust, not even if you let us down. I know you, Bobby. I know this."

"You gave it your best," Jerry said. "You always do. It's who you are."

"If I've learned anything from these past weeks, it's this," Candace said. "Fall down seven times, and get up eight."

Celia reached inside the pocket of her jeans and came out with a folded slip of paper. "I'm probably the last person who should be talking to you about God. But Brent said I should find passages that speak to me, write them out, and carry them around with me. Let God speak through them, if He will. I found this yesterday."

Brent covered his eyes with one hand.

"It comes from the thirty-first psalm. 'In you, Lord, I have taken refuge; let me never be put to shame. . . . Since you are my rock and my fortress, for the sake of your name lead and guide me. . . . Into your hands I commit my spirit; redeem me, Lord, my faithful God. . . . I will be glad and rejoice in your love, for you saw my affliction and knew the anguish of my soul.'"

No one spoke.

Celia flattened the paper on the table, running her hands over the surface. "It seems to me that even when I don't understand it, even when part of me wants to laugh this off, if I can just manage to hold on and wait, I feel . . ."

"Peace," Jerry supplied. "Rightness. Even when the world says it's impossible."

Brent reached over and took Celia's hand. His eyes were wet. "Whatever happens to the film, Bobby, know this. I have lived in a time of miracles great and small."

"I wouldn't trade this gig for an Oscar," Candace agreed.

heirs was an odd sort of first date.

To begin with, Liz was an hour late picking up Stanley because she needed to phone a few more friends and ask their help in praying for Bobby Dupree and the Shoestring project. She and Stanley met at a service station six blocks from the church, after Stanley's truck broke down while on his way to trade it in for a car more in keeping with what a pastor should be driving. Whatever that was. When Liz met him after the tow truck had left, Stanley's first words were, "I feel like I just plumb broke the old girl's heart."

Having raised two sons and one former husband, Liz knew enough not to point out that they were talking about a twenty-three-year-old truck. "I'm so sorry, Stanley."

"Either that or the angels who've been holding the thing together decided their job was done."

They stopped at the Cowpoke Grill, a hole-in-the-wall off the highway, and dined upon the world's undisputed king of hamburgers. They then drove to the Houston prayer meeting. They did not talk about each other or what they might or might not be entering into. There wasn't space. The only thing they could focus on was their friends.

Their worries were shared by all in the prayer meeting. They talked about it in the futile irritation of people paid to solve problems. But the entertainment industry was a closed system, where few of them had any usable connections.

One man said, "I've got a pal up in Chicago who's invested in a chain of them whatchacallems."

"Multiplexes."

" 'Course, I can't ask him to put something on the screen that's gonna remind folks of what you sweep off a stable floor."

Liz said, "I've seen about ninety seconds of whatever they call the filming."

"Dailies," Stanley filled in. "They were great."

"They gave me chills," Liz agreed.

Their leader that evening was the president of a regional insurance company. "So first we need to know if we have a product to work with. When do they expect to finish up?"

"They've wrapped the shoot, according to Brent. They're midway through postproduction. Tim Crawford's doing the score."

"I can't imagine Tim Crawford putting his stamp on something that isn't top drawer."

"I'm telling you," Liz said. "I think they're producing a real winner here."

Stanley added, "They were hoping to release around the first week in September."

The insurance company president was busy making notes. "Let's assume for the moment Bobby's group has come up with a solid product. So there are two problems he needs help with. The first is, can we help him find theaters that would be willing to show his film."

"What about this distributor business?" someone asked.

The company chief waved that aside. "Bobby Dupree has either bought or set up two dozen corporations. He can put the thing together, if he's got a reason to. No, we need to focus on our two problems."

"So what's the second?"

Liz supplied, "Getting the word out."

"That's it in a nutshell," their leader confirmed. "It doesn't matter how many theaters we can feed his way. If people don't know the film is coming out—"

Stanley leapt to his feet, sending his chair crashing against the wall. "I am a complete and total ninny!"

The insurance company president had led a relief convoy of thirty-two semis into New Orleans the week after Katrina. He was not easily shocked. "You have something for us, brother?"

"I am such a fool." Stanley searched the boardroom. "Anybody got a phone?"

"You mean other than the one hanging from your belt?" Liz asked.

"Oh. Yeah. Sure." In his haste to make the door, Stanley stumbled over a pair of feet and almost went down. "Y'all gotta excuse . . . I need to find—"

The door slammed shut.

Somebody said, "Looks like the Spirit's launched that guy out of bounds."

"Something sure put a spark under his saddle," another agreed.

revor sat next to a very frightened Brent. He knew the man's fear was unfounded. But this moment was not about logic. It was about getting his friend ready to go up there and save the day.

Of course, having all their hopes and dreams riding on what Brent said, not to mention the future of Bobby Dupree's company, was enough to give anybody a severe case of the willies.

Brent asked, "Why are you smiling?"

"No reason, mate."

"There's nothing funny about this."

"Quite right."

"This is serious business."

"Most assuredly."

"So wipe that silly grin off your kisser."

"No one says *kisser* anymore. The word's grown all dank and moldy."

Brent shut his eyes and leaned his head against the wall behind his chair. Furrows of strain ran from his eyes to his hairline. "I can't believe I let Bobby convince me to do this."

They sat in the corner of the stage. Beyond the curtain rose a gentle bedlam. The Austin Convention Center was playing host to the largest gathering of evangelical pastors in the world. It had originated as an Orlando convocation, the brainchild of a major youth organization's founder, who thought there should be a weekend retreat restricted to pastors and church leaders. Non-denominational. No political agenda. In the nineteen years since they had started, the gathering had grown from several hundred to almost twenty thousand attendees. Each year, the steering committee gathered and prayed and fasted for three days. At the end of this period, they announced the theme for that year's convocation. Pastors were invited to come and deliver talks. Each senior pastor who spoke was balanced with an up-and-comer. This year's theme was "Beyond the Comfort Zone."

Stanley Alcott's predecessor had volunteered his church as this year's host organization. The downtown convention center was the only place in town large enough to hold the gathering. The group had finished their Saturday dinner and were filing back into the arena for the final lecture. Only tonight there was no lecture to be heard.

Trevor leaned close enough to his friend not to need to raise his voice. "Here's a scoop, mate. You've already got the inside track on this gig."

Brent cracked one eyelid. "I almost understand what you just said."

"Job done. Tools up. Hands washed. Tea's milked. Biscuits dunked. End of another good day. All you need to do is walk out there and sort out the intro, and right sharpish. Then go find your seat and let the film do the rest."

"It's that part about walking out there that's got me stumped."

"I admit it's a fair old trek from here to there. But there's something you have to remember, lad. You're not alone in this. Not by a far cry."

Brent had both eyes open now. "All I've ever wanted is this.

All I've ever been good at. The only place I've ever felt truly comfortable. Just another wounded bird surrounded by others exactly like me. All of us sharing that strange and incredible chance to grow wings of celluloid. And just for a moment, only the length of that one take, we can rise up together and fly."

Trevor felt the wind catch in his throat. He swallowed hard and managed, "Do you know what makes a great director? It's not a fellow who finds the proper angle and shoots the right scene. I grant you, such fellows are a rare enough breed. But a *great* director, now, he has that and something more. Do you have any idea what I'm referring to?"

"None at all."

"Well, then, pay attention, because I'm about to utter a mountaintop pronouncement. A great director, dear boy, is someone who *galvanizes*. Who encourages even when dealing out the harshest criticism. Who can take an unlikely assortment of odds and ends and draw from them a work of beauty." Trevor patted Brent's knee. "Working with you has brought me as close to greatness as I have ever come."

Tim Crawford spoke from behind them. "I'd give that a big amen."

"So what I suggest, mate, is we bow our heads and pray for you to recognize just who you have become. And then I want you to stand up and walk the red carpet down to the altar of publicity. And stake our Lord's banner front and center."

———•———

Having Tim Crawford walk out unannounced created quite a ruckus. The crowd was up and cheering in a wave as his name passed from person to person. He stood bare-headed and alone, his favorite Gibson strung around his neck. There was no podium. His face was up on the screens looming on either side of the stage. He strummed a note and the sound echoed from massive speakers rising to either side of the giant empty screen that now acted as backdrop. He waited until the audience quieted somewhat, then launched straight into "I'll Fly Away." Lyrics replaced his face on the screens, and the whole world sang along.

He led them through a couple more resounding favorites, then said, "Most of y'all have heard about Shoestring Productions and their project *Long Hunter*. Those of you who know the legend of Daniel Boone know the title was Boone's nickname. He was called that not because of the length of his musket, as many now like to claim. It was because he led his hunting parties and his families further than any frontiersman had ever been. He did so because he felt his God called him to lead the way into a wilderness where no settler had ever ventured. Out into the forbidden territory. Out where there were neither maps nor guides. Out into peril and death from a thousand different dangers."

Tim Crawford slid his guitar behind his back and went on, "I started on this project because I could hear my granny, the woman who first opened the Bible for me, telling me this was something that needed doing. But I've found myself in something a lot bigger than just making a film. I'm in the company of a modern day Long Hunter."

Tim Crawford turned and said, "Brent, why don't you come on out here and let the folks have a look at you."

Brent's legs managed to carry him out and across the endless stage. His battery pack bumped in his jacket pocket. A dozen of his own shadows tracked his movements on the white screen behind him. His hands were as moist as old sponges. He was certain the mike pinned to his lapel picked up the pounding of his heart.

Tim wrapped one burly arm around Brent's shoulders and said, "Folks, I asked to be here today just so I could stand on the stage with this man. Y'all know him, or know of him. Y'all know he was broken. Some might have heard he was also saved. What I have discovered is that God has taken these broken shards and made a vessel into which He could pour his greatness. Ladies and gentlemen, I count it an honor to introduce the director and star of *Long Hunter*, Brent Stark."

The arena was four levels high, and arched on the sides like arms raised at the elbows. From where he stood, every seat seemed full. Brent had no idea what exactly he was going to say until that moment. "A recent Gallup poll stated that over two-thirds of Americans claim they are practicing Christians. Forty percent of those polled said they were evangelicals. That makes somewhere around a hundred forty million people. But where are they? They're certainly not in our churches. No. They are in our movie theaters. They are in front of their televisions. They are lining up to buy the latest game console. You don't have to look any further than your living room to know that this is an entertainment-driven culture. This is not supposition. This is truth.

"But we live in an era of moronic films and self-destructive story lines. What we tried to do here was offer an alternative. Create a story that was derived from the best of our past, in hopes of stimulating a different take on our future.

"Many of you from Texas will recall what the studio system recently did to the Alamo. They made the story cynical, self-serving, politically correct, and void of heroes. You watch. Galaxy Studios will soon release their own Daniel Boone film, entitled *Iron Feather*. I am certain their take on Daniel Boone will only be more of the same. The studio does not dispute this. In fact, they brag about it.

"It's time we reclaim our right to take pride in our nation. It's time we lifted up our heroes and our heritage. This is our version of a truly great man.

"The problem is, we have been shut out of the Hollywood system. No distributor will touch our product. They claim it's because the film is no good. You folks are going to be the first to ever see the finished version.

"If you find it to be as good as we think it is, we ask that you pray to see if you feel called to help us out. We don't know what you can do. We don't know precisely what to ask for here. All we feel able to say is, please, if you like the film, take it to the altar in prayer. Because without your help, we are done for."

Brent started to walk away, then turned back and added, "If you want my opinion, we have fashioned something special here. Something that deserves a chance. This is not only about a small start-up Christian outfit being shut out of the Hollywood system. This is about an entertainment system that has no room for our values. Thank you. Enjoy the show."

Brent and Trevor and Tim walked down to the front row, where Stanley and Liz sat with Bobby, Candace, Celia, and Jerry. There were quick embraces all around, and words that Brent really did not hear. All he clearly caught was the sincerity in their voices and their features. The assurance that he had not shamed them up there.

The lights darkened. The audience stirred and rustled and whispered. These church leaders had come to hear one of their own. Instead, Stanley had given up his evening as host pastor. Stanley Allcott, the man who had gone from prison to the pulpit of a major evangelical church. This should have been his night to shine, to demonstrate that his church was right to have awarded him this position. Instead, they got this.

Brent could well understand why they squirmed.

Then the hands appeared on the screen. They had gone back and forth over whether to add music, to score this with some inspirational tract. Instead, at Tim's insistence, they had left it as it had been originally. The man's hands folded the Bible shut and tied the tattered Book with binding twine. The cord rustled over speakers twenty feet tall. Then came the rush of wind, the swoop that Tim claimed sounded to him like the Spirit walking on tongues of flame. And the word *Shoestring* was formed with the cross at its heart.

In letters five stories tall.

It was the first time any of them had seen the concept on anything larger than the studio's flatscreen.

Bobby Dupree leaned over his hands and wept.

Tim Crawford had done them proud. His grandmother's favorite instrument opened with a melody like a rose-hued dawn. A country duo joined in. Not singing words nor following a tune any could name. Yet it all sounded hauntingly familiar, as though Tim had managed to capture some core essence to a thousand familiar gospel tunes, distilled it down to a thread of sound elevated by a pair of voices, now joined by a pair of violins, now by a dozen more voices, now a hundred, now a full orchestra. All humming a wordless hymn to a bygone era. To the heart of their shared beginnings. To the day they now lived.

The film ran four and a half minutes beyond two hours. Brent had wanted to cut another ten minutes but could not find them. Now, as he sat in his first audience and saw it from a distance he had never found in the editing room, he felt that he had done right not to cut further.

The final scene was one of his favorites. Boone sat on the porch of his cabin, one of over a dozen he had carved from the wilderness with his hands and his family's help. His wife sat beside him. He talked of the next wilderness still ahead. Thieves disguised as tax men had stolen all but forty of the thirty thousand acres deeded to him by a grateful nation. Boone was world famous, yet too poor to afford a second mule. He had nine towns and three counties named after him. He had been lauded in Paris, London, Moscow, and Washington, places he had never been. Royalty he had never met spoke of him in awe.

Boone's rocker was on the west-facing porch next to his wife's, his face etched by more than one more sunset. He stared at mountains he could not see. They had been named the Rocky

Mountains, and they called to him.

Daniel Boone was eighty-four years old.

He would never see those mountains.

The credits rolled. Tim Crawford sang a third and final time. Only this time it was a cappella. Not even his faithful guitar kept him company. Just a lone voice, singing about wind and freedom and frontiers and God.

The lights rose. Brent could not bring himself to look around, for fear that he would find half of the seats empty.

There was no sound.

Liz wiped her eyes and whispered, "Stand up."

"What?"

"Go on, brother." Tim Crawford used both hands to clear his face. "Don't keep your fans waiting."

Brent had to use the arms of his seat to rise to his feet.

The applause grew and grew and grew. Brent stood in utter shock, until it occurred to him to ask for some company.

They joined hands. Trevor and Candace and Jerry and Bobby and Celia and Tim.

The applause went on forever. Or so it seemed to Brent.

few weeks later, Liz carried her fourth phone call of the morning into the bank's elevator with her. When two early arriving ladies and one sleepy man crowded in, Liz said, "I'll have to get back to you." She shut the phone and sighed. Just past seven and already one of those days.

Then she realized what the ladies behind her were whispering about.

Liz turned around. "Are you talking about *Long Hunter*?"

"Yes, ma'am."

"What have you heard?"

"Our pastor was at some meeting a while back. He said it was the first time he'd cried at a movie since he was nine years old."

"Our pastor's wife says she still dreams about the woman who plays Boone's wife. I can't remember her name."

"Celia Breach," Liz said.

"Don't you know the director?"

"Brent Stark. Yes. He's a dear friend."

"Did you see the movie, Ms. Courtney?"

"I wept like a baby."

"Is it true what the pastor said about Hollywood not giving them a chance?"

"They couldn't find a distributor."

The young man offered, "My church is buying out the theater."

The elevator pinged for their floor. Liz exited with the others. "What did you say?"

One of the young women replied, "Our pastor urged us all to go that first weekend. He says it's important. I don't remember exactly why."

The young man said, "They're opening in six hundred theaters. Which is, like, nothing at all. The only chance they have to get a larger number of theaters is if they pack out the first weekend wherever they can."

"That's right," the woman said. "I remember now. The pastor said we all need to go on opening night."

Starting down the hall, the young man called over his shoulder, "Go back to him and tell him the church ought to front for the tickets."

Turning toward her own office, Liz added a silent amen.

"The thing has taken on a life of its own," Stanley told her that night. "My youth pastor was home with a sick baby and couldn't attend the convocation. Even so, he's taking two hundred students on the strength of a pal's word."

"Would your youth pastor happen to be the young man by the buffet table who is trying hard not to stare at me?"

Stanley turned his head and squinted.

"Don't look."

"If I don't, how am I supposed to answer your question?"

"Stop smirking."

"I'm with the finest looking woman here. What am I supposed to do, weep?"

It was a double milestone sort of date. Tonight marked their first month's anniversary of dating. And it was the first time Liz was seen as officially in the company of the pastor at a church event.

Liz couldn't figure out what to do with her hands. "So I'm getting stared at by total strangers."

"Honey, what did you expect?"

"Telling myself what to expect and living it are two different things. You know a lot of these folks are now assuming I joined the church to chase you."

"You're probably right. And there's nothing I can do about it but show them how much I care for you."

Her fidgeting eased. "You say the sweetest things."

"I've been practicing that line all day."

"Pastors aren't supposed to fib, Stanley."

"It's the honest truth. I knew this was gonna be a tough one. There's a cluster behind you who are going to town. My least favorite board member is probably telling them about the last church we were involved in. Now the heads are shaking. The lady just got to the juicy bit. I was hoping to find a way to tell you how much it means, your coming like this."

The monthly church supper was far too large to fit inside the social hall. The outdoor tables were lost beneath a summer deluge. Lightning streaked the silver curtain falling outside the glass doors, the rumbling causing the littlest kids to squeal. The crowd stretched down the connecting hallway and half filled the gymnasium.

Liz reached across the table and took hold of Stanley's hand. It might have been the thunderbolt that followed, but a lot of the people around them went very still. "You are a dear, sweet, good man."

A young man with a scraggly goatee and a teen's energy

rushed over, caught sight of them holding hands, and said, "Whoa."

Stanley said, "Cue the youth pastor."

"I can definitely come back later."

"Sit down, Mike." Stanley added his second hand to the mix. "Allow me to officially introduce Liz Courtney."

"I guess you realize this is getting some kinda serious attention."

"We noticed," Liz said.

Stanley said, "I'm going to need to say something to the church about us, Liz."

"Go wild."

"Oh man," Mike said. "Is this cool or what."

"By the way, Mike," Stanley said, "the lady's seen the film. You can ask her about it."

Mike's energy notched even higher. "Is it as good as they say?"

"Better."

"We're working on getting a couple hundred people to go the second night now," Mike told them. "I just heard the multiplex is shifting to three screens. You mind if I say something to the folks here?"

Stanley said, "I think everybody's probably already aware that the film opens in two weeks, Mike."

"Can't hurt."

"No, I suppose not. But first things first." Stanley gave her hand a final squeeze and rose to his feet. "Time to address the troops."

He made his way to the mike at the room's far end. He greeted the people, led them in a prayer, and then paused. Stanley had a special way of claiming the pulpit. Liz was personally convinced it was part of his appeal, how he leaned his beefy forearms on the podium, allowing his hands to drape over the edge, and talked to the people in a soft, comfortable rumble. "We are a family. And that's why Liz and I are here together tonight. To introduce you, our kin in Christ, to a change that's happening in our lives. We've known each other for a long time. There's a remarkable history between us—some serious pain, and a great deal of joy. And we've started seeing one another. I don't . . ."

The applause caught them both by surprise. When it finally died down, Stanley went on, "That means more than I can say. We're both adults, and we know there's a lot of ground yet to cover. The good Lord tells us to focus upon this day alone. But from my side, I got to tell you, my affection for this fine lady is growing stronger every day. And it's getting harder with every passing hour not to think about the future."

he studio called it the triple whammy, a tactic devised by Sam and derided by their competitors. A few other studios wished they could do it, but not many. These days, almost all studios were run by corporate clones and pinhead accountants and lawyer-sharks in striped suspenders. Sam Menzes was the last of a dying breed, a gambler willing to put his own chips on the table and throw the dice.

Of course, doing all he could to load the dice in his favor was just business, Hollywood style.

The normal way of introducing a finished film was to line up a series of test screenings. The audiences were asked to fill in cards with their responses, and a few viewers were held back to talk at length with the marketing clones. Sam loathed the process with a vengeance. It was the sort of tactic an accountant would think up, all caution and layers of marketing reports between them and the firing squad. The only time Galaxy introduced a film that way was when there was internal disagreement over structure and they wanted the audience's help in deciding which way to go.

The Sam Menzes approach was to go for the surprise factor.

In the run-up to opening night, his team held three simultaneous screenings. Tonight the Academy's largest screening hall hosted nine hundred film critics and cable lollipops and guests, flown in from all over the country at Sam's expense.

Shari's secretary, Emily Arsene, and Leo Patillo were all doing duty at the bar tables set up in the massive foyer, from where Shari hoped they could garner initial responses. Shari herself had been ordered by Sam to represent the studio, along with Raul Solish, the director, and *Iron Feather*'s costars, Colin Chapman and Billie Rondelle. This was not the official launch, the so-called charity event where thousands of camera flashes would light up the red carpet. This was the critics' turn.

The out-of-towners had virtually filled the Beverly Hills Hotel. They arrived at the screening in a convoy of gleaming limos and would depart the same way. The foyer bar sported a fifteen-foot ice sculpture of a frontier hunter right down to the flintlock musket, and spouted vintage champagne. The buffet held mountains of caviar and lobster tail and fresh sturgeon. Tables to either side of the door groaned under the weight of gifts to be handed out at departure time—the gift bags resembled those handed out on Oscar night, an allusion to the prizes Galaxy hoped the film would win. Included in the pile of goodies was a dual DVD set of longer interviews with each of the principals and all the film's trailers. The on-air critics could cut and weave as they chose without the expense or energy of actually having to spend time with the people.

Nothing was too good for the critics.

Shari and Billie and Colin and Raul made their way down the battery of TV cameras and smiling on-camera talent. A bevy of studio PR lackeys held the interviews to sixty-second spots. Shari followed the parade, bringing up the end.

Carey McGraw from *Evening Entertainment* met her with a smile. Shari had intentionally given her friend the last spot and extra time with each of the principals. Carey shook her hand briskly. "Ready?"

"Just a minute." Shari handed over a card.

"What's this?"

Shari turned her back to the camera and pushed the mike Carey held well away. "Sam is having a few friends of the studio over tonight. They'll have a screening first and then dinner will be served. Afterward they'll have a private Norah Jones concert."

"Sam is inviting me?"

"No camera, of course." Shari patted her arm. "Consider it payback for the good press you've given us on this film."

Carey slipped the card into her pocket. "It's good to have friends who know how to say thanks."

Shari turned back around and smiled for the camera. "I couldn't have said it any better myself."

Shari left after the screening but while the party was still in full swing. Jason joined her, along with Emily and Leo. The limo was ferrying them the short distance from the Academy head-quarters to Grauman's Theatre, where a select audience of local trendsetters were being treated to a first viewing of *Iron Feather*. The three principals—Billie, Colin, and Raul—were driven straight to the Menzes residence. Shari would join them shortly. But first she wanted to see the faces leaving the theater. The marketing guys had wired the place with infrared cameras that constantly scanned the audience's response to certain scenes. Two dozen moles would drift with the departing crowd, gauging their responses. But Shari wanted to see it for herself.

Leo made himself a drink from the limo bar. "Anybody else want something?"

"You better lay off," Emily warned. "We've still got work to do."

"Work, schmerk." Leo pulled hard on his glass. "What we've got on our hands is a full-blown winner."

"The critics seemed pleased," Shari agreed.

"They weren't pleased," Jason said. "They were blown away."

"You're sure?"

Jason took Shari's hand. "There are a lot of times you need to doubt in this business. Tonight is not one of them."

Leo smirked at the sight of them holding hands. "And I thought it was just a matter of time for you and me to be an item."

Emily laughed out loud. "News flash. Shari's after bigger game."

"What, you're saying I'm not prime material?"

"Not even afternoon soap material."

"I'm crushed."

"Sorry, kiddo. Better you hear it from a friend, though, right?"

"Oh. Is that what you are?"

Shari leaned her head on the seat rest and sighed. Jason squeezed her hand. "Happy?"

"Very. And tired."

"You should be. You've earned a rest. Soon as this thing is launched," Jason told the others, "we're sailing down to Cabo."

"Nice," Leo said. "You got room for a third?"

"No," she and Jason said together.

Emily asked, "Any word about the competition?"

Leo snorted. "If you can call it that. At last count, *Long Hunter* is slated to open in four hundred theaters."

Shari sat up straighter. "I thought they didn't have a distributor."

"Shoestring has opened its own division," Jason replied. "I heard they were up to six hundred screens."

"Four, six, what's the diff? We're going to bury them."

"When did this happen?" Shari asked. "Their setting up their own distributor, I mean."

"Couple of weeks ago. I sent you a memo."

"No you didn't."

"What's the matter?" Jason asked.

"Six hundred theaters. That's a lot."

"It's nothing," Leo said. "They'll be gone in a week."

"Leo's right," Jason said. "*Iron Feather* is opening on, what, three thousand screens?"

"Thirty-seven hundred," Emily corrected.

"It's not just the number. It's the initial impact," Jason said. "Your film is coming out first and strongest. You'll get all the publicity. You'll come up top in the ranks."

Leo said, "They had some church group meeting in Austin."

"Who did?"

"I wrote you about this, Shari. Some church thing, is all. They've hooked up with some of the indie cineplexes. They'll play one week to empty houses and then vanish."

Emily said, "All it means is they'll be able to claim a theatrical release instead of a straight to DVD."

Jason watched Shari's face. "What's bothering you?"

"I don't like hearing this after the fact, is all."

"And I'm telling you, I sent you a memo," Leo insisted.

"It's not just that," Jason said. "Is it Lizu?"

"Who?" Emily asked.

"Shari's grandmother."

"Sure, we met. She's one sharp cookie."

"She is still worried," Shari said.

"Did she tell you why?"

Shari wished she could just blink her eyes and clear away the fog of worry. Instead, her grandmother's quietly insistent voice floated so clearly Lizu might as well have been in the limo with them. "She still thinks they could be a threat. Back before the shah fell, my grandfather was governor of a province in Persia. This was before my father was born. By the time he came along, my grandfather had first been the shah's ambassador to Pakistan and then took a position in Tehran."

"Wow, we're in the presence of royalty," Leo said.

"Let her finish," Emily said.

"Back when he was regional governor, they had some problem with missionaries. The local Muslim clerics wanted them gone. But the missionaries were Americans and the shah was concerned about upsetting the American government. So nothing could be done officially. But the clerics wouldn't leave it alone. Finally my grandfather gave them the okay to cause a riot. They burned down the churches and beat the missionaries pretty badly. They all left. Problem solved, or so everybody thought. Only ten years later, when the shah got into trouble, they discovered the problem hadn't gone away at all. The province was a hotbed of underground churches. There were hundreds of them. And hundreds of thousands of Christians. Living right under the imam's nose."

Leo rattled the ice in his glass. "You going somewhere with this?"

"Probably not," Shari agreed. "I thought I'd put the whole discussion behind me. But hearing about Shoestring putting together six hundred theaters rattled me."

"And I'm telling you I sent you the memo."

Emily said, "Let's let the memo thing die a simple death, okay?"

"So what—" Jason started.

Emily's phone chimed. "I thought I turned this off." She glanced at the screen and said, "It's the boss."

She hit the button. "Yes, Sam. Yes, it went great." Emily smiled and said, "She's right here."

Shari accepted the phone. "Hello, Sam."

Sam Menzes was a very happy man. "You've done us all proud, Shari. The initial responses are astonishing."

"We're on our way to Grauman's now. I should have more for you when we get to your place."

Sam brushed it aside. "Audiences will believe what we tell them. The critics are essential. You have them on our side. PR reports nothing but good things came from tonight's viewing."

"Raul and Colin and Billie made the film."

"I will thank them in the appropriate manner. But it's time you accepted your own kudos. I gave you the ball and you ran with it for a touchdown."

She glowed but could not keep herself from confessing, "I'm concerned about *Long Hunter* gaining a theatrical release."

"Four hundred screens is nothing."

"Jason has heard six."

"Anything under fifteen hundred means they're not able to cover all major markets. They'll have a week of sporadic audiences, perhaps two. Then it will fade into history."

"I hope you're right."

"Mark my words. You've put that Tennessee street urchin right where he belongs, in the ground right beside his little film. I can hear the dirt hitting their casket. Forget them. Gauge the reaction at Grauman's and then get on over here. There are some people I want you to meet."

Shari shut the phone and related what Sam had said about Shoestring. Emily agreed, "They bury the bodies still warm in this town."

"Meet some people," Jason said. "Sam Menzes wants to personally introduce you into his circle."

"Remember me when you hit the peaks," Leo said.

"You'll always be my special guy, Leo."

"Huh. She says this while she's got a dead solid lock on another man's hand."

They pulled up in front of the old-style theater awning. Building-sized posters were already going up for the upcoming release of *Iron Feather*. Shari stepped from the limo and took a moment to drink in the sight.

Jason draped one arm over her shoulder. "Your name isn't on this one. But it will be soon."

"I don't need the fame."

"No, and that's just one more reason why you're so special." He smiled just for her. "Ready?"

"Yes." And she was. If only she could erase her grandmother's nagging whisper, the night would be perfect indeed.

alaxy Studios held their official release at the largest theater in LA, a new Westwood behemoth. The reception afterward was at Chasen's. The stars walked the red carpet while mammoth klieg lights spun pillars into the night sky. A massive banner for *Iron Feather* stretched above the restaurant entrance. Portable bleachers had been set up to either side of the red carpet, specialty items trucked in for just such an occasion. The bleachers were jammed with screaming fans.

Shari stood just inside the restaurant's entrance and watched the last limo arrive, the process as carefully choreographed as an invasion. One of the bouncers in a tuxedo and headset opened the rear door. The film's male lead stepped from the limo. The fans' screams reached a fever pitch. Shari winced at the almost painful din. Colin Chapman paused long enough to bathe in the adulation. He waved and smiled and turned with the slow regularity of a tango dancer, aware that any jerky movement would come across badly on tape. The camera flashes were a constant silver strobe.

Carey McGraw of *Evening Entertainment* did a quick interview there on the red carpet. She and the star shared a for-the-cameras laugh over how he could not hear her question for the screams. What Colin said was unimportant. The scene would play well on the next day's show. Which was crucial. Everything depended upon a huge opening weekend. Such early hints of a hit would drive the initial numbers even higher.

Emily was suddenly at Shari's side. The older woman hid herself in the doorway's shadows, made almost black by the camera lights outside. "I just got word of the reviews."

"And?"

"*Hollywood Reporter* and *Variety* are both giving us front-page slots. Ditto the *LA Times*."

The weeks of tension ballooned in her chest. "What?"

"It's all good. And gets better. All three are calling the Shoe-string project a wash."

"You're sure?"

Emily slipped three folded sheets into Shari's pocket. "Save it for your bedtime read. They tried to contact Shoestring for a comment. Nobody even bothered to respond. They're saying forget the theatrical release. *Long Hunter* is just another second-rate, low-budget, straight-to-DVD stink bomb."

"Any word on the number of theaters?"

"Still holding steady at six hundred. You can stop worrying now."

Shari turned back to the night. "Not a chance."

Emily backed away as Colin paraded past and entered the restaurant to prolonged applause. Shari waited for Carey McGraw. The television presenter came in patting her makeup, her professional smile set firmly in place. The on-air presenter told Shari, "That is going to run as our headliner for tomorrow night."

"Excellent." Shari stepped back into the shadows Emily had just vacated, drawing Carey with her. "I have something for you."

The woman's eyes sparked. "If we're doing it in the dark, it must be dirt."

"It is. On Brent Stark."

"Excellent." The journalist laughed gaily. "I'm still upset over how that Dupree fellow dissed me on the air."

"This is your chance for revenge." Shari handed over a mini-disk. "My people have dug up some never-before-seen footage from Stark's accident. The Shoestring director being led from the wreckage of his Aston Martin. His arrest picture. And the best for last, Brent being taken away from his sentencing in shackles."

"I've got chills. This is an exclusive?"

"Yes."

Carey's face might have been fresh and eager and as young as money could make it. But the eyes were ancient. "What do you want in return?"

"Nothing," Shari replied. "For now."

"I can live with that." She smiled brightly. "What's a little debt between friends?"

Shari smiled back, the message sent and received.

"You heard Shoestring has refused to give any further inter-views? And they're not showing the film to critics?"

"Yes."

"That can only mean one thing. The film is a total bomb." Carey McGraw patted her pocket. "All your efforts may be totally unnecessary."

"Maybe. But I want to be sure."

"I hope Menzes knows what he's got in you." She spotted someone behind Shari. "Here comes your Prince Charming. How about an interview with the couple of the year?"

"This is not our night."

"Some other time, then. Something tells me you two will be around for a while."

tanley? It's Brent."

"What time is it?"

"Just gone six where you are." His friend sounded dead asleep. Brent said apologetically, "I thought I'd just catch you before you left for the AA meeting."

"I've had to give it up."

The news caught him hard, an unexpected uppercut to his heart. "What?"

"I know. It was tough on me too. But running a church this size is all-consuming."

Brent felt a keening loss. "Who will run the group?"

"I've got a good man in place there. And they've got a strong one started over here, in case you want to come join us in the 'burbs. But you can always call me, brother. You know that."

"It sounds to me like I've got to choose a different time."

"Yeah, I didn't get in last night until well after midnight." Stanley hesitated, then added, "I went out with Liz."

"Our Liz?"

"I guess you could say we're an item."

There was no reason why the news should have sounded

anything but excellent. Even so, he had to force himself to say, "This is great, Stanley."

"Yeah, you sound thrilled."

"No, it's not you two. My world's been rocked pretty hard, is all."

Stanley's voice resonated with a pastor's ability to draw the world into focus and be there for another. "What's happened?"

"They're burying us deep before we even release."

"Who?"

"The Hollywood crowd. *Iron Feather* opened last night. The critics raved over the film."

"Now give me the second half."

Brent's room was on the twelfth floor of the Nashville Marriott. The city's awakening din rose up from below. Bobby Dupree's office building was directly across the street. He watched a few early arrivals enter their offices and settle in to just another day. "They dug up some old news footage of my bad old days."

"The accident?"

"That and the arrest and my sentencing. Some pictures I've never seen before. There was one of Celia being pulled from the wreckage." Brent dragged one hand through his hair. "It was pretty bad."

"I'm sure it was. And I'll tell you the simple truth, brother. You deserve better. But right now, you've got to hold on. Don't let go."

"I'm not . . ." Brent sighed from genuine pain. He turned from the window and sank onto the floor between the beds. "I'm so worried about Celia."

"From what I've seen of the lady, she's already handled this and has moved on. Regardless of that, you need to focus on what's most important here. Tell me you understand."

"The eternal in this moment."

"There you go." Stanley gave it a minute, then said, "I hear there's a lot of action around your film. My church group has basically prebooked the theaters that will be showing *Long Hunter*. I hear the same thing is happening in a lot of other places."

Brent tried to put some enthusiasm into his response. "That's great, Stanley."

"I hear there's a groundswell of support building on the Internet. Trying to get people packed in the opening week. That's pretty important, from what I hear."

"Either we get in the top ten films released that week or we're toast."

Stanley led them in a word of prayer, then signed off. A busy pastor headed into another overfull day. Brent cradled the phone next to his chest. His mind kept going back to the news. Stanley and Liz. An item.

He was drawn from his reverie by a knock on his door.

He got up to find Celia standing in the doorway holding two Styrofoam cups of coffee. "I didn't see you at breakfast."

He felt everything drain away. All energy, all his remaining hopes. Every last one. "Oh, Celia."

"That's what I thought. Can I come in?"

He stumbled back a step. Celia stepped around him, saw the cell phone and the Bible on the floor between the beds, and said, "That looks comfortable."

Before he could formulate an objection, she had slipped down so her back was against the bed opposite his. She pulled a top off one cup. "Black, one sugar. Right?"

He stood there, mute.

"Come sit with me, Brent."

He forced himself over and down. "I'm so very, very sorry."

"Here. Drink."

He did so, though he tasted nothing. "Why are you here?"

"Don't be silly. Where else should I be?" She wore an outfit similar to what she'd been wearing when he had first seen her, back at the beginning of this adventure of theirs, an off-the-shoulder sweater and stone-washed jeans. Her hair was pulled sternly back from her face. She looked equal measures teenage beauty queen and timeless wisdom. "Candace and I slept through the first airing. I only heard about it at breakfast. Which is why I'm so late showing up."

"I don't know what to say."

"I know." She held out her free hand, the impossibly long fingers with their rose-colored nails.

He stared at it.

"Hold my hand."

He did so because she ordered it, astonished that the touch did not brand him.

She said softly, "Was it awful?"

He could not force down another swallow. Brent let her take the cup from his limp fingers. "I hadn't seen it before."

"Prison spared you some things. I couldn't get away from it. The press hounded me for months. The pictures . . ."

He rubbed his face. The skin felt numb beneath his fingers. "I thought I was . . . you know . . ."

"Ready. Strong. Able to take it and handle it all by yourself."

"Not by myself."

"No." She moved the Bible to one side and slipped over so she was seated next to him. "But without me."

"How could I ask you to help me through this?"

"Because we're friends. Aren't we?"

"I don't deserve you, Celia."

"Funny." She draped one hand over his shoulders. "I was just thinking the same thing."

"Can you ever forgive me?"

She leaned her head on his shoulder. "If you'd asked me that a couple of months ago, I'd have said no. I never could. The pain and the loss and who I was to begin with were all just too much to handle."

He wanted to see her face. But he didn't want to move. Her hair smelled of shampoo and springtime. "And now?"

"Everything is so new I can scarcely accept that it's happening. That it's really me saying the words."

He heard his swallow, a thrumming beat of hope. "What words?"

"Are you going to make me say them?"

"Celia, I can't even bring myself to ask you. Much less demand."

She snuggled closer still. "Then I'll tell you. Hope. Forgiveness. Trust."

The thrumming began down deep in his gut and rose to clench his heart in shivers as strong as the words she'd spoken.

She pulled a fraction away from him. So as to reveal to him eyes he had seen in a thousand closeups. And yet it seemed to him that the color was somehow new. A shade he had never seen before now.

Celia whispered the last word. "Love."

t Bobby's insistence, the crew stayed together for the release date. Bobby took over two B&Bs and the Marriott Courtyard near his home. Brent and Celia and Jerry and Trevor and Candace filled the Duprees' upstairs bedrooms. Nobody felt much like celebrating, but no one refused his invitation either.

He put together a down-home party for the evening. The crowd grew to include several busloads of extras with their pastors in tow. The church buses filled the road leading down to the Dupree home. A local crew came in to do a Carolina barbecue, slow-roasting a pair of hogs in his backyard, serving up potatoes and corn fritters and washtubs of coleslaw. Lemonade by the pitcher. A bouncy castle for the kids. Frisbees and dogs and laughter and nerves aplenty.

Brent heard the same thing so often the words became imbedded in his brain. Theirs was a great God.

Whatever that meant.

Even so, there were hugs and smiles and genuine happiness on almost all the faces that night. Regrets too, of course. But still, to feel anything other than deflated was a triumph.

Brent bade the others an early good-night and enjoyed the

first unbroken night's sleep since starting the final edits. Or so it seemed.

He came downstairs the next morning to tears.

Candace and Celia and Darlene Dupree stared at the small television set above the microwave with wet faces. Bobby Dupree and Jerry both looked poleaxed. "What's the matter?" Brent asked.

Celia sniffed loudly and walked around to give him a hug. "Good morning, sleepyhead."

"Bobby made us let you sleep," Candace said. "We didn't want to, but he insisted."

"I ain't never seen anybody as tired as you were last night," Bobby agreed. "This fire won't be going out for a while."

"Why is everybody crying?" He stared at the television. A line of people were photographed from above. A newscaster was saying something, but the words didn't fit. "Did somebody die?"

"No, my darling. That's us."

Brent looked down at her. "What did you call me?"

Celia smiled through her tears. "Darling, did you hear what I just said?"

"I heard all right." He gathered her up in his arms. "Oh boy, did I hear."

"Would you get a load of that," Bobby said.

"It's about time," Candace said.

"I'll give that a big amen," Jerry agreed.

Darlene said, "Somebody pour the man a coffee and tell him what's happening!"

Brent managed a double sip without letting go of Celia. The woman in his arms said, "Are you awake now?"

"About as awake as I've ever been."

"Okay. Then very carefully." She pointed at the screen. "That. Is. Us."

He could not stop smiling. "Us."

"Yes, Brent, honey. Us."

He stared at the screen. But all he saw was people. "Sorry. I'm not tracking."

For some reason, that caused them all to burst into laughter. "What is wrong with you people?"

"Not a single solitary thing." Bobby wiped his eyes. "Oh man. Look at that boy's face."

"I'm thinking sunstroke or serious love," Candace said.

"Us," Celia repeated. *"Long Hunter."*

The day froze solid. "What?"

"Those are people waiting to see our movie."

Brent turned from the screen. Inspected each face in turn. Just to be sure. "You're not just saying this, are you?"

"I've been watching this for an hour," Jerry said. "It still hasn't sunk in."

Brent set down his mug. He was afraid his fingers would not be able to keep hold. He leaned one hand on the counter. The other he used to keep Celia tight. "That was the line from last night?"

"Does that look like nighttime to you?" Celia hugged him harder. "This is *now*."

He searched the kitchen, found the clock over the stove. "It's eleven o'clock."

"It sure is," Candace said

"In the morning."

"Right as rain," Bobby said.

Another scan of the faces, then back to the screen. The crowds were replaced by a smiling announcer. "Where was that?"

"Everywhere," Celia told him.

"Dallas, Atlanta, Jacksonville," Jerry started, "Richmond, Charlotte, Nashville, St. Louis. We got shut out of New York and LA. But most other places are exactly the same."

Candace said, "People have been waiting for hours."

"We opened in six hundred theaters," Jerry said. "The announcer just said we've already doubled that number, and we're pushing aside the competition like it doesn't even exist."

Bobby said, "The office switchboard is near about jammed. All those Hollywood folks who did their dead-level best to bury us are lining up to have a chat."

"Business as usual," Candace said, "adjusted for inflation and Hollywood."

Bobby went on, "You want to talk to 'em, be my guest. You want to ignore them, that's fine by me."

"I've got to sit down," Brent said.

Bobby dragged over a kitchen stool and clapped his director on the back. "They threw everything they could at us. Right down to the very last minute. They attacked and they slandered and they burned. And look where it got 'em." Bobby Dupree was dancing in place. "You know what you're looking at there?"

"A hit," Jerry said. "We've definitely made the top ten for this weekend."

"And now playing in twelve hundred theaters," Celia said, keeping him close by standing next to his chair.

"Not for long," Candace said. "I bet they double the number by next week. Or triple."

Brent stared at his friends. And felt his own face go wet. He wanted to say the word but could not find the strength just then. But it was all right. They knew what he wanted to say.

Miracle.

onday morning, Shari Khan got ready for what she assumed was her last limo ride. It was the first time she had asked the studio guys to pick her up at Jason's. He had left for the airport at dawn in the Land Rover. They had argued while he packed about what it all meant. For Shari, the lines of people snaking beneath the helicopter spotlights were the gathering for her own funeral. Jason chided her for overreacting, then grew increasingly angry when she did not come around to his way of thinking. He had phoned her after hitting the freeway so they could continue quarreling. She heard him do curbside check-in, knew everyone in line could hear him say, "This is Hollywood, Shari. If you're going to make it here, you've got to accept that some things don't go the way you want."

"Sam Menzes does not go in for second chances."

"So change studios."

Her throat grew raw from confessing, "If I leave Menzes, all I have is a few months out of the mosh pit."

"That's absurd and you know it."

She had heard his change in tone. Jason grew not merely hard. But impatient. A man on the move who had no time for those who were unwilling to move with him. Jason usually saved it for the recalcitrant star who was one inch from being dropped.

It scared her as bad as the previous evening's news. "All right, Jason."

He paused. Having her agree was clearly not expected. "You'll do it?"

"You're the expert." She hated her submissive tone. The falseness of it left her feeling physically ill. "If you say it, it must be so."

"That's right. I've been around this jungle for a long time."

Shari inspected her hands, as though making sure all her fingers were still present. "I need to go."

"I'll call you tonight."

Shari phoned the studio, then went through all the proper motions. She showered and applied her makeup and chose an Ungaro suit. As she walked through the kitchen, the phone rang. Shari knew who it was long before she heard her grandmother ask, "Have you eaten anything?"

"Please."

Her grandmother sighed. The woman was far too wise to say she had told them and told them. That the snake was not dead merely because they had chopped off the head. Instead she asked, "What does Jason say?"

"That I am overreacting." She spotted the limo pull up the drive. "My ride's here."

"Wounds heal, my darling."

"I'll call you tonight." Shari set down the phone, thinking how certain wounds were too deep, the damage too great, to ever mend cleanly. Shari slipped on the biggest sunglasses she owned, a pair that masked most of the top of her face, and headed out.

The driver might have smirked, or he could simply have been polite. "Nice place, Ms. Khan."

"Thanks, Jimmy. Could we go straight to the studio, please?"

"No problem. The trades are on your seat."

Shari could almost hear the hiss of steam rising from the pages. Her fingers were singed by the act of lifting the dailies. She flipped to the weekend summaries. A cry of bone-deep pain slipped out.

"Something wrong, Ms. Khan?"

Shari opened her mouth to respond, but could not find the air.

The driver slowed and glanced back. "Ms. Khan?"

She moaned, "Just drive."

"Sure thing."

Shari dropped one daily and picked up the second. The news was the same. Every Monday morning, the dailies carried the critical weekend stats. There were five numbers of crucial importance. One was general placement, where the film stood in the top ten. Next was the number of theaters playing the film. It was essential that a major release hold steady for at least three weeks, because the international distributors used this as the measuring stick upon which to gauge how large an opening and budget to give the project overseas. Third was the total revenue the film had made over the three-day weekend, and fourth was the per-theater weekend gross. Fifth was the film's total revenue since its release.

Shari flung the second journal to the floor and picked up the one segment of the *LA Times* the driver had left for her. The only section that mattered. "It can't be!"

"You say something?"

"Drive!"

It couldn't happen. But it had.

After only two weeks, *Iron Feather* was no longer in the top ten.

It was not even listed on the page.

Gone.

Vanished.

And at the top of the page, in the number-one slot in all three papers, was *Long Hunter*. What was more, the number of theaters carrying the film had *exploded*. Almost thirty-five hundred. And the per-screen revenue was out of sight.

Despite everything she had thrown at them, the film was destined to become one of the biggest grossing films of the year.

Her eye was caught by the headline beneath the weekend list. "Shoestring Project Buries Major Studio."

She groaned again.

This time, the driver said nothing.

Her phone rang. Shari did not even glance over to see who was calling.

The phone stopped, then started again. The ring sounded like a drill to her brain. Shari's hands were unable to keep hold of the pages.

She felt as though her internal organs had been excavated and left to rot on the freeway. She had never dreaded anything as much as facing the day ahead. She had seen such moments before, of course. It was part of studio lore. Her former boss had come in and moved about like a ghost for a week and a half before the memo arrived from Derek's office terminating his contract. The jokes had made the rounds before lunch.

Now it was her turn.

The limo driver's phone chirped. He answered, then said, "Ms. Khan."

"Not now."

"I've got Mr. Menzes' secretary on the phone."

She forced herself to lean forward and accept the phone. "Khan."

"Hold for Mr. Menzes."

The secretary might have sounded more cheerful than normal. Shari neither knew nor cared. She did her best to straighten in the seat.

The chief came on the line. "Shari."

She was caught off guard. To her recollection, he had never

before called her by her first name. "Sir, I don't know what to say."

"I can well understand the sentiment. The question is, what are we going to do now?"

"Sir?"

"We have *Snowbound* approaching principal shooting. What I want to know is are you still interested in being the studio's point on that project."

Her mouth worked, but no sound came out.

"You still there?"

"Sir, Mr. Menzes, there is nothing I want more."

His voice deepened, roughened. "Are you absolutely certain about that?"

She squinted against the day's fierce glare. But the way ahead became no clearer. "Absolutely. I'm your girl."

"That's what I wanted to hear. I keep a bungalow at the Beverly Hills Hotel. I like to think of it as my secondary office, kept for just such special moments as this. I suggest we meet there."

A chill rose from her gut. "If that's—"

"I'll phone the desk and alert them you'll be arriving. I'll meet you there in an hour."

On leaden legs, Shari walked toward Sam's bungalow—as fine a poolside apartment as could be expected for three thousand dollars per night. Shari let herself in, hit the light, and stood a foot inside the door. She could go no further. The massive bed was visible through the sliding doors. It taunted her.

Turn and run.

She had never heard voices before. But the words were so powerful she felt them echo about the empty room.

Turn and run NOW.

She glanced at the phone. Maybe she could call her

grandmother. But what would she tell her? How could she ask for advice? How could she even admit she was considering such a move?

Shari found herself recalling the confrontation with Bobby Dupree on the courthouse stairs. She wanted to scream with frustration and pain and rage at a man who was three thousand miles away. Even so, the man and his burning eyes crowded into the room. It was almost as though she could hear him shout the words, feel him slip the oversized card into her fingers once more.

Leave this place.

Now her grandmother's face shimmered before her eyes. The dark gaze, the knowing expression, the depth of pain hidden beneath the old woman's polished exterior. Perhaps Lizu Khan had not endured this one particular agony. But something. Oh yes. The old woman bore her own secrets. *Remember the price,* she had said again and again.

Was this the price of stardom? The cost of rising to regal status?

This time the voice was quieter, a mere whisper that came and went in an instant, soft enough for Shari to pretend she had not heard the unspoken message at all.

Flee while you still can.

he night was the same, only different.

The Oscar party was at Liz's home again. This time, Brent stayed the distance, remaining in the living room through the entire ceremony. He and Celia regaled the others with memories made funny by the distance and the love that surrounded them.

Afterward, he walked a path illuminated by moonlight and stopped where the house lights were blocked enough for him to revel in the expanse of stars. *Iron Feather* had copped two Oscars, including Best Actor for Colin Chapman. Brent had seen the phenomenon often enough not to be surprised. The Hollywood crowd was notorious for rewarding films and actors on Academy Awards night that the public had scorned. It was their way of getting back at the audience that told them they were out of touch. No mention had been made of *Long Hunter*. Not even in the jokes.

Even so, it hurt.

Still, Brent managed to watch the show with a sense of pleasant detachment. He was back in Austin only to pack up and move to Nashville. The film company was offering advance bonuses to everyone willing to go with Bobby's long-term contract. The amount was not enough to move him back to Bel-Air. Not that he would ever want to go. But enough to have him spelling a word that he hasn't used in a long time.

Future.

As in, his own.

"Brent?"

"Down here."

Celia glided down the path toward him. Her hair shimmered like a halo. Her hands danced in the moonlight. "Are there snakes?"

"Too cold."

"Are you sure?"

"Come here, lady. I'll keep you safe."

She folded herself into his arms. "You say the sweetest things."

They walked the frosty earth down to where the river flowed in easy winter majesty. Celia studied the currents for a time, then asked, "Are you all right?"

"I'm fine."

"Stanley was worried. About . . . you know."

"I felt disappointed and at peace, all at the same time."

"I understand exactly what you mean," Celia said. "You know what occurred to me back in there? Maybe we should set up awards all our own."

"Now who in their right mind would want to see a thing like that?"

Brent feasted on her smile, her gaze, and his own feeling of completeness. "How was it for you tonight, being on the outside looking in?"

She took a firm two-armed grip around his middle. "There's no place I'd rather be than right here, right now."

"Same here. I feel more than fine. I feel rich. I feel blessed. I feel . . ."

Celia squeezed him tighter. "Tell me."

"I feel in love."

She was so close he could feel the tremble from her ankles to her hairline. "I'm glad it's not just me."

"Marry me, Celia."

The request astonished them both. Celia was quiet so long he feared she was trying to think of a way to turn him down gently. Then he realized, "You're crying."

She nodded, tears streaking her pale cheeks. "But I'll marry you anyway."

His eyes filled in response. He leaned in close and kissed her. "Hey, I'll take that over an award any day."

Be the first to know

Want to be the first to know
what's new from
your favorite authors?

Want to know all about
exciting new writers?

Sign up for Bethany House newsletters at
www.bethanynewsletters.com
and you'll get regular updates via e-mail.
You can sign up for specific authors or
categories so you get only
the information you really want.

Sign up today